Never Were Such Times

Also by Nancy Livingston:

Death in Close-Up
The Land of Our Dreams
Death in a Distant Land
The Far Side of the Hill
Incident at Parga
Fatality at Bath and Wells
The Trouble at Aquitaine

Never Were
Such Times

NANCY LIVINGSTON

St. Martin's Press
New York

A-1

Library of Congress Cataloging-in-Publication Data

Livingston, Nancy.
    Never were such times / Nancy Livingston.
        p.   cm.
    ISBN 0-312-05902-7
    I. Title.
PR6062.I915N4   1991
823'.914—dc20   90-28540
                                                                      CIP

First published in Great Britain by Macdonald & Co (Publishers) Limited.

First U.S. Edition: June 1991
10 9 8 7 6 5 4 3 2 1

Prologue

In ancient times this part of Suffolk had few inhabitants. Those there were had travelled long distances. They settled in glades among the trees, or close by the rivers. Dense forest provided roots and berries but when the people discovered flints buried in seams of chalk and learned how to split and sharpen them, the men became hunters, bold enough to explore further.

Vast glaciers melted; huge stretches of water cut them off from the mainland of Europe but the people here were content. This was their territory now, it was home. They'd traversed it so often, bare feet had marked out tracks; the Peddars Way, the Ichnield Way.

They bartered flints for pottery; they learned to clear trees and make space for corn. There was peace. Their children grew tall. Then came invaders who'd discovered another secret, iron, which could be made into swords. After that the people of Suffolk had to learn to defend themselves; above all, how to survive.

Chapter One

1885 The Bride

The night before her wedding, Sybilla Unwin sat preening herself in front of the mirror. Silvery fair hair in tight curl rags framed a square, rather pugnacious face that simpered back. There were candles burning on either side of the attic mirror – an unheard-of extravagance! Lily, the kitchen maid, kept glancing at them nervously.

'I shall get up real early tomorrow an' pick flowers while the dew's still on 'em. That way they'll stay fresh all day. You shall go round to my Enoch with a rosebud, Lily. You shall tell him I sends my love with it, an' 'tis for his buttonhole.'

'He's so handsome, Syb! I can't hardly bear to look at him.'

'Hush! Tomorrow, 'twill be my husband you're talking about. 'Twould be improper for you to say such things after that.'

Lily was fifteen. She perched on the end of the bed they both shared and gazed in awe at the nineteen-year-old parlourmaid. Such sophistication, such a gulf opening up between them: matrimony! The security every girl craved.

'I promise I won't even think like that after tomorrow, Syb. If'n I should pass Mr Porrit in the street, I shall look away so's I shan't be dazzled. Just think . . . this time tomorrow you'll be a married woman. Will you feel different?'

' 'Course I will.' Sybilla gazed at her reflection complacently.

'How will that be, d'you think?' Sybilla considered.

'I shall feel respectable . . . real proud to have such a good-looking husband.' Joy overcame poise and bubbled to the surface. Sybilla bounced to her feet. 'I'm such a lucky girl, Lily.' She hugged the kitchen maid and twirled her round the narrow room, 'Lucky, lucky, lucky . . .!' They collapsed in a giggling heap on top of the wedding finery. Lily heard something snap.

'Oh gawd, Syb! That was a bone in your corsets!'

'Oh, no!'

Worn and darned, they were still Sybilla's most treasured possession. She cried in despair, 'I been keeping these specially!'

'I know!' A sympathetic tear oozed down Lily's cheek; they were a symbol of Sybilla's other great achievement.

'When she give 'em to me, the Vicar's sister said she wasn't giving me no *tip* for maiding her, that would be too much to expect . . .' Lily nodded, she knew the words by heart for the tale had often been retold.

'She said I was to brush my teeth reg'lar to keep my breath sweet –'

'And your nails, Syb, she said not to forget your fingernails.' Sybilla frowned at the interruption.

'Which I ain't. An' then she give me these corsets because she said she had no further use for them but she had no doubt they would stand me in good stead,' Sybilla finished triumphantly, 'Which is why I kep' 'em for when I got married.'

'We shall have to mend 'em. Otherwise the broken bit'll dig in somethin' cruel. Come on, I'll undo 'em for you.' Lily began to unpick stitches. 'Fancy bein' a lady's maid for two whole weeks!'

'Which I was,' Sybilla agreed proudly, threading her needle. Lily looked at her soulfully.

'D'you think I'll ever get the chance?'

Sybilla's courtship had been as fond and foolish as the girl herself. Conducted with propriety – the vicarage cook saw to that – it had begun in the High Street of the small Suffolk town of Brandon.

10

After an initial bold glance, Enoch Porrit's custom whenever a pretty girl went by, he had pursued her out of impulse, knocking one day at the vicarage back door. To see him standing there was, in Sybilla Unwin's naive eyes, as good as a declaration! Blushing furiously she invited him in and pointed to a chair beside the kitchen range.

Enoch was astonished. Effrontery had never paid off so well before. It had been raining, he'd been on his way back to town, all he'd craved was shelter and here he was warm and dry with a plateful of freshly baked scones. It was against all the rules, they both knew that. Lily was terrified but by the time the cook, Mrs Heyhoe, returned to the kitchen after her afternoon nap, Enoch Porrit was established, if only in Sybilla's imagination, as her Young Man. She was prepared to defy the world to keep him.

'I invited Mr Porrit for a cup of tea as he was passing,' she told Mrs Heyhoe.

Did you so, Enoch thought to himself, that's the first I knew of it. He poured hot liquid into the saucer and blew to cool it. Over the rim, he saw Cook's expression; she didn't believe it either.

He never intended to repeat the experiment; Enoch's taste in females was for those with more spice. But the scones had been fluffy and, within a month or two, curiosity got the better of him. As he was leaving on this occasion he asked casually, 'You got a bit put by?'

'I got a pair of linen pillowcases in my bottom drawer,' Sybilla boasted, 'an' cotton sheets, all embroidered.'

'How much *money* you got?'

'Twelve pound ten shilling in the bank.'

'How much!' It was beyond his wildest dreams, equivalent to a year's salary for a labouring man.

'Father was an old skinflint. He threw Jeremiah and me out to earn our livin' soon as he could, but when he died, there was ten pound for each of us. Mother never knew he had so much.'

'But how did he get a hold of the money?'

'He once found a big gold chain in the road . . . boasted he'd got plenty for it at the pawn shop, not that he gave us a penny. "Finders Keepers" he used to say. But he knew when the hotels in Bury wanted pheasant or a nice juicy rabbit,' Sybilla explained artlessly. 'He'd a pleasant way of talkin', I don't suppose anyone asked where he got them from.'

As an amateur thief and poacher himself, Enoch was jealous. He'd never made half as much. Twenty pound!

'I don't hold wi' banks,' he said sulkily.

' 'Tis the safest place for money, Enoch.'

'But can you get your hands on it again?'

' 'Course I can,' Sybilla told him tenderly. What an ignoramus the dear chap was!

There'd been no betrothal ring; Sybilla remedied that omission herself after hints had failed. She walked the six miles to Thetford and, greatly daring, withdrew two shillings and sixpence. The jeweller assured her the stone wouldn't fade provided she didn't immerse it in hot water and the gold would come up like new with a rub of the cleaning rag.

The ring hung round her neck until the following Sunday. She and Enoch were in the habit of dawdling after the evening service, the vicar's cold supper having been left ready.

' 'Tis a ruby stone. D'you like it, Enoch?' She'd undone her blouse to get at the ribbon and he glimpsed the soft pearly flesh inside. His grip was rough as he pulled her close and began to nuzzle her. 'Stop that!' Sybilla cried sharply, 'Folks can see us.'

'Let's go by the river where they can't.'

She was immediately nervous. Once before when she'd agreed, Enoch had shocked her. His mauling on that occasion had been so rough he'd torn her bodice and they had had *words*. Sybilla was both flustered and dismayed, such behaviour was outside her experience. In Cook's magazines, gentility was a byword.

'Will you promise me then?' He grinned but didn't speak. 'Please, Enoch.'

'Oh, stop your fuss. You want it same as me.' But she didn't, and on her wedding night Sybilla discovered she wanted it even less.

By then, another event was causing far more consternation among certain of the town's authorities; it had begun when Sybilla's brother, Jeremiah Unwin, was taken ill.

Jeremiah hadn't had his sister's luck. He'd had a much harder life, apprenticed as a farm hand by his skinflint father. His inheritance had come too late to save him. Married by then, living in a tied cottage with four young children, escape was impossible. As a consolation, Jeremiah had spent his ten pounds on books.

Night after night, he read aloud, impressing on his children the need for education to escape a similar fate. A quiet, gentle man in contrast to Sybilla, Jeremiah determined that his two boys, Chas and Albert, should break free.

A few weeks before Sybilla's wedding, illness struck the family. After twelve days of violent headache and fever, realizing his wife was similarly afflicted, Jeremiah could stand it no longer. In despair, for he'd very little money left, he sent his elder boy, Chas, to fetch the doctor.

The physician's first thought was that putrid fever, which had been causing such havoc in Thetford, must have spread. In dusty heat with Chas hurrying to keep up, he rode out to the cottage, cursing inadequate sewers that made each summer a lottery. When the temperature rose, as it had this year, so many were doomed to die because of impure water.

But when he entered and saw his new patients, the doctor was aghast: this wasn't putrid fever, this was catastrophe! Not the slightest hint must be allowed to slip out. Jeremiah Unwin, his wife Barbara and the youngest of their four children were exhibiting symptoms of the most malignant form of smallpox!

Within hours, his orders had been acted upon: Chas, Albert and Polly showed no signs of infection yet, but this might only be a matter of time. Accordingly they were despatched in a closed carriage to the isolation

13

hospital. As for Jeremiah's only other relative, Sybilla, the doctor sent word to the vicarage that on no account was she to attempt to visit the cottage, nor could Polly be her bridal attendant the following Saturday.

Sybilla hadn't spoken to Jeremiah since harvest time. When the corn was in, the poor were permitted to glean what they could in the fields. It was strictly forbidden for vicarage staff to join in, but such was Syb's determination to increase her savings, she had mingled with the rest that hot day and found herself working alongside Jeremiah. 'What you doing, Syb? Vicar won't like it when he finds out.'

'Do be quiet! An' don't you let on you've seen me, d'you hear.'

After a while Jeremiah had asked more gently, 'You still encouraging that chap, Syb? He nearly got caught down Thetford Warren. The keeper got one man but t'other poacher ran off. Keeper swore to the magistrate it were Porrit.'

Sybilla remembered the warm-skinned bodies concealed in the game pantry. The rabbit pie consumed surreptitiously, with herself so proud of Enoch's cleverness.

'For what we are about to receive,' Cook had murmured as she picked up the carving-knife, 'may the Lord make us truly thankful and whatever else – keep His Nibs upstairs from finding out.' Sybilla and Lily had gasped at the audacity but Enoch had sneered.

'That's the way, Mrs Heyhoe, tha's what it's about. Take what you want and doan' get caught.' Cook eyed him for a moment or two before she handed him his plateful.

'An' are you really going after another silly tiddly little rabbit, Enoch Porrit?'

'Maybe so,' he replied carelessly, 'Give us some more o' that gravy, there's a good soul.'

'You could find 'tis a weasel you got hold of?' Enoch leaned back, savouring the first succulent mouthful. Sybilla butted in, eager to show off.

14

mended stays and w
either side, the cor,
had not the slightes
temper flared. Hov
jealous, like her sis
this fine figure of a
the same . . . she'd
lips Enoch had. The
making her oddly un

From the chancel
but before she could
woman. In her ecst:
something unpleas:
the curve of her b
skirt.

It was outrageou
groping hand hard.
laughter! Miss H
come-uppance! Wha
Porrit? As for the
Enoch had made he
never! But she was

The doctor ordered
lines between Lond
worded instruction:
Jeremiah lingered.
torpid weather, f
possible.

Unaware, all thoug
mind, Sybilla's em
day progressed. Th
to the mystery of th
too young. Althoug
naivety, she prefer
consequences.

Sybilla had consi
intervened. Revea
sister-in-law? But a

'No one catches weasels, Mrs Heyhoe. Too fierce, they be. They can bite your finger through if they goes for you.' Explaining country ways made her feel superior; Cook was from Bury St Edmunds, she couldn't be expected to know. To Sybilla's surprise, Enoch had laughed so much he nearly choked.

'There you are, missus, there's your answer!' He leaned forward, crashing chair legs down against the stone flags, using his knife for emphasis. 'But if't did turn out a weasel, 'twould have to be tamed. Till it learned for certain 'tis only a tiddly rabbit tha's wanted.'

Sybilla turned the doctor's brief message over and over, discussing it with Lily before telling Mrs Heyhoe. There'd been a rumour in the town that Jeremiah was sick, but it was unthinkable for Sybilla to ask for time off whilst working out her notice. Barbara would have to manage as all the women did. Even if it were the pox, as gossip whispered, why should Sybilla worry? Jeremiah was stupidly fond of his wife, he wouldn't care if she lost her looks.

The fact that a doctor had been sent for worried Sybilla more. How could Jeremiah afford that luxury on ten shillings a week? She decided she wouldn't lend him a penny, even if he begged her. Serve him right! Such a waste, frittering away all that money on books.

When told of it, Mrs Heyhoe looked at her thoughtfully. 'Will you delay your wedding, Unwin?'

'Don't see why I should . . .' They were making polish to clean doorknobs throughout the house. Sybilla stirred the powdered whiting and oil as Cook grated in flakes of yellow soap. The girl was less confident because the doctor's words had been so abrupt. 'Jeremiah might be better by Saturday, there's no telling,' she declared optimistically. 'What do you think I should do, Mrs Heyhoe?'

In a rare burst of honesty, Cook said slowly, 'If I was your family, Unwin, I'd forbid you to marry Enoch Porrit if'n he was the last man on earth,' which virtually settled any lingering doubts the silly girl had.

All the same, it wa
her family to witn
miah to be taken
impertinence to cri
who couldn't bear
prize. No doubt t
prevented from b
tossed her tight cu
this disappointmen

It didn't occur to
Sturdily healthy he
staff, she'd never k

Her mind still fe
her gentle brother
faults. How ridicul
most handsome ma

The night before
untroubled sleep
doctor and a collea

In one way, the au
tunate. Jeremiah's
lying farmland, ea
over, every trace
they could do was v

Rumour persiste
wedding, folk spec
matter. Then one
barber's – a rare
ahead – Sybilla U
brother was in dan
as well enjoy the fu

Then as now, an
diversion. Fancy P
'Twas more than
Expectancy rose as
church.

Sybilla had despat
the rosebud bound

Eagle, sipping ginger beer while groom and his drinking cronies laughed raucously within, Sybilla was more disturbed than she cared to admit. Why had the congregation laughed like that?

As for Enoch, his opinion of women was simple; they were for men's use, like dogs, although not as easy to subdue. They asked for it, smiling and inclining slender bodies to show him what was on offer. When they screamed he was hurting, that was all part of the game. Sybilla was the worst sort, she had tantalized him.

Later that night, in the small terraced cottage for which she had paid one month's rent in advance, the new Mrs Porrit lay rigid on her side of the bed. Her cheeks were wet. The last time she'd wept like this was when her father had turned her out at fourteen, to earn her living. She'd been lucky then, to be offered employment at the vicarage. Hitherto, Sybilla had believed in luck; wasn't that how she'd first encountered Enoch?

Beside her, the red lips slack, her husband slept. He would be there when she woke. He would be beside her for the rest of her life and, if the vicar were to be believed, throughout eternity as well. There was no going back.

Wide awake now, Sybilla Porrit faced up to what she'd done. She'd married a brutal cruel man who didn't love her. Enoch had never claimed to, to be fair; until now she'd pretended it didn't matter. He would grow to love her, she told herself sentimentally; why else had he continued to call? Now she knew. Tonight he'd stripped away pretence, taking her by force and hitting her when she tried to pull away. 'That's for what you did to me in church!'

Equally frightening was the way he'd deceived her about his ambitions, which she'd assumed were the same as her own.

Sybilla had spent so much of her life making plans, she'd forgotten to listen to anything Enoch might have to say. They would remain in this cottage a month, she'd decided. During that time, Enoch would work night and day to earn 7/6½d each for their fares and then they doctor, never mind anythin' else. Please, Mr Godwin, stop 'em burning his bits and pieces. There won't be a farthing to spare, not with Jeremiah sick for so long!'

These worries added to her agitation. She'd have to part with some of her savings to help Jeremiah.

'Go and see the doctor,' Godwin urged, 'he can tell 'ee better 'n I.'

In growing despair, Sybilla hurried through quiet Sunday streets. At the surgery door the housekeeper was hostile.

'When you las' see your brother?'

'Not since gleaning.' The woman made a quick calculation.

'You can come in then. You be safe enough now.'

Sybilla was frightened. What had happened? Why wouldn't anyone tell her? The housekeeper refused to say another word.

She was too nervous to question the physician. When he asked about her contact with the family, Sybilla replied in a whisper. He stared out of the window. Eventually he began to speak. She was so shocked she could barely comprehend.

'I deeply regret, Mrs Porrit, that your brother, his wife and their baby daughter are dead. The last to pass away was your brother, Mr Jeremiah Unwin. He died in the early hours of this morning. It was a Christian death, despite the pain.'

In the void, one thought occurred to Sybilla; Jeremiah and I were suffering together . . . he was dying . . . I was being forced by Enoch Porrit. The doctor continued.

'Your brother died with one hand resting on the Bible, which had to be burnt, of course. Indeed, every single item in that cottage must be considered contaminated. I gave instructions nothing was to remain. I recommend destruction of the property as well . . . Unfortunately, I was over-ruled.' The memory still vexed him. 'I have insisted it not be used for habitation until a full twelve-month has passed, however.'

Sybilla's white face reminded him he had been remiss. 'In view of your recent marriage, these events must be

27

especially poignant, Mrs Porrit. Pray allow me to express my felicitations as well as my condolences. The funerals will be held tomorrow morning. Until then, I must ask you to be discreet. You understand why we were unable to send word to you earlier, I trust?' Slowly, through her numbness, Sybilla focused her gaze on him.

'Even if it was scarlet fever . . . I don't see why you had to burn the furniture. They only had two chairs.' She remembered the excitement when Jeremiah returned from Thetford having bought real furniture, 'They cost ten shillin' – why did you have to burn those?' Passion broke through her fear of officialdom, 'I want to see my own brother before you close the lid!'

'Good God, that's impossible!' The doctor leaned across urging her to understand. 'It was smallpox, Mrs Porrit, and thank Heaven we have managed to contain the outbreak. It was providential that your brother's dwelling was remote, also that the three elder children were isolated so speedily. They have escaped infection and can now be discharged. How thankful we can be that three poor orphans will now have a home.'

'Beg pardon?'

The doctor either didn't hear, or affected not to.

'You and Porrit can collect them after the funeral. It would be better if they didn't attend the obsequies. Normal, er, reverent formalities, will of necessity be kept to a minimum. You will be doing your Christian duty, Mrs Porrit.' This was sincere at least. Sybilla would be relieving the parish of three unwanted charges. As a member of the Poor Law Committee the doctor saw it as extremely providential. He rang the bell before she could object.

'So I can't see Jeremiah . . .?' Sybilla was indeed finding it difficult to marshal her thoughts. She had a vague notion that, even in death, her brother could offer badly needed comfort.

'Dear me, no!' The doctor pulled himself together. 'Lead-lined coffins, Mrs Porrit,' he said emphatically. 'The authorities will bear the cost, no need to concern yourself about that. Sealed, naturally. The babe to be

28

interred with its mother. No necessity to follow the cortége, no necessity whatsoever! Outside the churchyard will be close enough. Set your thoughts upon those three dear children who remain rather than your poor brother, Mrs Porrit. What a comfort *they* will be to you and your husband in the years to come.'

Which meant he obviously didn't know Enoch, but she'd no strength left to argue about that.

It was late when she returned. Enoch had learned of the deaths at The Ram. More jibes there about his newly married state hadn't improved his temper. Neither had a cold hearth with no meal ready on the table. He began to storm as soon as Sybilla lifted the latch.

She ignored him and went through to the scullery, staring out at the darkening sky. 'The funerals are first thing tomorrow. I shall have to get some blacks.' It was as though she hadn't heard a word.

'So?'

'I can't go to the bank, like you wanted.' He was immediately suspicious.

'You're not trying to cheat me, Syb?' Despite her exhaustion she spun round.

'You're not stoppin' me dressin' decent when it's Jeremiah they're buryin'!'

'No, no,' Enoch protested, 'Don' see why you has to go, though. Not if there's a chance you might catch the pox.' He sneered, 'I wouldn't want you to be marked, Syb.' She was relieved but careful not to let it show.

'You don't intend goin' to the funeral then?'

'Got to think about my health and strength now I've got a wife to support. You an' me can go to the bank Tuesday instead. Nothin' to stop us doing that.' Enoch had enough money left for one further evening's carousel. 'Wha's for supper?'

Despite her tiredness, Sybilla announced after the meal she had a further call to make. 'The vicar needs to know which are Jeremiah's favourite hymns.' It was her first lie since she'd married but she knew there would be many, many more. Enoch was indifferent.

29

'You go if you wants . . . I shan't come.'

At the sight of her, Mrs Heyhoe sent Lily upstairs and listened intently. How Unwin had changed! A bruise under one eye and now she stumbled over words as she tried to explain what she wanted.

The scraped-back braids were another surprise. Unwin had always been particular about her silvery fair curls, they'd been her best feature. In Cook's opinion there had been too many but now . . . Mrs Heyhoe sucked in plump cheeks. Fancy anyone so young make herself look so plain? Sybilla finished speaking.

'So tha's it. D'you think you'll be able to help me, Mrs Heyhoe? I needs a favour badly.'

'I reckon so. I owe you that much, Mrs Porrit. I do indeed. I'm truly sorry about what's happened. Your brother was a kindly man. I only met him the once but 'twas a pleasure to watch him with the children.' This was balm to Sybilla's sad heart.

'As for owin', Mrs Heyhoe, you don't owe me nothin'. I've brought trouble on myself. I didn't listen to Jeremiah nor you when you tried to warn me. Now Jeremiah's gone . . .' her voice wobbled, 'I must learn to manage on my own account.' Mrs Heyhoe unbent a little further.

'Is Porrit treating you . . . decent?' she asked delicately. Sybilla's expression froze.

'I shall be ready for'n next time,' she whispered, 'Las' night he was in liquor by the time he come to bed . . . Even so . . .' A sob interrupted, she blew her nose vigorously. 'If'n 'e do try hurtin' again, I hev promised to tell the magistrates.'

'Oh, my!' Mrs Heyhoe had never heard a rash threat like that. 'Will they listen, d'you reckon?'

'I've got to stop him some'ow,' Sybilla cried, "e don' know his own strength.' It might have been a worn-out drudge rather than a girl only twenty-four hours married. 'As for the rest . . .' Sybilla admitted despairingly, 'all Enoch wanted was my savings. You guessed that, didn't you, Mrs Heyhoe? 'Twasn't affection. He ain't got none o' tha' for me. But come Tuesday — when he thinks he's a gettin' hold of my money — well, he's not. I don't know yet how I shall stop him but I'll manage it somehow.' She gave a brief, hard smile, 'On Tuesday Enoch Porrit'll find out 'tis a weasel after all, not a tiddly little rabbit.'

It was worse than Mrs Heyhoe had feared. She was anxious to do what she could.

'Here,' she urged, 'take this but see you bring the pot back. 'Tis a bit of casserole left over from His Nibs' dinner. Put dumplings in an' 'twill do for tomorrow night's supper, when you got five mouths to feed.'

The fact that she'd won an ally renewed Sybilla's strength. There was a warmth between them as Cook took her hand in farewell. 'Remember to hold your head up, Mrs Porrit. 'Tis important for folks to see you do that. An' don't let *him* mither you if you doan' feel like it. He's got to learn to do without occasionally, all men have.'

It took courage later, when Enoch pulled back the bedclothes and fumbled with her nightgown. As calmly as she could, Sybilla said loudly, 'There was some of Jeremiah's things they 'adn't noticed . . . books and such. Seemed a shame to let 'em be burnt, jes' 'cause of tha' stupid doctor.' It was her second lie and it came more easily than the first.

'Wha'?' Enoch drew back fearfully. 'You didn't bring the pox back here!'

'Might not hev been the pox. The doctor wasn't certain.' She turned that she might see and enjoy the fear, 'He wondered if it might not've been the *plague* that killed 'em. But you don' need to worry, Enoch. I didn't do more than touch one or two of them books . . .' she was lying to an empty room. With profound relief, Sybilla Porrit lay back in her bridal bed and slept.

Chapter Two

A Disposal of Effects

Chas and Albert lay hidden among the branches and stared down at the graveyard. The curious had gathered as they had two days previously, but this morning the mood was cautious, people stood further back. Beyond the churchyard wall volunteer gravediggers waited uneasily. The vicar defended himself from corrupt flesh with a handkerchief well soused in vinegar. This he clutched to his nose, his prayerbook balanced on his other palm, and the acrid stench wafted up to where Chas, high in the tree, clung to the trunk with his other arm firmly round Albert.

When they'd left the hospital, the three hadn't been taken home as expected but to the union workhouse. Here they'd been given ill-fitting black garments and told to wait. No one thought to ask if they'd had breakfast. When sanctimonious guardians first broke the news that their parents and baby Amy were dead, all they could think of was how hungry they were. In a quavering voice, Chas asked if they might have a bit of bread and cheese and the guardians pronounced them 'unnatural' and 'unfeeling' in consequence.

Last night they'd been separated, sleeping in dormitories with other hopeless, doomed human beings. Today, sniffing the first fresh air and sunshine for weeks, the three had bolted like heifers newly let out to pasture. Polly, hampered by her skirts, was quickly recaptured but the boys remained free. They'd been drawn to the churchyard nonetheless, fearful and close to tears.

Down below their Aunt Sybilla poked a finger inside the tight collar of her hastily purchased 'blacks'. As instructed by cook, her back was ramrod straight. Today was to be a testing time, she couldn't afford to let sorrow interfere, that indulgence would have to come later. She bit her lip and pushed away all memory of Jeremiah.

Last night Mrs Heyhoe had given sound advice. Nevertheless, it behoved Sybilla to keep her wits about her; there were battles ahead which simply had to be won. Even thinking about them frightened her and she squeezed Polly hard.

The child whimpered and Sybilla ordered sharply, 'Be quiet!'

The vicar paused in his gabble. His eyes watered and now he made them worse by wiping them with the vinegary handkerchief. Up in the tree Albert whispered, 'Is he crying for our mam?'

'No. 'Tis only us do that.'

'Poor ol' Pol . . . she'm frightened down there by herself. Shall us go down?'

'No.' Chas was adamant, 'Us'll get walloped.'

'Be still,' Sybilla muttered again at the hapless Polly.

Despite her resolve Sybilla found herself thinking of Jeremiah. How he had watched the door whenever Barbara was gone from the room for more than an instant. What must it be like to be loved like that?

'Forasmuch as it hath pleased Him . . .' His Nibs had scarcely taken more trouble over the words of her wedding service. The Unwin family had no cause to be grateful to him.

All in such a short time, too; anger began to pulse inside. Fate was so unjust! Sensing her tension the vicar glanced up from the page a second time. His former parlour maid had lost her attractiveness, he noticed. Women of that class took so little trouble once they'd ensnared a man.

At that moment Polly almost succeeded in jerking free. Quick as a flash, Sybilla slapped her.

'Be still, I said!'

Immediately she heard in her mind Jeremiah protesting.

'Be gentle. 'Tis my little maid, Syb,' and she dug her nails into her palms as anger wavered dangerously close to grief.

Seeing the service stop, one of the gravediggers moved forward and caught the vicar's eye. He sighed. The commital wasn't finished, there'd been no proper prayers but the sooner both coffins were under the earth, the better. In his infinite mercy, the Almighty would surely understand.

Up in their tree, the boys flinched at the slap. Albert was indignant. 'Why did Aunt Syb do that? Polly ain't done nothing.'

'Aunt Syb's in a temper,' Chas gazed down on the crowns of various black hats. 'I expect it's because Enoch Porrit done a bunk.'

'He was here when everyone else arrived,' Albert would always be fair, 'an' I heard someone say there was a danger of con-tag-ion if any of us got too close.'

'It 'ain't that. Aunt Syb hev found out why no one else wanted to marry 'im, tha's why she's in a real tizzy,' Chas confided. 'She hev discovered how he's a real lazy devil.'

This was adult wisdom, overheard and repeated. Albert gave a shiver. Whatever his flaws, their new uncle was large and probably as quick with his fists as his bride.

'She got savin's . . . Enoch Porrit's been tellin' everyone. One of 'em in the dormitory las'night, he'd heard 'im in The Five Bells. Aunt Syb ha' made a fool of 'erself an' no mistake.'

Adult gossip spread fast but to repeat it was treason. Albert hunched his shoulders against a possible thunderbolt when, with a slither and a thump, the first of the lead-lined coffins dropped into the grave. As he saw this, the hot ball of sorrow in his throat burst and unmanned him. Loud sobs shook their perch.

Chas whispered urgently, 'Hold on, ol' bor!'

'Mam!' There was no stopping Albert now, he roared with terror at being only twelve years old and knowing for a certainty, he'd lost the only love he'd ever known, 'Mam, come back!'

The Poor Law Committee faced Sybilla across a table; the

34

town clerk, the Receiving Officer, the doctor and, most reluctantly because he preferred to avoid unpleasantness, the young vicar. In a corner at the back of the room were the sole chattels of those he'd just buried; three sad-eyed children, whose fate was about to be decided. Their misery was so intense, he shifted his chair to avoid seeing their faces.

The thought popped into his head that if only they'd died too, the committee wouldn't be faced with this problem. The same thought had occurred to the Receiving Officer. He had nothing but contempt for the poor. Destitute children shouldn't be allowed! Parents had no business dying without making provision. It left this committee with the thankless task of persuading the female opposite to do her Christian duty. She looked stubborn. He scowled. What a damned nuisance the whole business was!

Polly and Albert were stained with tears. Chas's were unshed but increasingly hard to contain. As for Sybilla, she breathed deeply to calm herself. What happened now would determine whether she would ever reach London. Matrimony was bitter as gall. There was only the future left to fight for. Despite what had happened, she would claw her way to freedom even if it meant outwitting the four men opposite.

When invited to speak she would be polite and mellifluous like a proper lady. Like the vicar's aunt, in fact; the only real lady Sybilla had ever encountered.

The topmost button of her collar had been undone to reveal a kerchief and this scrap of colour drew attention to her hazel eyes; it was a deliberate ploy devised by Mrs Heyhoe. Sybilla took a deep breath and began.

'I can't afford to support those dear children, gentlemen, an' that's the truth of it, though it do make me ashamed to have to admit it.' She lifted her veil to dab her eyes and one fair tress, reprieved and re-curled for the occasion, drooped against the cheap black poplin.

'You're their only living relative, Mrs Porrit,' the Receiving Officer said severely.

'D'you think I don't *want* 'em, sir? You can't believe I

would willingly see my brother Jeremiah's little ones go on the Parish?'

As this precisely summed up their thoughts, none could think how to reply. Sybilla sighed and fingered the curl.

'All I'm able to do, sirs, is provide the three dears with a *Home*, by using every penny of my savings. 'Tis what I 'ad put by for my old age. For buryin' in fac'. But every penny shall be spent givin' these little uns *A Roof*.'

She'd got their attention now all right.

'It was money left me, sirs. My dear dead father put me out when I was fourteen even though he didn't need to, but bein' an old skinflint which it sadly turned out he was, me an' Jeremiah left home in obedience to his wishes. Jeremiah was 'prenticed for farm work 'n I went into service with the good kind reverend here . . .' She paused to bestow gratitude with those hazel eyes.

'It only came out that father'd got this money hid under the floorboard after he died. Mother never knew. They reckon 'twas the shock of findin' out she been sleepin' above a fortune tha' killed her so soon afterwards, him havin' been mean all their married life. But as the Good Book says, you can't take it with you. The Lord must've 'ad a special purpose in clasping' my dear father an' mother to 'is bosom, leaving me the money to provide *A Home* for these dear children. Ten pounds is what it amounts to, gentlemen.'

At this deliberate lie, Sybilla paused instinctively to allow God to strike her dead. Nothing happened. God was all-knowing, he knew it was over twelve pounds not ten, but he hadn't been much help so far and she'd given him his chance. She continued with increasing confidence.

'I shall have to get us another place to live, me and Porrit havin' only the one bedroom at present, gentlemen. 'Tisn't right for two boys and a maid to sleep along o' Porrit an' me . . . being newly married as we both are.' Embarrassment was evident and she sought to spare their blushes. ''Tis all right, gentlemen, I do know of a house I could buy with three rooms upstairs.' The vicar plunged in to divert her.

'Are we to understand that you are offering to provide . . .?'

'A Home, sir, yes.' The aspirate was once more given full value, 'As my share of the responsibility. But that's where the problem begins. It'll take *all* o' my money. I shall need help for victuals an' clothing. It makes me sad to have to admit this an' I 'ope you'll all understand . . .' Her gaze travelled and gathered them into her confidence; they waited apprehensively. 'Porrit is not a *reliable* provider.'

'One moment. Perhaps you would join the children, Un-Mrs Porrit.'

As she moved out of earshot, it suddenly occurred to Sybilla that these men sitting in judgment had wives. In the privacy of their bedrooms, they probably behaved just as Enoch had done. How disgusting! No longer nervous, she scowled with cold hostility. Beasts! If a dog tried to bite at least you could kick it, but women had no redress – why had Mrs Heyhoe never warned her? How had she managed to rid herself of Mr Heyhoe?

The vicar quailed as he saw the implacable face. Unwin – Porrit as he must now learn to call her – had changed from a silly parlour maid whom he scarcely noticed into a very determined young woman. Certain remarks made that morning by his cook as she served his devilled kidneys, came back to him now. He repeated them to the committee.

The Receiving Officer wiped his kerchief over his forehead, muttering. 'What concern is it of *ours* if the woman has married a wastrel? Provided she has sufficient to buy a house – I must say I find it extraordinary that a woman of that class has money to throw around!'

'Only ten pounds, Mr Pettigrew. She told my cook the best use was for the benefit of the children.'

'Thank heaven she has the sense to buy property. But why can't her husband support them? I fail to see the difficulty.'

'The man never was nor ever will be reliable, as cook herself confirmed.'

'I repeat, that is no concern of ours.'

'Who is he?' asked the clerk. 'Do we know him?'

'Enoch Porrit.'

'Ah, yes . . .' The name jogged the doctor's memory. He remembered an unwanted baby with the same moist red lips and bold eyes. 'I've – come across him.' Why on earth had this woman married such a man? She didn't look like a fool. The vicar guessed his train of thought.

'She was always headstrong,' he said sadly, 'No one could dissuade her. However . . .' and he hesitated because cook's final words had made him uneasy, 'Mrs Porrit has let it be known she will publish any grievance abroad . . . that is to say, if she considers we treat her unfairly here this morning.' The Receiving Officer frowned.

'I don't follow?'

'She has announced she will complain to Thetford magistrates if we do not offer adequate assistance in view of her own generous provision of accommodation.'

'The devil she has!'

The threat cast a chill. Outside, the quiet ancient landscape was deceptive. In this small town as in neighbouring communities, people were capable of expressing discontent. Nearby Thetford had spawned Tom Paine, who'd set the world ablaze with his defence of the Rights of Man. All these thoughts and more passed through the minds of those sitting round the table and the atmosphere changed to one of disquiet. There were uncomfortable coughs as they strove to adjust their attitudes.

'I suppose the woman has a point.' The doctor remembered it was he who'd ordered the bonfire of Jeremiah's possessions. 'Those children might have been better provided for had we not had to destroy their inheritance. I must say I was impressed by Unwin. One doesn't expect to find a love of learning in a labourer. The house had plenty of books –'

'Books!?'

'He certainly believed in educating his children –'

'That sort of indulgence is all very well,' the Receiving Officer was indignant, 'but it's we who have to pay the costs of burial!'

'We were bound to do that by law,' the doctor reminded him, 'it did not come out of our own pockets –'

'Be that as it may, we are not here to subsidise the lackadaisical!'

'Gentlemen, please.' The vicar remembered he was the peacemaker, 'I think we're all agreed the woman's request is not unreasonable.'

'It's Porrit we're worried about,' retorted the clerk.

'I believe Mrs Porrit was intimating, as far as a woman's sensibility permits, that our *moral* support is also required. As a good shepherd, I shall watch over her and the children.' This would not be a drain on the Parish funds, the Receiving Officer nodded in approval. 'Moreover, I shall ensure Porrit understands that we will not permit one farthing of our liberality to disappear down his throat.'

'Good Heavens, I should think not!' The Receiving Officer looked on Parish Relief as his own money, which made it wellnigh impossible for him to part with it. 'Twopence per week each for the two youngest? There's no reason why the elder boy cannot work. Bird-scarers are always in demand.'

'He's still at school. Although well-grown he is only thirteen years old.'

'His father was a farm hand!'

The doctor persisted, 'Unwin was also an intelligent man, as I have said. Had he not been forced to earn his living in a menial occupation, he might have achieved far more. His desire, expressed to me before he lost consciousness, was that both sons should remain at school and eventually attempt the scholarship.'

'But it is we who now have to pay for such whims!' The rest of the committee waited for the Receiving Officer to calm himself.

'One or two years at the most,' the clerk said, 'that is the most we are obliged to provide. Once the eldest has reached Standard V we will have done our duty. By then it could be that Porrit . . .' he looked across at the stiff figure sitting beside the children, 'he may reform, his character may change for the better,' he murmured.

'And provide for them, you mean?' the Receiving Officer asked, 'Well, she'll bring him to heel if anyone can, I'd say.'

'Reform him as a loving wife should,' the vicar reproved. 'Who can deny the hand that rocks the cradle rules the world?'

'Hmph!'

Sybilla walked away, richer by two shillings and sixpence per week. It had taken nearly an hour. The Receiving Officer's blood was ready to boil but she'd stuck to her guns. Twopence would only pay for schooling, it wouldn't feed growing children. They needed clothes as well as food even if she was prepared to turn and mend. She wouldn't budge from her target and eventually she wore them down.

When she rose, Sybilla discovered the battle had taken its toll, her legs felt incredibly weak. She hustled the children outside before the committee could change its collective mind or her strength give way altogether.

The vicar would have been disappointed if he'd been able to read her thoughts. Sybilla had no intention of filling a cradle, let alone rocking one. What mattered was achieving her ambition of going to London. Anything which interfered with that was to be avoided at all costs. She hadn't been able to avoid taking in these three children, but at least she'd secured an income for herself. If ever that were withdrawn, she'd rid herself of them.

Meanwhile there was pressing business to attend to.

'I got something private to do. You three stay out of Porrit's way till I gets back, d'you hear.'

'Yes, Aunt Syb.' She'd only walked a short way but was conscious of being watched. She turned. The children still stood there, they hadn't budged.

'Be off with you then!'

'What about our dinners?'

'We'll have summat to eat when I gets back. Mind you don't go near the river.' She waited until they'd disappeared before setting out on the Thetford road.

40

Chapter Three

A Woman of Property

The bank manager shook his head. 'Any property would become the joint possession of you and your husband, madam.'

'But 'tis my money! What my father left me and what I hev added to since I were fourteen!' Emotion robbed Sybilla of grammar, not of her wits. Sensing the man was adamant, she changed tack swiftly. 'I would share my last farthin' with my dear husband, naturally, but 'e do hev 'is little weakness, poor soul. An' now I'm expected to provide for these dear children as well . . .' She raised her eyes to heaven. 'If I get took, d'you know what would happen? Porrit would throw 'em out in the street. He'd sell up everythin' so's he could go drinkin' an' that's God's truth.'

The manager had never come across such frankness before; he wanted the earth to open and swallow him up. As it adamantly refused to do so, he shrank back against the wall and resorted to banalities.

'I shall respect your confidence naturally, madam. I'm sure some form of protection could be devised –'

'Can you write me a paper sayin' I intends to buy this house I've told you about, then I can show it to anyone who asks?'

'Express your intentions in the form of a letter? I think that would be possible.' He flattered himself that at last he understood this simple country woman. It was unusual for one of her class to be a client of the bank, nevertheless she would make an amusing anecdote with which to regale his London colleagues. He smiled benevolently.

41

'My clerk will draft a suitable document for you to pass to your solicitor.' Sybilla saw she was expected to look grateful and ducked her head submissively. This chap obviously thought she was illiterate but what he'd suggested sounded about right. All she really wanted was headed writing-paper filled with impressive copperplate because Enoch Porrit couldn't read.

'Er, have you a man of business to whom we might address this document?' the manager hinted delicately. 'If not, perhaps I might recommend –'

'Just you put the name an' address of the house I wants to buy,' Sybilla slid a scrap of paper across the desk, ' 'Tis all there. An' I shall need ten pounds to take with me. You get me the money while your clerk does the letter.'

He tried to dissuade her but Sybilla knew her quarry. If rumour was to be believed, the owner – a young widow – had been left penniless. How could *she* resist two brand new, crisp five pound notes? The sight of them made Sybilla salivate.

When the letter and notes were safe in her bag, she began the walk back home in fading afternoon sunlight, planning the next step very carefully indeed.

Wavering shafts of light between the trees made a pattern on the long straight line of the road. Sybilla trudged on, resolute yet nervous, her cheap black skirt swirling in the dust. She'd never in her life had to make such far-reaching plans, nor carry them out unaided, but they were her only hope. Enoch Porrit must not be allowed to drag her down. If she gave up now, she'd end up a penniless drudge, worn out before her time, spending her winters in the workhouse because her man wouldn't or couldn't provide. Sybilla gritted her teeth. Self-respect demanded she keep her nerve – hadn't she once been a ladies' maid?

Persuading the manager had been easy but the widow was a different proposition. How to wheedle a girl she'd known during her schooldays? Sybilla shrugged off doubts and stepped out jauntily. She'd managed to secure a weekly income from parish funds thanks to Mrs Heyhoe's advice. A vulnerable widow shouldn't prove too much of an obstacle.

Curls were tucked out of sight, the collar was fastened as were black cotton gloves. A virtuous wife, that was Sybilla's role on this occasion, and why not? It was indeed virtuous to use her talents to best advantage, according to the Good Book.

Chas, Albert and Polly gravitated to the river bank as naturally as waterfowl. This part of town was unfamiliar, associated with rare walks on summer evenings after harvest. Chas remembered the warnings his father used to shout and shouldered the same weighty responsibility today. 'Mind you don't trip, Pol. Watch your step down there, it's slippery.'

'My boots is too big!'

Their own clothes had been burnt; these black garments supplied by the workhouse were hot and ill-fitting. The boys at least had had their hair cropped, which was welcome in summer heat. Polly might have lost hers too, had not a nurse offered to wash it twice over with Sunlight soap. It had been combed daily for lice and now honey coloured and clean it hung down her back under the hideous charity hat.

Out of habit, Chas thrust his hand in what should have been a familiar darned pocket but it wasn't there. That darn had always reminded him of Mam. She'd mended it after he'd brought home a sharp fossil. She'd never patch or sew for him again, nor would father be there, full of enthusiasm whenever there was something interesting to discuss. The enormity of their loss overcame him and this time he allowed a tear to slide down his cheek.

'Chas . . .'

'Yes, Pol?'

'Do we have to live wiv Aunt Syb?'

'There's nowhere else for us to go. We can't go back home.'

'There is . . .' Albert insisted vigorously. 'There's the workhouse, tha's what him with the watch-chain was *whisperin'* about but the bald 'un couldn't hear 'cause of his belly. "Speak up, why doncha", the bald 'un said,

43

"Those children cannot understand. They look half-witted to me." '

Chas marvelled how his skinny brother could take on a character. In knickerbockers cut down from a pair of old trousers, Albert's legs stuck out like scarred twigs. His stockings were rucked around his boots and he swayed to and fro, feet braced to support an imaginary stomach, one thumb in his armpit as he recited what he'd heard.

' "Nother burden on the parish, no doubt?" "Certainly not," says baldy, "not while they hev a livin' relative. H'I 'ope I know where my duty lies when it comes to the h'a, public purse." '

'D'you think Aunt Syb *wants* us in her home?' As usual, Polly had gone directly to the nub of the problem. Wide shadowy eyes gazed enquiringly, 'Will she be fond of us?' Chas swallowed.

'Not *fond* exactly,' he admitted, 'but she didn't make no more fuss when they said she could have half a crown. An' she agreed Albert and me were to go back to school,' he added with relief. He was sensible enough to realize what it meant to forego education. Polly's anxiety increased.

'What 'bout me. Ain't I goin' back to school?' Shoulderblades shifted beneath the scratchy skirt. Chas would never lie to Polly. On the other hand, to reassure her wouldn't be fair either. Aunt Syb had made no promises concerning her.

'Oh, look!' Albert gazed entranced at the opposite bank, 'There's chaps swimming over there!'

'Crikey!'

It was a tempting spot, where the little Ouse meandered until it disappeared in a bend behind an oak wood. On the opposite side the bank was fringed with reeds which stretched out to meet waterlilies, so thick they lay like flat green saucers, the sluggish current slopping over them occasionally.

A gang of boys whooped in and out of the reeds. One, braver than the rest, gulped in air, dived beneath the lily pads and shot up several feet away, upsetting the resident frogs.

'Best not stare, Pol,' Chas ordered swiftly, 'they ain't got

44

no clothes on.'

'They don't look different from you nor Albert.'

As if hearing a cue, Albert pulled the flannel shirt over his head, yanked off boots and stockings and began wrenching at his buttons.

'What you doin'?' demanded Chas, 'you can't swim!'

'I can try. I'm too hot.'

'No! You're not goin' in that river!'

'You can teach me, Chas.'

'I want to swim too!' Polly reached for her hatpins. Chas grew alarmed.

'Listen, the pair of you. None of us is going in that river because Aunt Syb wouldn't like it. We're not supposed to enjoy ourselves today anyroad!' But the hat was already at Polly's feet and she was struggling out of her pinafore. Chas was scandalized at the thought of what might happen next. 'You can't take your clothes off! Not when there's boys about!'

He was so engrossed in preventing her, he didn't notice Albert was already naked. There was a splash and his brother was in the water, gasping and flailing his arms as he tried to stand up in the soft oozing mud.

'Come out this instant!' roared Chas.

'Can't.'

'What?'

'Can't stand up ... Me feet keep slipping!' The tough rope-like lily stems twined round his legs and the sharper reeds cut his skin. 'Chas!' It was panic. On this side, the current was stronger, sweeping him with other detritus towards the wide curve of the bend.

On the opposite bank the gang stood fascinated and mute.

'Catch a'hold of him, can't you!' Chas implored, 'He's my brother!'

'Chas!' It was Polly, terrified, imploring. 'Get him, Chas. Don' let him drown!' The whimper, a soft animal keening grew shrill as Polly sank in a heap, both arms round her knees. 'Please, Chas, don' let Albert die!'

There was a flurry as the one good swimmer in the gang plunged through the lilies and set off in pursuit.

45

'I hev lost the dearest brother a woman could ever have, as no doubt you've heard. He was a beautiful man . . . as good an' kind as your Joe.' Her former schoolfriend's lip trembled but Sybilla pretended not to see. 'Jeremiah's dear wife and their baby were took as well. 'Tis a most dreadful sorrow and burden 'pon my heart, as I know you will understand.' The widow blew her nose, puzzled as to why such a distant acquaintance had seen fit to call, especially on such a tragic day, and ventured a question.

'I did hear of it, Syb – Mrs Porrit. Was it the pox? Folks round here have been saying it could've been scarlet fever even. That must've been terrible for them poor souls.' Sybilla placed a mysterious finger to her lips.

'The Lord gave, and the Lord hev taken away,' she announced sententiously, 'Don' do for us to ask why he done it. One of life's awful mysteries, the vicar said. An' the doctor hev had all Jeremiah's things burnt. Every stick of furniture, all the plates an' cups broke into pieces an' thrown away.'

'How dreadful!' Sybilla's regret was equally sincere.

' 'Tis so wasteful, Mrs Helliwell, being as now I'm left with three children to rear . . . an' the worry of havin' lately married Enoch Porrit into the bargain.' Mrs Helliwell thought it tactful to make no comment about that. 'Not a patch on your dear Joe, I'm afraid.'

'No.' There simply was no comparison.

'An' how's your dear little baby? Getting to be like his father?'

' 'Tis a girl, Mrs Porrit.' Sybilla gave herself a mental pinch.

'Of course she is! How could I forget when one of the las' things her poor dead father did do was come to the vicarage with her baptismal names. What a lovely day tha' was, when she were christened. Wasn't it the very next day when Joe was shelterin' from the storm tha' the tree split and come down on his dear head . . .?' The widow's tears confirmed it, thick and fast. 'So young,' Sybilla deflected her grief towards practical considerations, 'Not enough time to provide for a family?'

'I don't know where to turn!' Mrs Helliwell's defences

collapsed altogether. 'I'm so embarrassed I can' even offer you a cup of tea, Mrs Porrit. There's no food 'cept what neighbours can spare. They say there won't be no union relief 'cause Joe come from outside the town boundary originally.'

And you just let them walk right over you, you silly woman, thought Sybilla scornfully.

'What about Joe's babby? She were born inside the town all right.'

'I were that upset an' frightened I never thought to tell 'em 'bout her till I'd left the meeting and was outside the door,' the poor woman choked, 'The words wouldn' come into my mind. I dursn't go back again!'

'Tut tut. 'Tis truly dreadful ... poor hungry little innocent.' Sybilla waited until further sobs had subsided before she said, 'But I come to help, if'n I can, Mrs Helliwell.'

'What ... with all your troubles?' The widow looked at her gratefully. Sybilla had a flash of inspiration.

'If we cannot help one another why hev we been sent down to this place, that's what I always say,' she announced for the first time in her life, 'Now then. Me and Mr Porrit, not expecting to be but two people until God sees fit, hev taken this dear sweet cottage by the river ... end of Willow Row – but not damp. Lovely little garden, with flowers. Rent's paid for the whole of the month. An' now, all of a sudden, there's five of us. But there's only the one room upstairs. Little Polly can sleep below but 'tisn't fair on Porrit, not with him an' me havin' to share with two growin' boys.'

She'd inadvertantly reminded Mrs Helliwell of joys lost to her forever, so hurried on before more tears could interrupt.

'There's ever such nice neighbours in Willow End. When I went down the garden first thing, the man next door did turn away and pretend not to see where I was goin'. Waited till I was on my way back afore he said good morning. An' he offered potatoes, freshly dug. Not many as do that.'

Mrs Helliwell nodded sadly. Her house had no immedi-

47

ate neighbours and the front garden was bordered by the London road.

'Pardon me asking, do you have trouble with your drains?' This sounded so officious Mrs Helliwell became alarmed.

'I don't think so. Why d'you ask?'

'Jes' something I overhead,' Sybilla replied enigmatically. 'Set me thinking about that dear little girl ... being as we hev had one or two hot days lately. Not that there's *ever* been any typhoid in this area ...'

Ten minutes later, the infant having been unswathed, examined and calmed by being put to the breast, Sybilla reached the crux of her mission.

'If only she could grow up, surrounded by flowers in a safe pretty garden. Rent is only one and sixpence and I could give you a good price for this place, my dear.' She withdrew the banknotes and slowly unfolded them. Black spidery engraving glistened against the whiteness. Promise to Pay the Bearer Five Pounds. Mrs Helliwell faltered.

'Joe paid over twelve pounds for this house, twelve pounds seven shillin'. I know because it took four years for us to save even though he was qualified.'

The late Joe Helliwell having served his apprenticeship and confident of his prospects had overstretched himself to provide a superior home. 'We'd already discovered it were more'n what we could afford,' his widow confessed, 'Joe thought we should take a lodger.'

'You *couldn't* do that now,' Sybilla was pragmatic, 'think how folks would talk now you're on your own. An' haven't you heard how prices have fallen?' she demanded. ' 'Tis wicked the way us poor folk gets robbed time 'n time again.' She smoothed one of the notes absently, reflected sunlight making a dazzling white lozenge on the ceiling. Gazing sentimentally at the baby, she said, 'Her's like a little flower, ain't she? Which of her names d'you call her by?'

'Gladys.'

'Aah ...' It wasn't long before the house was hers.

The day had been long but it wasn't over yet. Despite her

victories, as she approached Willow End and saw her husband waiting, Sybilla's heart sank. He was hers and she his forever; if only she could have her time over again!

And now there were the three children; how could fate be so unfair? She'd never get to London at this rate. Sorrow for Jeremiah was replaced by anger. Why shouldn't Sybilla have her chance?

'I shall get rid of 'em soon as ever I can,' she promised herself, 'I don' want no children, growing ones an' all, what'll need feeding.' The parish half-crown was forgotten in her self-pity. ' 'Tis wicked, demandin' I should take 'em in – I don' deserve such a burden!'

Gone was married poise; Sybilla was back to being a nineteen-year-old girl, full of frustrated tears.

She prepared the meal in silence while Enoch complained loudly over the day's events. 'The vicar come 'round this afternoon 'n told me I'd got to go to work!' Indignation overflowed, 'God damme, wha' business is it of 'is?' Cups rattled as he thumped the table. Stirring the dumplings, Sybilla allowed herself a moment's satisfaction; she hadn't expected such a speedy result from the Poor Law Committee.

'I had to manage as best I could this mornin', Enoch. They badgered me with questions after the funeral.'

'What sort'a question?'

'About Jeremiah's children, I had to tell 'em we hadn't got no money comin' in till you got back to work.' Enoch's face grew mottled.

'I'm goin't to give 'e a hiding, my girl, one you'll never forget!' Sybilla tried not to quake as she saw the belt in his hand.

'The Receiving Officer said 'e'd call,' she said quickly. 'They could ask for their money back so you'd best not mark me.' Enoch's eyes narrowed. In the small room, his stale breath nauseated her.

'What you talkin' about, wha' money?'

'The Parish says 'tis our duty to take the children. They're givin' us two 'n sixpence a week towards their keep.'

Enoch smashed his fist into the chimney wall,

bringing down plaster.

'I'll not 'ave any of 'em in my house!' he roared, 'An' no one's goin' to tell me wha' to do.' His words took away her fear. This was her cottage, paid for with her money; how dare Enoch claim it was his when he hadn't contributed a penny.

' 'Tis already arranged. They'll be here any minute so sit down an' I'll dish up.' She took the pot through to the scullery. Through the window she could see three small figures huddled beside the privy.

Opening the back door, she called sharply, 'Where you been all this time? Get inside!'

Chas held onto Albert with Polly squeezed in between. 'Face up to it like soldiers . . .' he whispered. It was one of their father's favourite sayings. Polly gave a little cry and Albert nudged her. Ahead, their aunt was silhouetted against the lamp. Behind her was the menacing shape of Enoch Porrit, still holding his belt. 'Stay out o' his way,' Chas quavered. 'Do what she says an' it'll be all right, you'll see.'

They stumbled forward until they reached the light, frightened, soaked, and guilty. Albert held out his offering of bruised willowherb and water lilies. 'I'm sorry, Aunt Syb. I was trying to learn how to swim.'

Blood and dirt mingled on his face. The close-cropped hair was full of weed and Albert had obviously used his shirt as a towel, it was so muddy. For Sybilla, it was the final straw. She'd spent the day at such a pitch of nervous energy, it had sapped her dry. These were no longer desperate, hungry children; all she could see were the three millstones round her neck forever and her control snapped.

She flung Albert's flowers aside, giving him such a clout it sent him reeling. Next she seized Chas and pushed him at Enoch. 'He deserves to be whipped.'

Enoch needed no second invitation. The belt sliced through the air in an arc and Chas screamed. Polly, shocked beyond belief, gave a high wail. Their terror brought Sybilla to her senses. Chas's face was a replica of Jeremiah at the same age, when their father had attacked him for no reason. What on earth was she

50

thinking of?

'No, no, stop!' she cried but her husband was enjoying himself and pretended not to hear. Sybilla pushed between them, forcing Chas into a corner. 'Doan' hit 'im no more, Enoch.'

The belt was raised, Sybilla put up a hand, the leather hissed, burning through the soft skin of her forearm. The pain was so fierce it made her retch. As the huge red weal began to sting, she staggered outside to be sick.

Later, arm throbbing and head aching with tiredness, she and Enoch lay on opposite sides of the bed with Polly curled up in a corner of the room. The boys, arms entwined in misery, were asleep on the floor below.

I've betrayed everything Jeremiah believed in, Sybilla thought bleakly. *He* never hit a soul in his life. As children they'd often clung together after one of their father's onslaughts.

'Tonight I was as bad as ever he was . . . I've got to start showing these three a bit of kindness.'

What did it matter if they were a hindrance, they deserved something of her. 'Have I still got it in me to be kind,' she wondered, 'after marrying *him*?'

'We're not keepin' 'em. Tha's my final word. They go on the Parish tomorrow.' There'd been a defiant note in Enoch's bluster.

'They'll tell people what happened. If they don't, I shall. Or the neighbours might. They was bangin' on the wall tonight or didn't you hear?'

'What of it?'

'The Receiving Officer could stop our money.'

' 'Twas you who said do it. Give 'im a whippin' you said!' As usual, Enoch refused to accept responsibility; with him it would always be someone else's fault. Sybilla was past caring. After only two days she couldn't remember what she'd seen in him apart from his bold, handsome face. Now he'd shown such cruelty it made her blood run cold.

Aloud she said, 'The parish won't take 'em back because of what I promised.'

51

'Wha' was tha'?' Her husband had pushed himself up on one elbow. She could feel his eyes straining to pierce the dark.

'I made a bargain, usin' my savin's.'

'What hev you done, Syb?'

'Doan' start shoutin' again, you'll frighten little Pol.'

'I don' care if'n the devil 'imself 'ears, wha' you done with tha' money?'

'Bought us a 'ome. We're movin' in tomorrow.'

He wouldn't be convinced until she produced her precious letter. Enoch ran his finger over the two signatures, hers and the widow's, unable to distinguish one from the other but recognizing defeat.

When she told him the house had cost every penny, he believed her, and what did one more lie matter? It had turned out as she and Mrs Heyhoe had hoped and planned, only yesterday – part of another age.

After his fury was spent, fury mixed with seething impotence that his wife should get the better of him because of her superior intellect, Enoch turned his back on her. Sybilla listened until regular breathing told her he was asleep. She wanted to give thanks for some kind of salvation, then remembered she'd renounced the Church of England and wasn't yet entitled to pray to the God of the Baptists.

Would the new church confer benefits? Could she persuade the minister to supplement her meagre half-crown? It was worth a try. Sleep began to overtake her.

For the last time, Sybilla stared at the stars through the tiny dormer. She'd only been here a few days but tomorrow it would be a different view of the sky, through the window of her new house. So much had happened it was unbelievable!

She yawned and sorrow flooded in, drowning a spirit left defenceless by tiredness; the time for grieving had finally arrived.

'Oh Jeremiah, I'm sorry I let him beat Chas. It won't happen no more . . . why did you have to die and leave me in this fix?'

Chapter Four

Kezia

The carter spotted the girl in the distance. It was his habit to deduce what he could about strangers. This one had been on the road too long; she limped and carried the small bundle as though it were heavy.

As he drew alongside, she looked up in mute nervous pleading. Taller than he'd first estimated, her body drooped under her shawl but she was clean enough apart from travel stains and appeared respectable, not more than sixteen or seventeen.

He jerked his head. She clambered up clumsily. He realized she was almost asleep on her feet.

They travelled another mile before he spoke. 'Going far?'

She misunderstood. 'I have a little money . . .'

He shrugged; the load was paid for. 'Glad of the company.' This confused her. She tried to slide a little further away along the bench. He snorted – as if he would!

The rhythmic clip-clopping mesmerized her and again her eyelids drooped. The carter satisfied himself she couldn't fall and returned to enjoying the day.

The sun rose higher. The white forehead beside him looked vulnerable. He was about to disturb her when he found she'd woken of her own accord. Wide grey eyes stared at him and he gestured up at the sky.

'Cover yourself. It's going to be hot.' She adjusted her shawl and thanked him.

'There's a spring where I usually water the mare, three

53

mile further on. But we'll not bide long. I want to be the other side of Abergavenny by tonight.'

'There's a railway at Abergavenny.' He couldn't decide whether this was a question.

'There is, yes. You can go down to Pontypool or up to Hereford. Which way are you headed?' The answer came reluctantly.

'To London.'

'London?' The mare's ears went up in an echo of his surprise. 'That's a distance for a young girl?' She didn't reply.

At the spring, he tried again. 'You got friends in London? It's a long way unless there's someone waiting.'

'There's no one. Not any more.' It was finite, hopeless. The carter paused in harnessing up the mare.

'Then why . . .?' But he was a married man with daughters and granddaughters. 'Eh, girl, it's not that, is it?' She went crimson.

'My boy was in the army, see.' It was a relief to be able to unburden herself at last, to a stranger. 'We were to have been wed next year if he'd come back.'

'Is there no one else?'

'Dad was killed down the pit. Mam and me went to live with Gran but there's so little money.' Not enough to support another mouth, apart from the shame a baby would bring.

'Where does your Gran live?'

'Llandefaelog.'

'You've not walked all that way!'

'I left yesterday morning.'

'Where did you sleep?'

'Under some trees. It was dry . . . I was warm enough.' The carter shook his head.

'What will you do in London? Can you speak English?'

'Oh yes. There's work to be had, so they say.'

'You'll need a place to live until you find a situation.' Her stupid innocence exasperated him. 'And what about when the baby comes?' The girl's courage began to fade.

'My boy was in a barracks in London . . . he wrote of Parks.' She pronounced the unfamiliar word carefully.

54

'Parks are locked up at night. You weren't planning to sleep beneath the stars by any chance?' When he saw she was, he clucked angrily and led the mare back onto the road. 'Climb up,' he ordered, 'we've a long way to go yet.'

The girl's name was Kezia. The carter introduced himself as Jacob Jones and sat there, brooding, letting the mare find the route herself. Human flotsam, that's what this child was; sucked towards the great Wen like spindrift on the wind.

By nightfall Kezia was exhausted. She made an effort to express her gratitude as the old carter urged her onto the train. He'd paid for her ticket and given her an address which he made her repeat aloud, convinced she would lose the piece of paper.

'It's my married cousin's sister in Fulham. Stick to those you know, that's my motto. Her husband was in coal-hauling at one time. I don't know what he does now; a bit of this, a bit of that. Don't be frightened by Lemuel's looks, it was nature's doing, not his. Tell Vida it was me that sent you. Send word home to your mam, she'll be worried sick until she knows what's happened. Promise me, now?'

Kezia couldn't make him hear above the steam but the carter watched her lips and was satisfied. He leaned forward and kissed the bony forehead. Bristles scratched the white skin.

'I'll pay you back every penny, Mr Jones.'

'Hush, girl . . . it's not necessary.' God alone knew if she'd even manage to keep herself let alone the unborn child. Jacob Jones sent up a prayer that they wouldn't both die on some hostile pavement. 'Look after the little one. Give my love to Vida and Lem. Goodbye.'

It was a scabby door in a small mews. A narrow row of houses, less than a dozen in total, squatting behind their taller, wealthier neighbours like the poor relations they were. This part of London was expanding fast; already the mews was overflowing with coaches, families and horses.

Kezia could smell London squalor thick and strong. There was a permanent fog at chimney level with no Welsh winds to blow it away. It concealed the sky and filled her lungs with soot. She could taste the dirt, the hem of her petticoat was black with it.

'Yes . . .?'

Don't be afraid, the carter had said, Lemuel can't help the way he looks. Kezia tried not to back away.

'Yes?' The speaker leaned forward, drawn by the pretty bony face, but when he saw the familiar repugnance, he wanted rid of her. 'What d'you want?' Her ear wasn't yet in tune with the accent but Kezia had rehearsed her reply so often, it came automatically.

'Mr Lemuel Meaney?'

'Yes?'

'Have you a room, if you please, Mr Meaney . . . a room to rent. A room,' she repeated again. An anonymous refuge where she could hide. Wordlessly she offered the paper with his name and address. Lemuel Meaney held it up to his one good eye, shifting his awkward body under the gaslight.

'A room, eh? That's rich! A room all to yourself – in London? My word, we are the lady! Here, this is Jacob's fist, isn't it? Vida, you there? Your cousin Jacob's sent us a girl all the way from Wales.'

His face with its unmatched halves so at odds with one another, swung round to face Kezia again. Greasy black hair hung thick on Lemuel's shoulders as if to compensate for the thin covering on his skull. 'Here . . .' the one all-seeing eye appeared to leer as he shoved his face close. 'You're not one of Jacob's own are you, not famb'ly?'

Kezia was so certain he was going to kiss her, she shrieked. The leer disappeared. Lemuel was stoney-faced when his wife came hurrying, demanding to know what the matter was. He said coldly, 'Your cousin Jacob wants to know if we can take her in.'

Vida pulled the girl inside. 'Let's take a look at you then. What d'you say your name was?'

'Kezia Morgan.' Flickering gaslight added to her pallor,

and the hair which had escaped the confining ribbon rippled in thick dark waves. Kezia slumped tiredly against the wall. Even so, she was head and shoulders above the muscular, swarthy Vida.

'You're nothing to do with Jacob then, not related?' The woman was obviously disappointed.

'Mr Jones gave me a lift . . . I told him I was on my way to London . . . I need somewhere to live.' Vida frowned.

'For how long? When would you be moving on?'

Moving on? Where? Kezia stared dazedly into the dark area which made up the whole of the ground floor as if it contained the answer to her problems.

The space, intended as a stable, was choc-a-bloc with evidence of Lemuel's various attempts to earn a living. Resting on its shafts was the big cart from his haulage days. Beside it was another, much more humble hand-cart. Stacked on shelves were tools; 'a bit of this and that' included carpentry, painting, plumbing, rag and bone, anything Lemuel could turn his hand to in an effort to feed and clothe himself and Vida – when he felt inclined.

There were mysterious sacks and wooden boxes, rolls of wire and lengths of wood, nothing that could possibly be of use had ever been thrown away. Dominating all of it was a rancid feral smell, a mixture of stale urine, animal fear and sawdust. Kezia's nose searched for the source.

A small cobwebby window let in enough light, now that her eyes had become accustomed, to see a rickety staircase which led to the living quarters above. Beneath, in deep shadow, were two wooden cages. She heard a rustling and red eyes gleamed like distant rubies.

'What is that!' She'd spoken in Welsh. Vida translated and Lemuel grinned. 'Ferrets. The white one's the female. She bit a rat's head clean off last week. He was big, too, twice the size of her. She's wild . . . the apple of my eye. Come and see.'

He lit a candle and walked across, stepping confidently over various obstacles. Kezia followed. As he held the flame high she could see snowy fur spreadeagled against the mesh as the ferret clung there on curved, transparent

57

claws. The small head moved constantly, delicate whiskers twitching as the ruby eyes followed every move of Lemuel's hand.

Beside the cage were scraps of meat. He shoved a piece through the mesh but, quick as he was, the female ferret moved faster. The candlestick fell to the floor. In the darkness, Kezia heard him curse.

Vida laughed, 'You don't feed them often enough, I've warned you before.'

Lemuel sucked his finger and spat out the mouthful of blood. 'They won't kill unless they're hungry. They're no use to me unless they do that.'

Behind him, Vida stood on tiptoe to turn down the gas. 'Go on up,' she said to Kezia, 'me and Lem can find our way blindfold.'

Upstairs the area was divided into two. A crowded room about twelve foot square provided living quarters. The other space was barely large enough to contain the old-fashioned brass bedstead.

Downstairs, despite the multiplicity of objects, there was order. Here, in Vida's domain, there was chaos. On the paraffin stove, two pans balanced precariously. Heat added to the stuffiness, but Kezia was suddenly aware of the smell of food. She was light-headed from hunger. She hadn't dare waste her money and it was over twenty-four hours since she'd eaten.

Around the stove were kitchen utensils including a worn kettle. Vida seized it and pushed Kezia gently out of the way. 'Take a seat while I see to supper.' Juggling with the pans, she watched the girl covertly. Hunched and apathetic she sat where she'd been bidden. What did Jacob Jones intend by sending her here? Someone who wasn't even family?

Vida brewed strong tea, added a dash of spirits and waited until Kezia had spluttered herself awake. She could hear Lemuel moving about below. He'd stay out of the way until she got to the bottom of this business.

'So . . . you met Jacob on the road and he gave you our address?'

58

The tale didn't take long. Kezia told her simply that she'd come in search of work. She didn't mention the baby or her dead soldier. Her pregnancy didn't yet show.

Vida nodded when she heard Jacob intended to write. 'He'll get around to that come Christmas ... Always does then, with all the *family* news.' The slight emphasis made the girl redden.

'Mr Jones was worried about me but I'll find a situation as soon as I can.'

'Have you a reference?'

'I've never been in service before.'

'What about a *character* or a letter from your minister?' Why this should cause Kezia to look embarrassed added to the mystery. 'How on earth d'you expect to find work?'

'I thought I'd ask at some of the big houses ... Mam taught me to cook and clean. I'm good at pastry...' Vida's expression made her falter.

'You've a lot to learn, my girl. You won't find anyone inviting a stranger in off the street and you can't stay here. Lem's not had much luck lately, we've no money. Can you pay for your keep?' Kezia, scarlet-faced, held out the slim purse. Vida was irritated.

'If that's all you've got, keep it. You'll need every penny.' That the girl obviously didn't understand her predicament annoyed Vida even more. 'Listen, before you can go into service you have to provide your own uniform – and you don't get any wages for a month. To go as a maid, you need morning and afternoon aprons, caps, print dresses and a plain black alpaca for when you give the parlour maid a hand?' She indicated the small bundle contemptuously, 'Have you got all those things? Of course you haven't. Even the skivvy needs to change her apron after she's finished scrubbing. So what have you brought? Anything useful?'

'My apron ... and nightgown,' Kezia mumbled. There was also a blouse which her grandmother had made for her sixteenth birthday, with a crochet edging to the collar. Kezia thought it the most beautiful garment in the world, but she had the feeling Vida would despise it.

59

'Lem can ask when he goes to The Musketeer. Someone might know of a situation. As for clothes, we'll go up Kensington way tomorrow – it's my half day – and do a spot of totting.'

What on earth was that? Kezia was too nervous to ask. Vida surveyed the cluttered room.

'You can sleep on the floor over there. We'll make a pile of the rugs and you can use your shawl.'

She wasn't going to the trouble of shaking the camphor balls out of her one spare blanket for an unwanted guest. Kezia began to thank her but Vida interrupted brusquely.

'Refill the kettle. Pump's outside, Lem'll show you where – and tell him supper's nearly ready. He'll need to wash if he's been cleaning out the cages.'

Mention of the ferrets reminded her; Vida opened the casement. 'Hey, Gyp!' she called softly. There was a scuffle, a yap from the backyard below. She tossed out a bone. 'Lem's terrier,' she said briefly, 'Whatever you do, don't try and make friends with it. Gyp's kept strictly for ratting, he's worse than the ferrets.'

When Lem had left for The Musketeer and she and Vida were preparing for bed, Kezia dearly wanted to strip to her skin but she felt too shy. She averted her eyes as Vida wiped her face and neck with a dingy flannel. 'Empty the slops outside and refill the kettle, Kezia,' she called as she went into the bedroom. 'Leave it on the stove ready for morning.' Kezia huddled quickly into her nightgown.

The rag rugs she lay on were grubby. She longed to fling them over a line and beat the grit out of them. Instead, she piled one on top of one another and tried not to feel itchy through her thin cotton gown. Her soiled petticoat hung on a chair. Filth was so deeply ingrained it sickened her. Tomorrow she would beg some soap – she couldn't bear to wear it in its present state, even though it was the only one she had.

She heard creaking from the next room. Vida was climbing into bed. Kezia rose quietly and pulled off her nightgown. She poured water into the one all-purpose bowl and began to wash, limb by limb, listening anxiously for the slightest indication that Lemuel had returned. A dingy towel hung from a nail. She dried herself on a corner of her shawl instead.

Growing bolder, she peeped outside. The small mews came to life at night. Light from sconces in the tall houses turned wet setts the colour of pewter. For a girl accustomed to the total darkness of a Welsh village, such profligacy was incredible. Gas used to illuminate a whole street! Who could afford waste like that? It was so bright, it outshone the moon.

Carriages came and went, the drivers ducking beneath the low arch, taking the gentry on their evening pleasures. In the mews, children darted with jugs of beer from The Musketeer. Each time the bar door opened, it added another layer of light and gaiety to the noise which bounced and echoed off surrounding buildings. Topping everything were the shouts from those who'd survived another grinding day. London was so terrifyingly alive! And here she was, a part of it.

Without thinking, Kezia rubbed a hand over her thickening waistline. The baby! Adam's child. Conceived on a bank of bluebells with Adam's greatcoat beneath her, and the crushed sappy fragrance intoxicating them both. Dear sweet lord Jesus, would she ever smell wild flowers again! Kezia had a sudden unbearable vision of Adam as he cried, 'Am I hurting you?'

'No, no!'

And when it was done, he kissed her eyelids, making all the rash promises of youth. 'I'll save every penny of my pay . . . We'll be married on my next leave . . . Be true, promise me now?'

'I promise. I love you.'

'Oh, Kezia!'

He'd been killed accidentally. Not gloriously dead in battle but carelessly by a comrade, who'd assumed a loaded musket was empty. When she was told, Kezia kept her grief to herself.

There was no point in telling anyone about the child, either. Adam's parents had objected to her when he was

61

alive, wanting better than a miner's daughter for their only son. It wasn't likely they would welcome her now that he was dead, nor would they forgive her sin, being strict Chapel.

So she nursed her broken heart in silence. Maybe her Gran had guessed about the pregnancy, Kezia couldn't tell. One night, when both mother and grandmother were asleep, she put her note on the table, stroked the dog for the last time and closed the door behind her. Had there been a face at the window to see her creep away? In the note she'd promised to write once she had a situation, to send money when she was able. She told them she knew she was a burden – and left it at that.

Looking out on the mews, Kezia thought again of the baby and as she did so, the image of the ferret, savage curved claws reaching up to tear tiny limbs apart, became frighteningly real. Kezia stifled a cry. She mustn't let fantasies crowd her brain. The cruel world outside had distorted her imagination. She must remain calm for the child's sake.

But how could she be true to Adam? What chance was there in London for a penniless girl to provide for an illegitimate child?

Chapter Five

The House on the London Road

It was small but, for Sybilla, it was a miracle of achievement. Overnight she'd risen the social ladder to unbelievable heights. Not even a lady's maid would be her equal now: Sybilla had become a woman of property!

When the time came to leave for London she wouldn't be hoodwinked into selling this house for ten pounds either, she'd demand nothing less than fifteen! For good measure, just suppose there'd been another miracle by then? Suppose she'd become a widow! There was nothing like hope to bolster the spirits.

'A real bay window!' She resisted the urge to measure the span with her arms. It was the only desirable feature in the otherwise small, square room; a wide sash with glazed side windows and folding shutters. Sybilla considered these old-fashioned. When she could afford it, she'd buy a Venetian blind with varnished wooden slats – the height of elegant perfection! The Queen was reputed to favour Venetian blinds in Osborne House. Sybilla gazed contentedly to where the lawn sloped down to join the London Road. Just to see carts bound where she was headed gave her a thrill. Buckingham Palace . . . she might see that too, eventually.

If the past few days had brought changes in Sybilla's life, this morning's events had left Enoch in a state of shock. He'd clung to the gate, refusing to walk up the short gravel path. 'We can't afford to live 'ere! What about furniture? You needn' think I'm buying any.'

'Keep your voice down, they ain't gone yet – Aah, here she is . . . Morning, Mrs Helliwell. An' how's that dear, sweet little babby?' Try as she might, Sybilla couldn't remember the infant's name. 'All ready for your new home then?' she cooed.

Enoch watched from a distance until Mrs Helliwell plus pram and pantechnicon had disappeared in a stately procession towards Willow End. He had nothing better to do so kicked idly at the flint wall which divided their property from the adjoining one.

A week ago he'd been boasting how he'd found a gullible fool to keep him in clover. That same girl had turned his life upside down. Not only that, she'd spent *their* money on a house they couldn't afford and taken in three unwanted children. Well, they could go straight to the workhouse, he wasn't prepared to argue about it. He'd said so last night, repeating it again this morning, which made it all the more infuriating that Syb should ignore him as though she were deaf. It came to Enoch suddenly – his wife was disobeying him! For one of his temperament it was the final straw.

All the same, memory of what *he* had done made him hesitate. The silence last night when the belt slashed her arm, the accusing eyes of those children, the livid weal and then the blood. Enoch kicked so hard, the toe of his boot split open and he swore, blaming this on Syb as well. Nor was there any prospect of his life improving. The present was bad enough but what of the future?

He glanced again at the house; the very sight of it added to his frustration. This wasn't a dwelling in which he could ever be comfortable. It amazed him that Syb walked in as though she belonged. Two-storied grey flint bordered by decorative brickwork with varnished window-frames all carefully wood-grained. The middle-class front door came complete with a letterbox and a proper lock. Enoch had never used a key in his life. He'd been born in a house where every door had a latch, he'd moved from there to Willow End. He could manage that type of fastening however drunk. Here he was in danger of being shut out.

What was worse, his life was no longer inviolate. From now on, night or day, those Guardians of the Poor, the blasted vicar or Receiving Officer were liable to drop by

64

and order him back to work. Enoch Porrit's happiness had been ruined by a stupid, pasty-faced girl – one he'd imagined malleable and eager to please – who'd tricked him into marriage by promising him her savings! She was frigid in bed. Blackest of all was the knowledge he was bound to her for life.

'I shall put tables an' chairs out there, when I can afford it. An' a sign above the gate –'

'We ain't really going to stay here?' Enoch whined. He'd changed tactics to cajole the Parish money from her.

'Of course we're staying, 'tis paid for, I told you. An' I want you to paint on it, "Teas".'

'What!'

'There's plenty come visitin' the town these days, an' next summer they say there'll be railway excursions from London. They'll need refreshments. Now, where have those boys got to? We've only got the loan of tha' barrow 'till one o'clock.'

She bustled past having dented his self-confidence still further: not only was Syb in charge, she'd obviously planned the future course of their lives without consulting him.

Enoch made no attempt to follow. Uncertain, bewildered, here he was in the wrong part of town away from his friends, with a wife he didn't love and those three little bastards who never stopped staring at him – he wanted to shove his fist into Syb's face, he wanted to kill her! Rage blinded Enoch and he stumbled outside.

'Gie us tha' money?'

'What money?'

'You know! Tha' half crown they give you.'

Today a stiff breeze presaged rain. The three children had arrived, panting, pushing the barrow with the few belongings piled upon it. Sybilla had been urging them to unload as quickly as possible. She kept her voice calm as she moved towards her husband. Neither he nor the children must know she was afraid.

'I can't give you any of that money, Enoch, 'tis for their food –' His hand landed heavily on her mouth. Polly screamed. ' 'Tis all right, maid,' Sybilla felt her teeth tenderly with her tongue. Thank goodness none were loose, she'd few enough left on that side. Enoch had been careful to avoid her sore arm, she realized sourly.

'He don't mean to hurt, did you, Enoch?' It was half-intended as mockery but weren't those the words other women used when 'keeping up appearances' in front of the children? Sybilla's jaw tightened; she'd sunk to the level of a beaten drab.

'Give us!'

There was no question of refusing him, he would only hit her again. She fished out sixpence. 'All of it,' he threatened, 'half a crown you said you got. Don' keep me waitin'.'

'What'll I use to buy vitals?'

'Tha's your lookout. Go 'n ask for some more.'

When she'd recovered Sybilla knew that, with cash in his pocket, she had at least won a breathing space but she was still shaken. After last night, she'd imagined Enoch would leave her in peace for a while. Would she have to make good her boast and complain to the Thetford magistrates? So soon? What had been said in heat now made her apprehensive. Would *they* listen? She could end up a laughing-stock.

She set the children tasks, leaving Chas in no doubt what would happen if these weren't done by the time she returned then, having scoured the rectory cooking pot till it shone, Sybilla set off with it to consult her own personal oracle.

The children were numb. From a loving home in which parents rarely shouted, Enoch's cruelty terrified them. Chas could feel where the belt buckle had cut his skin. If Aunt Syb hadn't intervened, would his uncle have carried on until the flesh was stripped from his bones? To a boy's fevered imagination, it seemed highly likely.

Polly and Albert watched him anxiously: he was the rock on which their safety depended. One of Sybilla's old aprons hung in folds around Polly's neck, making her a scarecrow. She and Albert were supposed to be scrubbing floors, Chas had been ordered to clean the windows, instead he looked down from the front bedroom as Enoch headed towards the old part of the town.

'He's going to drink all the money they giv' her for *our food*.' The words were slurred because of a shivering fit. School and the fever hospital had been the toughest experience of life so far; nothing had prepared Chas for Enoch's violence.

'Will it be like last night when he gets back?' Nightmares had left Polly with smudges under her dark eyes.

'We'd best get started. We got to finish before she comes home.' No point in inviting trouble.

Albert attacked the floorboards frenziedly, holding the scrubbing-brush with both hands and working his body up and down. The burst of energy didn't last. Polly tried to wipe away excess water with an over-large mop. Chas continued to stare outside. 'Don't reckon I can stick it if he starts on me again,' he said, his teeth chattering in another fit. He'd expressed their terror into words. Polly hugged herself tightly and Albert bit his lips to prevent them trembling.

'It might not be so bad next time . . .' but his optimism faded. 'What's going to happen?' Chas was troubled. Albert and Polly were his responsibility; his father's last message had been to confirm it.

'He didn't hit either of you –'

'He might!' Polly's wail was piercing. 'He might next time. What are we going to do, Chas!'

'Run away.' The prospect was frightening but it was the only solution he could think of.

'Could we manage?' Albert asked chokily.

'We'll have to, one day.'

'You won't leave me behind?' Polly's tears joined the puddles on the floor. Chas pulled himself together and blew his nose.

'Listen, we'd best get the jobs done while I think where we can go. We'll stick together, whatever happens.' Polly was immediately satisfied. Albert began attacking the floor and he was left to worry on his own. 'One thing I am going to do though, an' that's teach the both of you to swim,' Chas breathed hard on the window pane and started to rub, 'No more of that silly drowning business.'

Mrs Heyhoe was less welcoming this morning. Part of her admired Sybilla's ability to survive but she'd never really liked the girl. It offended her propriety that a parlour maid, who'd originally come for advice, should now behave as her equal. Nor could she abide constant demands for help. Mrs Heyhoe had already decided to occupy the morning with training Sybilla's successor. Slightly put out, therefore, she sent the new girl upstairs while she dealt with her visitor.

Without being aware of it, she was jealous of what the former parlour maid had achieved. Unwin should've been cowed; instead, she'd ended up owning a house. Chas, Albert and Polly were another matter, however. Mrs Heyhoe was indignant when she learned what had happened to Parish funds.

'He'd no business stealing that money! I'll see if there's scraps left over for their suppers. Imagine, hitting you until you give it him! You're not to come begging every day, mind.'

Sybilla prudently ate humble pie and gave every outward sign of finding it wholesome. She thanked Cook effusively and submitted her new plan for her inspection.

'It seems to me it could happen each time Porrit finds out I got money. So I can't rely on Parish funds, I got to earn some as well. An' what come to mind was that picture in one of your magazines – two men on pennyfarthin's – d'you remember? All sweaty, they looked. As if they could do with a glass of sasparilla. There's more'n more of 'em about the town these days. Some come a long way. I expec' they're just 'bout dyin' for a drop of tea.'

'And you're aiming to provide?'

'If'n I can.' Sybilla wondered if she dare confide another matter. 'I didn't let Enoch know exac'ly how much the new home cost, Mrs Heyhoe. It was ten pounds – which was a bargain for 'tis worth fifteen. I kep' something back, for furniture and such. I hope you'll not tell anyone? The

Receiving Officer wouldn't give me another penny if he knew. As long as Enoch thinks I'm skint, he won't try and beat the rest out of me ... 'twas a sin to lie but you understand why I did it.'

'I do, Mrs Porrit.' Ten pounds? The girl got her head screwed on all right.

' 'Tis the drink, you see. Cash is liquid down my husband's throat. An' it makes him so brutal ...' The injured arm was suddenly conspicuous. Sybilla waited, confident of Mrs Heyhoe's reaction.

'That bandage don't look very tidy.'

'I had to manage as best I could, the children were too upset. All I had was this rag.'

'Would you like me to ...?' Sybilla leaned forward.

'Mrs Heyhoe, I didn't like to ask. It hurts real bad ... I'm worried to death 'bout it.'

She had to grit her teeth but it was worth it. Once the wound had been exposed, Cook's anger grew. Any reservations were overcome by the sight of puffy, torn flesh. Sybilla had to submit to a poppy-head fomentation before soothing ointment was applied. After consuming a restorative glass of sal volatile she eased the conversation towards her objective.

'I was thinking ... about my husband's weakness.' Mrs Heyhoe forebore to ask which particular one. 'If'n I could provide him with home-made wine of an evening it might stop him spending all our money at The Five Bells. I remember you telling me it don't cost nothing to make ... an' maybe Enoch wouldn't get so excitable with wine, not like beer. You said it had sent the vicar to sleep once, when he was getting fidgety. It never put him in a temper, neither.' Mrs Heyhoe frowned severely.

'That depends on how you make it, Mrs Porrit. 'Tis a secret, how to brew good wine and not everyone has the *discretion* to know when to offer it.' Sybilla held her tongue. 'It takes experience to judge who to give to ... and how much.' There was a long pause while the rocking-chair went back and forth.

'I remember what happened to the constable that time,' Sybilla murmured softly, 'when he kept hanging round this kitchen. Always under your feet, you said he was, an' then you offered him a glassful to teach him a lesson.' Despite herself, Mrs Heyhoe found herself smiling. Sybilla leaned forward conspiratorially. 'I never told everyone why he come to ride his bicycle straight through the front hedge but I knew all right.'

'Missed the gate by twenty yards! Never come back, thank the lord. Yes, that was my rhubarb,' cook reminisced, 'with a drop or two of brandy stirred in to hide the smell of laudanum. I needed to get rid of him that time because my pork loin was spoiling in the oven. I knew if he was woozy enough he'd want fresh air. Trouble was, I overdid it.'

She weighed Sybilla up carefully. 'You don't want to do that, not even with your husband. My wine is too powerful to risk making a mistake. There was a woman in Bury one time, kept giving her man too much . . . when his kidneys failed the doctor gave out it was her fault. Folk pointed the finger. She's still a widow. Other chaps dursn't take a chance on her.'

Widowhood was such a beguiling prospect, Sybilla fought to keep the eagerness out of her voice.

'A glass or two couldn't do no harm, surely? It might put a man in a sleepy frame of mind, an' quieten his temper. 'Tis Jeremiah's children I worry about.'

'Of course you do.' They both knew this wasn't her real purpose. Cook handed her guest a cup of tea and took a step nearer the truth. 'Children can be a mixed blessing in this world, Mrs Porrit, not always welcome. An' a hot-blooded man can be a trial, so I've heard.' Delicacy forbade further probing; Sybilla sipped her tea.

'He don't know his own strength when *beer* hev inflamed his brains,' she admitted, 'tha's when he either hits me or won't leave me in peace. He won't give over neither, whatever I says.' Mrs Heyhoe looked at her speculatively.

'You can have a couple of bottles to start you off. I might show you how to make it, in time; we shall have to see.' The implication was obvious, nothing untoward must occur. Sybilla smiled her gratitude.

'I can't pay at present, Mrs Heyhoe, but I was thinking

70

. . . This new girl who you say ain't up to much . . . if I was to train Polly the way you taught me. She'd be just what you was looking for in a year or two.' Mrs Heyhoe considered.

'Won't you be needing her when you're doing afternoon teas? You'll be baking cakes and scones and such, running in and out with trays all the time.'

Sybilla intended that someone else should do that chore. Polly might turn out to be pretty. With Enoch's inclination towards her sex, the sooner the child was in a safe haven, the better; she owed that much to Jeremiah.

'And what about the two boys, Mrs Porrit?'

'They'll be kept busy, helping with the washing,' Sybilla said, revealing another stratagem. ' 'Tis a long time till next summer. I might try one table to start with for 'twill be next year before I can afford to buy four more chairs. If I'm to provide meantime, I shall have to take in washing. Albert can fetch an' deliver, an' Polly can help with the mangling. Chas can earn his keep on a farm, like his father used to. I hope you'll consider me for linen, Mrs Heyhoe. You remember how I used to get a nice crisp edge on all His Nibs' cravats? 'Specially if the new girl ain't up to much.'

'Maybe.' One thing at a time; changing a launderer was a serious business. As she showed her out, Cook asked curiously, 'What'll you do if Porrit does keep taking the money?'

'I don't know,' Sybilla admitted, 'I'll have to think of summat or we'll starve.'

'Why not tell His Nibs?'

' 'Twouldn't be right, not now I'm joining the Baptists.' Mrs Heyhoe was appalled.

'He won't like that! Not after what he's done for you.' This annoyed Sybilla. Any achievements were her own; in her eyes the man of God was partly to blame for her present predicament by not warning her about Enoch.

'He never 'elped. He should never hev married me to Enoch Porrit. All that talk when he called me to his study that time – how was I to know what he meant? "Porrit's infelicitous carnal inclinations" – he should hev given me a dictionary if he'd wanted me to understand. What lies

71

Enoch did tell in church an' all. "Love and cherish"? "Honour"? I'll tell you what, Mrs Heyhoe, the only true promise he made was "till death us do part". I'm stuck with him and His Nibs knew I would be – but he never said so plain even though I took him his tea every blessed morning.'

Mrs Heyhoe watched the stubborn figure march off down the drive, the set of her shoulders as defiant as ever.

Ah, but would you have listened if His Nibs had spoken out, she wondered? Leopards are not renowned for changing their spots, neither was Sybilla Porrit. She would always demand her own way and pay no heed to the consequences. What Mrs Heyhoe didn't yet understand was that this same obstinate streak would eventually prevent Sybilla from going under.

Albert and Polly alternately danced or dawdled along the road as they made their escape. They'd debated the morality of taking the heel of a loaf from the pantry. 'It was intended for us,' Chas reasoned, 'I heard Aunt Syb tell Uncle Porrit.'

'If'n it's still there it's 'cause he didn't want it then,' Albert pointed out.

'Right,' Chas stuffed the bread inside his jacket. 'All set?'

'Yes!' Polly's eyes were shining. 'We really are going to run away – and you won't leave me behind?'

'No.'

'Cross your heart?'

'An' hope to die . . .' The words hadn't held any meaning previously. Chas shrugged off remembrance of yesterday's funerals. 'Come on, let's get started.'

They set out in mid afternoon. Evening crept up stealthily as excitement gave way to trudging, and with it the wind. Branches swooped down, dried leaves made a harsh scolding chatter. Polly began to falter. 'We're nearly there,' Chas urged.

'You said it was a special place, with hidey holes.'

'It is . . . you'd remember if you hadn't been so little.'

72

It had been a golden day. Mam with the new baby at her breast, laughing delightedly as he and Albert climbed to the top of the old earthworks and rolled all the way to the bottom. Time and time again they'd done it until they could no longer move. They'd curled up like tired puppies for a nap. Father had woken them. 'Time to explore. This is where the Old 'Uns used to come for their flints so tread carefully.'

He led the way. He'd learned it from his father who'd learned it from his, the same way all the legends were handed down over the centuries. Forcing their way through gorse and scrub they crossed undulating ground, both boys haring down hollows and up the other side. At the bottom of a deeper incline, they sat cross-legged to hear the ancient story. Father had found each of them a special flint. Chas's had the impress of a tiny, long-dead starfish, half the size of his fingernail; Albert's had the spiral of a fossilized snail.

They listened intently to tales of Gods and Romans, of treachery and devastation, of a peaceful time when fathers and sons came here for flints to fashion into tools, of a terrible time when invaders killed the people and the land was stained with blood. The boys gripped their flints tightly. Any minute now an invader with a sword might appear over the lip of their hollow and they would have to defend themselves!

Chas examined his flint more closely. It had been honed to a fine sharp edge ready for hunting, according to father. He ran a finger along it, and cut himself. Drops of blood fell onto the sandy soil as though the Old Uns were set on answering any disbelief.

Chas had glanced nervously over his shoulder, half expecting to see another boy, dressed in furs, an axe in his hand. Common-sense reasserted itself but not before father had noticed and smiled quietly to himself.

They held on to one another as they made their way back to where Mam waited patiently. But why be afraid, Chas had reasoned with himself? Such ghosts, if they existed, would be friendly. In the sunshine of that far-off afternoon, he almost believed he could hear echoes of their

73

laughter among the distant trees.

They returned via the spot where father had discovered the flints. Jeremiah Unwin paused, stopped and pushed a halfpenny into the crevice. Copper glinted in the sunlight before it was hidden. Albert had rushed ahead to show his mother his fossil but Chas held back to ask about the coin.

'To propitiate Old Grim,' father told him seriously.

Would they need to propitiate the Gods today? They hadn't a single coin between them.

'Come on,' Chas called urgently, aware how late it was. Polly was hesitating. In the gloaming the earthworks had a menace he hadn't been aware of before. Albert remembered the picnic.

'Are we going to play? We did before.'

'No. We're going to find a place to sleep and then we'll make a fire to keep warm, like they did in ancient times. Polly can see to the food. You and me are going to be hunters from now on.'

'Kill things, you mean?'

'Why not?'

'You don't mean – rabbits?' Albert and Polly were speechless. This was strictly forbidden; poachers were sent to prison.

'It'll be all right if we don't tell anyone,' Chas sounded braver than he felt. The other two still stared. 'Well, we got to eat something. I'm hungry.' That was a mistake.

'So am I!'

'Ssh, Pol!' Why look over the shoulder now? The spirits weren't here today – were they? 'You two find the firewood,' Chas ordered abruptly. 'Don't lose sight of her, Albert. I'm going to look for somewhere to sleep.'

Sybilla was too wrapped up in her own concerns to be worried at first. She was annoyed to discover the children were missing but at least they were out of Enoch's way, which was a relief. Not that there was much chance of him returning early. With all that money in his pocket, he'd be standing treat to every layabout in the town.

74

It was when she discovered the loaf had gone that Sybilla became annoyed. She'd give them a slap for taking that. With a bit of dripping, that would have done for tea. A daddy-long-legs buzzed round the empty safe. Sybilla flapped at it idly. The lazy little devils hadn't made much of a job scrubbing in here, she'd scold them about that too as soon as they got back.

She wandered into the kitchen. There were one or two items of furniture here which Mrs Helliwell hadn't been able to accommodate. The widow had hinted she wouldn't mind a little compensation but Sybilla had turned a deaf ear. As she saw it, they were part of the fixtures and fittings.

The front parlour was bare. As soon as she could, Sybilla intended to buy an aspidistra to put on a bamboo table in the centre of her bay; that would furnish the room and make her the equal of every fine lady in the land.

Upstairs, her trunk and Enoch's spare boots were lined up neatly in the main bedroom. Tonight they would all have to sleep on the floor. Sybilla had earmarked that first precious half-crown for palliasses. Now her beautifully embroidered sheets would have to be pawned instead, and God alone knew how she was going to provide food. Cook's scraps would be made to last as long as possible.

By nightfall, she was concerned for the children. She searched as far as Willow End, then along the riverbank. None of the gang of boys had seen the three today. Back at home, finding Enoch hadn't returned, Sybilla pocketed her pride and went for help.

The constable knew the way of small boys; he'd been a powerful force in various young lives over the years. He lit his lantern, adjusted the shutters and set off. Searching the fields at a discreet distance from the isolated farm cottage that had been their home didn't take long. Doors and windows remained barred, the doctor's notice was still in place; local people hadn't been tempted to venture here, neither apparently, had the children.

There was one other place where they might try to hide, though . . . the constable cursed at the thought of the bicycle ride ahead.

Albert and Polly hadn't found much wood. At first they'd been excited by the place Chas had chosen, but when a bat squeaked low, Polly declared it was haunted and he had to find another, shallower hollow. It grew colder, the wind freshened. Chas had to coax the fire to keep it alight.

'I want to go home!'

'How about some food. You're in charge of that, Pol.'

'I'm so cold!'

'This wood's too damp. Where did you put the loaf?' Polly pointed to where they'd gone to first; in the gloom, it was difficult to distinguish one mound from the next.

'Over there, I think.' Chas got to his feet. 'You're not leaving us!'

'I'm hungry too, you know. Albert'll look after you.'

'We'll come with you.' Albert grabbed one hand, Polly the other. 'We'll stick together like you said.' A disembodied booming voice boomed out of the darkness.

'Hallo? Anyone there?'

'Aaah!' Polly surpassed herself. 'AAAAH!' The lantern's beam shone on Albert. He let out a bellow.

'The Old 'Uns hev come for us!'

Dratted kids, thought the constable. 'Here, hold your noise, and stay where you are.'

Chas and Albert each got a clip on the ear but neither cared. The constable didn't lay it on like Enoch. It was enough for Albert to sob out the story of the belt for him to gaze at them thoughtfully. He raised the lantern above their heads.

'Show me what he done!' Shivering, Chas pulled up shirt and vest, revealing the scar.

' 'e didn't ought to,' Albert insisted loyally, 'Chas didn't do nothing, 'twas me fell in the river. Chas helped fish me out.'

'I don't want to hear 'bout that. 'Tis fools that go in tha' river when they don't know how to swim. Come over here.' The huge bulk, the constable's ghostlike face above the glimmer and his reassuring warmth as he bent closer made them draw near. 'Now then, you listen to what I has to say. You're to come along an' not give me any lip. I

76

promise to see you're all right once we get back.'

'Will 'e hit us again, mister?'

'Not if you behaves yourself and doesn't run off.'

'Oh, no!' There were goblins and goodness knows what out in that darkness.

'I'll tell 'im how you didn't really mean to run off,' Polly reached up to whisper earnestly.

'Mister, Uncle Porrit can't prop'ly understand when he's full of beer. Will you make sure he does?' The constable nodded impressively.

'Don't you worry about that, maid. I 'as a way of makin' folk understand me. Come on, up you get.' One massive arm scooped her onto his shoulder. 'Put your arms round my neck and you two, catch a hold of my tunic.' They set off at a stumbling walk on either side of his bicycle. Above them, clouds raced across the moon.

When Enoch finally returned, the hastily convened reception committee were waiting for him. He'd swaggered most of the way, determined to reassert his authority, but the sight of constable plus vicar, plus Sybilla's newly bandaged arm, so white under the oil lamp, made him snarl.

Had she actually gone and done it? Reported him to the authorities? He'd beat her raw if she had! A man could do what he liked when it came to a wife, she'd be begging before he'd done with her. He was so consumed by anger he scarcely heard the vicar begin. Only gradually did the words sink in.

The children had run away because he'd frightened them? So much the better. Let them go to the workhouse where they belonged. Enoch opened his mouth to tell the vicar so but the man wouldn't let him speak.

With each sentence, the vicar held up the shackles of Enoch's life for him to inspect, that he should comprehend their weight. Those marriage vows had been sworn in front of witnesses. He had undertaken responsibility for a wife, it was only Christian therefore to accept her three orphaned relatives as well. It had been a criminal act to steal public money. His last chance of avoiding gaol was to return to work, in support of his new family.

As he heard this, the ferment of hate inside Enoch nearly exploded.

'If I hear one more complaint against you, Porrit, I shall see to it that you appear before the magistrates.' Safe in the knowledge the constable would protect him, the vicar leaned forward until they were only inches apart. 'I shall condemn you from the pulpit. People in this town will learn the full extent of your depravity.'

What about my arm, thought Sybilla indignantly, when's he going to scold Enoch for that?

But the vicar wasn't interested in the rough and tumble of marital bliss; his responsibility ended with the Poor Law fund. He continued his homily a little longer before taking up his hat. When he'd gone it was the constable's turn.

'Porrit.'

'Wha'?'

'You didn't get catched down the warren that time.'

' 'Tweren't me.'

'Of course it were. Now you listen. Poachers who wallop little children sometimes has nasty accidents, 'specially in the dark.' The constable moved so that his bulky shadow spread across the wall as high as the ceiling. 'If'n I hear you been using that belt again, I wouldn't fancy your chances if you 'n I should happen to bump into one another one dark night . . .'

He picked up his cape. 'Here, missus, buy the children supper.' He put two pennies on the table, jerking a shoulder at Enoch. 'Next time he helps himself to your purse, do what my mother used to, pick up your rollin' pin.' The back door closed behind him. Enoch Porrit faced his wife across an unbridgeable void.

'I 'ope you're satisfied.' The words had no real meaning, there wasn't a scrap of hope in Enoch's voice. But when Sybilla considered the question – she discovered she was indeed, satisfied.

She'd converted her savings into property, thus protecting them. As bricks and mortar, their value would increase. She could survive, meanwhile, by taking in washing, and next summer there was the glittering prospect of providing afternoon teas. Best of all she'd managed to hang on to the rest of her money.

Did anything else matter? Certainly not the new tight bitter lines round her mouth. Why bother about her looks? She knew for a fact love wasn't worth a candle; from now on all her energies would be directed towards reaching London.

Romance had been an illusion. A brief memory of Jeremiah and Barbara made her pause but Sybilla thrust the image aside. Their marriage had been different. Enoch didn't know what love meant, he wasn't capable of understanding. She, on the other hand, would learn to manage without.

As for her husband's brutality, at least he'd been cut down to size. She recognized that any money he earned from now on would be spent on himself, but so be it. She'd manage to keep herself and the children, somehow. She had the wine for emergencies, with luck she wouldn't get pregnant. All in all, a week which had begun badly had started to improve. No point in provoking him, though.

She asked politely, 'Shall we go to bed, Enoch? You'll want to be up early now you're going back to work.'

He watched her turn down the wick. He was a man of limited resources and those had been emasculated. He'd lost his mastery over every situation. He could still demand his rights over his wife, and would, when he felt inclined. But where was the pleasure in going to bed with this woman, especially now she was no longer afraid?

He'd have to work because *they* would hound him if he didn't. As for poaching, that surge of adrenalin when he darted down hidden Breckland paths, outwitting the world – he could feel it begin to ooze away. From now on there would always be the spectre of that bulky figure with his bulls-eye lantern, waiting for him in every patch of shadow.

For the first time, the bully in him experienced fear. All life's savour disappeared. Enoch wanted to kick out, to crush, to kill even – but in his new-found despair, he recognized the futility of smashing so much as a tea-cup. Leaden-footed, he followed his wife dutifully up the stairs.

Chapter Six

A Providential Situation

One small attempt by Kezia to show gratitude to her new hosts misfired badly. When Vida returned from the Battersea bottling factory to enjoy what was left of her half-day, her neighbour was on the lookout. 'That girl's run the pump dry.'

'What?'

The woman indicated the bedroom windows. 'She's still at it.' They could see Kezia polishing the bare panes.

'Where's my curtains?'

'She's hung them in there.' Vida peered through the open mews doors; the shafts of Lemuel's haulage cart were laden with washing. 'First it was your carpets, then the bedding. She's stoned the step an' all. It's not spring cleaning time – what you trying to do, Vida? Show us all up?'

On the ground floor, the feral smell had almost disappeared. Lemuel had shut the small window tightly when they'd first moved in, nailing it fast. It had been flung wide open and both ferrets stood erect, bodies pressed against the mesh, muzzles quivering ecstatically at the onrush of fresh air.

'Don't you two start thinking of escaping,' Vida warned them as she climbed the stair. 'I'm back,' she called. 'What the devil have you been up to, Kezia?'

It was familiar now, to see the girl blush. She'd bundled her hair under a cap and wore a sacking apron over her pinned-up skirts – even so she was attractive. She also looked younger still in daylight. Could she be as much as sixteen? Vida demanded crossly: 'Our house not good enough then?'

'Oh, no!' Hands went out in supplication, 'I wanted to please you.'

'Don't bother,' she said tiredly. There was floor space where there hadn't been before. Their possessions were neatly stacked instead of lying where they fell. 'I hope Lemuel can find his belongings, that's all.'

'I can show him where everything is . . .' Kezia was deflated. It had been a colossal mistake. All she'd done was draw Vida's attention to her own slovenliness.

'If there's any water left in that pump . . .' Vida eased off a wornout shoe, 'I could do with a cuppa.' Kezia fled downstairs with the kettle. On her own, Vida marvelled. The walls had a yellow pattern underneath the dirt, she'd forgotten that.

Totting, it turned out, was bewildering. It consisted of shouting loudly as they pushed the handcart through Kensington, demanding any old rags, clothes or iron. If a child ran out with an offering, Vida offered a bowl of comfits immediately. 'Help yourself and God bless you, my dear,' but when a young shop assistant hurried after them, asking money in exchange for two worn pans, Vida smiled blandly. 'I only wish I could, young sir. I'm working for an employer. Mean? You wouldn't believe. Quality is what I'm after, you see. Those ain't exactly top class.' He disappeared without even a sweetmeat as consolation and Vida whispered triumphantly, 'Those'll fetch threepence as scrap, you see if they don't.'

Kezia clung to a shaft of the handcart, deafened by Vida's shouts. They had one encounter with an organ grinder who yelled at them to clear off. In the next street two ladies were distributing religious tracts. Vida accepted one, simulating gratitude. 'Thank you kindly, madam. I wonder if you could help us? My poor cousin here . . . come from Wales without even a spare chemise . . . She has to earn her living see, but she can't, not without proper clothes.'

To Kezia's shame, Vida had insisted she wear the

81

hessian apron for their outing. She'd also been told not to speak. 'Act dumb,' Vida ordered, 'try not to blush, neither. It makes you look healthy and we want people to feel sorry.'

The younger of the two ladies glanced enquiringly at her companion. 'I think our maids might have cast-offs, don't you, Miss Travers?' Vida jumped in quickly.

'We could come back after dark so's not to embarrass you.' Miss Travers was already insulted.

'You may attend our Mission as is right and proper,' she retorted. 'We do not permit beggars at our address. It is unseemly for young women such as yourselves to solicit in the streets.'

'Beg pardon, madam . . .' Vida abased herself even further and Miss Travers appeared mollified.

'Your circumstances certainly appear unfortunate,' she admitted grudgingly to Kezia, 'and it is true our Mission was founded to aid the destitute. We do not permit riff-raff, however. Every applicant must be of excellent character and Godly habits.' She frowned severely. 'We seek to nurture the soul not the flesh.'

'The soul must come first,' Vida agreed piously. Her ankles were swollen, her stomach rumbled and she was ready to give her soul for somewhere to sit, but judging by Miss Travers' expression, the body was merely an offensive necessity.

'The flesh must be scourged in order to save the soul!' Miss Travers cried. To this Vida could not respond; against her will she was forced to deny her flesh daily. 'We do provide a small amount of sustenance,' Miss Travers admitted and at this Vida perked up. Food as well as clothes! With luck she could pinch enough for Lem's supper. Miss Travers sniffed at the thought of those provisions. 'Not enough food to gorge the body,' she warned, 'just sufficient to prevent faintness.' Indeed it had been the sound of starved bodies collapsing during the services which had forced these fervent Mission workers to provide any nourishment at all.

'Forgive us, ladies, we had to do as best we could, which is why we come here today,' Vida murmured ingratiatingly. 'My cousin needs to earn her crust. To do that, she needs proper garments.'

'Has she a situation?' The younger woman gazed at Kezia compassionately.

'Has she a tongue in her head,' snapped Miss Travers. 'We must not interfere, Miss Williams.'

'If you did happen to know of a place?' Vida switched her charm to the impressionable one, 'My cousin's ever so willing and very good at housework. In a respectable establishment, of course.' Miss Williams appealed to her companion.

'Wasn't it the Massingham housekeeper who handed in that advertisement today?'

'The Massinghams . . .?' Vida asked innocently.

'Across the square. Number eighteen.' Miss Travers snorted. 'As to respectability, that we cannot guarantee.' She didn't explain so Vida looked again at Miss Williams.

'It is a *theatrical* household. Mr Massingham is the manager of a company as well as being its principal actor.'

'A company which includes his wife and daughters, who exhibit themselves daily – on a public stage.' Miss Travers' view of such depravity was plain but Vida was overjoyed; a situation for Kezia had fallen like an apple into the palm of her hand.

'Those garments you spoke of, madam?'

'Not so fast, miss,' Miss Travers replied tartly, 'The Mission door opens at 7.00 pm for prayers. Food and clothing are distributed *after* our act of worship.'

'Seven o'clock, madam,' Vida repeated fervently, 'Will there be hymns?'

'Of course.'

'I love a hymn, madam. We shall be counting the hours.' She hustled Kezia plus the cart down the street. 'First thing tomorrow, when you're kitted out, we'll try our luck at number eighteen.' Kezia remembered her former warning.

'But will anyone employ me straight off the street?'

'I told you – act Welsh. I'll do the talking. We'll say you lost your last reference and you've been living with us ever since.'

Vida wasn't one to analyse her feelings but a girl who could look attractive in an apron, whose fetish for cleanliness meant she smelled as sweet as a daisy, wasn't someone she wanted near Lemuel any longer than necessary. 'I'll make sure the Massinghams take you,' she promised.

The strain of constantly speaking English had left Kezia feeling drowsy. The Mission hall was warm. She would've fallen asleep if it hadn't been for Vida's elbow. They arrived early to be sure of the front row, even so they'd had to force their way through a desperate, hungry crowd. Kezia tried not to feel guilty for those whom Vida pushed aside. There was another jab in her ribs.

'Look attentive,' Vida hissed, 'Don't nod off when they start preaching!' But as soon as Miss Williams began at the harmonium, her worries were over. A familiar hymn roused such uncontrollable feelings, Kezia's tears fell copiously. She sang her heart out. Miss Williams heard and was touched. After the service she handed over several cotton wrappers.

'You need not fear catching anything from these,' she told Kezia earnestly, 'we insist our maids disinfect every single garment donated here. I hope you soon find a situation, my dear. Don't hesitate to come back if there's a difficulty.' Kezia bobbed and hurried outside after Vida.

She wasn't allowed to keep her bounty. Back at the mews, Vida inspected each wrapper as Lemuel munched purloined bread and cheese. 'Kitchen maids don't need nice things. You can keep the faded ones but these're worth a couple of bob and Lem hasn't had much luck. We did take you in, remember. You'd have been on the pavements if we hadn't.' Kezia tried to conceal her disappointment as Vida told her husband righteously, 'Kezia showed me her money when she first got here but I didn't ask for a penny.'

'I've about three shillings left,' Kezia confessed, embarrassed.

'How about treating us to a jug of beer?'

'I'm not that thirsty, Vee. She should keep it if that's all she has.' Lemuel shifted awkwardly but his wife had lifted a jug down from the shelf.

'You'd like to give us a treat though, wouldn't you, Kezia? To say thank you.'

'Oh, yes . . .'

When she'd gone, he said shame-facedly, 'She may not be family, Vee, but she did give this place a good clean.'

'She didn't have to, showing me up in front of my friends,' Vee said angrily. 'Besides, I'm worn out after all that walking round Kensington.' She watched caustically as her husband took one of the prettier wrappers and added it to Kezia's small pile. 'You know your trouble, you're too soft.'

Kezia emerged from the small side door. It was the time of evening when the area came to life. The lamplighter had finished his round. Beams shone down including one from high above the colourful red-cheeked face of The Musketeer. Where two shafts met they created a luminous yellow patch on the cobbles. Clutching the jug Kezia gravitated towards it.

She paused to watch one of the coachmen negotiating an elegant carriage under the arch. He ducked and cursed when one of the greys skittered. Inside a tall house that overlooked the back of the mews, the owner of the carriage contemplated the evening ahead over a seltzer. His womenfolk, waiting for him in the drawing room, wore elaborate bustles padded with horsehair, lined with taffeta, festooned and draped, the cascading trains so stiffly pleated, they were forced to perch on the edge of their chairs. Trapped women, caged as much by their gowns as their situation, mere chattels of those whom they'd married. Like their menfolk, they gave no thought to those who occupied the congested area behind the house.

It would have amazed all of them to learn that those who lived in the mews worked because they'd no other choice. What mattered in the mews was survival.

The evening meal was over. Doors opened and children

spilled out of the overcrowded living quarters. Some tied a skipping rope to a tethering ring. Others gathered by the arch, eager and expectant. There was a cry of 'They're here!' and suddenly everyone was outside.

Kezia heard the mandolin before she noticed the dancers. The door to The Musketeer opened suddenly, making her blink, and there they were, four of them in silhouette, poised like statues. A gipsy girl rattled a tambourine. The shimmer of sound was a signal for the audience to shush one another. The gipsy ran round the group, removing shabby overcoats and Kezia gasped. Underneath, the statues wore vividly flounced skirts and tight bodices. Without collars their faces could clearly be seen, highly coloured with rouge and paint – but these weren't women, they were men!

The tambourine rattled again and this time the statues struck a pose, arms held high. A chord from a mandolin was echoed by the high clear note of a pipe and slowly the dance began. As they came to life, their limbs moved to the music, but beneath blue painted lids, the statues' eyes were lifeless.

The beat quickened, the dance became a whirl of colour and movement, utterly strange. A week ago, Kezia had never been further than a Welsh village, now she was breathless. She caught the excitement, she wanted to stamp and clap like the children. The tempo increased to a crescendo. There was a tumult of silk fringes and cartwheeling bodies and then, just as quickly, it was over.

Pennies showered onto the cobbles. One fell beside Kezia. Automatically she bent to pick it up but the gipsy girl moved like lightening. Strong fingers seized Kezia's wrist, eyes blazed as she spat at her, 'Bloody thief!'

It was dark next morning when Vida shook her awake. Outside, rain fell heavily. To Kezia, hurrying through it with no protection other than her shawl, it was as though last night had never been. Everywhere was grey, the empty wet streets, the faces of the homeless huddled in doorways, not a scrap of colour anywhere.

As she followed Vida down the steep curving steps to the basement of 18 Colnbroke Square, SW7, homesickness weighed down on her as never before. Hitherto she'd lived among friends. In London she knew only Vida and Lemuel and now they intended to cast her adrift.

Kezia was sick with longing for familiar things, for high Welsh mountains with craggy blue-grey slate jutting through green grass. This façade in a brand new square of identical houses rose like an alien white cliff face above impressive pillars, a formidable cold landscape. She was desperate to escape, to let herself be borne away with the swirling leaves. Her heart thudding, she remained mute as Vida pounded on the door. Beneath pavement level, gleaming white gave way abruptly to grimy red brick.

They waited and Vida cursed as rainwater seeped down the back of her neck. Kezia gazed up at the railings curving overhead and imprisoning her. Inside her womb, the foetus quickened. The door opened and a voice enquired, 'Yes?' Vida pushed her inside. Her career as maid-of-all-work had begun.

Within a month, it felt to Chas and Albert as though they'd always lived on the London road. Life at their parents' cottage was part of another life. Outside the window there was no wild scabious, poppy or marguerite, the sun no longer shone. With ever increasing rain, laurel and privet dripped in sorrowing sympathy, for circumstances hadn't improved. The first blow came when the vicar discovered Sybilla's change of allegiance.

A Baptist indeed – it was nothing but an insult! Had he not been her ever-loving Shepherd? He it was who'd been responsible for urging her idle husband back to work. The Receiving Officer shook his head when he heard; such ingrates would never learn. He reconvened the committee to suggest the voluntary support be withdrawn.

The following week Sybilla was ordered into line with the poorest of the parish and given the regulation dole instead; one pound of flour plus 3d a day. A grand total of one shilling and ninepence to provide for herself and three children. That night she complained to Enoch. 'Serve you right,' he jeered. 'Send 'em back to the workhouse, I've told you often enough.' But she wouldn't be beat, she owed it to Jeremiah.

There was no question but that the children had to help. After one brief argument, Chas knew the end of education was in sight. Provided Aunt Syb could find a certified job of work, he could be withdrawn from school – and she spared no effort to find him one.

First it was a Saturday labouring job on a farm. From seven in the morning to seven at night Chas cleaned all the boots, knives and forks, helped with the milking and turned the handle of the churn before cleaning out the byre and stables. He returned home exhausted with 2d, which he was ordered to hand over to Sybilla.

Chas's Sunday task was to clean the stove. Newspaper was spread to catch soot from the flue. This was followed with an hour of elbow grease as he blackleaded oven and chimney hood until the shine was rich and deep. After emery-papering the steel fender he finished off by polishing the brasswork. When that was done he had to help Polly with the upstairs rooms which left precious little time for study.

Albert spent his spare time helping with the laundry. That first winter he never seemed to be dry. When he was indoors he was surrounded by steam; delivering or collecting, his instructions were that the tarpaulin was to protect the washing, not himself.

As for Polly, Sybilla's training meant her education was curtailed. Mondays, she scrubbed collars and postled sheets. Tuesdays she yawned over her school desk. Wednesdays she stood on a box, swapping irons endlessly on the stove, trying to avoid burning her fingers as her arms began to ache.

The school attendance officer turned a blind eye; it was always the same with poor families. Registers reflected the farming cycle in this part of the country. No doubt these three would disappear for weeks at a time during sowing or harvest even if it was against the law.

A change of religion brought little consolation for Sybilla. She found the Baptists austere. As for practical assistance, prayers were offered but little else. Perhaps, had her material approach to life not been so obvious, the congregation would have warmed to her, but marriage to Enoch had honed a once naïve girl into a sharp-tongued woman chasing every penny with London, always London as her relentless, secret goal.

Two of the upstairs rooms in the new house were rented out for a total of four shillings a week, linen and candles included. This sum was hoarded and all that could be saved, concealed in the bank account. The house was cared for – that was Sybilla's investment – but as for the children, she had little time or affection to spare for them.

Deprived of female company apart from visits to Mrs Heyhoe, she grew shrewish. The plain Baptist chapel wasn't to her taste any longer; she found much to criticize compared to the stately fourteenth century parish church. As for the length of the sermons, His Nibs always knew when to finish, Cook could depend on him not to let lunch spoil. Here, the minister cared neither when nor what he ate. His congregation grew ever more restive but his sonorous voice went on . . . and on. Matters finally came to a head when the subject of baptism arose.

Sybilla knew of the ritual; total immersion in the river with the congregation lining both banks and giggling children kept at a distance. Her mistake was to imagine herself immune. 'I been Christened when I was a babby,' she protested.

'Mrs Porrit, you cannot be received into our church if you do not profess your faith and submit to having your sins washed away.' Sybilla's temper was short.

'Tha's all right for *girls* standing about in their wet shifts. 'Taint decent for married women.' She'd seen what had happened to one plump maiden and had described the impropriety indignantly to Mrs Heyhoe. The minister blenched. No one before had spelled it out so crudely.

'Mrs Porrit! During the ceremony our thoughts will be on Higher Things!'

'They wasn't las' month. I saw everyone staring at Molly Peck. Silly girl should'a kept more of her clothes on underneath 'stead of showing what she was made of.'

Discussion ended abruptly. The minister was adamant, Sybilla obdurate. Finally there was nothing else for it but to renounce Baptism in favour of Methodism. About the same time, her faith in the prophylactic power of Cook's wine was shaken as well.

Sybilla's schemes for earning money meant that only one bedroom remained unlet. Despite her fine words to the Poor Law Committee, Chas and Albert still slept under the kitchen table and Polly had to share with her aunt and uncle after all.

There hadn't been space or money for a bed. She slept on two chairs tied together, a pillow for a mattress, a cushion under her head and an old blanket as a coverlet. Every night she tried to fall asleep before Enoch returned. Sometimes she was unlucky, especially those nights when he demanded his marital rights.

As a child in the tiny farm cottage, Polly had shared her parents' room. She remembered soft murmurings heard from her cot, her mother smiling, reaching down with loving arms to hug and caress a wakeful child; she knew she'd been included in their joy.

Here Polly pulled the blanket over her head to shut out the humiliation. Her aunt's protests created an image of marriage which began to haunt her. She tried to explain to Chas but he didn't understand. He and Albert were simply thankful to avoid Enoch Porrit's attentions.

Polly knew her aunt measured out wine for Enoch occasionally; she was too young to understand why. But a month or two after the last bottle was emptied, her aunt's temper grew very short indeed. She announced she was off to the vicarage and might be late back.

Mrs Heyhoe offered her guest another scone. 'Don't see it could be anything else.'

'No.' Sybilla's face was drawn and grey; facts were facts. 'What you going to do?'

'Get rid of it.' Mrs Heyhoe took on a disapproving tone.

'Can't help you, not to commit a mortal sin, Mrs Porrit . . .' But this was hypocrisy given what had passed between them already; on reflection Cook felt ashamed. She masticated slowly. 'There are ways, so I'm told,' she admitted eventually, 'I've been lucky, never having been in a certain condition, but some women claim to know what's what.'

'I'm not sure who to ask . . .' Sybilla waited but cook couldn't volunteer a name. 'Nor what it costs?' Again, silence. 'Whatever it is, I shall have to pay.' It was a risky business but there was an even greater danger as far as Sybilla was concerned. '*He's* found out about it.'

'Oh, dear!'

'He says he wants a son . . . even promised to stay off the beer. He didn't of course. Managed to stay sober for a couple of days, tonight it was back to normal.'

'What'll he do when he knows that you . . . You know?'

Sybilla shrugged. 'What can he do?'

'Mmm.' In the silence Mrs Heyhoe stirred more sugar into her tea. 'You want to be careful how you tell him afterwards. He won't be none too pleased.' Sybilla hid her fear behind tightened lips. 'He don't deserve a son, anyway, not the way he treats young Chas.'

'Enoch keeps on about sending all three of 'em back on the parish when he's got one of his own. Tha's another reason I'm not going to give him one.' There was an even darker fear. 'They say it can be bad sometimes, Mrs Heyhoe.' Cook admitted she'd heard the same.

'It ain't always possible to have another after, so I believe.'

'Thank God for that.' Sybilla finished her tea and stood up, 'Laundry's a penny extra this week, by the way. The price of starch hev gone up again.'

Chapter Seven

A Time to be Born

Being a house-maid meant spending each day servicing the fabric of the Massinghams' house, rising first every morning, creeping downstairs to light the kitchen stove then cleaning and re-laying the remaining fires in the large ground floor reception rooms.

It included preparing breakfast for the rest of the servants, attending to six bedroom fires, scrubbing kitchen and scullery floors plus the flight of steps which led to the front door. Every carpet then had to be sprinkled with wet tea-leaves to lay the dust, before being swept clean using a small stiff brush.

In effect, Kezia spent the greater part of each day on her hands and knees cleaning the treads, balusters and banister rail of a staircase which rose from the ornate hall through the four storeys, taking care to step aside whenever anyone wished to go past.

It was a day which began at 5.30 a.m. and finished when the Massingham family retired after returning from the theatre. A week included six full working days. (On Sundays Kezia wasn't expected to clean the front steps.) Once a month she had a half day off on condition she was back indoors by 9.00 p.m. Her wages were £14.0.0d per annum. Out of this she had to supply her uniform and provide for her old age.

If anyone spoke, it was to remind Kezia how fortunate she was. Unemployment was high due to the constant flight from countryside to town in search of work. Employers could pick and choose. She had no *character* but now she had a situation. Under the circumstances how could any girl fail to be grateful.

Kezia was fortunate in one respect; she shared the tiny end attic with only one other person, the nursery maid, Rose.

Rose had been equally lucky. Both mother and sister had died of tuberculosis, she had the same waxy complexion yet she'd managed to avoid detection when obtaining her present position. 'Because the last two girls walked out, that's how I got this place. One didn't even wait for her money.' Kezia was amazed. 'When you meet the children, then you'll understand why she did it,' Rose warned darkly.

The Messinghams were 'artistic'. The trouble was their temperaments were allowed free reign. Out of the public eye, they rampaged, caring for nothing or nobody in their path, particularly when audiences failed to come up to expectation. These tantrums caused a high turnover among the staff and in the beginning, terrified Kezia. On her first half day, she returned to the mews for advice and was told to stick it out. On no account was she to risk losing her first situation.

So when faced with hysteria on the stair, Kezia curtsied, eyes downcast, and kept her thoughts resolutely Welsh. That way wild shrieks remained incomprehensible. Even when Master Wilfred Messingham, annoyed at a lack of response, grabbed Kezia by the hair, she managed to stay detached and let herself go limp as he shook her. Slightly unnerved at having an inert body at his feet, that gentleman uttered one or two magnificent *bon mots* (written by someone else) and disappeared upstairs leaving Kezia to resume her work. She did so with care; by now she was more concerned for her child than herself.

Every month she undid gathers so that the wrappers remained loose-fitting. No one remarked on her increasing girth for who stopped to take notice of a maid? Kezia developed a rhythm to her work which slowed as her bulk increased, but as long as she finished by bedtime, that was all that mattered.

Rose was always busy – the infant Massinghams were a 'handful'. During the day the two saw little of one another. The sun wasn't up when Kezia rose, they dressed and undressed in the dark, washing hurriedly in the freezing little attic. In an age of modesty there was little discussion of bodily functions and Rose was unaware of Kezia's lack of periods.

On her half days, Kezia went for timid walks, usually ending up at the mews for she was too nervous to explore. Those 'parks' Adam had described must be the garden squares, she decided, barred to such as herself. She watched through the railings as governesses paraded their charges past dingy rhododendrons, laurel and plane trees. She tried to imagine them through Adam's eyes but it was no use; they brought no joy. In her heart she would always yearn for green turf and Welsh mountains.

Maybe it had been summer when Adam was here? Next spring there might be primroses to gaze on, which would lift her spirits. Spring! Kezia hugged herself. Then there would be Adam's child to love.

Vida was usually at the bottling factory when she called. If Lem was about, he was happy to let Kezia clean their living quarters. In return he made them both a cup of tea. He seldom spoke, unless it was to tell her of Gyp or the ferrets. Once he let her hold the female one while he cleaned the cage. Kezia tried not to be afraid of the beautiful squirming body with its sharp teeth and claws.

She always left behind screws of paper containing two penn'orth of tea and a piece of sugar loaf, by way of payment. Once a month, she kept her promise to the old carter and wrote a letter home. It was difficult to find words her mother and grandmother would understand. How to describe the masses of new white, porticoed houses, each containing the same acreage of turkey carpet according to Rose. The incredible number of people in London, too – there were different strangers every time Kezia walked abroad – and endless pavements without a flower anywhere. Her grandmother, who'd never left Llandefaelog, would never be able to comprehend. Not once did Kezia mention the baby, nor did she give an address.

As Christmas approached, Rose began to speculate. 'I might ask my brother if I can go over there for my dinner. He and his wife live in Holborn.'

'Oh yes.' It could have been the moon.

'They've got this room over a shop. Tiny really, but I have stayed with them once before. What about you? You going to your friends?'

'I don't know.' Lemuel hadn't suggested it.

'That's if we can have Christmas Day off.' Their problems were solved when the head house-maid told them this was impossible.

Christmas was, for Wallace Massingham, an occasion to impress the world with his bonhomie. His actor's voice boomed even louder, his personality filled the house – he was Christmas; the embodiment of a bounteous season. Daily the Press were sent descriptions of his dinner-parties with a list of important guests.

Nightly, it seemed to Kezia, mounds of dirty plates and cutlery grew and multiplied as if defying her to finish, while every morning she now had to rub carpets with cloths wrung out in vinegar, to clean up the wine stains. The festivities became more frequent and merged into an endless stream of people, trampling mud across the hall, soiling every tread of the staircase en route to the drawing room, determined to be merry. By Boxing Day, Kezia was last in a row of tired domestics, lined up by the Butler in order to receive their annual 'gifts'.

There had to be an audience for such a presentation, Wallace Massingham couldn't function if there wasn't. Tonight's was made up of admirers. There were bursts of applause at imagined Massingham generosity, for Wallace had a flamboyant way of describing each wrapped parcel. The lack of response among the servants was commented on disparagingly. Scarcely a muttered word of thanks from any of them!

The line dwindled until there were only Rose and Kezia left. Rose stepped up onto the dias. The actor/manager flung his arms wide towards Rose. 'Dear little Jessie, Happy Christmas! Ladies and gentlemen, this child is as dear as my own Mélisande . . . Come, Mélisande.' His actress daughter scowled but complied. Wallace Massingham, an arm round each girl's shoulders, rotated them for the benefit of the assembly. 'They might be – sisters!' He paused, not for applause this time but so that all might see how moved he was. 'Two young girls . . . the bloom of youth upon their cheeks . . . on the threshold of Life itself!' The parent in him suddenly recalled that Mélisande was now nearing twenty-seven. 'Youth' was perhaps an exaggeration. He dropped the pose and demanded, 'Come, hand me Jessie's gift.'

Mrs Massingham had also played her part many times before. Automatically she selected the larger of the two remaining parcels.

Wallace Massingham presented it regally: 'Take this – token, my dear Jessie – of our blessing and our love.' It should have been gold or frankincense. Back once more in the attic, Rose discovered it was myrrh.

'Flannel!' It was four yards of a particularly virulent shade of salmon pink. 'The stingy blighter! It should've been a dress length – that's what I got last year when I first come here. What they given you?' Kezia unwrapped her two yards of calico. 'At least you can make an apron. What am I supposed to do with this?' But flannel was just the thing for a baby's skin.

'Swop?'

'If you like.'

As they exchanged, Kezia asked, 'Why didn't you tell him your real name?'

Rose pulled a face. 'I wanted my present first. You know what he can be like. If I'd interrupted he'd have taken the parcel back. If I'd known what was in it, mind, I'd have told him right enough! Cor, they're so mean in this place!'

Spring was very late that year. Dirty snow froze hard and however frequently streets were swept, more dead birds littered the gutters. Passers-by remarked on the sad fact. Stiffening corpses of the homeless were dealt with more speedily, so that delicate sensibilities might be spared. By late February, everyone was desperate for the sun.

The jug of warm water carried up to the attic each evening was frozen solid by morning. Up and down the passage, servants were preoccupied in keeping warm, rubbing chapped fingers and resisting the urge to do the same with chilblains. Bouts of Massingham temperament grew less. There was now a serious problem facing them: audiences were sparse. If the weather didn't improve – and the bookings – they might have to close! Plans were hurriedly advanced to revive a popular old chestnut, guaranteed to fill the house.

At eight months, the child lay low and warm in Kezia's womb. She withdrew into her own private world, living for the pleasure of each small movement inside. Despite hard work, the food here was plentiful. An increased blood flow freshened her pink cheeks. Lugging buckets of coal had been a problem but the pantry boy, captivated by her blossoming, was eager to help and Kezia adapted her stance when doing her cleaning, to ease the ache in her back.

As mornings grew lighter, Rose marvelled at her size. 'Don't know how you manages it, you must eat an awful lot of grub, Kezia. I'm skinny, whatever I do.' Kezia didn't reply.

She didn't know how to calculate the date of the baby's birth but it must be soon, her body told her that. For the first time she began to consider what might happen. Joy over the child had occupied her thoughts. Since leaving Wales, so much had happened, one day at a time was all she could manage. Now, thinking about the future, Kezia began to be frightened. There was the matter of the birth itself; she hadn't the slightest notion how babies came into the world. Her belly button was swollen – would it burst open like a bud and let the baby out?

Finally, she asked Rose. It was late in February and the Massingham children had been querulous all day. Rose undid her garters, rolled down her stockings and pulled her nightgown over her head. 'Gawd knows, Kezia,' she

97

yawned. 'Why d'you want to know?'

'Just – interested.'

'I could ask nurse, I suppose?' That was too risky.

'No, thanks.'

'God bless.' Rose was asleep within minutes. Kezia pondered. Perhaps Vida would be at home next time she called? Her eyelids drooped, sleep was beckoning. If Vida wasn't in, perhaps she could write a letter and leave it for her? But it was more than two weeks before Kezia's next half day and by then the seed planted by Adam was fully ripe.

The attic stairs were uncarpeted, as was the passage. Rose's footsteps clattered. She had fifteen minutes to change into her afternoon dress and apron. Nursery tea was at five sharp, followed by that blessed period of rest when the children went downstairs to be with their parents. She opened the attic door. 'Hallo? I thought it was your day off?' Kezia lay on her side of the bed, sweaty-faced.

'I got stomach ache . . . Rose?'

'Yes?'

'Could you run a message for me?' Rose's face fell.

'Oh, Kezia, it's me only chance to put me feet up –'

'Can you go round to Lem and Vida in the mews?'

'Is it urgent? You can go and see them next month when you're better.' Kezia's face contorted in a spasm. 'Here, you all right?'

When the contraction had passed, Kezia whispered. 'Promise you won't tell?'

'Tell – what?'

'I think I'm having a baby.' Rose's mouth opened into a huge round O. She took in a great gasp of air.

'Oh, gawd – Kezia! You ain't, are you?'

The minute hand crawled round the face of the nursery clock. Infant actors and actresses who had learned petulant antics from their parents, rehearsed their repetoire for the benefit of maid and governess. Today, for some inexplicable reason, when the nursery-maid returned she behaved with tremendous ferocity. There was an aston-

98

ished howl. The governess's eyebrows shot up. 'They'll tell milady the minute they get downstairs.'

'So what,' Rose said curtly, 'spoiled brats.'

'Ssh! Little pitchers have big ears.'

'And they'll get those boxed an' all. Come here, Miss Alexandra, your ribbon's undone.' Rose retied it, yanking the miniature crinoline straight above the white pantalets, 'Off you go,' she ordered. 'Be good. Mama and Papa have a First Night tonight.'

Like the rest of the staff, Rose was apprehensive. These occasions meant taut nerves and even worse exhibitions of temper. Now she'd got this incredible situation upstairs on her hands, she still could hardly believe it! A baby? It simply wasn't possible. As soon as she could, Rose hurried back to the attic. Kezia's back was arched and she'd ripped the sheet in an effort not to scream. Rose was terrified.

'Gawd . . . What's going to happen?'

'Don't know,' Kezia panted, 'It's got to come out somehow. Find Vida, Rose. Quick as you can.'

Left alone, Kezia clenched her teeth in an almighty effort to fight the pain. Contractions came in waves, surging through her, lifting her into realms of agony she hadn't known existed. As each ebbed away, she lay clammy with cold sweat and fear, terrified at her plight.

Despite her resolve, she cried aloud. But supposing someone heard? If anyone reported it, the head housemaid would dismiss her immediately. She and her sin would be left to die on the icy pavement, no one would care. Adam had been her only love, now there was no one to protect her. In utter despair, Kezia clung to the bedstead, sobbing his name.

Rose ran through unfamiliar streets as though the devil were after her. She hammered at the door of the mews. When she saw the misshapen face, she knew she'd found the right address, 'Is Vida in?'

'She's at work.'

'Oh, no, please no!' She had to confide in someone. 'Kezia's having a baby and I don't know what to do.'

'What?' The idea was slow to take root. Lemuel frowned, 'What d'you mean?'

'Kezia – she's having it right this minute!'

'What d'you mean – baby?' The girl wore a white frilly cap, she was probably from some hospital but she must be mistaken. 'Kezia's not pregnant.' Rose seized him.

'She is, she is! Listen, she's in our attic and she'll yell the house down unless I do something.' She shook him, her face working frantically, 'I . . . don't . . . know . . . what . . . to . . . do – can't you understand? Someone's got to come and help. Kezia might die!'

Pieces of a jigsaw began to slip into place; Kezia's stance on her last visit, how she'd clutched her back, how swollen and puffy her face had been. Her thick woollen shawl had concealed her figure, he'd wondered at the time what was wrong. Lemuel Meaney nodded slowly.

'Come inside a minute while I think about it.' He couldn't be rushed, Rose could see that. She must stay calm and ignore the churning inside. She followed him up the rickety stair and sat. Once she was stationary, Lemuel began to pace the little room.

'Let me think who there is . . . you say you don't know what to do?' Rose shook her head dumbly. Her mother had never discussed the facts of life, nor her sister.

'Got it!' Lemuel smiled his leery grin and picked up his hat. 'Shan't be a tick.' At the head of the stair he called, 'I'm going to Number Eight. She's had five, she'll know.' He disappeared and Rose was left to wait.

Kezia had lost control over her body. A short while ago she'd been aware of doors banging along the passage. The two ladies' maids who doubled as dressers to Mrs Massingham and Mélisande talked excitedly as they left for the theatre. Kezia managed to bite her lip to stop herself crying out as they walked away. After them went the second house maid who was always on duty at First Nights, to hand round the champagne. The head house maid would have gone by now anyway to spend the evening with her fishmonger beau in Hammersmith.

Knowing she was alone brought a tiny respite. Kezia

relaxed tense fists but when the pains began again she hadn't enough strength to stop herself screaming. Once begun, each moment was worse than the last and threatened to tear her apart. She couldn't go on! Her body arched again, heels digging into the mattress and hot liquid gushed between her legs. This time she wept for shame.

Cautiously, the attic door opened. She was conscious of Rose with a strange woman standing beside the bed. All she could see was the woman's dirty face with its cheerful toothless grin. The woman still wore an apron under her coat and when she grinned, the warm oniony breath had more than a hint of beer. Kezia stared dully, at Rose.

'I've wet the bed.'

'Oh, Kezia!'

The strange woman chuckled. 'That's good. Means you're not far off. Let's have a look at you then?'

Rose said nervously. 'It's all right, Kezia. This is Mrs Macguire. She's a friend of Mr Meaney and she knows what to do.'

'Pleased to meet you,' said Bridie Macguire.

'Where's Vida?' The strange woman had lifted away the torn sheet and began to fold it. Another contraction and Kezia ceased to care about anything, 'Take it out, please!'

'What, dear?'

'She wants you to get the baby out,' Rose cried, 'I don't know how you're going to manage it, her belly button isn't nearly big enough.' Bridie Macguire's eyebrows shot up and she began to laugh.

Rose asked helplessly, 'Kezia is having a baby?'

'Of course she is, but it's going to come out the same way it went in, like all babies do. Now take off your shawl and give me that basket.' Rose watched as Bridie selected the cleanest from a bundle of Lemuel's rags.

'How does it do that then?' she asked innocently. She didn't hear the answer because of Kezia's sudden scream.

When it was over, Bridie said, 'Tell Lem I need a bucket of hot water.'

Rose backed away. 'I'll fetch it. He's keeping cavey outside.'

'Much good will that do,' Mrs Macguire said, grim for

101

once at the danger they were in from any staff passing by. 'Just pray to the Virgin that this baby comes before anyone else turns up.'

As she toiled up and down the stairs, Rose gave thanks instead for a First Night. The Massinghams always held court at the Savoy Hotel for a celebratory supper; after being on duty there as well as at the theatre, the staff then returned home, very late indeed.

Up in the attic, Bridie Macguire had given Lem the task of gripping Kezia's hands. When Rose appeared, she called sharply, 'Leave that now, I need you as well. Come over here.'

Beside the bed Rose gasped at the bent knees and the particular part of Kezia's body that lay exposed. When she spoke it was in a very small voice indeed. 'Is that – a baby?'

'It's the head of one all right,' Bridie felt inside gently, 'The cord's round his neck – don't push! She doesn't seem to understand me, you tell her.'

'Me?'

'Yes! Otherwise she'll strangle it.'

Rose knelt by the pillow. On the opposite side, Lemuel clutched Kezia's hands for dear life. Rose lifted the matted hair away from the pallid face. There was no recognition now, Kezia was oblivious to everything except the pain.

'Kezia . . . you'll hurt the baby if you push . . . And please, please don't make so much noise!'

'Aw, let the poor thing shout,' Mrs Macguire's brawny arm held Kezia firmly as she eased her fingers between the cord and the head. There was a cry of sheer agony. 'Sorry, my girl, it's the only way. Now, don't fight it any more – PUSH!'

'Push, Kezia, push hard!' begged Rose.

From where he crouched, Lemuel muttered, 'What a mess . . . what an awful mess!'

'PUSH!' Kezia strained. 'Come on, girl!'

It felt as if she were expelling the entire contents of her body.

'Look, look it's coming . . . it's a baby!'

'I'm going to be sick!'

'Clean as a whistle . . .' Mrs Macguire eased it onto the

102

bed and tied two rags deftly before slicing through the cord. She supported the tiny squashed head, 'Where's some more of those rags?' Without looking at what was on the bed, Lemuel thrust a handful in her direction. Bridie wiped away the mucuous, 'Now then my lovely, don't disappoint us.'

She cradled the baby in her apron, rocking it gently, stroking first the cheeks then the throat. Nothing happened. 'Open your mouth for me,' she crooned, forcing the tiny lips apart with a grubby finger. She blew into the mouth, then the nostrils. Rose watched fearfully.

'Is it dead?'

'Hush!' Mrs Macguire slapped once, twice. Rose shouted instinctively, 'No! Don't hurt it!' but the baby gave a shudder and cried.

Lemuel was allowed to wait outside while the afterbirth was dealt with. Such horrors – he'd never felt so ill! Thank God he and Vida had been spared. The door opened and Rose handed him the bucket full of unspeakable filth. 'We tip the rubbish out by the door where you came in. Use the back stairs and mind no one sees you.' Swearing under his breath, Lemuel crept away.

Kezia was suffused with a warm, loving lethargy. She watched them hazily, the baby in the crook of her arm wrapped in the salmon pink flannel. Rose moved quietly, putting the room to rights. Mrs Macguire grinned down at her. 'Now you know how babies get here, eh?'

'Yes . . . thank you.'

'The name's Bridie.'

'Thank you Bridie.' The woman moved a fold of the cloth to see the tiny face.

'Have you thought of a name?'

'Esther.'

'Well, I don't suppose you were intending taking her to church.' Bridie Macguire licked a thumb and sketched the sign of the cross. 'In the name of the Father, the Son and the Holy Spirit, I name you Esther.' She bent closer to examine her features. 'You're going to be as pretty as your

Ma, God help you.'

There was a discreet tap and Rose opened the door. Pale-faced, Lemuel stood there.

'Can we go? Vida will be home soon.'

'In a minute. Where's that basket of yours?' Lem came further into the room and gave it to her. Mrs Macguire smoothed the scraps of cloth that filled it. 'It'll do. She'll be snug as a kitten in there. I'll put it beside the bed, Kezia. You can reach her easy when she needs feeding.'

'It used to be Gyp's but he grew too big.'

'So will Esther in a month or two,' Bridie said, being practical. Lemuel was agitated.

'We should get back,' he insisted. 'Vida will be worried.'

'You'll have a tale to tell her tonight all right,' Bridie chuckled. She gave Kezia a few final instructions and gathered up her belongings. 'How long do you two think you can keep Esther a secret?' she looked at the two of them, curiously. 'Babies cry, you know, you can't stop them doing that.'

Kezia appeared not to have heard the question.

'I can't pay you any money, Bridie,' she apologized.

'I don't charge. When you feel up to it, you can give my place a good clean, like you do Vida's, that'll settle the account.'

'When *can* Kezia get up?' asked Rose, 'She's supposed to work again tomorrow.' Bridie assessed her patient.

'She can't do that, she needs to rest. Today's Wednesday . . . think of some excuse for her till Friday, that'll be soon enough. You're a lucky girl, you had an easy time. There's many who don't.'

Lucky! thought Lemuel.

'We'll manage,' Rose said bravely. Kezia looked at her gratefully.

'You can't keep a baby hidden,' Bridie Macguire moved nearer the bed. 'We all make mistakes, my dear, but they're best put behind us. Why not give Esther up now? Lemuel and me could take her to the church and leave her there. The nuns would look after her, she'd not starve.' Kezia's eyes grew big; her saviour had turned into the devil, come to tempt her.

104

'No!' She hugged the child, terrified the woman would reach out and snatch her, 'She's mine! I'll look after her, I'll never let anyone have her!'

Bridie straightened up. 'When *they* find out downstairs it could mean the workhouse. Babies die there.'

'No!' Kezia gazed at the treasure in her arms, her precious link with Adam. 'I'll never let anyone send her there, either.' Bridie looked significantly at Rose.

'It's Our Lady of the Sorrows,' she murmured, 'when she changes her mind.'

Vida wasn't at home when Lemuel returned. Instead, the occupants of the mews had gathered in excited groups to discuss the explosion in Battersea. There was a message for him from the bottling plant, giving the list of hospitals at which survivors might be found.

Chapter Eight

A Time to Leave

The following day a weary, sweaty Rose hauled herself upstairs with a plate of food and Kezia learned for the first time about the accident.

'One of Bridie's kids come round,' Rose explained, 'Vida's in hospital but there's nothing to be done, seemingly. "Act of God" they're calling it. The factory boiler exploded.'

'How dreadful!'

'Vida was standing right next to it. They think she could go blind.' Kezia's own grey eyes widened in distress; imagine never being able to see the blue sky again.

'That's truly dreadful, Rose ... how will she and Lemuel manage?'

'Never mind them, it's us you should be worrying about. I can't keep doing both our jobs. The housekeeper's been nagging, asking if what you've got is infectious.' She managed a tired grin. 'I told 'er you 'ad the ear-ache terrible bad and you'd be back at work tomorrow.' She sank down the bed and pleaded, 'Do you think you could, Kezia? It's bedlam downstairs, all of 'em shouting and hollering. Something went wrong at the theatre by all accounts. I don't know what exactly but there's such a carry-on, you'd think the world was coming to an end.'

That was an understatement. The Massinghams smouldered as never before, igniting wounded pride with volcanic flashes of anger. To a man, the critics had been merciless: why should such a hackneyed piece be revived, they'd demanded, and so cheaply? Wallace Massingham and his company deserved their contempt.

The entire production was condemned from shabby scenery to inadequate acting. As for Miss Mélisande Massingham's performance in the ingénue role – here the press outdid one another to produce the most scathing epithet, proving not for the first time there wasn't a gentleman amongst them.

The day after their verdict had been delivered, Kezia left the safety of the attic for the first time. Fears for Esther obsessed her. Every half-hour or so, she sneaked back upstairs to satisfy herself the baby was well. She'd no sooner gone down again when she went rushing back, imagining she'd heard a faint cry.

In her weakened state, her mind played tricks. The protective cocoon she'd woven during the past few weeks vanished, leaving her vulnerable. Reality pressed in from every side. Alone in a vast uncaring city, how could she care for her child? Bridie Macguire had been right; far better to hand her over now before she grew too fond. Yet as she leaned over Gyp's old basket and hot tears splashed down, Kezia knew it was already too late; she couldn't bear to part with Esther, she'd as soon kill herself. Now there was Vida to worry about as well, for how could *she* manage? Leaden-hearted, she closed the attic door and crept downstairs to finish her tasks.

Her obsession with Esther made her oblivious of the Massinghams' fury. If anything, this anger had increased during the past twenty-four hours. The newspapers had had a devastating effect. Last night's audience had been thin and those who were there had cat-called and booed. Miss Mélisande's temper, never reliable at the best of times, had finally given way. She'd marched down to the footlights, arms akimbo, and to the gallery's delight, attempted to scold them. It had been most unwise.

Today the Massingham family's initial reaction to the critics, that of stunned disbelief, had faded; now all their energies were concentrated on revenge, on assuaging injured pride. They hurtled past Kezia as she attempted to clean the stairs, leaning over the banisters and shouting at one another, bawling up from below, shifting the blame this way and that, enunciating cutting remarks about one another's thespian abilities; most irate of all was Mélisande.

Hitherto, friends and family had assured her she was an ornament to her profession. To be described in the papers as 'amateur and vapid' and then publically jeered by a gallery claque was not to be borne! Humiliation festered. Mélisande Massingham flung open every door in the house in an effort to catch anyone repeating the libel or, worse still, laughing behind her back.

Was she not the bearer of an immortal flame? Last year in Paris she had visited the theatre. Alexandre Dumas had been in an adjoining box and on the Odéon stage itself, Sarah Bernhardt. That night Mélisande Massingham had floated above Boulevard pavements, full of passionate adoration; she too would become a great actress, the world would be at her feet, she would be – adored! Nothing would prevent it.

Returning home, she modelled herself on the young French actress and tried to buy a puma. When that enterprise failed, she had a chaise-longue installed in her room. On it she spent long secret hours in front of her cheval mirror. And now, after all that effort, *The Times* had judged her performance 'shallow'!

Mélisande demanded her father defend her honour in a duel. Wallace Massingham told his daughter to go to the devil. She sought out her brother but Master Wilfred, angry at being described as a 'buffoon', declared he'd always known his sister couldn't act. It was too much for a sensitive nature to withstand! Exhausted, Mélisande sought the solace of her chaise-longue, quivering on the verge of a scream.

The door to her room was ajar so that all might pity her distress. She sank down gracefully but catching sight of her reflection, decided the left profile better expressed her agony. She rose and noticed for the first time a maid, cleaning the landing carpet.

'Stop staring at me!' Kezia looked up, startled. 'I said –

don't stare!' Kezia obediently returned to her dustpan and brush.

This indifference was too much. Miss Massingham screamed and flung a vase. Her aim was far more accurate than her performance had been and caught Kezia on the temple. Half-stunned, the girl remained on her knees, trying to staunch the blood with her apron. Miss Massingham screamed again, this time in fright at what she'd done.

'She made me do it! She made me – do it!'

Had no one arrived to stop her, Mélisande might have been tempted to exhibit the full range of her inflections. Mercifully her mother was quick to react.

'What's going on? What on earth's the matter now?' Mrs Massingham had little sympathy to spare this morning. One critic, caustic over the most *imperceptible* of fluffs ('If Mrs Massingham cannot remember her lines, it is high time she quit the London stage for good'), had been so vehemently cursed, she felt drained.

She was also recovering from her husband's pronouncement; on examining the forward bookings Wallace Massingham predicted that, short of a miracle, their theatre would be dark by the end of the week. A play which had never been known to fail before – how could it have happened? Mrs Massingham swept into her daughter's bedroom and glared. Mélisande continued to sob.

'Oh, for heaven's sake – stop that noise!' Mrs Massingham, it must be remembered, had once been a tremendous Hecuba; it was comedy that was her downfall. At present however she could exercize her proper talents, 'Stop it, I said!' That same roar had once halted Priam. Mélisande choked, gasped, and pointed.

'She *made* me . . . do it.' Kezia's head throbbed and she leaned against the wall. Mrs Massingham turned and saw one of the house maids with blood pouring from her forehead.

'How disgusting! What happened?' Kezia heard her own quiet voice as if from a distance.

'Miss threw a vase at me, milady.'

'She *made* me –'

'Yes, yes. Do be quiet, Mélisande!'

But seeing Kezia slump, Miss Massingham realized her own position was open to question. Attack appeared to be the most reliable form of defence.

'How dare she faint! It is *I* who am insulted!'

'Pray be silent, Miss!' thundered her mother and to Kezia, 'Go and clean your face immediately, you're not fit to be seen.'

Kezia tried to stand. Doors were opening up and down the landing and curious faces peeped out. Rose hurried down from the nursery to join them.

'You all right, Kezia?' she muttered, terrified. Mélisande, tender at the implied criticism, began to shout.

'She deliberately stood there – and stared!' Rose half-lifted Kezia to her feet.

'Let's get you upstairs.'

'I cannot live under the same roof as those terrible, staring eyes!' Mrs Massingham had had enough.

'You – whatever your name is – apologize to my daughter.'

Clinging to Rose, Kezia repeated dazedly, 'Miss threw the vase . . . I don't know why, milady.'

Mrs Massingham thrust the now hysterical Mélisande back inside her bedroom, returned to her boudoir and summoned the head house maid.

Up in their attic, Rose said, 'You've done it now, Kezia. You should never answer back.' The baby lay between them on the bed. 'What you going to do?'

'Ask for a character, and to pay me what they owe. It wasn't my fault, Rose.'

'Since when did that matter? They'll claim it was because of Miss's nerves.'

Faint from childbirth and loss of blood, Kezia asked weakly, 'What about mine?'

'Servants don't have any, they can't afford 'em.' There was a knock at the door. 'Quick! We got to hide Esther – pull up the covers!'

'No . . . not any more.' The time had come to make a stand even if Kezia knew her circumstances were desperate. She lifted out the baby, thrust her few possessions into Lem's basket and wrapped the infant in her shawl. The knocking became impatient, the door opened and Mrs Massingham's personal maid stood there.

'You're to come downstairs and be dismissed, Morgan. Here . . .' She advanced a step. 'What you got there!'

'She's mine.' Kezia cuddled her daughter tenderly, adjusting the shawl to protect her. 'Will you bring my basket, Rose?' The lady's maid goggled as the little procession went past.

On the landing Rose said half-chokily, 'Wait a bit.' She wiped away some of the blood from Kezia's face, 'Can't have you looking like you been in the wars. Chin up, gel!'

The lady's maid suddenly realized what she'd seen and what it meant; she ran ahead, down the passage. They listened to her shriek, 'A baby! They've got a baby!'

'I don't suppose we could've kept Esther a secret much longer,' Rose tried to sound brave.

'They won't blame you for any of it?'

'I hope not! I can't afford to lose my place.' Rose kissed the tip of her finger and placed it on the baby's cheek. 'Bye-bye, my lamb. Come on. We'd best get it over.'

Downstairs they went, first the uncarpeted flight, then the haircord thread which led to the nursery level. The drugget changed at the curve of the landing, where it could be seen from below, to the rich red turkey pattern. Every inch Kezia had swept a dozen times, each brass stair-rod polished; now she acknowledged for the first time how much she loathed the work. Life must have something better to offer than this – senseless drugery? It wasn't much, this tiny spark of independence, but it rekindled her courage.

They arrived outside Mrs Massingham's boudoir.

'Shall I take Esther?'

'All right.' Kezia sounded calm but her heart was pounding. She tapped and on being bidden, entered the room. Mélisande, having assumed her most tragic pose, leaned beside her mother at the bureau. The head house

111

maid waited a respectful distance away. Mrs Massingham waved a languid hand.

'Proceed.' The head house maid bobbed and picked up a small pile of coins to give to Kezia.

'Your wages, Morgan. Less three shillings towards the cost of the vase. Be thankful it wasn't more valuable.'

'We have, of course, deducted a week's emolument in lieu of notice,' Mrs Massingham addressed the bureau rather than look at Kezia. 'As for your disgraceful refusal to apologize to Miss Massingham, that . . .' She indicated an envelope on the blotter, 'is all the character we can give.'

She waited while the head house maid passed the envelope across ceremoniously. Outside, excited whispering had begun among the staff but Kezia was too absorbed with the inscription to notice.

To Whom it May Concern.

Inside was her passport for the future: she had a character at last! Mrs Massingham had begun speaking again − 'We shall require you to leave immediately −' when the interruption came.

'My lady!' Bursting with indignation, her personal maid had flung open the door and pointed a quivering finger at Rose, now cuddling Esther, 'Look what these wicked creatures have been hiding upstairs!'

Kezia ignored the shock and horror. She walked over and held out her arms for her baby. Catching sight of Mrs Massingham's expression, she almost laughed: milady was comical in her disbelief.

'My daughter's name is Esther. She was born in this house while you were at the theatre . . .' There was a strangled noise from Hecuba followed by absolute silence among the rest. 'Whatever else happens to her, Esther's never coming to work here,' said Kezia quietly, 'Never.'

With her basket under one arm and holding the baby carefully, she descended the forbidden main staircase. She crossed the hall, opened the front door and went down those steps she'd scrubbed so often, out of their lives for ever.

Behind her, Miss Mélisande Massingham began an

attack of hysterics which would have won her the critics' bouquets.

The biting March wind tore at Kezia's spirits. By the time she'd reached the Mews, her spirits were low and her energy gone; she could scarcely drag herself along. She crossed the road, went under the arch and managed the last few yards. The small side door was unlocked. Kezia climbed the wooden ladder, Lemuel sat at the table, his head in his arms. He was sodden with tears.

'Vida . . .' he began when he saw her, but couldn't continue.

'Is it – very bad?' Kezia was frightened by what the answer might be.

'They won't know till they take off the bandages . . . she's hurt so bad! They give her laudanum but it don't work. Her skin's all burnt see, nearly to the bone. My lovely Vee . . . it's terrible.' His own tears began once more. Over the past few days, Lemuel Meaney had seen too much human suffering. Kezia marvelled. Adam had been beautiful but Lemuel was so ugly it hadn't occurred to her he was capable of the same deep, tender feelings.

'She tries to stop herself crying out,' Lemuel went on, 'they tell her she'll only make things worse . . . She's full of spunk, my old girl, she don't half try.' He wiped his face on his sleeve. 'You been chucked out then?' He didn't sound surprised.

'Yes, but it's all right. They've given me a character. I'll get another situation soon as I can.' Kezia showed him the precious envelope. 'Until I do, can I stay here? I could look after you and Vida. And Esther, of course.' Lemuel regarded first her then the baby sombrely.

'You'll do all that? On your wages? I ain't got nothing, not even this week's rent. Vida's always paid that. There's no work to be had just now . . . I don't know how we're going to manage.'

His next question chilled her: 'You sure they give you a character? It sounds to me more like you was dismissed?' A shadow crossed Kezia's face.

' 'Twasn't my fault, what happened,' she said to

reassure herself, 'They gave me what money was owing. We'll have enough until I find another place.' Lemuel was obviously still full of doubt. 'Here,' Kezia urged, 'this is my character, see for yourself. It's not sealed.'

'To Whom it may Concern . . .' Carefully, so that he didn't dirty the paper, Lemuel unfolded the reference.

'Well?'

He looked up at her. 'You ain't read this yet, have you?'

'No.' He pushed it across. Words shifted and slid in front of Kezia's eyes.

'Dismissed without a character . . . abused her position . . . provoked Miss Massingham into an attack of nerves . . . destroyed valuable property . . .'

'An' you reckon you'll get another situation? With that?' He was sad rather than sarcastic. Kezia trembled.

'It was Miss who threw the vase.' Lemuel didn't know or care what she was talking about. He indicated the baby.

'They found out about her, of course.'

'No. They didn't even know she'd been born. When Rose and me took her downstairs, that's when they found out.' His ugly face crinkled a fraction.

'Must have been a bit of a surprise for all concerned when you did. An' you still thought you'd get a character out of 'em once they knew? A baby an' no wedding ring? Bit of a simpleton, ain't yer? Didn't they teach you right from wrong in Wales?' Kezia was fiery red. 'It ain't no business of mine how you got yourself in the fam'bly way,' he said brusquely, 'but you have got to learn sense.'

She hung her head.

'How are you going to manage, with a baby an' all?' The thought of leaving the safety of this small room terrified her.

'Can I stay, just for a little while. Until I find work.'

He was dubious. 'Depends what Vida says. We'll ask at visiting time.'

They tip-toed into the waiting area with the rest of the cowed crowd, too abashed to speak. Beeswax and carbolic were so pungent one or two sneezed. Peering over

114

shoulders they glimpsed the public ward through the heavy, glass-panelled door; each bed aligned with military precision, sheets tucked in so tightly the occupants were scarcely able to breathe. All the patients lay deathly still for fear of giving offence while those in authority creaked with starch.

'One visitor per bed. Ten minutes, that is all. No one is permitted to touch the patients.' Lemuel shambled across the polished floor. Clutching Esther, Kezia watched breathlessly.

Vida's bed was in a distant corner, she didn't need the light. Bandages hid most of her face. Where her scalp had been burned the hair was cut off. Kezia could make out dark tufts in between the white bandages. The nurses had finally relented and given her a rubber plug to bite on when the pain became too great. Kezia was too far away to see where Vida had bitten her lips raw in an attempt not to scream.

Lem reached over to kiss her forehead. A nurse called sharply, 'No touching!' Sheepishly, he murmured, 'How are you, old girl?'

'Right . . . as ninepence.' It hurt even to speak, he could tell.

'That's the ticket. Kezia's here. She's had a baby.' He waited but there wasn't any reaction. 'The day of the accident she had it. You was too poorly, that's why I couldn't tell you before. Bridie Macguire helped, an' I give a hand as well. I kep' cavey outside the door.' Vida made a strange noise, whether of pain or ridicule that he should do such a thing, Lem couldn't tell. 'She's brought it to show you,' he said and before he could stop himself, 'pretty little thing, she is.' Too late he remembered how Vida had always wanted a child.

'That's why she left Wales, I often wondered,' she murmured. Lem relaxed a little: she obviously hadn't guessed, nor did she seem particularly upset.

'Her chap got killed,' he explained. 'His parents didn't approve, an' her mother ain't got much, not enough to keep her and a baby.'

'Ah . . .'

'She told it all to Jacob Jones, that's why he sent her to us. The thing is, Kezia needs somewhere to stay now . . . I said it was up to you Vee.' Lemuel listened to the painful, ragged breathing. 'She's lost her place an' I don't reckon she'll find another very soon,' he added gloomily.

It was a long time before Vida spoke and he asked anxiously, 'You all right, old girl?' She told him yes, to comfort him. He saw the Sister snap open her fob watch. 'I told Kezia she should come an' ask you herself,' he muttered and hurried off to the waiting room. 'Be quick,' he ordered, 'Visiting time's nearly over.'

Kezia sped across the ward. Sitting the regulation eighteen inches from the bed, she found herself tongue-tied. There was no familiar face, nothing but bandages. Below the tufted scalp and round the chin, Vida's skin was scorched as charred paper. Swollen lips moved but the sound was difficult to make out.

'You been . . . a naughty girl then?'

'I loved him. We'd have got married if he'd come back.' Kezia saw the Sister pick up the handbell. Fear unlocked her tongue. It was vitally important that her child had a home. 'Vida, I got nowhere else to go.' One hand lifted slightly.

'Let me have a feel of her . . .' Swiftly, Kezia held out the baby.

'She's called Esther.'

'You'll both have to sleep downstairs. And you'll have to see she doesn't upset Lem.' Gratitude made Kezia oblivious to fear; what did the ferrets matter now she and Esther had a roof. She brushed Vida's hand with her lips.

'Thank you for being so good to us,' she whispered, 'I'll look after you as well, Vida, that's the other thing I wanted to tell you.' Despite her pain, the older woman laughed. She gazed through the permanent mist at the haggard young-old face looking at her so earnestly.

'Don't make promises you can't keep, girl.'

'But I will. You helped me. I'd have died if you hadn't, we both know that. Now it's my turn to care for you and Lem.' The pain came back with a vengeance, obliterating all other thought in Vida's mind.

116

'We'll see,' she muttered as the bell tinkled peremptorily. Visitors were shooed outside, including Kezia. Vida lost sight of her. 'Care for you and Lem.' What a rash promise, the girl had no idea what it meant.

'The thing is,' said Chas seriously, 'you 'n me've got to think things out. So give over play-acting and come and sit down.'

'In a minute.' They were on the river bank opposite the big house. As always Albert was on the look-out for gentry, currently in residence for the otter shoot. 'Look out, here's a couple of 'em coming now!' He was so thin, his teeth chattered in the cool breeze but that was forgotten when there was money to be earned.

He capered about to attract their attention as the gentlemen wandered down to the water's edge, eyeing them intently. As soon as they stopped to watch, Albert took on the character of first one, then the other, stroking an imaginary beard, setting gaitered feet down daintily amid the mud and finally, clowning an imaginary argument which culminated in one man pushing the other into the water.

Full of embarrassment, Chas pretended not to see – but as usual, it worked. At first annoyed, then forced to laugh, and when Albert popped up gasping out of the river in front of them, happy to thrust hands into pockets in search of coins.

This time there was a bonus. The wife of one man appeared on the terrace behind, calling imperiously that her husband should join her for tea. The instant she'd disappeared, Albert scrambled up onto the bank and became the haughty dame, shading his eyes against the light and whisking an imaginary train behind him. The husband tried to stifle his laughter but for sheer impudence, tossed another sixpence. Albert gave an exaggerated bow and dog-paddled splashing back to the other side. Learning to swim had so far proved extremely beneficial.

'You'll catch your death,' Chas said sourly. It was too

117

early in the year for the river.

'Never!' Albert towelled away with a bit of rag. 'I'll run about a bit and get warm.' He scampered up the towpath and back, alternately transforming himself into Sybilla then Enoch in the midst of one of their rows.

'Will you be still!' Chas scowled. 'I got something important to say.'

'What?' Albert hopped on one leg as he pulled on a stocking.

'I don't think I can stick it any more. I'm always so blessed hungry! You are too, ain't yer?' Albert paused.

'A bit. But not like you. I ain't grown so much.'

'If only she'd give us more grub – she's so mean!'

There was no denying it, Syb's miserly housekeeping left all of them wanting more. Chas's eyes were big in his bony face. The past two months he'd put on inches and his body craved extra nourishment. Working dawn to dusk bird-scaring had taken its toll, too. Albert examined him closely.

'You down in the dumps, bor?' Chas rounded on him.

'What d'you expect? They're working me to death at that place. All day in the fields and then no grub when I gets home 'cept a bit of bread.' Albert was alarmed.

'You ain't going to die, Chas?'

'If I don't gets proper vitals, I might.' A fistful of muddy coins appeared under his nose.

'Here y'are. You go an' buy what you want.'

'No thanks. Those are yours. You earned 'em.' It made Chas bitter that he should work so many more hours and end up handing his tiny wage over to Syb. Once she discovered what Albert was up to, no doubt he'd have to do the same with his booty. Until that happened, however, his brother was rich.

'You can have all of it but just let me keep twopence back for Pol. I want to get her something.' Chas had no present for her birthday.

'What you giving her?' he asked jealously.

'She needs a new frock.' This was undeniable, Polly had grown as well. Chas was scornful.

'That'll cost more'n a bob or two!'

118

'I know!' Albert stood on his dignity. 'When I got enough she can have one. Meantime she can have two pennorth of ju-jubes. From both of us,' he added generously. It was a sweetmeat of which he was particularly fond. Chas accused him.

'You reckon she'll share, doncha?'

'Pol ain't mean,' Albert conceded, 'not like Aunt Syb.' He pounded his arms against chilly flesh. 'What you going to do then? You got any ideas?'

'Nope.' Chas kicked the turf. 'Can't think prop'ly when I'm starvin'. Got to do something though.'

'Hey, there's Pol now. We ain't late are we?' Chas squinted at the sky.

'Nah. 'Snot teatime for hours.' They watched her approach. Today there was no eager smile when she saw them. They waited. She sat, hugging her knees and staring at the river.

'We're to go round an' ask Mrs Heyhoe if she'll give us tea.'

'Damme, no!' It was Albert's latest word, picked up from the gentry.

'Don't swear,' Chas chided, 'What's up?'

'Aunt Syb's poorly.'

'She was all right this morning.' Polly gave a quick shake of the head.

'Not now she ain't. Soon as you'd left this morning, she sent me to fetch old Ma Figgis . . . When *he* come home for his dinner'n saw Ma Figgis's dog, he started shouting an' kicking it.'

'Why?' It was a harmless animal, well known about the town. Polly shrugged.

'Ma Figgis come down to see what the fuss was about 'n he went for her as well. She told him to hold his noise.' This was incredible bravado.

'Bet he didn't!'

'Yes, he did. He stopped when she give him something to hold.' Polly described it reluctantly. 'I thought it was a skinned rabbit at first, ever so tiny . . . Ma Figgis had wrapped it in a bit of blanket.'

'Was it big enough for a pie?'

119

' 'Twasn't a rabbit, 'twas a baby.' Albert stared in amazement.

'Where'd she find that?' Chas was practical.

'Ma Figgis must've brought it with her if no one else come to the house.'

'It was dead.' They stared at her solemnly.

'You sure?'

'She told Uncle Porrit to ask Mr Summers to put it in someone else's coffin. Said it would cost one 'n sixpence but it was a human soul and had to have a Christian burial. Uncle Porrit started crying . . .'

This time the boys were speechless. Crying? Enoch Porrit? For no reason at all, Polly wiped her eyes as well then said crossly, 'Do hurry up. Mrs Heyhoe won't give us no tea if we're late.'

They pondered her tale as they made ineffectual attempts to tidy themselves. 'One 'n sixpence is a lot,' said Chas. 'Wonder whose baby it was?'

'Aunt Syb hates babies. Wonder why Ma Figgis give her one? You'd have thought she'd have known,' Albert said, puzzled. Polly examined him critically.

'Mrs Heyhoe won't let you in, all covered in mud.'

'I'll stand behind Chas,' he promised. 'If I breathe in I'm nearly as narrow an' she'll never even *see* me boots.'

Once admitted at the vicarage back door, they were wiped down with a damp rag and ordered to sit at the kitchen table. Questions began but for some indefinable reason none of them felt inclined to answer. When asked, Polly replied simply that her aunt wasn't well. Mrs Heyhoe seemed mysteriously to understand. No mention was made of the dead baby.

'How about your Uncle Porrit?' Chas had finished a second helping of stew and, without asking him, Mrs Heyhoe now served up a third. 'Is he behaving hisself?' she pressed. Out of deep gratitude, Chas made an effort to be sociable.

'When he come home this afternoon, he was upset, so Pol says. I think it was because of Ma Figgis's dog.'

'Ah . . .'

The gravy was so lovely Chas let his bit of bread wallow on the plate to absorb every drop before picking it up and licking the residue off his fingers.

'Maybe it wasn't the dog. Maybe it was 'cos his dinner wasn't on the table,' Albert speculated. 'Uncle Porrit allus shouts if it ain't. An' if Aunt Syb was poorly so he knew he'd have to wait . . .' It sounded weak but it was the best he could think of.

They watched as Mrs Heyhoe returned to the stove and opened the oven door. Inside there was a large plum duff. Round the table, there was ecstacy.

'Can we come here next time Aunt Syb's poorly?' Cook regarded Albert enigmatically.

'I wouldn't count on it if I were you.'

Chapter Nine

Changes 1887

'Esther? Come here. Don't go where I can't see you.' Vida peered into the stifling, simmering cauldron of the mews. There were no outlines now, just blurs. This summer, white hot sun combined with the odours from the stables to make her new half-blind world overpowering. The surrounding houses, tall and indifferent, penned in heat and stench alike. Vida was learning to adapt but there was no denying this endless heat added to her misery.

Sweat broke out whenever she moved today, voices had a whining edge brought about by endless, breathless days. Uneasy now about the child but unwilling to summon help, she listened for the chuckle and tinkling bells that Lemuel had fastened to the leather harness. The reins had somehow become detached from her chair.

There was no real danger, Esther never crawled far. She was playing a game she'd devised when she'd discovered Vida's weakness: that of moving only a few feet away. Once she did that, she was 'hidden'.

'You naughty girl, where are you?'

Heat didn't affect her as it did the adults in her world. Esther stretched her arms to greet the sun as soon as she opened her eyes every morning.

'Come here, you little varmint, do as aunty Vee tells you.' Another, larger shape blocked out the light as Bridie Macguire scooped up the child. 'Who's a wicked girl, pretending not to hear?' Bridie scowled as she planted a kiss and the little girl crowed with delight. 'It's frightened you're supposed to be, not laughing at me!' She placed her where Vida could touch her. 'Will we ever

122

be cool again, d'you think?' The scarred face lifted towards a molten sky as Vida Meaney sniffed the air.

'It's hotter than ever today, I reckon.' Bridie sank down on an adjoining stool, pulling up her skirts to let the air reach her swollen, veined legs.

'It's doing me no good, that's for certain. I can't stand this sort of weather, it makes my skin itch. Kezia not back yet?' Bridie knew already but waited until Vida had shaken her head before saying, 'She works, that one.'

'So she should.' Vida was quick to fend off imagined criticism, 'Lem can't support us on his own.'

'Is he out totting today?' It was Bridie's opinion, shared by many in the mews, that Lemuel Meaney was a lazy devil. He could turn his hand to most jobs but a regular daily routine he found uncongenial. He'd slackened off considerably since Kezia had come to live with them.

'Rag and bone don't bring in much,' Vida said defensively, 'not these days.'

'No but every little helps, doesn't it?' Bridie answered bluntly.

Everyone knew of Kezia's promise to care for the couple. Bridie had guessed Lemuel would take advantage of it. The girl's few shillings couldn't provide for three adults and a child. If Lem had begun to take his cart out again, so much the better; it would relieve the strain.

Until now no one had expressed the neighbourhood disapproval aloud to Vida; for her friend Bridie to be the first to do so was a blow.

'Lem's not totting but he is working,' she announced, thankful to have something to boast of. 'He's ratting up Chelsea way. They've sent for him three times already this week.' Bridie grinned and mopped her face.

'Those folk can turn their noses up at the likes of us but let vermin come crawling out of the river, then it's a different tale. I heard there was typhoid too, in Chelsea?'

'Yes but Lem's very particular about that,' Vida replied quickly. 'He washes hisself before ever he touches that child. He'd never risk hurting her.'

'Dotes on her, doesn't he,' Bridie agreed. 'You've only to see his face when she runs to him of an evening. Wish my

123

Tom felt the same. I've only to tell him I've fallen for another for him to drink himself stupid. If my kids could have ate what their father's poured down his throat all these years . . .' She shook her head ponderously. 'All the same . . .' she reverted to her theme, 'it's a pity Kezia has to work *so* hard.' Vida shrugged. She had other problems to worry about that.

'She doesn't complain.'

'I don't suppose she does. Always grateful. Nicely spoken an' all.'

'Hmph!' Kezia still had her looks. Vida was sensitive to the way people drew back on first meeting her now, almost as quickly as they did from Lem. We're equally matched, she thought bitterly, a pair of freaks. Bridie Macguire gazed at the resentful face. She guessed a little of what her friend felt.

'I don't suppose anyone's told you lately, Vida, but Kezia's nothing but skin and bone.' Vida was silent. 'She can't be much older than my Alberta but you wouldn't think so to see them together. She's still cleaning up West, I suppose?'

'Every morning after she finishes at The Musketeer.'

'Doesn't get in till late, neither. Esther must be in bed by then.'

'Me and Lem see to her,' Vida protested. 'We do everything needful. He feeds baby and I gives her her wash.'

'Shame for her mother though, ain't it?' Bridie pressed. 'There's not much pleasure having them, but you might as well enjoy seeing 'em grow, especially such a pretty little scrap.'

She fussed over the child to make her laugh, snatching an occasional glance. Vida's near-sightless eyes stared at infinity but she didn't respond. It was a difficult situation. Bridie sighed.

Since losing her 'character' Kezia had been forced to scrub floors. The trouble was, Vida didn't consider it unjust. Hadn't she been the one to find Kezia a good situation? It had been the girl's own fault for losing it, but now Bridie's words made her uneasy.

'If there was a chance of something better . . . there

124

ain't, Bridie. You know that. Kezia has to take what she can get.' Bridie spoke cautiously.

'She never refuses work but she's doing too much. She's wearing herself out.'

'So what am I supposed to do about that?' Vida asked shortly, 'I can't work and it takes Kezia all week to earn three or four shillin'.'

'If there was something nearer, to save the long walk up West. Waste of time that is.'

'She ain't got a reference. Not one blooming word to say she's honest and trustworthy.' This was Bridie's cue.

'They need someone at The Coachman's and they're willing to give her a trial.' It was a small café, round the corner from the mews, open all hours and patronized by cab drivers. 'The last girl lived in,' Bridie hinted, 'I was thinking how much nicer it'd be for you and Lem if Kezia had a place. She'd be just a step away and she could bring Esther during daytime but take her home at night.'

Vida understood immediately: she would have the pleasure of the child, but Kezia wouldn't be there in the evening for Lemuel to gaze at.

'It's not up to me what Kezia does,' she said with a show of reluctance.

'She's bound to ask your opinion, you know that. Kezia values your advice, I've heard her say so many a time.' Bridie could flatter now that her suggestion was being considered, 'I thought you should be the one to tell her about it. She'll listen to you more than she would to me.' This was an effort to bolster Vida's pride. 'She'll have to do the "rough" as well as cook and wait at table but after what she's been doing, it'll seem like easy work.'

'Trouble is, can we afford to let Kezia go?' Vida said candidly. 'I ain't never told you before, Bridie, but it's her money that pays the rent. Lem ain't managed to earn enough since my accident. It ain't his fault,' she insisted loyally, 'he's just never had the luck.'

'I daresay Kezia'll want to offer you something for looking after Esther, and now you say Lem's in a more regular line of work . . .'

'It won't last,' Vida was fatalistic. Bridie grew

125

impatient; Lem shouldn't be allowed to give up. Her husband, whatever his faults, stuck at whatever he could find and brought in sufficient for Bridie to skimp and scrape her way through the following seven days.

Besides, the whole neighbourhood knew that Vida must have a nest-egg even if she was being coy about it. The time had come for honesty. Bridie asked bluntly, 'How much did the factory people give you then?'

Vida wrinkled her forehead. 'What d'you mean?'

'When they come from the bottling plant a couple of weeks ago? Kezia had taken you and baby for a walk so it was Lem who spoke to them.'

'He never told me!' There was a brief, dreadful pause then the stool scraped as Bridie got to her feet, anxious to be gone.

'I expect he forgot,' she said awkwardly. 'It must've slipped his mind.' Both knew this was impossible but the truth was unthinkable. 'You won't forget to tell Kezia about the job at the Coachman's?'

She would keep a lookout herself. Goodness knows what sort of row there'd be when Lem returned – fancy him keeping the money and not saying a word! Vida would make him pay for it. Near blind she might be but she had her strength and the same fiery temper; they'd all learned to dread Vida's tongue.

Bristling with anger, Bridie gave Esther a final hug. Rules were strict in this community: you could cheat outsiders to your heart's content but to steal from your own kind was heinous.

She would keep Kezia occupied this evening. It was time to think of the future, the girl had more than repaid her debt. Fond of Vida though she was, it was wrong for Kezia to become a slave when Lemuel was capable. Vida had supported him in the past, now it was his turn. When Tom Macguire returned, he was invited to share Bridie's wrath.

'That Lem Meaney deserves what's coming to him – fancy keeping Vida's compensation money. It's all she'll ever get now she can't work.'

'Wasn't much, if what I heard was true,' Tom replied. 'They offered a sop to ease their consciences, that's all.'

126

'I don't care how little it was, it belongs to Vida. She's suffered enough for it. Imagine Lem stealing it – he must've known he'd be found out?' Tom Macguire shrugged.
'Lem wouldn't think of that. Money changes a man, haven't you noticed? 'Specially when you've never had any, never had the feel of it in your pocket. Lem probably *meant* to give it Vida. But when he got a hold of it, heard it jingling, everything changed.'
'I hope there's some left,' Bridie said tartly, 'I tell you, Tom, a farthing'd be welcome in that house. I peeped inside today. They've pawned almost everything since Vida's accident. Downstairs is nearly empty. The tools are gone, all that spare wood he kept for his carpentry – he must've sold it. All Kezia's got for a bed is a rug on the floor beside the cot that Lem made for Esther. 'Tain't good enough.'
'It's none of our business, gel. Keep your nose clean. You'll get no thanks if you interfere.'
'Kezia deserves a bit of luck,' Bridie said stoutly. 'She might find herself a nice young cab driver working at the Coachman's. Esther needs a father.' Tom was brusque; he'd troubles of his own.
'Never give up do you? Here – Lem ain't pawned his handcart?'
' 'Cause not. He needs that for totting.'
'Comes in handy for flitting an' all,' her husband muttered after a pause. Bridie whipped round.
'What did you say? You ain't never gone and lost your place again!' she cried but Tom Macguire was already on his way out.
'Just going to stretch my legs,' he called as he headed for The Musketeer. Bridie Macguire cursed long and loud but it was no use, she knew the signs. Vida wasn't the only one with a coward for a husband. She went to the head of the stairs and called to her daughter.
'Alberta, take the sheets round to Uncle's and try and get five bob on them. Your father's lost his place and if we don't pay the rent this week, we might have to flit.'

Kezia stood at the water's edge. It was dusk, the only time of day she could call her own. As always she was

127

anxious to be back home with Esther, yet to stand here in a park such as Adam had once described, was to know peace.

It was nearly two years since they had made love in the bluebell wood. She watched now as other young soldiers, arm in arm with pretty girls, walked up and down the bridle paths. It was a shock to realize they were probably the same age as herself. Kezia could scarcely remember what it was like to feel young.

Two pigeons were squabbling near her feet. Outside the park, carriages were heading west along Knightsbridge, their lamps shining butter-yellow in the gloom. Kezia understood the pattern of London life now but she'd never be a part of it. She still yearned for the space and quiet of Wales. Out of habit, she glanced up at the sky through tired summer leaves. Humid weather lay like a blanket across her face.

As usual today, on her way to scrub office floors in Regent Street, she'd passed the painted faces of those who'd given up the battle to stay decent. The stifling damp was merciless to cheap finery and rouge. Beside the railings of Green Park, all along Piccadilly, women wilted, their once youthful skins glistening with sweat as though with tears. Memory of them haunted Kezia. Suppose she had to give up the struggle? Since childbirth her body wasn't strong. If she couldn't continue working would she end up offering herself for sale on the pavements of London?

She remembered the sweet-faced lady who'd played the harmonium at the Mission. Wealth protected her from the realities of life yet it was the Mission women who doled out charity. Charming and concerned though most of them had been, how could any understand? Dare she apply to them again?

Kezia dismissed the idea. She recalled their attitude to those whom they described as 'fallen'. The shrill demands for public avowals of penitence from desperate souls grovelling in front of their kid-shod feet. Hers was a great sin, Kezia acknowledged it; she'd broken a sacred commandment. According to the church she was damned, as was Esther; the price of forgiveness would be a lifetime of expiation. Yet how could this be, argued a voice inside? Was it likely God would create a perfectly healthy child in order to destroy it? How could it be a sin to bring Adam's child into the world? Surely a man was entitled to his posterity?

No doubt those righteous Mission ladies would demand the fruits of sin be given up – but Kezia couldn't do that, either; the bond between her and Esther grew stronger every day.

Having come full circle with her fears, Kezia straightened her back: she would not give in, it would be a betrayal. If Adam was denied her she would cherish Esther in his place, with all the love of an overflowing heart. Ignoring her weariness, she set off once more towards Fulham.

In the mews, doors were wide open to catch whatever breeze there was. Lassitude following the heat made parents careless and children ran unchecked. On the lookout, Bridie Macguire called softly, 'Have you a minute, Kezia?' Lemuel Meaney had only just returned, she must delay the girl as long as possible.

'Esther will be waiting for me.'

'She's asleep. Didn't I pop in just now and see that her dear little eyes was closed,' Bridie fibbed blithely. 'Sit down, I've something to discuss.'

Chairs and stools were dragged outside and Kezia sat.

'They need a girl round at the Coachman's, just the sort of work that would suit you.' And before she could protest, 'Don't be worrying about references. I've told them who you are and that you're reliable. That's all that matters to them. They're expecting you at ten o'clock tonight; it's their quiet time.'

Taken by surprise, Kezia was silent. The Coachman? Not more than two minutes' walk from the mews – a small square window that fronted onto the pavement – a constant stream of customers – and the most succulent fragrances whenever the door opened ... not to scrub floors for a living – was it possible?

'You'd be living-in,' Bridie told her, 'Esther as well. Vida could see to her during daytime. She'd like that. But you'd be out of old Lem's way and she'd like that even more.' Kezia went scarlet and Bridie said, 'Now then . . . I'm not suggesting you've anything to be ashamed of, but you know how it is with Vida nowadays. She imagines what she cannot see, and she always was one for imagining the worst.'

Instinctively they glanced towards the open front door at the end of the row. Bridie wondered whether to mention the missing compensation money but decided against it. By now, Lemuel Meaney would be emptying his pockets, swearing that he'd never meant to take a farthing, and Vida would be informing him that from now on, he was the only breadwinner.

She returned to consideration of Kezia. With a shock she realized just how thin the girl had become. Shoulder blades, fragile as birds' wings, poked up sharply beneath her clothes. She looked far too tired, even her voice sounded old.

'It's kind of you, Bridie, very kind, but how can I desert Vida and Lem? They need every penny I can earn even though it hurts Lem's pride to accept.' Bless your heart for being a simpleton, thought Bridie angrily.

'Now you listen to me, Kezia. It's time you thought about Esther. Lemuel's perfectly capable of supporting the two of them. With you there, he's not had to make the effort but I've got a feeling, after tonight, he might see things differently. In fact, I'm sure of it.'

'He's made some lovely toys for Esther!'

'I know. And what happened when Vida suggested he make some more to sell from the barrow? Lem couldn't be bothered.' Kezia defended him.

'He took us in, Bridie. Esther and me wouldn't have survived without their kindness.'

'You've repaid ten times over,' Bridie scolded. 'Think of the future. What'll happen to Esther if you fall sick, eh? They'll feed you at the Coachman's and you'll get scraps for her. It's a busy place but you'll manage once you've got your strength back. Why not give it a try?'

Why not, indeed? After the past few months, it sounded wonderful. A room of her own in which to care for Esther. A door to shut out the cold cruel world. Kezia's heart beat faster at the thought she might not get the job. Ten o'clock before she could apply; one whole hour to wait. She rose to go.

Bridie didn't attempt to stop her; Vida must have dealt with Lemuel by now. She caught her briefly by the hand.

'I spoke up for you at the Coachman's. They're not worried about a "character".' A smile lit up Kezia's tired face.

'You're so kind. It seems as though I'm forever in your debt.'

'Nonsense.'

She watched the quiet, dignified manner in which Kezia walked past open doorways, nodding politely; a fixture in the life of the mews, yet she must be lonely.

'It's high time she found herself another man,' Bridie told no one in particular, 'one who'll be a father to that child.'

Kezia entered quietly in order not to startle Esther. As always her heart leapt joyfully when the child's chubby arms reached through the bars of the cot. Kezia gathered her up, murmuring soft loving words of Welsh. Beyond them, the ferrets chattered behind the wire mesh, full of excitement after their blood sport in Chelsea.

She soothed her daughter back to sleep and for the first time became aware of the quarrel overhead. Vida, loud and accusing, then Lem, defending himself and placatory at the same time. Apprehensively, Kezia climbed the stair.

They were so full of passion, neither noticed her. Lemuel stood, twisting the cap he always wore, holding it in front of him as if to stave off Vida's anger. Fury had transformed the scars into livid blotches against her skin. 'I don't believe you, Lemuel Meaney – you're lying! You've spent the money, that's what it is! Haven't I suffered enough?'

'I keep telling you, they was gentlemen, Vee. That was the trouble. I couldn't stand up to them. They wasn't exactly offering, neither – they argued me inside and out –'

'I'll never be able to see properly again!'

'You can see a bit though, can't you?' he pleaded. 'It's not as though you're completely blind.' She lunged towards the sound of his voice.

'Don't, Vee, please! You'll only upset yourself.'

'It's because I'm ugly, that's the reason, isn't it?' she shrieked. 'It's that Welsh bitch you want, not me. You can't stand the sight of me, that's why you couldn't be bothered to ask for compensation.' Tears filled Lemuel's eyes.

'Kezia's got nothing to do with it, Vee. I couldn't stand up to them, like I said. I wish there was a better reason – I was too ashamed to tell you afterwards. Too scared. I should've known you'd find out.'

Vida snorted. As if such a secret could be kept in the mews! Lemuel tried to make her understand.

'One of 'em, a proper toff – he wouldn't sit down in case he messed up his trousers – kep' saying how the nurses had took good care of you at the hospital – I couldn't argue with that, could I?'

'But that was a public ward, Lem. Anyone's entitled to go there, even the destitute. What about my compensation?' The old cap was twisted out of all recognition by now.

'They had this paper, you see, Vee . . . kep' saying how to prove negligence would mean going to a court of law – I couldn't face that –'

'I could've,' Vida sounded ominous. 'I would've managed, somehow. What did it say on the paper, Lem?'

From where she watched, her head just above the level of the top step, Kezia waited with a sinking feeling, for his reply.

'It was all written out. They said all I had to do was sign an' that would be an end of it. No more worries about making a statement or going to court. On your behalf, as your husband. "Per pro". They was very polite and explained what that meant.'

'And you signed?'

132

'For your sake, Vee, so's you wouldn't have any more bother.'

'How much?'

'Pardon?' That was foolish. She grabbed at his neckerchief and pulled so tightly, Lem fell on his knees in front of her, clawing at her hands. 'Please, Vee, don't!'

'How much did it say on the paper? Don't pretend you didn't read it.'

'There was a lot of wherefores –'

'How much was they going to pay!'

'Five pound. But it could've meant going to court . . .' The whimper trailed away as Vida turned her puckered scarred gaze on him. He loved her, she knew that. As much as he was capable of loving anyone, Lem loved her. But he was weak and she was strong.

Now she asked the terrible question: 'Weren't my eyes worth five pound, Lemuel Meaney?'

Kezia crept below. She crouched beside the cot in the humid dusk, listening to Esther's quiet breathing. Eventually, Lem rushed past, wiping away tears, on his way to seek solace at The Musketeer. She listened to his boots striking the cobbles and, summoning her courage, mounted the stair once more. Vida sat, hands tightly clasped, staring into empty space. When she spoke this time, her voice was harsh.

'You're late.'

'Yes . . . shall I make us a cup of tea?'

'There's none left, nor sugar.'

'I bought a pennorth on my way home.' It added to the heat to light the paraffin stove but Kezia brushed sweaty drops from her forehead.

'Bridie come round here earlier. There's a job going at the Coachman's,' Vida said abruptly. 'You could live in.'

'Yes, she stopped me as I went by. It sounds a good situation . . .' Kezia couldn't keep the longing from her voice, 'but I won't go if you need me, Vida.'

'We'll manage. Lem'll have to stir his stumps. I can look after myself, mostly. All he'll have to do is earn regular money. I'll see that he does from now on.' There was a new steeliness which was chilling. Vida had lost her raucous cheerful bounce.

Kezia asked nervously, 'Would they let me have Esther over there?'

'Not in daytime. You can bring her back here to me. Come round and collect her at nighttime. The last girl they had got five shilling. Tell them you'll do the "rough" as well and ask for threepence extra.'

Vida waited; Kezia emptied the precious tealeaves into the pot and stirred. When she put the cup between Vida's fingers the older woman said, 'Lem and me'll be better on our own. I'll see he works hard from now on. He'll have to do what I ask if there's no one else. You bring Esther here in the mornings, she's no trouble.'

'Thank you.'

'You can pay me half a crown but we won't tell Lem. He'll not drink that away – I shall need it for the rent.'

'Yes, Vida.'

Kezia recognized she would still be contributing; Lem couldn't be relied on, even now.

'Suppose they won't take me?'

'You see they do. It must be nearly time for you to go round there?'

'Yes.'

'Tidy your hair then. See your face is clean.' There was no need, Vida knew, given the girl's fanatical attitude to cleanliness but the new firmness was there to stay. 'It's time you found a place of your own, Kezia.'

'I'll do my best.'

'Come over here a minute.' Vida ran her fingers over the thin face. 'Bridie's right, you're nothing but bones. See you eats the leftovers when they offer them. Men don't like skinny women, there's nothing to warm the bed on a winter's night. Find yourself a smart young cabbie. Esther needs a proper father, not Lem fussing over her, pretending she's his.' Kezia understood: it wasn't that Vida was jealous, she was denying Lemuel every pleasure as part of his penance.

'Yes, Vida.'

The time had come to move on.

134

Chapter Ten

The Way Forward, Autumn 1887

Chas set off at first light to walk the fifteen miles to Bury
St Edmunds. Excited, half crying at the enormity of what
he was doing, he climbed down noiselessly from the
hayloft. Boots in hand, he tiptoed across the stone-
flagged barn floor and shushed the sheepdog in his
kennel.

Mist swirled about the flinty sandy paths, muffling his
footsteps. He was alone in a silent world, all the familiar
landmarks gone. In his nervous state the engulfing
softness appeared a threat, likely to stifle him; but as the
sun rose, his spirits lifted. He strode out firmly. There
was no going back, the die was cast. He'd taken an
irrevocable first step towards a new life.

His father had once described offering himself at the
hiring fair at Bury. This had given Chas the idea. He'd go
there but not to seek farm work, he'd had his fill of that.
Besides, when it was discovered what he'd done, he'd be
dismissed and no farmer would consider him after that.
That knowledge made a constriction in his throat which
nothing could dissolve. He brushed away unmanly tears
and scolded himself into a positive frame of mind. It was
the right decision, he'd been weighing the pros and cons
for weeks. All he had to do now was find alternative
employment; that, or starve. That thought depressed him
again.

The warmth soon went out of the day; clouds rolled
across the wide Suffolk skies. It began to drizzle, then to
rain. The piece of sacking over his shoulders was soon

soaked. He couldn't waste time looking for shelter, he must press on if he were to reach Bury in reasonable time. He'd allowed himself four or five hours to find work but would that be enough? It had to be; Chas suddenly realized the journey was taking longer than he'd estimated. He must reach home again before dark. He'd no money for food or lodging, nor dare he return without an offer of employment. From now on he had to fend for himself. Aunt Syb would wash her hands of him that was certain. Last night, to reinforce his courage, he'd slipped away from the farm and found Albert. Swearing him to secrecy, Chas had revealed his scheme.

'You're not to tell a soul. I shan't come back without I've got summat.'

'Suppose no one'll have you?' Chas attempted bravado.

'Always work to be had in Bury, that's what father used to say.'

'He used to tell as how they dropped the wages at the end of the hiring fair so that men were forced to accept whatever they could get. Wicked, father said it was.' Chas blazed at him.

'Give over, will you! Ain't I got enough worries already? Don't tell Aunt Syb where I've gone, neither.'

'Take me with you. You promised we should always stick together.' Chas relented.

'Depends what I can find, bor . . . but I will try. You and I shall be together like I said, if'n it's possible. Don't tell Pol, though. She cannot come, that's for sure, and there's no point in her fretting over it.' He sighed. 'I wish there was summat. She's no better than a skivvy, the way Aunt Syb makes her work . . .' He shrugged. 'There ain't nothing for her as I can think of.' Albert agreed sadly.

'Maybe we shall earn enough to send for Pol. Maybe we could set up house, buy her a new frock even.' If wishes were horses, beggars could ride, thought Chas sadly.

'See you don't say nothing.'

'Not a word, cross my heart.'

Father had also described to them the churches and abbey ruins of Bury but Chas wasn't prepared for their immensity. Down Angel Hill they ranged, towering monuments dedicated to St James and St Mary, together with the Norman gateway leading to the sprawl of the ruins. Chas was drawn towards them, seeking comfort.

Sybilla had dragged them to many different churches in her search for charity. Currently they attended a Sunday School where Albert, ever the optimist, hoped to acquire sufficient good conduct points to be included on the annual picnic.

Staring up at the church of St James, Chas saw that this building was as stern as it was strong, yet it offered sanctuary to the sore of heart.

He traced a line of carving with his finger, a perfect curve of stone chiselled by some long-dead craftsman. Tears threatened again – born out of frustration this time. He had made such efforts to acquire skills, studying by candlelight, teaching himself what he could, reading anything he could lay his hands on. The farmer's wife loaned him her Bible, provided he always washed his hands first, but books designed to show him alternative ways of earning a living, those were beyond Chas's reach.

He leaned his forehead against the wall remembering his father's precious volumes, cherished like jewels, all of them burned to ashes. Chas hid his misery by clinging to the stones and through them he felt vibrations; someone inside was playing an organ. He felt a longing to immerse and refresh himself with music and set off timidly towards the west door. Catching sight of his reflection Chas abandoned the idea. Shabby and mud-stained – no verger would permit him to enter.

The recruiting sergeant lounged on a bench in front of the Three Feathers. He was an expert at spotting likely ones, especially those still wet behind the ears. He sized up the muscle and sinew approaching him now, just as a farrier might assess a horse.

'Thirsty?'

Chas glanced round warily then wandered across, attracted by the friendly tone. He was conscious of a dry mouth and the hours which had elapsed since his last slice of bread.

'Landlord! Fill 'em up, if you please. Come far?' The northern twang was difficult to understand at first.

'A fair way.' When he realized the group were all in uniform Chas hesitated, but to depart now might be thought uncivil. Even as he paused, a brimming tankard appeared.

'Sit yourself down, there's plenty of room.' The sergeant put out an arm as if to guide him in onto the bench; in reality, it was to feel the breadth of shoulder beneath the sacking. 'You're wet through!'

'Yes.' Chas shivered.

'Hungry?'

'Oh yes.' The sergeant jerked his head and a soldier spun quickly on his heel. A bowl of meaty broth appeared as speedily as had the ale.

'Got a trade?'

'I'm 'pprenticed to a farmer.'

'Trying your luck in Bury? Hoping for a new employer?' Chas reddened.

'I'm seeking other work entirely, sir.'

'Uh-huh.' It was like plucking a ripe fruit. The sergeant made a shrewd guess; this fool had left without permission so would be out of work by this evening. He didn't bother to hide his derision. 'You must've had dozens of offers,' he mocked, 'a smart young chap like you.'

'I've not had one so far, sir.' Chas was too busy eating to notice any cynicism. The sergeant signalled for the tankard to be refilled.

'Healthy, are you? And strong?'

'Oh, yes.' He stopped licking the spoon to explain, 'You have to be fit to work with the plough. 'Tis heavy, right enough, even though most of our land is loamy. Over in the fens, now, that's worse. There's clay there as well as peat.' The sergeant indicated the empty, shining bowl.

'What's the matter, don't the farmer's missus feed you?' Chas blushed again, this time in shame of his appetite.

'Only the leftovers. I don't get meat while I'm

138

'prenticed, just a bit of cheese. It's not sufficient.' It distressed him to be disloyal to his employers – hadn't Mrs Booth shown him kindness more than once – but the sergeant wasn't interested.

'Three square meals a day, that's what the army reckon a man deserves. Hot food, no half measures. Tot of rum to give you courage. And a healthy life, twice as healthy as what you're used to. Am I not right, lads? Then there's the travel: how d'you fancy seeing the rest of the world? India, anyway.'

'India!'

'Fuzzy wuzzies, my boy. Got to remind them they're part of the empire. Mustn't let them get the upper hand; remember what happened at Calcutta? Respond to authority, natives do, especially when it's wearing the uniform of one of her gracious Majesty's regiments of foot. We've been commissioned – due to leave at the end of the month. It's a chance that'll never come your way again, my boy. Ever heard of the North West Frontier? Ever sailed through the Bay of Biscay? Ever been on board ship, come to that?'

Chas was round-eyed. Imagine going halfway round the world – as far as India!

'To be under sail . . . now there's an experience. Fills a man's lungs, makes him *feel* ten foot tall. Ever seen flying fish, lad? The way when the sun's on them it turns a shoal into a sparkling rainbow skimming over the water . . .'

The corporal's eyebrows went up but he knew better than to laugh. Recruits had a shock coming if they thought they'd spend their days leaning over the rail watching out for coloured fish!

'Yes, whenever I come home . . . and the girls hear tell of the sight I've seen . . . It's not the uniform that get's them, lad, it's the *experience*. They can't resist that. Worth gold, experience is. Not married by any chance?'

'Oh, no!'

'That's good. Marry in haste, repent for the rest of your life, eh?'

'I daresay.'

' 'Course, you do. *Experience* comes first, lad. See the world. Learn. Fill your mind with sights that no one else has a chance to see – and let the army fill your belly. Let it turn you into a man. See if I'm not right.'

Within the hour Chas had taken the Queen's shilling, obtained the promise of a place for Albert, been examined and pronounced fit by the regimental doctor and had been measured for the uniform of the Northumberland Fusiliers.

He skulked about the lanes until it was late, slipping into the garden the back way and hiding behind the privy. He gave his private whistle. Sybilla heard it as well but gave no sign. She waited until Albert had melted through the scullery door before following him.

The summer dusk was moist after the rain, the earth soft beneath her feet. Sybilla moved unobserved. From beyond the shed she heard the whispered conversation and Albert's squeak of excitement, 'India!' She was equally astonished but held her tongue. India . . . what had Chas been up to? Moments later Sybilla understood.

'If you wanted to join, why not go to the training camp at Thetford,' Albert was demanding. 'They'd have taken you right away.'

'Because she'd find out, stupid. That's why I went to Bury in the first place . . . so's she wouldn't know.'

'And you joined the army there?'

'That's right . . . and there's a place for you.'

Sybilla was astonished; she'd never credited Chas with having the initiative but here he was, persuading Albert to do the same. It was ridiculous, of course. Albert was far too young. She was distracted by wondering if Jeremiah would have agreed to let Chas go? But Sybilla Porrit had long ago learned to smother her conscience.

Consider the benefits: she'd have no further responsibility for either boy – India was beyond the moon as far as she was concerned. Why, she might never see them again!

Imagine never having the worry of how to provide the next meal? Sybilla turned it round another way: the army was the perfect solution, why hadn't she thought of it? Chas and Albert would be far better off seeing the world than remaining in this backwater. 'Jeremiah wouldn't argue against that . . . he'd be glad for 'em.'

She was complacent at having so easily discharged her obligations. Had she not done what the church demanded, behaving like a Christian in cherishing three unwanted orphans? She'd keep Polly, of course. The girl had turned out to be useful, cleaning up after the lodgers, baking bread, ironing. She'd have to collect and deliver the laundry too, once Albert left home. Out of habit, Sybilla made a virtue of necessity: it would do the girl good to have a bit more fresh air.

Come next summer Sybilla planned to add more tables to her front garden. Polly would have to give up schooling because there'd be so many more teas to serve. People flocked to Suffolk during the summer, thanks to the excursion trains.

As for Enoch Porrit, Sybilla had learned to ignore him. He still demanded his "rights" and on one occasion, stared as if seeing her for the first time. Sybilla demanded to know what the matter was. He was sober for once. 'I was thinking of our baby . . . and wondering how you could ha' done such a thing.' She shrugged: what was past, was past.

He repeated the question, this time she turned on him. 'That child would've been yours so why should I ha' wanted it? It would've reminded me of you whenever I looked at it. If'n it had grown, it might've behaved like you. Some other girl would ha' suffered as I have. Best thing was not to let it live. I've never regretted it, even if 'twas a sin. Ma Figgis reckons I can't have another, either. If you wants a son, Enoch Porrit, you must find some other fool to bear it, for I never shall. An' it makes my heart glad to say so.'

After that, Enoch's drinking and wenching was done in Thetford. He told himself he didn't care if Sybilla got to hear but in truth he was half afraid of her, she'd become so hard. When she told him she couldn't have another child, he could have sworn she gloated.

As for Sybilla, her philosophy was simple: she'd been a fool but she'd survived. If she could reduce her husband to impotence with a few scathing words, it compensated in some degree for the scar she still carried on her arm.

On those nights when, out of despair, Enoch still tugged at the buttons on her nightdress, Sybilla told him to be quick and closed her eyes. It never took long, thank goodness.

On the other side of the privy, Chas was whispering again.

'We'll have to be careful, Albert. Farmer Booth'll be round soon –'

'He come already, at breakfast time.' Chas swore softly. 'What did he tell Aunt Syb?'

'He kep' threatening the law on her an' asking for the 'prentice money back. She offered me in place of you because she said he couldn't have a farthing of it. He refused to take me – he said I was too skinny.' Albert flexed non-existent biceps indignantly. 'See that? I ain't skinny!'

'We'll have to fib tomorrow about your age. I told the sergeant you were sixteen.' Albert gasped and Chas scolded, 'Look, you want to come with me, doncha? You want to see India as well? By rights we've got to have Aunt Syb's permission but she'll never give it so don't let me down when I tells a lie.'

'I won't. I'll stand ever so tall and straight, Chas. An' I'll frown. People do that when they get older.'

'You behave yourself or I won't take you at all,' Chas said severely. 'When we get to Bury, you do exactly what I tells you. The sergeant said we was to be there by ten o'clock so see you're ready to leave as soon as it's light.'

'Yes, Chas.'

'It's three days before we can start training. They gives us passes an' all we has to do is turn up at the railway station. I shall have to hide till then, and you'll have to smuggle me out some grub.'

'I'll manage. Where will you go?'

'In the woods by the river.' There was a pause and when Albert next spoke, it was in a much smaller voice.

'Chas . . .'

142

'What?'

'We will tell Pol afore we go, won't we? She'll be ever so upset.'

'We'll leave her a note,' Chas said firmly. 'I know you. You'd let the cat out of the bag soon as you spoke – and that could mean Aunt Syb finding out. Neither of us would get away if that happened. She might force me to go back to Farmer Booth.'

On her side of the privy, Sybilla was tempted to call out that she would do no such thing but she remained motionless and silent.

'Chas . . .'

'What now?'

'It'll be all right? Sailing all that way?'

' 'Course it will. It'll be an experience. The chance of a lifetime.'

'I meant – being on a boat for weeks and weeks.'

'You ain't frightened, bor . . .? Look how good you are at swimming.'

'That's true.' Albert's volatile nature immediately switched to optimism. 'I'm the best swimmer there ever was an' if I finds the army doesn't agree with me, I can always nip over the side an' swim back home.'

Out of habit, Sybilla went to confide in Mrs Heyhoe. In the rectory kitchen, under the influence of strong tea, she told the tale as she had reconstructed it. In her version, it had been her suggestion from the beginning that Chas should enlist. 'Why shouldn't the dear boy see the world, Mrs Heyhoe? It'll be the chance of a lifetime, I told him. What my dear dead brother Jeremiah would have wished for him if he'd been spared.' Cook wasn't fooled.

'I did hear that Farmer Booth come round demanding his 'prentice money . . . He's been putting it about that Chas run away not just from farming but from you and Porrit as well.'

' 'Tis a wicked lie. That boy loves his home. Porrit ain't troubled him for months, I seen to that. No, 'tis the farming Chas don't find to his liking. I should have minded what Jeremiah told me years ago . . . He swore

143

farming was nothing better than slavery, 'specially if you wasn't your own master. If Jeremiah hadn't married so young hisself, an' if he hadn't had those three little lambs so quick, why then he'd have never become a labourer. 'Tis likely he'd have gone for soldiering instead.'

'Hmm!' Cook's chair rocked to and fro. 'Pity you didn't remember all that afore Chas was 'prenticed.'

'It slipped my mind,' Sybilla assured her blithely, 'I was that pressed for ways of feeding them dear children, I couldn't think of nothing else. An' Farmer Booth's wife promised me she'd cherish Chas like one of her own, which she have done near enough 'cept for the matter of his victuals.' Sybilla sought to divert her friend considering the matter further. 'How's His Nibs, today?'

'All of a lather.'

'Oh?'

'The new missus is in a tizzy as well.'

'Don't do for her to get excited, not while she's carrying.'

' 'Tis on account of Canon Greenwell who's staying here. I told you he was always off digging where the Old Uns used to live? He wrote to the newspapers saying he'd discovered where prehistoric man dug for flints. Missus showed me where they'd printed his letter.'

'That ain't a discovery,' Sybilla was annoyed, 'anyone here could've told him, 'tain't no secret.'

'Ah, well . . .' Cook sucked at a loose tooth. '*He* didn't know. He come here from the university and discovered it all for hisself.'

'Ain't that the way? Folk spend five minutes poking about an' when they find what we've allus known, they claim it's summat new. Of course it's where the Old Uns used to dig – it's where old queen Boudicca chose the flints for her chariots.' Sybilla's indignation subsided as quickly as it had arisen. ' 'ere, do the Canon want to know any more? I'll tell him what I can remember for sixpence.' Cook was dubious.

'He likes finding out for hisself.'

'Save him a lot of digging,' she insisted.

'Yes, but you ain't been to university. It'd spoil it for the

144

Canon if you was to tell him. He likes to think he's cleverer than us.' To placate her, Mrs Heyhoe refilled the tea-cups. 'What about Albert, then? What'll he do once Chas has gone for a soldier? I did hear how Farmer Booth turned him down when you offered him instead?' Sybilla was angry that gossip should have spread so far so quickly.

'Albert wants to go to India along of Chas.' The tea-pot was suspended mid-air.

'You're never going to let him! He's too young to enlist, surely?' Sybilla became vague.

'I couldn't say, I'm sure. The army's willing to take 'em straight from school nowadays, I believe. They must be desperate to come recruiting in Bury.'

'But he's only a tiddler is Albert! He's not growed tall like Chas.' Sybilla became anxious. Mrs Heyhoe now had an obstinate look which she remembered well. If Cook decided Albert was too young to enlist, she was perfectly capable of telling His Nibs. *He* was always seeking an excuse to interfere in other people's lives. Suppose he took it into his head to go to Bury and tell the recruiting sergeant Albert's date of birth? Sybilla might end up with both boys back on her hands, which would never do. She set herself to charm cook into silence.

'You know how it is with those two, Mrs Heyhoe. David and Jonathan they are, allus has been. If'n I was to try an' prise 'em apart, why the thought of what that might do to Albert really upsets me. An' you wouldn't stop him leaving, no matter what.

'D'you know what I think he'd do? He'd run off. Whatever obstacle you put in his way, he'd go to the other end of the world if'n it meant being with Chas.' Sybilla put her head on one side and smiled. 'The way I see it, I shall let 'em both go to Bury tomorrow. It may be as soon as the army claps eyes on Albert, he'll be sent packing because he *is* too little. But suppose they have got a suitable position for him? You once showed me pictures of boy soldiers in one of your magazines. Why then, he and Chas will be happy together. But if you or I was to try an' spoil their chances, they wouldn't thank us now, would they?'

'Hmm . . .' Mrs Heyhoe didn't trust Sybilla when she

145

smiled like that but she couldn't fault the logic. 'So what are you going to do?'

'Sit tight,' Sybilla answered promptly. 'They might both be back by tomorrow night an' that would be an end of it.'

'Chas won't. He couldn't if he wanted to, not if he's taken the Queen's shilling.'

'But it is what he wants, Mrs Heyhoe. 'Twill be the making of him, Albert too, shouldn't wonder.'

Cook had been out-manipulated and resented it. She rocked and brooded, then an idea began to form. The last kitchen maid had been dismissed and a replacement was badly needed, especially since the new mistress had odd notions concerning hygiene. The kitchen had to be cleaned twice a day – such nonsense!

'I'm run off my feet, and that's the truth. The mistress says, bring a new girl into the kitchen, Mrs Heyhoe, one you can train, and I shall be more than happy to pay her wages.'

'Well, why not do as she says?' Sybilla said carelessly. 'You can have your pick. There's plenty as'd be eager to come here; a good situation with food and board thrown in.' She'd fallen into the trap and Mrs Heyhoe smiled with satisfaction.

'Polly must be ready for training by now. You always said how she'd be just the girl for this place, Mrs Porrit.'

Sybilla could've kicked herself! She couldn't wriggle out of it this time. She remembered every detail of their former conversation.

'She would be ideal,' Cook repeated, 'an' God knows I need another pair of hands. She'd be well trained; a proper kitchen maid when I'd finished with her. I'd even show her my recipe for Paradise pudding.' Most women would have been overjoyed for their nieces to be shown that.

'We'll see,' Sybilla temporised, 'Polly will be right upset once Chas has gone.' Cook looked at her narrowly.

'You are going to tell her? So's she can bid her dear brothers a proper farewell.'

'I swore I'd keep it a secret as long as Chas wants me

to,' Sybilla extemporised. 'Besides, now he's decided he wants Albert to go with him, it'll be a terrible shock for dear little Polly. I shall hev to comfort her and take her mind off her sorrow. She won't be fit to learn puddings nor any other such thing, not for a long while.'

Mrs Heyhoe gave a withering look. There were half-truths and necessary fibs, but for Sybilla to pretend she cared anything for Polly was outrageous. Nor was it selfishness that made Cook demand Polly as a maid, it was concern.

Without her brothers Polly would be at the mercy of both Sybilla and Enoch. Cook was far from ignorant of the amount of work Sybilla expected and Enoch wasn't the sort of man she approved of as an uncle.

'I tell you what, Mrs Porrit: I won't say a word to His Nibs about Albert, even though we both know he's too young ... provided you sends Polly round here.' The stubborn face defied argument. 'You can have a day to console her first,' she added sarcastically, 'if you think it necessary.'

Sybilla agreed, she couldn't afford to do otherwise. But as she rose to take her leave, Mrs Heyhoe passed on an invaluable piece of information.

'A sad business about Mr Fowler.' Sybilla looked blank. 'Hadn't you heard. He got took early this morning.'

'Never!'

'He did. Such a fine, healthy looking man, too. Half past three this morning Mrs Fowler sent for His Nibs. *He* was upset, being got out of a warm bed. Said she should have gone for the curate, especially when it come out the Parish'll have to bury the man.' Shock piled upon shock. Sybilla sat down again abruptly.

'I thought Mr and Mrs Fowler were comfortable. She always sent all her linen for laundering, never kep' anything back.' Mrs Heyhoe nodded sagely.

' 'Twas all a front, seemingly. So's folk'd *think* they were doing nicely. But as soon as her husband expired, Mrs Fowler come out with it. She don't know where to turn for a halfpenny, she told His Nibs. As for a funeral, she's having to apply to the Parish for everything, even his coffin.'

'Dear me!' Sybilla was genuinely astonished but her mind was working very fast indeed. Mrs Heyhoe rocked, shook her head and pronounced her verdict.

'What they had, they spent, seemingly. Funeral's next Tuesday morning . . .' Her guest appeared lost in reverie so Cook looked pointedly at the clock. 'Must make a start on the vegetables. I shall be glad when Polly's here to give me a hand and no mistake.'

Sybilla made her farewells absent-mindedly. Outside, she paused. The Fowlers had a small house out towards Mundford. Such a property was bound to increase in value, it would make a better home for her nest-egg than the bank. Sybilla needed that to grow into a healthy sum before she departed for London.

It wouldn't mean much of a diversion, either. She'd had a message asking her to call on Mrs Helliwell at Willow End, but that could wait. Still hidden by the vicarage hedge she lifted her skirt and removed her emergency sovereign from its hiding place before going to pay her last respects to the late Mr Frederick Fowler.

His relict clung to formalities of death. The door-knocker was shrouded in crêpe and straw was spread thickly on the front path, to muffle the harsh sound of feet from dying ears. It was a delicacy not normally enjoyed by the less affluent and, in Sybilla's opinion, sheer waste. If your husband was dying, why fritter money away?

Mrs Fowler greeted her with red eyes having spent the morning with creditors. Mrs Porrit wasn't a close friend, but anyone who could share her burdens was welcome. She poured out her woes then, recollecting the decencies, suggested Mrs Porrit might like to see the corpse before partaking of a glass of something.

In the darkened dining room, Sybilla contemplated the waxen features. What a silly fool Mr Fowler must have been. There was evidence of extravagance on every side and now . . . not even a shroud to call his own. Here there were flock wallpapers, knick-knacks and brass fire-irons, even a piano with frills covering the legs for modesty's sake.

She moved discreetly to a china cabinet and scanned the contents. Her knowledge wasn't great, but at the vicarage she'd learned to discern good from bad. Despite the gloom, one or two pieces looked acceptable. Now was the time to strike before Mrs Fowler had time to recover. Sybilla began to feel excited.

She neglected to offer up a prayer for Mr Fowler's soul but went in search of his widow. Declining the wine – which gained her hostess's gratitude for there was so little left in the bottle – Mrs Porrit made her offer. The cottage and certain of the contents for seventeen guineas, cash. It would mean borrowing for she hadn't that amount in her account, but the rent Sybilla intended to charge would more than repay any interest.

'I should want that extra bit of land thrown in,' she pointed to the grassy untended stretch beyond the hedge, 'that's part and parcel of the property anyway.'

'Frederick paid an additional sum for it,' his widow faltered. Sybilla shook her head.

'I shall need every square inch if I'm to make the place pay, Mrs Fowler. And you shall have the whole seventeen guineas tomorrow morning. Cash, like I said. Here's one now, to show I mean business.'

The gold coin produced the reaction she had anticipated. Gratitude that her spouse could now have a decent burial made Mrs Fowler incoherent and Sybilla quickly shook hands before the woman could reconsider. As she got to the front door, Sybilla paused as if an idea had just occurred.

'My dear, can I make a suggestion?'

'Please do, Mrs Porrit.'

'As I was beside your dear husband – what a lovely corpus he do make, to be sure – those bits of china you have in the cabinet, they must be worth a few shillings? Why don't you sell one or two, to help you out of your difficulties.'

'Oh, I couldn't do that! Frederick inherited the porcelain from a very dear uncle.' Sybilla lifted pious eyes.

'An' have you prayed for guidance, Mrs Fowler. Have

you asked your late lamented, not forgetting his uncle, what they would do, given your sad circumstances?' Before the tears could restart, she said quickly, 'Shall I see what I can manage?'

'How d'you mean, Mrs Porrit?'

'I has to go to Thetford tomorrow, to visit the bank. Supposing I takes a little piece to show one of those shops on King Street where they sell nice things? They might give a decent sort of price for it.'

'Would you?' Mrs Fowler obviously found the very idea of a commercial transaction abhorrent; Sybilla almost laughed.

'Dear Mrs Fowler, what are friends for at such a time? If'n we cannot help one another in our hour of need . . . as the Bible tells us to.' Uncertain where that particular reference might be found, she moved purposefully towards the dining room, 'Shall we just take a couple of pieces from that cabinet?'

They crept inside, fearful of disturbing the inert presence. Sybilla indicated those she'd spotted.

'Just the one, perhaps,' Mrs Fowler glanced nervously at her husband, convinced of his disapproval. 'That little shepherdess came from Germany, I believe. It's very old. I remember Frederick telling me so.' Sybilla rejoiced silently at her ability to discern the best.

'I shall do what I can,' she promised. She felt uneasy in the corpse's company. 'I must go now, but I shall be back here tomorrow to let you know what I got for it.'

Half a mile further on, Sybilla sat under a hawthorn hedge to do her calculations. The net result left her deeply satisfied. There was also the additional piece of land. She had just the person in mind for that, but first there was the request to call on Mrs Helliwell.

The widow and her child were in the garden. Gladys had turned out to be plain, as Sybilla had predicted, but this didn't prevent her enthusing.

'Ain't she bloomed just like a little flower?' she cried rapturously. 'Didn't I promise she would, Mrs Helliwell?' The widow couldn't remember and was distracted by other anxieties.

150

'I don't know how to put it to you, Mrs Porrit. I have tried, truly I have, but I don't know where to turn.' Sybilla was smug.

' 'Tis money, is it?' she asked directly. Mrs Helliwell's lip began to tremble. 'Now, don't upset yourself, my dear. What are friends for, that's what I allus say.'

'I couldn't think of anyone else to turn to,' the widow burst out, 'you having helped me before. I've sold all I could, Mrs Porrit, all the best pieces of furniture left me by my dear husband –'

'Deary me!'

'But now there's nothing left and the rent's due again on Monday!'

It was fate, Sybilla decided; a fair return for having been forced to give up Polly to the vicarage.

'Now, I won't offer to *lend* you money, Mrs Helliwell, for that'll only make matters worse.' She watched with cool indifference as the woman's fear increased. 'What I am going to offer is work, for which I'll pay you fair and square.'

'But, what can I do?'

'Goffering. You know I runs a small laundry business with the help of my niece, Polly. Well, she's to be trained. I've arranged for her to go as kitchen maid at the rectory, which means she won't be able to help me no more. You'd have to fetch and deliver, mind. Collect what's ready for ironing every day and deliver to customers the following morning, that would be the way of it. I can only offer twopence a load, but if you works hard with your iron, you'll soon earn enough for the rent and for to feed you an' Gladys.'

It would mean fifty hours or more a week to achieve that but Mrs Helliwell wasn't as adept at calculations. She began to spill out her thanks. Sybilla cut her short.

'First thing Monday morning, you come to our back door. Don't let me down.'

The widow said humbly, 'Oh, I won't, Mrs Porrit, and thank you a thousand times.'

'Here's sixpence to tide you over. We can set it against your first week's wages.' Without realizing it, Mrs Helli-

151

well had bound herself to the meanest spiral of pay Sybilla could dare suggest.

There was one more errand before Sybilla could return home. She walked round the back gardens of the Willow End to see if her former neighbour was tending his plot. The fact that he was, and that the results of his labour were a delight to the eye, added to her satisfaction. She inhaled the scent of phlox, roses and lavender and admired the prolific vegetable patch before coughing to attract his attention.

As on that first, disastrous morning of her marriage, the man gave a slight, polite bow when he saw her. Today he doffed his old hat again and Sybilla warmed to him.

'I don't suppose you remember me.'

'Mrs – Porrit, isn't it?'

'That's right. Me and my husband used to live next door but we took a house on the London road.'

'Ah, yes.'

'An' now I have took another house, not for us, but for to rent out. It has a bit of land with it.'

'Indeed.' His quiet gentleness was in such contrast to the men Sybilla normally had dealings with, she automatically became more genteel.

'Excuse me taking the liberty . . . this is a very nice garden you hev.'

'Thank you, Mrs Porrit.'

'A bit more land would mean you could grow more.'

First elation then a shadow crossed the man's face.

'That had always been my ambition,' he admitted, 'to grow fruit in addition to vegetables. But as you can see . . . there's no more space here.' He glanced at the back bedroom window, 'Not until the Lord sees fit . . .' he murmured, slightly furtively, 'I dare not venture far from Willow End.'

'Bless the name of the Lord,' cried Sybilla, not understanding, but thinking privately, 'Blast!' Was this chap turning out to be one of those wretched evangelicals? She'd once made the mistake of attending such a church.

152

'I was looking not for to *rent* the land, 'tis scarcely big enough for that. Not more than half an acre, I'd say . . .' She saw his eyes light up again. ' 'Tis only a step, wouldn't take you away from Willow End for long. And what I was hoping for was someone who'd grow vegetables – or fruit – and let me have a share. No charge for the land at all.' She'd originally planned to demand half the harvest but Sybilla's ideas were undergoing a sea-change. Such a charming man . . . how old was he? Fortyish? Such lovely manners, too! She'd only demand a quarter of what he could produce, she didn't want him to get a bad impression.

'Why not take a look at it,' she urged, 'see if'n it looks suitable for a fruit garden. 'Tis on the Mundford road, where Mr an' Mrs Fowler live.' His eyebrows went up.

'Mr Frederick Fowler who . . .'

'The very same. God rest his soul.' It was the man's turn to say Amen and he did so quietly.

'I'm helping his widow out by taking the house an' land off her hands,' Sybilla told him ambiguously. 'If'n we cannot help one another when we are in trouble . . .'

'A Christian act, Mrs Porrit.' He'd made her uncomfortable.

'Yes, well you have a look and see what you think. I shouldn't want anything but what you could spare. A few taties, greens and such. For to feed my poor brother's children.' She wouldn't be able to claim to be doing that much longer. Oh, well.

The man bowed again now the interview was at an end. Sybilla felt very much a lady when he did that. A thought occurred to her. 'I don't recollect us having been introduced, not prop'ly . . .?'

'Henry Durrant, ma'am. At your service.' Sybilla gave a gracious nod.

'Pleased to make your acquaintance, I'm sure.'

As she walked back along the river bank she pondered on an unjust fate: why couldn't she have met someone like that? As she turned down the High Street she thought with even more regret, if only I'd *waited*! Pausing to let a

153

cart go past, unbidden came the idea, if Enoch Porrit was to die, she might marry again!

Did Henry Durrant have a wife? 'I shall find out,' Sybilla promised herself, 'I shall find out everything about him.'

Later that night, in her best writing, she penned the advertisement for a Thetford shop window.

TO LET: furnished accommodation, clean and comfortable, bedding included. Suit professional gentleman and housekeeper. No children. Gardener kept.

It was a mite premature but Henry Durrant had as good as promised he'd take over the land.

The recruiting sergeant was accustomed to turning a blind eye but this was too much. 'You're never sixteen! Put your hand on that Bible and swear you are.'

Albert, facing front, hands rigidly to his sides, asked, 'Permission to speak, sir.'

'Swear it!' The voice sounded dangerous. Albert swallowed.

'Beg pardon but it was the monkey nuts what did it, sir.' The sergeant's face turned to stone. Chas closed his eyes. Albert had done it this time.

'Monkey nuts . . . what monkey nuts?'

'What Aunt Syb fed me. She found them in a paperbag on the Thetford round. They wasn't supposed to be for 'uman beings. They was intended for h'a parrot, sir. Intended to help it grow feathers.' Among the listeners there was a tendency to giggle.

'And are you going to unbutton your shirt and show me your wings, boy? Because I got a piece of advice. Start flapping them now and get out of my sight!' There was a menace that Albert had come across before. Terror made his voice shake.

'Soon as Aunt Syb give me red meat instead, sir, I begun to grow proper. Ask Chas, he'll tell you. Soon as she stopped feeding me them nuts. An if'n the army feeds me like I should be fed, I shall grow even more. End up a giant, I shouldn't wonder.' At this, one of the listeners exploded. Quick as a flash, Albert addressed him in the tones of an officer he'd just seen.

'Have a care, my man. You-ah, are in danger of-ah, ridiculing a po-tenshul mighty-ah force.'

The mannerisms were exact; he'd transformed himself into the pompous little man, imaginary cane under one arm, equally invisible yet over-large moustachios quivering with indignation. Even the sergeant guffawed but he was quick to recover.

'Have I given you permission to stand-easy!' he bellowed.

'Beg pardon, sir.'

'We've had enough tomfoolery. Be off, back home to your mother. We don't cradle-snatch in the Fourth, even if we are short of numbers.'

'Permission to make a final request, sir.' It was as pathetic as from a man about to be hanged.

Despite himself, the sergeant asked, 'Well . . . what is it this time?' Albert indicated the figure of Chas beside him.

' 'e needs me to look after him, sir. Like I allus promised mother I would.' Arms akimbo, torn between anger and wanting to laugh, the sergeant loomed over him.

'Just how d'you propose to do that? Fight off lions, I suppose?' This time Albert was utterly sincere.

' 'Course I would, sir, if they was attacking Chas. We ain't never been parted since mother and father was took. Please, sir, let me go with him an' be a soldier.' There was a swift consultation among those surrounding the sergeant, who had to agree they were short of a mascot at present. Slowly, reluctantly, he began to nod his head.

The doctor was scandalized; this recruit barely met the minimum height requirement of 5'3". He agreed, grudgingly, that the boy might still grow. The tailor grumbled at having to fashion so small a uniform, but Albert didn't care. He was in the army, he and Chas would be together. He took the oath, which surprised him. It wasn't until the following day he realized the

155

magnitude of what he'd sworn; he had promised to slay the Queen's enemies and if need be, lay down his life in defence of his country. Nothing but death, or so it seemed, lay ahead. It was a daunting prospect.

On the appointed day, he crept out of the house at dawn, full of suppressed excitement at the forthcoming train journey. Albert wanted to announce to each garden bush – they were his responsibility now. On behalf of Her Majesty, he would defend them, he and Chas. It was incredible; last week he'd had the cane at school, now he was under orders to go and shoot fuzzy wuzzies. Amid the jumble of whirling incoherence in his brain, one thought suddenly emerged to stop him in his tracks: did he actually want to go? Was it, in fact, A Good Idea?

From behind her bedroom curtain, Sybilla watched uneasily. She'd been wakeful, which was unusual. What was worse, her sluggish conscience had given her twinges. Albert was still a child it insisted, she should intervene while there was yet time.

Sybilla vacillated. He would be with Chas, which was what they both wanted. She had no reason to reproach herself, she argued. But in the dark hours those reasons returned, one by one to haunt her. Now she waited apprehensively: had Albert changed his mind?

It flashed into her head that, gentle though he was, Henry Durrant would have disapproved of her behaviour. He wasn't stupid like Enoch Porrit. Against the pillow, her husband snored to remind her she was still bound to him. His mirrored reflection, dim in the dawn light, showed the sensual red lips slackly apart, revealing yellow, neglected teeth. Henry Durrant's teeth were evenly set in healthy gums. Drat it, she wasn't married to him. She was shackled to a man she didn't love. All the same . . . and once again Sybilla floated off into a daydream.

In her imagination marriage to Henry would mean an end to 'nastiness'. He wouldn't maul her when he was drunk – the very idea of Henry Durrant becoming inebriated was ridiculous. Instead, Sybilla saw herself at a nicely laid table, pouring tea out of a china pot, Henry sitting opposite, linen napkin neatly tucked into his waistcoat. And later on . . . In bed? Naturally he would wear a nightshirt, as a gentleman should. Nor would he be in too much of a hurry to take it off. In fact, it might be up to her to suggest a chaste kiss occasionally. This prospect was so delightful, Sybilla's conscience began to prick in earnest: lust was an avoidable sin.

There was also the problem of Polly. She would wake this morning to find both her brothers gone and only a note of explanation to console her. Sybilla had seen Albert sneak off with a page torn from her laundry book. Her pencil too had been borrowed and then returned, the end well chewed.

As she waited now for Albert to make a move, Sybilla suddenly heard Jeremiah's voice loud inside her head: 'They're my sons, Syb, both my boys . . . Don't let them come to any harm . . .' She jerked her head, to try and dislodge the reproach. It cut through her daydreams bringing her wide-awake. At that same moment Albert made his decision. Quick as a flash he vanished through the hole in the fence.

' 'Tis out of my hands now,' she whispered fearfully.

Jeremiah's presence was so real, she drew back, afraid his ghost might appear on the other side of the window pane. Instead, a magpie flew down to strut on the grass below, shrieking his call of abuse.

157

Chapter Eleven

Defenders of the Empire

Albert and Chas were euphoric at the novelty of the train journey; their spirits rose even higher when they joined the rest of the regiment at Chatham. Albert's excitement at leaving the only place he knew, seeing unfamiliar countryside outside the carriage windows followed by towns thronged with people and finally, London itself! It was all too much and reduced him to a squeak.

Two weeks under canvas brought a diminution of excitement. Every minute of every day was governed by orders. They had no time to stand still, not an hour of the day without a summons from the bugle, above all they were not allowed time to think or reconsider their decision. At the end of the fortnight they were herded onto the troop ship at Greenwich. By this time there wasn't a man amongst them who, when hearing the sergeant shout, didn't jump to obey. Had they but known it, however, the good times were past. After leaving the shelter of the land the weather changed. Lying on their bunks, feeling very ill indeed, the first serious doubts began.

Deep in the bowels of the boat in the worst cabins of all, recruits were stacked on palliasses, two abreast in three rows. Six human beings with scarcely a foot of headroom nor eighteen inches between them. There were no portholes for they were well below the water-line. Above their heads was the crash and thud of hooves; officers' horses were valuable and merited well-ventilated quarters. They also had predictable habits; urine dripped constantly through the cracks.

Below, if a man wanted to rise and stretch his legs, the rest had to remain in their bunks. The cabin roof was so low, not even Albert could stand upright. Worst of all, the bunks didn't remain horizontal. As the wind freshened they tilted, hurtling their miserable occupants against the bulwarks as the vessel plunged her way across the Bay of Biscay.

In the most airless bunk of the six, Albert made a vital discovery: he was prone to seasickness. At first Chas was sympathetic but after four days stumbling to and fro with a bucket, he became impatient.

'Try and make an effort, bor . . .'

'Aaah!'

'You've got to get up today anyway, it's an order. There's rifle drill.'

'Let me die, Chas, I won't be no more trouble to you then.'

'You must get up, you could be on a charge else.' Albert stared at him, bloodshot sunken eyes in a grey face.

'If I manage it, will it mean I can go on deck?'

'Dunno about that.' Deck was a privilege, reserved for higher ranks. 'I wish we could, though. I'd like to see those flying fishes the sergeant told me about.' But mention of anything remotely connected with food brought back queasiness.

'Aaah . . .!'

'Oh, give over,' Chas said, annoyed, 'there can't be anything left inside you by now.'

'Yes, there can!' came the doleful reply, 'quick!' As the pail was shoved under Albert's chin, the clanking noise reminded others of its use and produced an automatic reaction.

'Aah . . .!'

'Aw, give us it next, Unwin, there's a good chap.'

'Over here, for God's sake!'

There was a watery sun when Albert emerged for his first breath of sea-air. The NCO jeered. 'Ready to tackle those lions then?'

159

Albert's knees trembled but he managed to croak, 'Yes, sir. Ready, sir.'

'And just how would you do that?'

'I'd tell 'em "Eat me first", sir. They wouldn't fancy Chas after that.'

Fresh air proved such a restorative he persuaded Chas to venture back up again that evening.

'We'll get punished if we're caught,' Chas warned, 'it's against orders.'

'Listen, I ain't going to reach India if I can't stop being sick. I'll end up being fed to those fishes.'

'Defend me against a lion,' Chas scoffed. 'If you let go that rail, you'd fall down – a pussy cat could finish you off.'

'Come on. Two quick gulps and I shall be able to eat me dinner.'

The marine sentry spotted them before they'd been on deck five seconds. 'Oy! What d'you think you're doing?' Albert straightened up smartly.

'H'estimating the depth of the h'ocean, sir!' The marine scowled. Albert tried to keep the quaver from his voice. 'H'estimating if'n I was to pinch my nose an' sink to the bottom an' run like the devil, whether I could make it to the shore, sir.'

'Hop it. Both of you.'

'A little bit longer, please, sir, to settle my stomach.'

'I'm going to the stern. When I come back, you two will not be here. Understood.'

'Yessir!'

Chas waited until he was out of earshot.

'Do you have to try and be funny?' he demanded.

'Can't talk ... could be me last chance ... to breathe ...'

'Could be mine as well,' Chas grumbled, 'if you go telling jokes to a marine.'

Misery gave way to monotony. Monotonous food, monotonous bells, monotonous orders every waking moment. There was drill six mornings a week and, on Sundays, church parade. They weren't allowed time to think on board either, the sergeant saw to that. By

160

nightfall they were too tired to care. They squeezed into the tiny space of the bunks, scarcely aware if a storm was brewing or not. They even grew accustomed to their own stench. The voyage took fourteen weeks. As they neared the end of it, Albert was shocked to realize verminous dirt no longer made him feel ill, he simply accepted it.

All the recruits had dreams; his and Chas's were of cool sandy soil trickling between their toes as they ran barefoot down the paths of Thetford warren, and the clean icy wind blowing off the Fens in winter.

The majority of Northumberland Fusiliers at this time had been recruited in Ireland as well as the north of England. The Irish were often tall, well-built men, used to outdoor work, driven from their homes by poor harvests or over-large families whom the land could no longer support.

Neither Albert nor Chas were tall; they felt affinity for the wiry men of the north-east, although they found the dialect difficult to understand. Chas marvelled aloud how well the Tynesiders tolerated the stiffling quarters. An ex-miner explained.

'Where we come from, you work down the pit. That's all there is, like. There's nought else for a man to do. You get used to a low roof, crawling on our bellies, day in, day out. We came away because we didn't want to end our days coughing our lungs up, like our fathers did. There's got to be something better, we thought.' Chas tried to imagine what it must be like working below ground, and shuddered. 'That's why we enlisted, anyroad. What's your excuse.'

'We was hungry,' Albert answered promptly.

'Ee, monkey nut, that can't be right. Look how you throw up everything they give you. Ungrateful, I calls it.'

'I ain't been sick for days,' Albert protested. 'I've got my sea-legs now.'

'Pride goeth . . .' an Irishman warned him. 'Say a prayer before it's too late. We'll be arriving in Bombay in time for the rains. Terrible storms they have there, according to the corporal; thunder, lightning, the lot.'

161

'I wouldn't mind a drop of rain,' the miner said wistfully. 'It's as hot as hell in here tonight.'

'Bombay?' Albert asked Chas. 'I thought you said we was going to Calcutta?' Chas shrugged.

'Maybe we are. Maybe they're close by, like Santon Downham and Brandon.' Albert considered their destination, about which he knew so little.

'Is India as big as Suffolk, Chas?'

'Dunno. Might be.' Chas searched schoolboy memories. 'It's got big rivers, I think.'

'Couldn't be bigger than the Thames,' Albert protested, 'Remember at Greenwich, how wide it was there? Must be the biggest river in the world. Here, d'you think there'll be wherries at Bombay?'

'Maybe. They got to get us off this boat somehow. Those horses can't be expected to swim, neither.' Lights out was called and the wick was snuffed. 'Night, old bor . . .' Albert yawned.

'Funny to think of wherries with fuzzy-wuzzies sailing 'em.'

'You'll be all right,' the ex-miner called softly. 'Eat monkey nuts, fuzzy-wuzzies do.'

Drill was designed to turn them into automata. They could clean and assemble rifles in their sleep and stow items in their packs in a matter of minutes. As fusiliers they were no longer expected to heft the huge old-fashioned haversacks that weighed seventy pounds when full, and half killed a man marching under a tropical sun. Now they had neat black canvas waterproof valises slung from belts and which rested in the small of the back, with pouches hanging on either side.

Old hands scoffed at the new-fangled uniform. Just over twenty years previously, the British army had fought throughout the bitter winter of the Crimea wearing short-waisted coatees that left the greater part of their bodies unprotected – how much more manly that had been than wearing these single-breasted tunics.

Some old soldiers even looked askance at the Oliver water-bottles. These would poison the regiment, like as

162

not. Nothing like the old wooden bottles for keeping water pure. Skinny recruits, especially Albert, thanked their stars for the lightness of the new metal ones.

He learned to stow his belongings for marching order; the serge great-coat in a tight roll, forage cap inside, with canvas straps crossed over his chest keeping everything firmly in place on his shoulders. With all this equipment on his back, bayonet to one side, trenching tool banging against the other hip, he found difficulty in standing upright and tried not to think what it would be like once ten pounds of emergency rations were added.

He and Chas were taught regimental tradition; other fusiliers wore plain sealskin caps or busbys, only the Northumberlands were entitled to keep the red and white horsehair plume. They learned, in theory, the various methods of killing the enemy; above all, they learned to obey without question.

The sergeant was no longer the friend of Bury St Edmunds. He was a martinet, a fiend, a bully whom they feared. When he spelled out the dire consequence of a lapse of discipline, there was absolute, petrified silence.

Albert lost all desire to joke. Body lice were now so numerous and rats so fierce, survival was all that mattered. As the lookout cried out that Bombay island was in sight, their NCO gave the order they'd been praying for: 'Prepare To Land'. Heavy monsoon clouds made the humidity almost unbearable. Rains were expected daily, hourly, but had not yet come.

Perhaps, had he been able to detach his mind from his immediate circumstances, Albert might have found something amusing. Instead, the nine buttons tightly fastened, encasing him in serge from neck to ankle, with boots inhibiting the circulation of blood to his feet, he was as miserable as the rest.

Fanned by the heat which blew off the land, the recruits crouched belov The inshore wind was laden with dust which irritated sh already blistered raw by the sun. The six of them tri to concentrate instead on descriptions passed down b iose who could see.

'Gateway to dia they call it.'

'There's two big stone towers on the shore.'

'Permission to drink, sir?'

'Certainly not.'

'Just a sip, sir.'

'No.' The last of the water taken on at the Cape of Good Hope had filled their bottles. Yesterday they'd grumbled at the brackish taste, now even thinking about it made it seem like nectar. Denied this relief, they licked their mouths with parched tongues to summon up saliva.

'Will we camp by one of those big rivers, Chas?'

'Maybe.'

'Wouldn't it be lovely an' cool. Like springtime at home.'

'Don't talk, save your strength.' But Albert had to talk, to escape a claustrophobia which threatened to choke him. Sensing this, one of the miners whispered softly, 'Hold on, monkey nut. We're nearly there.'

Polly hadn't been able to shake off her desolation on the day of their departure. The two she loved most in all the world had deserted her. Albert's note, read and re-read, had struck her as incredibly daring at first. She'd been amazed that the two of them should think of escaping from Aunt Syb. Only gradually did it dawn on her that she'd been left behind. When she realized that, Polly was overcome. Tears obliterated Albert's careful writing. She kissed the note and tucked it inside her bodice to comfort her broken heart.

That same morning, after a sleepless night, Sybilla felt irritable. Forbidden thoughts of Henry Durrant kept returning and made her edgy. The sight of Polly's stricken face fuelled her unreasonable temper. Instead of consoling the child, she turned her back on her. Memories of Jeremiah's voice were put aside; she couldn't bear the sight of those shadowy, sad eyes. Polly summoned up courage, believed it was up to her to break the terrible news. Would she be caned for it?

'Chas and Albert have left home, Aunt Syb. They've run away to join the army and go to India.'

'You were lucky. They never left me no note.'

164

Realization was slow but, when it came, Polly was stunned. Did that mean – as surely it must – that her aunt had known of the scheme beforehand?

'If you knew they were planning to go, why didn't you stop them?' Sybilla whipped round, angrily.

'Don't you speak like that to me, miss.'

'You could've, if you'd wanted to!' Polly had recovered and was shrill, 'You could've stopped Albert going! You didn't want to though, did you? You were glad to be rid of them!'

Sybilla had been denying the truth for so long. For Polly to bring it into the open and accuse her of it was unpardonable: Sybilla slapped her hard.

Polly neither moved nor let out a cry. She stood, ashen-faced, a great red patch forming on her cheek. 'I hate you,' she whispered passionately. 'You couldn't have stopped Chas, he was that desperate to get away. But if you and Uncle Porrit hadn't made Albert so unhappy, he wouldn't have gone.'

The voice was such a bitter echo of Jeremiah, Sybilla backed away against the dresser.

'There was nothing I could do,' she blustered, 'they allus had to be together.'

'I could've looked after Albert, you know I could. He should have stayed on at school and made something of himself. You could have stopped him if you'd wanted to,' Polly whispered accusingly.

She didn't realize there was still time to retrieve Albert from the army's clutches but Sybilla did. Despite her temper, she was anxious. If Polly so much as uttered a word to anyone in authority ... To divert her, she swallowed her chagrin and attempted to wheedle.

' 'Tis the best thing that could have happened to your brothers, Polly. You wouldn't want to spoil it for them? The chance of a lifetime, that's what Albert said.'

That phrase, copied out in Albert's 'best' writing, told Polly everything.

'You knew from the start, didn't you Aunt Syb? You must've done if you knew what Albert put in his letter?' Sybilla opened her mouth to deny it but closed it again.

165

Of course she knew; she'd followed Albert whenever he'd slipped down the garden to speak to Chas, she'd listened to their plotting. She wasn't going to admit it, though. She began to fuss over the laundry baskets.

'You'll have to do the deliveries now Albert's gone . . .' Polly turned her back in anger and despair; did she have to be so cruel!

Polly couldn't understand why her brothers had betrayed her, that was worst of all. If they couldn't take her with them why hadn't they let her in on the secret? If only there was someone she could talk to.

Out of defiance she went to the table, cut two pieces of bread without asking permission and ladled on dripping.

'That's right, eat up. Got to keep your strength up now you're doing the delivering,' Sybilla said fatuously. She was nervous as to what the girl might decide to do next.

The small rebellion was quickly annihilated. Enoch, not yet aware of the boys' disappearance, stumbled downstairs. When he saw Polly, he remembered the significance of the day.

'She's been told she's got to go to the vicarage.'

'Not yet.' Sybilla pulled a warning face.

'Good riddance, I say. One less mouth to feed.' Polly was confused.

'What does Uncle Porrit mean? There's no laundry to take to Mrs Heyhoe, not this morning?' Sybilla couldn't avoid it any longer.

'Uncle Porrit means you're going to the vicarage – to live. To be trained as a kitchen maid. If you're a good girl, they might make you parlour maid, just as I was. 'Tis a fine opportunity, Polly, any girl would be glad of it.' Polly stared, the earlier tears still wet upon her cheeks. 'When you've done delivering, come back for I shall have a parcel ready. A present for Mrs Heyhoe for being so kind as to take you, and some new clothes for yourself. There's one of my old skirts you can have. It'll be smart enough to wear in the afternoons provided you turns the seams so the shiny bits don't show. And a piece of stuff to make an apron. Mrs Heyhoe is a fine cook. You're a really lucky girl, Polly.'

166

'Who says I'm to be a maid?' Polly demanded fiercely, '*I* don't choose to go and work there!' Her stare included both of them. Enoch lost his temper.

'Don't you look at me like that or you'll feel the back of my hand!'

'Quiet! She's upset,' his wife warned. 'She's just found out both the boys have gone.'

'Gone? Where? What d'you mean? What are you talking 'bout, woman?' Sybilla couldn't be bothered to explain.

'Leave Polly be,' she said brusquely and tried again to placate her.

'It'll be an opportunity for you. If you learn to please Mrs Heyhoe –'

'What about my schooling?'

'That's over,' Enoch said loudly, ' 'taint worth wasting money on a girl. I shall tell the inspector you has a good position then he's bound to let you go.'

'The Parish is willing to pay for me!' Polly cried desperately. She could see it was useless. Even so, this was her home. 'I don't have to go, I belong here.'

'Not any more,' Enoch said flatly. Sybilla tried a different tack.

'Widow Helliwell's sore pressed these days. I've told she can help with the laundry instead. She can earn extra doing the fetching and carrying that you've been doing. You wouldn't deny the poor woman the opportunity, Polly?'

Sybilla recalled that she'd never paid Albert or Polly a farthing for any of these chores but unpleasant thoughts were easily smothered nowadays. 'The dear soul deserves to be helped,' she cried, anxious to deflect any such thoughts in Polly, 'what with little Gladys to feed, an' the rent to pay.'

Polly bit her lips tightly; after years of hard work they didn't even want her. The prospect of being at Mrs Heyhoe's beck and call was suddenly frightening. Out of despair, she pleaded, 'Can't I stay? Please!'

'No.' Enoch was adamant.

'Father didn't intend any of us to go into service . . .' It was subdued but it reached Sybilla.

'Just be thankful I've found you a respectable place. Four or five years with Mrs Heyhoe and you'll be as well trained as any girl. You'll make someone a good wife, someone who'll look after you . . .' This recalled her own experience and made her sharp.

'Be off with those baskets and see you come straight back. Mrs Heyhoe wants you over there by teatime.'

Rebellion trembled but, this time, remained hidden. Lately Polly had dreamed of becoming a governess. The one employed at the Manor had appeared in church in starched striped calico and a straw boater. How Polly yearned to be as smart! Instead she was the shabbiest girl in her class. Slowly, sadly, she faced up to the new reality: Chas and Albert had escaped; to become a governess was out of the question. From now on there was nothing else for it but to accept her fate.

Mrs Heyhoe composed her features for Polly's arrival, stern and forbidding, designed to instill apprehension in a new employee. The sight of Polly's woebegone face changed all that.

'There's no need to be so sad . . . Here.' She enveloped her in a brief, fierce hug, 'Come inside. I've just put the kettle on. We shall sit down and have a nice cuppa tea.'

'Chas and Albert have run away. I shall never see them again!'

'They'll be back, never you fret, my dear.'

'If you knew as well,' Polly sobbed, 'why didn't you do something. Albert's too little to be a soldier.' Drat Sybilla Porrit, thought Cook. Goodness knows what lies she'd been telling this time. She tried to soothe her.

'There, there, Polly –'

'Chas would've gone away but what's going to happen to Albert? There's snakes in India – he could get bitten and die!'

'Now then!' She hustled her new charge into the kitchen. 'Sit at that table, Polly. Are your hands clean? Would you like a slice of my lardy cake?' She didn't wait for an answer but set a tempting plateful in front of her. It wasn't her usual practice, she must be growing soft;

annoyance with Sybilla increased. 'When you've finished, we'll take your things upstairs. I don't believe you've seen inside this house before?'

'No.' Polly swallowed a sob.

'It's a nice house, and you must learn to be polite. It's "No, Mrs Heyhoe" or "Yes, Mrs Heyhoe" in future. As for you, we shall call you Porrit –'

'My name's not Porrit, I'm Polly *Unwin*!'

'Bless my soul, I was forgetting your poor dear Ma and Pa,' Cook admitted. 'Now, this house takes a bit of looking after, 'specially with a new mistress. She come with some silly notions but we're getting rid of them, bit by bit. She's in an interesting condition, which helps. It takes her mind off whether the picture rails have been dusted. Not that you should miss them out, mind. You must stand on a stool and dust them every other day.

'Mistress won't expect you to be maid of all work. You'll do what's right and proper as I sees it, apart from when the parlour maid has her day off. That's when you'll help out upstairs.'

Mrs Heyhoe made that sound like an adventure but it wasn't the same as being a governess. Polly sighed. The tea had partially thawed the ice in her chest. She clutched the mug and, despite her resolution, tears began to flow again. 'Chas and Albert never told me they was going,' she wept, 'they didn't even say goodbye. Just left a note.'

The precious item was thrust into Cook's hand, the writing now decorated with so many watery marks it was indecipherable. 'The chance of a lifetime, Albert says there,' Polly explained seeing Cook was having difficulty. She added sorrowfully, 'He shouldn't have gone, Mrs Heyhoe.'

'I quite agree.'

Cook realized she would have to tackle the subject. 'I shall speak so you knows how I feel, and then we needn't talk of it again. Your aunt should've gone to Bury to talk to the recruiting officer. Maybe I should've spoken to His Nibs too, when I found out, only I didn't. It's too late and I'm sorry. What's done is done.'

Polly's eyes grew round at being treated like an adult. She nodded solemnly that she'd understood.

'This is between ourselves, Polly. It mustn't get out.'

'No.'

'Your Aunt Syb is set on going to London, always has been, even before she married Porrit. She made a mistake doing that but it hasn't stopped her wanting. If anything, it's made her more determined, that's why she was anxious to be rid of you three. When she's saved up enough, I reckon she plans on leaving Enoch Porrit behind as well.' Mrs Heyhoe shook her head, 'Your aunt always was a fool; wouldn't listen to any advice.' She snatched a look at Polly, wondering if she'd gone too far but the girl appeared preoccupied.

'I suppose that's what makes Aunt Syb so mean? She can't bear to spend a penny. This morning, she kept some money that properly belonged to Mrs Fowler.'

'That's a dreadful thing to say, Polly! That's as good as accusing your aunt of stealing.'

'But it's true. She boasted she'd sold an ornament in Thetford belonging to Mrs Fowler – Aunt Syb got five shilling for it but she only give Mrs Fowler half a crown. She said it would teach the silly woman not to know Meissen from pot.'

Cook said slowly, 'May she be forgiven! That poor woman.'

'Aunt Syb told me I'd learn all about porcelain, working here.'

'If I ever hear that you are following in your aunt's footsteps . . .!' Polly straightened up abruptly.

'Father taught us right from wrong, Mrs Heyhoe.'

'I'm thankful to hear it, indeed I am.' For a moment she wondered if she'd made the wrong decision, insisting on Polly as a maid. 'Hurry up and finish your tea.' Polly put the mug down daintily.

'I expect it's because Aunt Syb wants to make more money,' she said, desirous of being sociable, 'that's she's bought Mrs Fowler's house as well.'

'What!' Cook was properly startled this time.

'As soon as the funeral's over, Mrs Fowler has to move

170

out. Aunt Syb is going to let the house to a gentleman.'

It was the final straw; Mrs Heyhoe practically burst with indignation. The sly varmint! The treacherous viper! Why, Sybilla Porrit must have gone straight round and bullied the bereaved woman into selling up before the corpse was in his shroud! 'Disgusting . . .' she exploded and again, more quietly, 'disgusting is what I called it and so it is. His Nibs shall hear of this all right!' Polly didn't care; one piece of cake remained on the plate, glistening with currants beneath the sugary glaze.

'Would that slice be going to waste, Mrs Heyhoe?'

'You can have it with a glass of milk before you goes to bed. Tomorrow, I shall show you how to make a lardy cake yourself,' she promised. 'Now, there's just time to put your things away upstairs before we has to start on their suppers.'

Polly hadn't had a chance to wonder where she would sleep; she discovered it was in the same room as Mrs Heyhoe, sharing the iron-framed double bed. She had to cling to the edge on her side, to avoid sliding down the deep incline made by Cook's buttocks.

Later that night, wornout with her new way of life, she undressed, watched surreptitiously by her new mentor. 'How long have you had that petticoat, Polly?'

'I can't remember.'

'It's fit for nothing but rags.' This was true but she didn't have another.

'It's clean, Mrs Heyhoe,' she said anxiously, 'I washed it Saturday like I always do.' It had been scrubbed so often the colour was indistinct. As she lifted it above her head another deficiency was revealed.

'Ain't you got no drawers, girl!'

'Only the one pair,' Polly was red-faced. 'If they're not dry the day after they've been washed, I has to do without.' Cook was outraged.

'But what happens if it's a windy day? And you're out in the street?'

'I has to keep a tight hold of my skirt, Mrs Heyhoe.'

Something would have to be done for the sake of

vicarage respectability but the revelations weren't finished yet.

'Surely to goodness you has a nightgown?'

'Yes, I clean forgot,' Polly said innocently, 'Aunt Syb give me one this morning and said to be sure to wear it.' This caused a further compression of cook's mouth while Polly rummaged in her parcel. Tomorrow, they would have to speak to the mistress for the girl couldn't work here, half-naked.

'You never wore that shimmy in front of your Uncle Porrit?' Cook hadn't intended to be so explicit but fortunately Polly didn't comprehend.

'I've grown out of it,' she apologized. 'I've let it out as far as it'll go . . . and mended it. Mother made it for me.' She stroked the almost transparent rosebuds edging the straining, shrunken neckline. 'It's pretty, isn't it?'

'It's too tight,' Mrs Heyhoe said tartly, 'It emphasizes your – chest.'

'Ah, here's the nightgown.'

Cook recognized a garment dating back to Sybilla's time at the vicarage. It hung in folds on Polly.

So, the girl had been sent with a total of three items of underwear plus a shawl, an old hat, one patched dress, darned stockings, Sybilla's cast-off skirt and a piece of stuff for an apron. No proper uniform at all. It was absolutely disgraceful.

She wondered if the mistress could come to the rescue? There had been much excitement when she first arrived with countless items of trousseau: two dozen pairs of frilled pantelets, a flurry of lace camisoles, lawn petticoats for summer, flannel winter ones, everything beautifully embroidered by nuns during a honeymoon spent in Italy. Mrs Heyhoe sighed; nothing there suitable for a kitchen maid. She would request a private interview nonetheless, something had to be done.

She watched as Polly kissed Albert's note surreptitiously before jumping into bed. 'What about your prayers?'

'I says them in bed, so's no one can overhear.'

'Not any more, you don't. You go on your knees like a Christian, and speak up. God's a long way off and he needs to hear.' And so do I, she thought.

Teeth chattering as flesh made contact with icy linoleum, Polly screwed her eyes tightly. 'God bless mother and father and little Amy. Please look after Chas and Albert, wherever they are,' she whispered. 'Don't let Albert get into trouble. Bring them both back as soon as possible, please dear lord Jesus. Amen.'

Mrs Heyhoe waited until she was back beside her. 'Tomorrow, Polly, you asks God to make you a good girl as well as all the rest. And you thanks him for all your blessings.'

Polly wondered what these were and decided it must be having dripping and lardy cake on the same day. The bed had a proper mattress with freshly ironed sheets, fragrant from lavender in the airing cupboard; it was something she'd never known before and she stretched out in luxurious enjoyment.

On her side, Mrs Heyhoe began to plan her course of action. First there was the matter of underwear, then, equally important, of Mrs Fowler's ornament. Mrs Heyhoe would send a message to Sybilla insisting the balance of the money be handed over – and threatening exposure if it wasn't. As for the house on the Mundford road, what to do for the best?

There was precious little apart from telling His Nibs, of course. He would speak severely but even that would not stop Sybilla benefiting. Anger increased. 'It's not as though the Fowlers were wealthy. *She'll* need every penny now her man's gone to his rest.' It was immoral. It was worse – it was a betrayal of a confidence, for hadn't Cook been the one to provide Sybilla with the necessary information?

'She's sly as well as wicked,' Cook muttered, 'persuading me to feel sorry for her time and time again because of Porrit . . . I'm glad I never showed her my recipe for mustard pickle.' It wasn't much consolation but it helped. Aloud she said, 'If you're a good girl, Polly, I shall teach you the secret.'

Slightly bewildered, Polly closed her eyes and slept.

Chapter Twelve

Home Thoughts From Abroad

Albert now knew for a certainty that India was larger than Suffolk. Much, much larger. He'd also discovered that Calcutta was a great deal further from Bombay than Brandon was from Santon Downham. As for the rivers...! His only previous experience had been the Little Ouse and the Thames. Compared to the ones which hindered their progress month after month now, those were mere streams. After the rainy season the regiment was frequently confronted with vast stretches of water over which a laborious bridge of boats had to be assembled and, equally tediously, dismantled afterwards.

The fuzzy wuzzies were a constant surprise. Albert still couldn't reconcile himself to perpetual brown skins and countless dark eyes which stared from pavements, dusty tracks and countryside as they marched past. No one could ever be lonely in India, he decided; everywhere he looked, there were more and more people.

At the beginning, he was in a constant state of astonishment. India was so different! He found it incredible that water-buffalo should be yoked to a plough, or stringy, dark-skinned women work alongside men in the fields. To Albert these were fragile butterflies, totally unsuited, not like the sturdy Breckland females he was used to. When these women walked past balancing huge water jars above slender necks, he wanted to close his eyes, convinced they were about to collapse at his feet.

174

Why did the people here keep building houses with thick mud walls which the annual rains almost always washed away? He tried and failed to describe these incredible things to Polly. In the end, he gave up. Without seeing for herself, he knew she wouldn't understand.

As for the heady rich stench of decay that was India, that too confused him. Old soldiers dismissed it as the smell of the East. Albert found it intoxicating. As soon as the first bugle sounded he would crawl outside to watch overnight hollows give off steam as the sun sucked away the dampness. It was a daily miracle, this miasma which was peeled away to reveal the mysterious primeval earth beneath.

Mysterious shapes formed and resolved as the morning mist evaporated. Men washing or defecating unconcernedly at the roadside, a woman crouched over her cooking pot or a holy man, naked apart from his stick, striding out purposefully towards some unknown objective. Albert didn't include a description of him in his letter. A chap had to remember his sister's sensibilities.

He did his best to give Polly some of the flavour but how to describe the girl who'd just passed by on the other side of the road this morning? A girl in a red sari and gold-bordered veil with jewels studding her nostrils, anklets chinking above bare feet and the inevitable load balanced on her head. Something about her reminded him of Polly. He tried to fathom what it was. Perhaps the very fact the girl was alone? The guilty feeling that he and Chas had left Polly so defenceless was a constant worry, even after six years.

Albert realized it was high time he finished his letter, ready for the collection. These days he ended with a phrase he'd learned from one of his colleagues which he considered highly sophisticated:

'Hoping this finds you as it leaves me, in good health.

Yr loving bro. Albert.'

He wanted to tell her that, despite the daily wretchedness of being in the army, it had been worth it. A Good Idea, in fact. Each time he hesitated to commit these words to paper, he didn't quite know why.

175

Once they'd had to cross a river by clambering hand over hand along ropes slung by the engineers between high rocks while a torrent raged through the chasm below. They looked on helplessly as several horses were swept away by the current. Elephants in the baggage train wisely refused to set foot in the water until led much further downstream.

That particular evening, exhausted by the day's toil, Albert and Chas had spied a dhooly containing one of the disgruntled horseless cavalry officers. They listened to the man issuing petulant contradictory commands until he finally allowed the bearers to set him down.

'I could just fancy a kip in that,' Albert said quietly.

'Don't be stupid!' They watched the officer stride off in the direction of the mess tent.

'Come on.'

Despite his reluctance, Chas followed. It was too tempting a prospect. The chief bearer still hovered but when Albert pressed a few *pice* into his hand, he too melted into the dusk.

The dhooly was large and lined with rugs. There were bolsters at either end. Chas and Albert sank down, grunting with pleasure. Chas's muscles were aching after their fifth soaking that day and he began to unlace his cracked leather boots.

'You'll never get those back on again tonight,' Albert warned. 'You should've taken them off afore going in the water. Doesn't do the leather no good, either.'

'Not all of us has a cushy ride,' Chas said tersely. 'Some of us has to jump to it without the option.' Albert grinned and filled his clay pipe.

'Told you what old Pomfrey said,' he reminded him, 'soon as he heard we was for Bhoperie, he warned us. "Get ready to strip off," he said, "Else you'll be wet through before nightfall." So I made sure I did.'

Pomfret, a veteran of Indian campaigns, had a nice way of earning an extra tot of rum in exchange for information, sometimes dubious but today surprisingly accurate. As a result Albert had volunteered for the baggage train and kept his feet dry.

176

The curtains of the dhooly parted briefly. The head bearer muttered, 'Captain coming back, sahib,' and disappeared. Chas was agitated but Albert removed his pipe and calmly extinguished both it and the lantern flame. Inside, it was now black as pitch. The officer, crawling on hands and knees, received an unpleasant shock as he attempted to enter.

'What the devil! Who are you? What in blazes are you doing in here?'

'I could ask you the same question,' Albert drawled, adding the refinement of the general's aide's lisp to his speech. 'In fact, if you don't remove yourself this instant, I shall have you horse-whipped.'

He could smell Chas's fear. Both of them kept perfectly still while the young officer repeated in stunned tones, 'Horse-whipped?'

This time the lisp had a cutting edge as Albert replied, 'Sequestering the *colonel*'s property is a punishable offence.' In the blackness there was immediate capitulation.

'I'm so sorry, sir, I had no idea – I thought this dhooly belonged to the medical staff.'

'If so, it was intended for the sick and wounded and not indolent officers. I trust your health is satisfactory, Captain?'

'Indeed yes, sir, thank you. I'm extremely well . . . er, goodnight, sir.' He backed away into the night. Chas expelled an anxious breath.

'You got a nerve!'

'Time we had a share of the better things in life,' Albert said placidly.

'What if he finds out?'

'He won't . . . provided we're out of here before it gets light. See you wakes me up early.' In the darkness, Chas swore softly. Why did it always end up his responsibility when Albert got them into a scrape? It happened so often nowadays. Increasing confidence had given Albert a careless attitude towards authority. Chas snorted irritably. His brother would end up like Pomfret, a perpetual private. And supposing Albert scuppered *his* chances of

promotion? All the same . . . soft carpet beneath his body
. . . a pillow under his head . . . wonderful!

They had landed at Bombay in the rainy season, the town
where English residents claim they bake for one half of
the year and boil for the rest. In the months that
followed, the fusiliers marched as far northwest as the
Rann of Cutch, one vast swamp following the monsoon,
then swung east round the edge of the Great Indian
Desert. Their role, never fully explained, seemed to
Albert and Chas designed to 'show the flag' but with no
other specific purpose. It was a marvel to the two of them
how the natives, so worn down by the daily battle to
survive, had once challenged British might.

Orders came for the regiment to march east, to
Jodhpur. Jaipur followed, then Agra and Delhi. A show of
strength was called for in Gwalior; at Lucknow, they
reinforced the garrison for several months.

Their first Christmas saw them, together with a
Gurkha regiment, assisting the East India company in
settling a pay dispute at Cawnpore. Afterwards, it was
north once more to Delhi where they were based for over
a year. Albert had written to Polly describing the great
marble tomb that had so impressed him on their first
visit. He and Chas bought a garnet bracelet from a street
vendor, promising light-heartedly to fasten it on her
wrist the first time they had furlough.

But new orders came and they were back on the road,
sometimes pitching camp in places they'd visited only six
or twelve months previously. 'Going round in circles,'
Chas grumbled. 'Don't anyone have any idea what's
what?'

Pomfret growled that in the British Army, very few
did. 'Muddling through, old fellow, that's the way it's
always been. All part of the great game.'

'What – great game?'

'Aah. No one's yet discovered what that is.'

They marched through the soft red dust of the hot
season and slithered over rutted hard-baked mud as the
land dried out after the wet. They went forward

178

half-blinded through hail storms, arms reversed, to prevent their muskets filling with water. They learned to pitch camp in the dark, and sleep as soon as their bodies touched the ground. They learned to strike those same tents within minutes when the bugle sounded.

They became adept at bartering for fresh food as they passed through villages and knew when to hoard the precious water supply. Their bodies protested at first but gradually became hardened. Sometimes their minds did as well. Sensitivity to the condition of a starving populace was not encouraged by the British army.

They learned to accept with stoicism the loss of a comrade, fallen victim to some unknown tropical disease and dead within hours of being taken ill. Older hands offered consolation as the firing party assembled to send a last sad volley over the coffin.

'Ain't got your number on it this time. Just be thankful.'

At such times Albert remembered his former, innocent self, attending Sunday School so assiduously to ensure he'd be included in the annual outing. He was on an outing this time all right. One that appeared to include the entire continent of India.

It was during their first year, after they'd been marching for several weeks, that he'd thought to enquire of Chas how long this particular adventure might last.

'You were told when you signed the paper.'

'Yes, but I wasn't listening, not properly.' Everything had been so exciting that day, lying about his age and his mind full of the possibility of escape from Aunt Syb.

'It's eight years before we can apply for a discharge.'

'How many!'

The consolation, when Albert considered the matter, was that he'd only be twenty-two when he got out – twenty-four according to official army records.

One promise made by the sergeant was kept; they were fed regularly. The food wasn't always wholesome, very often it was rancid from the heat, but at least it filled their bellies. By the end of twelve months, Albert was above the regimental minimum height. By the end of twenty-four, Chas, tall and lanky, had full moustachios.

So far, they hadn't fired a bullet in anger except over the rioting crowds at Cawnpore following the increase in food prices. Most of the time it was sufficient for the regiment to arrive in a town for order to be maintained, although rumours continued to reach them that trouble was expected in the Punjab.

Albert always wanted to know the reason for everything they were asked to do. Being so long in India hadn't dulled either his curiosity or his perception. Why, for instance, did they have to enforce rent collection among natives so poor their children died of hunger? Why support a Maharaja so rich, he weighed himself in pearls? These, intended for distribution to the needy, ended up lining corrupt pockets. 'Which everybody knows about,' Albert protested indignantly, 'so why turn a blind eye? Why don't someone *do* summat?'

He had learned a smidgen of sense. His more provocative remarks were made well away from official ears but why, most of all he wanted to know, was the British army marching hither and yon in this vast foreign land? Why couldn't the fuzzy-wuzzies manage things for themselves? There were enough of them, for heavens sake.

'You know why. It's our Empire, that's what,' Chas answered wearily. 'And you can't stop them fighting among themselves – you've seen how they slit each other's throats if they've got a tiddly little grudge. We don't carry on like that.'

'Not nowadays, maybe,' Albert conceded. 'We did once. Remember when father told us about that banner; "Blood or bread this day in Brandon"? Bet there was fighting then all right.' Chas was adamant.

'We've got to keep the trade routes open so's everyone can have a decent cuppa tea.'

'We ain't had one of those for weeks. This water's filthy. Tastes to me like a dead buffalo fell down that well.'

Chas spat out a mouthful of liquid.

'Just a thought,' Albert grinned, 'might only be a bit of cow dung, nothing to worry about.'

They were enjoying a rest day which, if they were

180

lucky, might include a delivery of mail. It was several months since they'd last written to Polly, plenty of time for a reply.

As usual they were making good use of their time. Three of them sheltered from the sun beneath a banyan tree; Albert, cross-legged with needle and cobbler's waxed thread, a leather pad strapped to his palm, was attending to three pairs of boots and some missing buttons from their tunics.

He wasn't as tall as Chas but he had filled out; legs and shoulders were muscular from over seven years of marching and carrying his pack. His skin was leathery, the tan emphasizing the inquisitive blue eyes. The sun had bleached his hair and eyebrows to the same silvery fairness as Sybilla's. Chas was darker but his complexion remained sallow. Because of his height, his build appeared slight, but thanks to the sergeant's enthusiasm for boxing prowess among the regiment, Chas was extremely fit.

Tea over, he began trimming his moustachios – his pride and Albert's secret envy – flicking bits of whisker at a lizard basking on the tree trunk.

Their companion, the tall red-headed Irishman who'd shared their cabin on the journey to India, yawned and got to his feet.

'Might as well wander across and see if anything's arrived,' he said with apparent carelessness. 'Could be too soon but you never know.'

'See if there's one for us, Paddy.'

'Of course.' They watched him go.

'Always on tenterhooks but it's never good news, not for him. Don't seem fair somehow,' Albert was sympathetic. 'I hopes he gets a cheerful letter one day. Either that, or his folks don't bother to write no more and put him out of his misery.'

'Comes of being part of a big family. At least we've only got Polly to worry about.'

'And Aunt Syb.' Chas hooted.

'Tough as that bit of leather, she is, bor! Don't waste your sympathy on her. Wonder if Pol got the scarf in time

181

for her birthday? We was a bit late sending it.'

'Soon find out. Twenty, eh? She should be as pretty as a picture by now.'

'You said that last year.'

'Well then, she'll be even prettier,' Albert said comfortably. 'We shall have to fend the chaps off when we gets back. Can't have them bothering our Pol.'

'She's had to do that for herself all these years. Wonder who *has* been taking care of her? Don't like to think of Enoch Porrit hanging around, not if she's grown to look like Ma.' Albert chewed on the end of the thread and squinted as he threaded the needle.

'Wish I could remember Ma. It's sort of blank when I tries to conjure up her face. As for Pol . . . Mrs Heyhoe would send Uncle Porrit packing. Fight off dragons, she would. Bung 'em in the oven and serve 'em up in a curry to the vicar. Hallo? Looks like it *was* bad news again. I didn't even see the dak gharry arrive.'

The Irishman slumped down heavily, causing eddies in the dust.

'What's up, old fellow?' They waited in respectful silence until he roused himself.

'It's my youngest sister Catherine. She's gone and emigrated.'

'Emigrated? You mean – left Ireland?'

'For good,' he nodded. 'We've an uncle went to America two years ago – she's gone to join him. But wasn't she my favourite sister? The reason why I joined the army? I promised her I'd save all my pay – which I have – and when I got home, she and I were to set up house together in Dublin. I swore she should leave that god-forsaken farm for ever.' He had tears in his eyes. 'I've kept my side of the bargain.' His frugality was well-known and those who knew the reason respected him for it.

'Eight years is a long time, 'specially for a girl,' Chas suggested tentatively. 'Could be she's found herself a chap? How old is she?'

'Twenty-one. And you're right, she has.' The Irishman fished the letter out of his pocket.

'A lazy good-for-nothing, snivelling little runt – I

182

remember him at school – Oh, here . . . ' as the second envelope fell out, 'I forgot. There was one for you as well.'

His sorrow was forgotten as they pored over the inscription, admiring as always, Polly's neat handwriting.

'Privates C and A Unwin . . . '

'I hope yours contains happier news than mine,' the Irishman said mournfully.

'Oh, yes,' Albert was confident, 'Polly'd never emigrate.' She couldn't, he thought with relief, they'd no relatives except in Suffolk, no means of escape for Polly. What a comfort to know she would be there waiting for them when this interminable outing was over.

Chas slit open the envelope and Albert squatted down to read over his shoulder. After the first couple of lines, the two glanced at one another.

'Henry Durrant? I don't remember that name?'

'I think I do,' Albert frowned. 'Didn't he live at Willow End? He had an old misery of a mother – I remember having to deliver their laundry.' Chas pursed his lips.

'But what's Polly want to write about him for? What she say again?' Albert read aloud in search of clues.

' "Mr Henry Durrant come round to tea. His mother died last November and left him a tidy sum . . . " ' He broke off, grinning, 'Hope Aunt Syb doesn't find out else she'd try and get her hands on it,' and went back to the letter:

' "Mrs Heyhoe told him how she is finding this cold weather hard to bear . . . " Cold?' Albert broke off a second time. The broad leaves of the banyan protected them but where the sun managed to penetrate, the rays scorched their skin. Chas took the letter and turned it over to check the date.

' "14 February," '

'Valentine's Day.' That made them both uneasy. 'Hope Mr Henry Durrant didn't come round that partic'lar afternoon for any reason.' Chas was suddenly jealous for the sister they'd left behind.

'Polly don't say anything about no Valentine. She probably wrote us because she thought we'd remember

183

the chap, that's all. Anyway, he's years older than she is. Must be old enough to be her *grandfather*.'

'I keep forgetting that,' Albert sighed, 'I think of people the way they used to be. Anyway,' he brightened, 'Mrs Heyhoe wouldn't let Polly do anything daft.' But again it occurred to them that Mrs Heyhoe hadn't been able to prevent Aunt Syb making a fool of herself.

'Why tell us about the tidy sum?' Albert asked, now increasingly anxious.

'Maybe we should warn Polly? Tell her not to be in too much of a hurry, 'specially over . . . well, over something like Valentine's Day. We don't want her to end up with the wrong chap.'

'If we tells her not to make any promises till we gets back,' Chas suggested, 'that should do it. She knows we'd only give her good advice.'

'The best,' Albert agreed stoutly. 'Besides, she knows how much we care about her. Does she say anything about the scarf by the by?' But Chas's attention had drifted from the letter. Suppose Mr Henry Durrant was in the habit of coming round often?

'How much longer we got?'

'Nine months and nineteen days. Or thereabouts.'

'As long as that?' Everyone clung to the pretence of not knowing; in their hearts each knew to the very hour. 'We'll write to her this evening. Polly's bound to realize how serious we are if we do it straight away. The gharry driver shall have it before he leaves in the morning.'

'Good idea.'

But the letter, mulled over and rewritten many times because of its delicate nature, took far too long to compose. Like the scarf, it arrived too late. Polly's next, sent a week after her twenty-first birthday, crossed with it; hers was headed, 'Willow End'. She signed herself,

'Yr loving sister,
Polly Durrant, Mrs.'

Chapter Thirteen

London Life, 1896

March was a month Esther loved; it signalled an end to winter, however cold and wet. On her mother's half day they would walk to various garden squares, staring at flowers through the railings. If her mother wasn't too tired, they'd venture as far as Hyde Park in search of fresh greenery, standing back shyly when the high and mighty swept past imperiously along Rotten Row. Their route home never varied; it always included the tall white-fronted house where Esther was born. From the opposite pavement the two of them would gaze up at the small windows under the roof and Esther would beg to hear the tale again.

As was her custom, Kezia would say, 'Our room wasn't one of those. They were for important servants. Rose and I had the smallest bedroom at the back of the house. Not much of a view, just roofs and chimneys.'

'Like from the top of Uncle Lemuel's house?'

'That's right. Uncle Lemuel was outside our room the night you were born, keeping cavey.'

'And big Aunty Bridie was there.'

'Bless her kind heart. If she hadn't come, I don't know what would have happened. Rose and I were so frightened. We didn't know how babies came into the world, you see.'

Neither did Esther. She had a vague notion that her beloved Aunt Bridie must have brought her here in a black bag. It was the received wisdom among her friends. Although she played with others in the mews, she

185

herself had never become a sharp-eyed London child; she'd inherited too much of Kezia's quiet shy Welsh spirit for that. Fortunately she'd managed to avoid her mother's melancholy, which had deepened in the years since Esther's birth.

'Now, Mam . . . it's not that bad,' she would insist with a smile. 'Look, did you ever see so many snowdrops? Spring's on its way. Soon there'll be daffodils.' Kezia would smile, watery-eyed in the bitter wind and wish, and wish . . . It was never any use. However careful they were with their money, there was never enough for the long journey back to Wales.

Esther had heard of that great adventure countless times. The mile upon mile her mother had walked, sleeping under the stars, until she was hailed by kind Jacob Jones, the carter. He was their one link with what Mam called 'home'. At Christmas he would sometimes turn up to bring them news.

Esther listened to the lilting sing-song conversation, occasionally hearing a word she knew but never enough to understand, content simply to see her mother smile. After his last visit, though, her mother had been extremely sad.

The old carter had shaken his head sorrowfully as he'd kissed Esther goodbye, his face scratchy against her own. He'd pressed his usual gift into her hand, two silver threepenny bits inside a length of pretty ribbon. The gift for her mother had remained unopened for a long time after he'd gone. Kezia had gazed into the fire instead. Eventually she began to speak of the bluebell wood and of Esther's father, Adam.

'He was very young and strong . . . Beautiful, too, to me anyway. He asked for my promise and I gave it, willingly; there'll never be anyone else. Then he went away and never came back. I don't know where they buried him, the letter didn't say . . . and now my mother's dead, so Jacob says. Your grandmother, Esther. Six months ago, it was. She's buried in the graveyard on the hill . . . I shall never see it.'

Kezia's voice, always soft, fell to a whisper. Esther held

her breath, not daring to speak, unable this time to offer comfort. It was too big a sorrow to brush away with kisses. But Kezia didn't weep. She stared unseeing at candlelit images on the walls of their small room, her thoughts hundreds of miles away.

'The last of our family, she was. Three years since *my* grandmother died ... now there's no one left. Nor any reason for me to go back.' Esther's small hand crept out to take hers.

'There is someone left – there's me. And we'll both go back one day.' Kezia gave a sob of a laugh but shook her head.

'Of course there's you, my darling. How could I forget? I meant – none of our own kin. But the reason I cannot go back is my mother's shame. She forbade anyone to speak of me – so Jacob had heard – the shame was too great. They say that's what killed her.'

The curse of bastardy again. Despite her youth, Esther felt a burst of anger. That stain ruined every aspect of her life, she couldn't ignore it. It had to remain a terrible secret. According to her mother she would carry the burden beyond the grave, there was no way she could rid herself of it – it was so unfair! And it hurt her mother even more.

Esther lived for sunshine and laughter, she turned her back defiantly on unhappiness. But now, according to kind old Jacob Jones, this same shame which so crippled Kezia had killed her unknown grandmother in Wales – why?

'I pray God my mother didn't die cursing my name,' Kezia cried sombrely.

'Oh, Mam! She wouldn't have done that now, would she? Not the kind person you've always told me about. Didn't you always tell me how she kept a lookout the night you went away, watching from her bedroom window until you were out of sight?'

No, Kezia wanted to explain, that was my grandmother. She was the one who watched so tenderly, but she couldn't read or write so we never spoke to one another through a letter. It was my mother, upright and

187

rigid in her faith, who refused to utter my name once she'd learned of the baby. She was the real reason I left Wales ... I knew in my heart she would never forgive. But why trouble Esther with this when she had never met either member of her family?

And now her mother was dead. On her knees in prayer, the Bible open on the floor beside her was how she was discovered, according to the carter.

There'd been no relative to follow the coffin. None who would know Kezia if she ever went back. The tiny hamlet was desolate, the remaining houses empty now because there was no work. No one in the entire universe to care whether she lived or died.

'Mam ... ' Esther sounded a warning note. Kezia gazed down into the dark blue eyes, Adam's eyes, and her black mood lifted a fraction. 'Come on, Mam. Say goodbye to the devil for me. He'd best be going otherwise I shall have to chase him with the frying pan.'

Esther, together with Bridie Macguire, had devised this silly game to banish Kezia's melancholy. It had begun when Esther was scarcely tall enough to lift the pan from its hook but she'd done so nevertheless, determined to make a 'big noise', to send the devil packing; that black dog which appeared without warning to sit on Kezia's shoulder and had troubled her more and more since the strain of Esther's birth.

There were many burdens to add to Kezia's sadness but amongst them was the fact that her daughter couldn't speak Welsh. During her childhood, Kezia had never been at home to teach her. When Esther was four years old, they'd walked as far as Eastcastle Street in the West-End of London, to a newly consecrated Welsh chapel where she hoped to enrol her child in the Sunday School. But the language class cost too much. How relieved Esther had been! She told her mother so during the long walk home – it was too far. Her plump little legs were sore. She didn't care if she never learned the language – home for her was London – hadn't she been born in that fine big house in Kensington. And now she belonged in the noisy, crowded cafe. Each and every customer was another of her uncles. As soon as Uncle Lemuel brought her back there each evening, didn't she put on her apron while Mam had a rest, and help serve them their tea?

Kezia smiled fondly; it was true. The regular clientele of cab drivers had known Esther since babyhood. Big, tough men, fierce in their protection of her. They brought the harshness of their life into the warm cafe with their coarse, rough attitudes but woe betide any who forgot himself so much as to swear in front of either Esther or Kezia.

Esther had learned their preferences for food together with the names of their cab horses in one great childish muddle. Laughter followed whenever she scurried to the hatch calling for 'Uncle Daisy beef and dumplings with extra gravy', or 'Uncle new dapple grey wants bread pudding.'

As she grew older, Esther not only ran to and fro, she also stood on a stool to dry the plates her mother had washed. Later, she learned to prepare vegetables. It didn't matter what time of day or night, there were always cabbies waiting to be served. The cafe closed at one a.m. or thereabouts, after the last customer had gone, re-opening at four every morning. One of the first sounds Esther heard in her sleep was the scrape of warped wood as the shutters were folded back and the door unlocked. Then came the sussuration of her mother's skirts as she dressed and slipped downstairs. When she heard that, Esther would turn over contentedly to sleep for another hour, until it was time to rise.

The elderly owner and his wife lived on the first floor. Kezia and Esther had one of two small attic rooms above, the other was used for storage, whilst on the landing between was a small screened-off area containing a wash-stand. Water had to be carried up from below.

Their tiny kingdom of a room had a dormer window which didn't fasten. Following several dry summers the building had shifted on its foundations. Window frames became distorted and one or two could never be closed again.

189

Esther didn't mind. An open window meant she could lean out and gaze at the street scene below. There was always something to watch, but on Saturday nights it could be exciting.

There was a carefree atmosphere on the one night when men and women had money in their pockets. Couples roamed the pavement, squeezing past horses at the water trough, jeering good-naturedly at stallholders in an attempt to make them lower their prices, waiting until the last possible minute to buy food.

It was an art perfected by the half-starved and impecunious. It began with feigning indifference to vendors anxious to pack up and go home. Customers lolled against doorways, watching hawklike as canvas covers were stowed and the naptha lamps extinguished. Then, as a bucket of scraps was emptied in the gutter and ravenous dogs pounced, a languid voice would cry, 'Give us three pennorth of neck then, cut as close to the tail as you can git.'

The constant battle to stay alive honed their wits. Children learned the ways early. From her vantage point Esther could see when an apple or a cabbage was stolen. Wicked, maybe, but necessary if you were starving.

How lucky she and her mother were to work at The Coachman! Esther had never known what it was to be hungry but there were days when Kezia didn't eat, when Aunt Vida needed her share of their food. It would never occur to Kezia to steal another portion.

Times were so often 'bad' for Uncle Lemuel. He would peer through the cafe's steamy window and her mother would hurry outside with a plateful of food. It seemed to Esther that times were rarely good as far as Uncle Lemuel was concerned. She knew that their responsibility included caring for him and Aunt Vida. Why, she didn't fully understand.

Vida and Lemuel used to shout at one another when 'times were bad', usually after her mother had paid their rent. Uncle Lemuel was always grateful, of course. When Aunt Bridie saw him looking pleased with life, somehow she always guessed what had happened and would scold

190

Kezia for being a fool.

Esther used to ponder these events from her window, especially on a Saturday night when beer and gin had taken hold and there were fights. Men, sometimes women, lay in the gutter. Once or twice Uncle Lemuel was there, joining in the singing. That was when Kezia pulled shut their curtains to block out sounds from inquisitive ears.

From her mattress, Esther watched the shadows on the ceiling. Once she had been afraid but Uncle Lemuel had shown her how to make animal shapes that danced. Esther imitated, twisting pudgy little fingers. She made up stories about Mr and Mrs Rabbit, chuckling when they became too ridiculous.

The occasional smart visitor climbed the steep flight to their attic; Aunt Rose, now an upper parlour maid in Mayfair and with auburn hair dressed exactly like the Princess of Wales. It amazed Esther whenever Rose declared she'd come especially to 'let her hair down' for not one strand ever escaped from that tight coiffure.

From Rose Esther learned of her mother's bravery. How Kezia had defied the terrifying Mélisande Massingham and the equally frightening Mrs Massingham before descending the hallowed front steps, baby Esther in her arms – 'Actually walked out of that front door without so much as a by-your-leave!' Rose would shake her head at the incredible memory. 'It was the bravest thing I ever saw.' Bridie Macguire had a different explanation.

'Your Ma was defending her pet lamb. You don't stop to think of the consequences when that happens.'

Finally there was Aunt Vida, who hadn't been present at her birth but for whom the night had been equally memorable because of the explosion. She was difficult to love. Esther tried not to cry out when her Aunt Vee gripped her hand too tightly, she knew it was because of pain behind those near-blind eyes.

Uncle Lemuel would speak of Vida's accident and of the way work eluded him as though Esther could not fail to understand. It surprised her when he claimed it hurt

191

to have to take money from Kezia, for Esther had never noticed any pain. Out of gratitude at her apparent sympathy, Lem persuaded a reluctant Gyp to balance a biscuit on his nose.

On dark winter days when Vida's scars ached ceaselessly, Lemuel would seek comfort from his ferrets. He showed Esther how to avoid being bitten when cleaning out their cage, how to whip up an egg with milk and water and dribble the mixture into a baby ferret's mouth. Shivering beside him in the gloom, Esther realized these were manifestations of love. Lemuel cared deeply for his animals. The mews might deem him a failure but there was a yearning inside for affection. She'd only to say, 'Aren't they beautiful!' for the ugly split-sided face to beam like the sun.

'Your mother's frightened of them, your Aunty Vida thinks they smell, but you an' me know different, eh, Esther?' Lemuel would pull on the thick leather glove and stroke the tiny darting head, 'Who's my beautiful gel?' he crooned softly, 'who's my wild one . . . '

Sundays were different. By midday, the cafe was shut. Chairs were stacked on the tables and the floor thoroughly scrubbed. When this was done, Kezia and Esther would change their clothes, put on their hats and walk round to cook lunch for Vida and Lemuel. At four o'clock, the high spot of the week arrived when Esther was allowed to run along to her Aunty Bridie's.

Bridie Macguire had become very fat indeed. Other women lost weight when their husbands had no work, not so Bridie. Worry increased her obesity. As her girth expanded, so the perimeters of her world decreased. She no longer ventured outside the mews. Her family were despatched instead. Once dressed in the morning, Bridie lowered herself, step by apprehensive step, to the ground floor where she stayed for the rest of the day.

If the weather was fine, her armchair was dragged outside onto the cobbles. Otherwise it stood in the open stable doorway from where she could survey the passing scene. Occasionally she would rise to visit one of her neighbours. For the most part, they visited her. On Sundays when Esther was expected, Bridie stayed in her chair.

Esther learned worldly wisdom sitting at Bridie's side.

'There's Mrs Birtle off to borrow Lem's cart. There'll be a flitting tonight, shouldn't wonder.'

'What's a flitting?'

'When you ain't got the rent and the bailiff's due. If that ever happens don't you ever wait to cry on his shoulder. Bailiffs don't come with no handkerchiefs, they come to take what's due. If you ain't got money – they'll have the furniture. And another thing . . . ' Bridie leaned closer to whisper, 'if you have got to flit, see you wear your best 'at.'

'Why?'

' 'Cause you might have to leg it and leave the blessed cart behind. If you're wearing your best togs, no one can take 'em off you, can they?'

'No, I suppose not.' Esther wondered aloud if it would ever happen to them. Bridie smiled reassuringly.

'Course not, dear, don't you worry. Your Ma's safe as houses working in that cafe. How long you been there now?' Esther wasn't sure. 'How old are you then?'

'Ten.'

'There you are. You been there nearly eight years. Part of the wallpaper, you two are. I don't suppose there's a cab-driver in London who hasn't tried your Ma's cooking.' Bridie sighed massively. 'Not that it's done any good seeing as she's turned 'em all down. She must have had more offers than most.'

'Offers of what?'

'Marriage, of course. To provide you with a Pa.'

'Oh, that.'

'Don't tell me Kezia's turned another one down?'

'I think so.' Esther frowned. 'There was this chap from Bermondsey, he has a roan cob. He's been bringing Mam flowers – that's a sign, isn't it?'

'It is,' Bridie agreed sadly. 'She's been and gone and told him "No," I suppose.'

Esther said carefully, 'I don't think Mam likes having

193

offers. She's had one husband, you know, only they didn't have time to get married. He was my proper Pa and his name was Adam. He was beautiful and strong.'

'Only he's dead.'

'Yes, and the letter didn't say where he's buried. That nearly brought the black dog back when Mam told me about it.'

'Did it so?' Bridie eyed the child narrowly. 'An' did you have to beat the frying pan to get rid of him?'

'I didn't have to. I keep a sharp lookout, the way you told me. I can spot if he creeps into the room nowadays,' Esther told her proudly. 'If I get there quick enough, I can chase him off before he jumps on Mam's shoulder.'

'Good for you, my darling. Run upstairs an' see if there's anyone to put the kettle on.'

'I can manage that by myself.'

'Well, you be careful. Don't want to end up like your Aunty Vida.'

'That wasn't a kettle, that was a boiler and she was standing right next to it, Uncle Lemuel said.' Bridie waited until Esther had gone upstairs.

'An' he deprived her of her compensation money but I don't suppose the lazy lummox told you that,' she muttered. She stared unseeing at roofs and chimneypots. 'You're a fool, Kezia Morgan. You're not strong . . . your looks are going – you can't expect to live for ever. Find yourself another man before it's too late, for Esther's sake.'

Chapter Fourteen

Skirmishes and Attachments

Sybilla Porrit's estrangement from her former ally wasn't of her choosing. Indeed, at first she couldn't understand how or why it had happened. It had begun years ago with that wretched Meissen ornament – Mrs Heyhoe had somehow discovered its true value.

Sybilla didn't obey Cook's exhortation to pay Mrs Fowler the additional half crown. Instead, she convinced herself she was fully entitled to keep the money. Had she not taken the trouble to sell the ornament in Thetford? She deserved something for her pains. She explained all this when she next met Mrs Heyhoe in the street. Cook didn't reproach her, instead she gave Sybilla an extremely old-fashioned look and walked away.

Then came the unpleasant discovery that she had indeed carried out her threat; the sale of the ornament had become common knowledge, also the circumstances surrounding the purchase of the Fowler's house. Acquaintances cut Sybilla dead and, if accosted, accused her of 'stealing from that poor woman'.

Sybilla was perturbed. She left it a week before her next call at the vicarage, ostensibly to see how Polly was faring. Seven days after her niece had departed, the parcel containing her entire wardrobe tucked under her arm, was long enough for Sybilla to obliterate all memory of what that parcel had contained.

There was a tense atmosphere when she arrived at the vicarage back door, as though they'd been waiting for her. She wasn't even permitted to sit. A summons, via

Lily, arrived almost immediately requesting Mrs Porrit to visit the mistress in the morning room.

Wreathed in smiles at this unexpected social recognition, Sybilla mounted the stair. What followed came as a shock. Far from exchanging pleasantries, the mistress lectured Sybilla on the impropriety of sending a young girl forth into the world without so much as a spare pair of – garments.

'You were responsible for Polly Unwin's moral welfare, Mrs Porrit. Had anything happened . . . ' the mistress reached for her eau de cologne, 'anything . . . ' she left it to Sybilla's imagination to fill the void, 'my husband would have denounced you from the pulpit, indeed he would.'

Sybilla could scarcely believe her ears. Hadn't she scrimped and saved all these years because of those unwanted orphans? Her life had been a misery half the time because she'd been so hard put to it to provide.

She began to protest but the vicar's wife lifted an imperious hand. She herself had had to provide Unwin with three pairs of drawers immediately – at this Sybilla was stunned, she herself only had two – and Mr and Mrs Porrit would now be expected to contribute a further twenty-five shillings(!) as a token against the amount spent on equipping the new kitchen maid with two aprons, two chemises, a cap, three pair of woollen stockings and a decent black gown.

Twenty-five shillings! Sybilla's blood fairly boiled! Didn't this woman know there was a perfectly good pawn shop in Thetford? Clothes could be had there for next to nothing. New clothes for Polly – what a waste!

She held her tongue. Although the wagging finger opposite didn't frighten her, anxiety overcame indignation: how far had this gossip spread? Mrs Nibs held sway in the town; her disapproval carried far more weight than any sermon preached by her husband. After the unpleasantness over Mrs Fowler, Sybilla knew she had to go carefully. To be condemned by the vicarage could result in total ostracism: no more lodgers, no customers for laundry, even the passing afternoon tea trade might be affected. She made one half-hearted effort to defend herself. In a pause she said meekly she had done her best but her niece had never shown any particular interest in clothes.

The mistress was made of sterner stuff. Polly's ecstatic gratitude at possessing the first new underwear since her mother had died, spoke volumes. Mrs Nibs renewed her attack on Mrs Porrit in acidic tones.

Sybilla capitulated in alarm. It was either that or she'd have no social standing whatsoever. She bit back her temper and grovelled, begging forgiveness for past sins and promising twenty-five shillings after she'd visited the bank. The mistress, although gratified, demanded one further penance.

'We have seen to it that Unwin is adequately clad, Mrs Porrit, but one more apron and cap wouldn't come amiss. Best cambric, if you please. We maintain a certain standard in this household.'

Sybilla ground her teeth. First three pairs of drawers and now two aprons! She'd never get to London at this rate. But she promised four yards once she'd been to Thetford. It was a convincing manifestation of penitence and the vicar's wife suggested they offer up a prayer together. At this, Sybilla was on her knees crying Amen before the other woman had risen from her chair.

Trespasses weren't completely forgiven but, as Sybilla wiped away non-existent tears, the vicar's wife bestowed a kiss and promised what had been said would remain confidential, between these four walls: her reputation was safe.

Sybilla's spirits rose immediately.

'Might I take this opportunity h'of mentioning a poor widow woman what I hev been doin' my best to help, madam. Widow Helliwell come to me in despair on account of she and her precious little flower Gladys, were starvin'. Out of charity, I provided employment h'and I'm gratified to tell you that thanks to my instruction, she's now become expert. Such a gloss she manages with gentlemen's starched collars, you can see your face in 'em.'

The mistress inclined her head gravely.

'You may have my husband's second best bands in next week's laundry, Mrs Porrit. After that, we must wait and see.'

Head held high, Sybilla passed through the kitchen, nodded to Mrs Heyhoe and Polly, before setting off for home. She'd survived, at a cost of twenty-five shillings plus four yards of cambric.

By the time she reached the London road, her self-esteem was back in place. She'd been misunderstood. Of course she hadn't been able to provide nice clothes when Enoch failed to hand over any of his wages. What a pity she hadn't thought to mention that during the interview.

If she'd told the truth about her marriage . . . My word, that would have opened the mistress's eyes! Mrs Nibs had no idea how the other half lived. Suppose her husband spent every penny of his stipend down at The Five Bells? This idea caused Sybilla so much merriment she almost choked. She paused in the shelter of a wall to recover.

Gradually, mirth gave way to indignation. Chas, Albert and Polly would've starved if it hadn't been for her! As for the humiliation at the hands of the Poor Law Committee – Mrs Nibs had never had to endure that, either. Next time she tried to give Sybilla Porrit a lecture on Christian charity, she would be told what was what!

In high dudgeon now, Sybilla slammed shut her garden gate. Rage distorted her features. It frightened one of her lodgers and sent him hurrying for sanctuary at The Eagle. But the day wasn't over yet. News had finally reached Mrs Fowler of the true price of her ornament; she chose this particular evening to visit Mrs Porrit to discuss the matter. Alas! Sybilla with her gander up was more than a match for one hesitant, nervous woman and Mrs Fowler went home, weeping.

A short time after Widow Helliwell made the mistake of calling to complain of her difficulty in earning enough to pay the rent, let alone buy food. Sybilla gave her very short shrift indeed. Employment would cease altogether if one more word was said; what would happen to dear little Gladys then, poor thing? Mrs Helliwell must simply work harder, faster! Goodness knows, Sybilla was doing all she could.

'Why, only this afternoon, I was down on my bended knees at the vicarage, persuading Mrs Nibs to entrust her husband's best linen – I hopes you don't intend to let me down, Mrs Helliwell? That woman may be a Christian but she struck a hard bargain. Whiter than snow, her husband's bands hev to be, before she'll agree to pay a farthing.'

Quivering, Mrs Helliwell retreated to Willow End and sought out the neighbour to whom she always poured out her troubles: Henry Durrant.

Sybilla now spent every idle moment dreaming of Henry. In her imagination he'd advanced from giving a shy nod to clasping her hands and looking deep into her eyes. Agreeable fantasies filled her mind. These began with Sybilla in deepest black and ended with her in elegant grey and lavender satin, standing at the altar.

It was defying convention to marry during the period of mourning but surely no one would object, not once they learned about Enoch? Anyway, if the Methodists proved difficult, Sybilla could always return to the Church of England. His Nibs could scarcely refuse, not after uniting her to him in the first instance. Which brought Sybilla back, resentfully, to the fact that her spouse was still very much alive.

How she came to be wearing black was extremely difficult to explain. Despite his habits, her husband enjoyed rude health; he was vigorous even though he now had a beer gut. Sybilla had never known him be ill.

She withdrew from reality, seeing herself with her left hand outstretched that all might admire the amethyst engagement ring. The ruby one had proved a sad disappointment. Sybilla had already chosen the next but this time it wouldn't be she who paid for it, Henry Durrant would do that.

In her heightened state, she read meaning into Henry's every word and gesture when he continued to call with his monthly tribute of vegetables. As he tried to summon up courage to explain he'd rather give up the piece of land – the soil was so sour – Sybilla convinced herself he was tongue-tied at being in her presence.

It was gratifying, of course, it showed gentlemanly refinement. Their genteel relationship was based on etiquette gleaned from Mrs Heyhoe's magazines.

If Henry Durrant were her husband there would be no hot drunken breath, no bruising on her body. Instead, tenderness would be followed by a polite request for a kiss and according to *Heart to Heart Chats*, replying to 'bashful Dora of Bradford', if one didn't wish to comply a discreet shake of the head was all that was necessary, gentlemanly lovers needed no further hint.

Gentlemen also learned to temper their ardour, Sybilla read, they could be relied upon to withdraw when faced with a lady's disinclination. If only she'd known *that* before she met Enoch.

She began to curl her hair on the days Henry was due. When summer came, she spent sixpence trimming her straw hat, but the object of her affections was finding his situation increasingly embarrassing. Matters came to a head following the death of his mother.

Henry Durrant emerged from that experience exhausted. Since his father died, his life had been dominated by this querulous domineering woman. He was employed as a clerk in a Brandon factory manufacturing quality top hats from the ready supply of rabbit pelts. His salary was sufficient for him to buy a house. Over his father's coffin, he proposed to his mother that they should go their separate ways: she to remain at Willow End while Henry would find a small property nearby. His mother was appalled. She demanded of her dead spouse whether he had ever heard anything so cruel?

As his parent was in no position to reply, Henry realized with a sinking heart what his mother had in mind. He refused to speak. Mrs Durrant's grief became hysterical. Half-lifting her husband from his casket, she declared she would die if Henry deserted her now, and as for leaving Willow End, so full of memories! What further cruelty was

Henry about to suggest!

Henry wasn't the man to stand up to her. He agreed they would continue as they were in the inconvenient, damp cottage.

After that, the lid was lowered and obsequies proceeded. Completely satisfied, Mrs Durrant took to her bed for the rest of her life, steadfastly refusing to see a doctor. Thus, years later, a genuine illness went undetected until too late.

This time the funeral proceeded smoothly. It was afterwards that the solicitor revealed what Henry had suspected all along: there was more in the bank than his mother had ever admitted. He was now, in the solicitor's words, the possessor of 'a tidy sum'.

As he wandered through the empty room, his mother's ghostly voice interrupted his thoughts.

'Don't let silly girls try and catch you, Henry Durrant. Stay at home and I'll look after you.'

'Don't waste your time with common people, Henry. Remember the Durrants were once carriage folk.' Henry came to his first decision.

All these years, his mother had done her best to emasculate him. Never mind; he would take one adventurous step every day for the rest of his life. He would begin tomorrow.

At forty-three, with thinning hair and a courteous, shy expression, Henry stepped forth into the pearly evening knowing the freedom of orphaned batchelorhood. Liberation left him weak-kneed. It also left him bereft of common-sense. A little too late he realized it might have been better not to mention his inheritance to his neighbour.

Framed by the gap in the laurel bushes through which Widow Helliwell was accustomed to tell of her troubles her disembodied damp eyes widened fast.

'Six hundred pounds! Oh, Mr Durrant . . . !'

Alas, within a few days, everyone marvelled. Overnight, Henry was transformed from one who was to be pitied into one who was eligible. Henry learned self-preservation fast. Despite the advice which came from every side, he dug in his heels. He wouldn't be precipitate, he would consider the options, then decide.

One matter was obvious however; the piece of land on the Mundford road. Despite his efforts, the soil gave very little yield, it would be a relief to hand in his notice. Once he'd summoned up the courage of course.

For months Henry had been aware of Mrs Porrit simpering whenever they met. He was shocked: a married woman had no business behaving like that. In the empty cottage, Henry brooded and it came to him suddenly that what he really needed was a wife. He could afford one. Not only for self-protection either, but for other reasons which had hitherto lain dormant.

He was aware Mrs Helliwell was setting her widow's cap at him for Henry wasn't a complete fool. Sadly, he found the snivelling Gladys repellent. Poor Mrs Helliwell, it never occurred to her that her child was unlovable.

He would look about for a house, he decided, one with a decent sized garden and then find a wife. While he grew flowers and all manner of vegetables, she would be in the kitchen cooking him a tasty supper. Later on, she would be waiting for him . . . Upstairs.

Meanwhile there was the matter of his mother's headstone. Not the lavish marble book inscribed with two lines of Mr Tennyson's *In Memoriam*, according to her instructions. All Henry was prepared to pay for since learning of her deception was a neat granite slab, heavy enough to keep her in place until the Last Trump.

Tomorrow morning he would go to the vicarage and arrange it.

It was Lily's day off so Polly answered the door. Mr Durrant had been unfortunate enough to choose a time when both the master and mistress were luncheon guests of the Bishop of Ely, so would Mr Durrant care to leave his card?

Mr Durrant admitted he had no card. Which put him in a different social category altogether. Although he behaved like a gentleman, his status was nearer her own; Polly risked a friendly smile.

They half-recognized one another from occasional encounters in Brandon High Street. He remembered she was related to Mrs Porrit. He expressed surprise that she had grown so tall. In her turn, Polly wondered aloud if he would care for a cup of tea in the kitchen, as Cook might know whether it was the verger who should be consulted in matters concerning headstones.

Mr Durrant was admitted. As he walked into her kitchen, Mrs Heyhoe saw a gentleman near her own age, possibly infinitesimally younger (she clung to being forty-nine) with beautiful manners. She never noticed the way he looked at Polly. Instead she told her kitchen maid to be quick and serve tea.

The nuances of Cook's voice were so familiar Polly knew immediately which tray-cloth she should use, which cups and saucers and, above all, which teapot. Esteemed visitors were offered Darjeeling brewed in the Sheffield plate. Henry, invited to partake of a second cup, tactfully agreed that such a pot added a certain something to the flavour.

He drank and bit into the first of Polly's rice cakes. His search was over, he need look no further. He'd never experienced such ecstacy before. Alas for widow Helliwell's dry caraway buns – this white butterfly fluttered down into Henry's stomach and came to rest there like a kiss. He was invited to have another, he patted his lips and murmured he couldn't resist: Henry was captivated . . .

Polly watched as Cook chattered on and on. Mr Durrant had a rather sad face in repose. She was well aware of his furtive glances in her direction but pretended not to notice, as was proper. More important was the manner in which Mrs Heyhoe was behaving; Polly had never seen her smile so much, nor rest her chin on her hand so coyly.

That night Polly listened. Beautiful manners were something Cook had always treasured, apparently, and those of Mr Durrant resembled the late Mr Heyhoe's in every particular. All of which came as a surprise. Hitherto Polly had been appraised of Mr Heyhoe's faults rather than his virtues.

Cook inspected first one clothes-hanger then another. Polly was asked her opinion of a blouse which had been kept for Sundays. She agreed it was equally suitable for weekdays.

She began to wonder – was it possible Cook was smitten? Gossip in the town claimed that her aunt too had become spoony over Mr Durrant, which was silly considering she was married.

As for Polly herself, she didn't feel anything. Since Chas and Albert had deserted her, she'd shut her emotions away. She thought again of the way Henry had glanced at her this afternoon. He reminded her of her father, the same quiet gentleness. It did occur to her that life with father and mother had been the happiest time she had so far known.

In his cottage bedroom Henry marvelled how Polly Unwin had changed over the years. Years ago she'd been a schoolgirl he'd scarcely noticed in the town, all eyes and skinny legs. He didn't know whether her legs were any fatter now but the rest of her was pleasantly rounded. She was taller, naturally, with the same shadowy thoughtful eyes. She'd bloomed into womanhood, in fact. As for her cooking . . .!

Henry's experience was limited: he knew what he didn't want. Polly was neither domineering like his mother nor careworn like Mrs Helliwell. She didn't simper like bold Sybilla Porrit, she didn't have muscular arms like Mrs Heyhoe. Best of all, while Cook talked, Polly remained silent. After ten years with his mother, Henry appreciated that trait as much as he did the rice cakes.

Polly was young but he'd had his fill of older women. He didn't give Mrs Heyhoe a second thought. How could any newfound batchelor of forty-three look kindly on a woman of fifty?

Polly's freshness was delightful. She wasn't pretty but her brown hair escaped from her cap in thick dark strands as she bent to refill the teapot. For the first time in years, Henry wondered what it would be like to remove the hairpins and let a woman's hair fall about her shoulders; Polly's shoulders. Would her skin be soft . . .?

He was free to lust timidly after the firm pinkness that lay concealed beneath Polly's cambric bib. He wouldn't rush; there was no need. He'd found the woman, now he would look for a house – for Henry continued to be methodical.

He would call at the vicarage at suitable intervals for he wanted to be absolutely certain of Polly's affections. He would be discreet. He didn't want to arouse her suspicions before they'd become properly acquainted. Above all he wanted to be sure of her reply. Henry Durrant shied away from the merest possibility of a rebuff.

Chapter Fifteen

The Heat of the Moment

Sybilla had by now reached the stage when to hear others speak Henry Durrant's name was essential to her happiness. Not when Enoch was present, naturally, but on every other possible occasion. When she went to Thetford, in the streets of Brandon itself, in any place where acquaintances could be persuaded to stop and talk. She never noticed how they remarked on her obsession behind her back.

On a visit to the vicarage, she was about to begin anew when to her surprise Mrs Heyhoe introduced the topic first.

'Mr Durrant was here Thursday.' Sybilla concealed her pleasure behind a doleful countenance.

'The poor soul, I expect he's still missing his mother.' She sighed affectedly. 'He must be terrible lonesome without her.'

'Hmmph!' Mrs Heyhoe was contemptuous. 'He must'a wanted to push the old besom into the river many a time.' Sybilla pretended to be shocked.

'Mrs Heyhoe, what a thing to say!'

'You should know ... doing their laundry all these years. I did hear she had a nasty smell about her at the finish. Not that Mr Durrant complained, 'cept to say she lingered too long.'

'He must still miss her,' Sybilla insisted valiantly.

'We got the impression he was thankful, didn't we, Unwin?' It was a rhetorical question. Without bothering to reply Polly rose to clear the teacups and begin setting out the pastry things. It was understood that a hint had to be dropped when Sybilla showed signs of lingering.

Today Polly made a leisurely business of refilling the flour sifter. Her aunt was making even more of a fool of herself over Henry Durrant nowadays; Polly was intrigued to hear what she might come out with next.

'Such a gentleman,' Sybilla sighed again.

'Lovely manners,' Mrs Heyhoe pursed her lips and ventured a further opinion, 'Still handsome, considering he must be wellnigh fifty.'

'Surely not?' Sybilla's gentility slipped in her astonishment. ' 'E can't be above forty-two or three. He's gone a bit thin on top, tha's all.' Cook snorted.

'He was working at Lingfords for years afore his father died – he must have been over forty then. And then his mother lingering the way she have. Three years in bed, he said. Told us how tiresome it was, her demanding to be waited on hand and foot.'

'Mr Durrant's not that old,' Sybilla insisted stubbornly, ' 'E can't be. I should know. I sees him every month when he brings our vegetables.'

'Well I saw him plain enough yesterday for he was sitting in that chair.'

Polly marvelled how Henry's age should become such a contentious issue. As far as she was concerned, he was middle-aged. From her point of view that wasn't necessarily a disadvantage; an older man might be more considerate.

Her thoughts on the subject, such as they were, centred on the nightmare sounds she remembered from her aunt's bed. She had tried to put them from her mind but found it impossible. She'd no intention of allowing any man to behave towards her as Enoch did. A quiet, undemanding husband was a necessity therefore. Other than that, Polly had no great expectations except that matrimony would be a means of escape.

Life at the vicarage was pleasant but she'd had enough. Unless she married, she'd be a maid for the rest of her life. As Henry Durrant's wife, she'd be her own mistress. Polly was naively aware she could dominate him for she guessed how fond of her he was. As for the rest, he was quiet enough; he would suit.

Her aunt and Mrs Heyhoe continued to argue. Polly found it ludicrous. Cook had put on weight lately. Irritation made her huffily red-faced and the newly demoted blouse was showing signs of strain.

The clock chimed and Polly began to mix the ingredients in earnest. Her aunt spoke as usual as though she were deaf.

'Does well, doesn't she? I always said Polly would make a good maid. You know, Mrs Heyhoe, looking back, I think of my time at the vicarage as the happiest years I ever spent.'

'If you hadn't been in such a rush to get married, you might still be enjoying yourself.' Sybilla ignored the barb.

'I would have ended up a lady's maid of course,' she said affectedly. 'That counts for something you know.' Mrs Heyhoe bridled.

'Well all you are now is Mrs Enoch Porrit and that counts for nothing at all.'

Polly's fingers didn't change their rhythm but she was amazed. Knowing her aunt's sharp temper, Mrs Heyhoe was taking a risk. Beyond the mixing bowl the kitchen knife lay exposed. Would it be better to hide it? Her aunt rose in a fury.

'What do it signify if'n I am married?' she demanded, 'What if I did make that one mistake? Don't mean I'm stuck with it.'

The knife clattered against the bowl. Mrs Heyhoe gazed open-mouthed.

'What do 'e mean, Mrs Porrit?'

'Nothing!' Furious at her own indiscretion, Sybilla grabbed her jacket. 'I didn't mean nothing by it – you made me lose my temper, tha's all it was, you silly old fool!' She hurried past them and down the passage. They heard the back door reverberate and then there was silence. Mrs Heyhoe was the first to recover.

'Don't use what's in that jug, get fresh water,' she ordered, 'that's been too long near the fire, it'll be too warm for pastry.'

208

When she'd recovered, Cook chortled. Fancy Mrs Porrit making a fool of herself like that! From now on they wouldn't be speaking to one another again. That was no hardship, it happened frequently. Mrs Porrit would have to learn to behave. Otherwise, Mrs Heyhoe might be forced to remind her of today's indiscretion.

She was quietly confident Henry Durrant would continue to call. He'd promised to return, he'd repeated it the other day when Unwin had handed him his hat. Yes, Mrs Heyhoe hadn't misunderstood. From now on she could afford to smile ever so condescendingly whenever she met Sybilla Porrit in the street.

As confidence increased, Mrs Heyhoe began to boast. Out shopping, she let fall casually that Mr Durrant was a regular visitor, that the mistress was aware of it and had given her permission. Which was stretching truth to its limit. The vicar's wife insisted on knowing the identity of every caller at her back door, but in view of Cook's age, didn't attach any other significance.

Mrs Heyhoe confided to those who asked that Unwin was present whenever Mr Durrant was there, for the sake of propriety. After that, all she could do was wait in happy expectation for Henry Durrant to make his move.

Polly realized how matters stood. She also knew that Henry was blissfully ignorant of them. It could become very awkward if Cook's hopes were raised too high. In fact, her own position might become extremely unpleasant. Perhaps she should drop a hint to Henry? But how, when Cook was always there?

Her chance came one cold February day when Mrs Heyhoe's chilblains were so painful she had to retire to rub them with camphor oil before she could face the evening ahead.

'You will excuse me, Mr Durrant. The backs of my legs are that ticklish, I keeps wanting to tear the skin off with my nails.' She smiled demurely. Henry tried to surpress a shudder at the thought of those legs.

'Please . . .' he murmured, 'I trust the oil will bring relief, Mrs Heyhoe.'

209

'Very kind of you, I'm sure.' She heaved her bulk upright, 'No, don't disturb yourself . . . ' But Henry was already holding the door open. 'Have another potato cake before you go, Mr Durrant, with some of Unwin's potted veal. It'll help keep out the cold.'

'Too kind . . . '

After she'd gone, neither of them spoke for a while. Polly made up the fire and offered the cakes, warm from the hob. Henry helped himself to two more, buttered them and asked shyly if she wasn't going to join him. Polly sat and considered how best to begin.

'Mrs Heyhoe has been a widow a long time . . . ' Henry nodded. 'She misses her husband for she's always talking about him.' He was surprised; he hadn't imagined cook capable of strong emotion. That too solid flesh conjured up images of food rather than passion.

'She says . . . ' Polly was slightly hesitant, 'that you remind her of him.' Henry frowned.

'Who?'

'Mr Heyhoe. You remind her.' He was dismayed.

'Why? In what way do I resemble him?' Polly had no idea. Henry was relieved. 'It must be difficult for any woman,' he said, warming to his task, 'especially one of riper years, to be alone.'

'Mrs Heyhoe doesn't want to be alone any more, she wants to get married again.' Henry decided enough had been said about Cook.

'Then let us hope she meets a good, suitable man who will reciprocate her affections – '

'She thinks she has,' Polly said urgently, 'she thinks that's why you come calling on her.'

'I? Call on her!' Henry's voice rose in disbelief and shock. 'She surely cannot believe . . . ?'

'Yes, she does,' Polly assured him. 'She as good as says so to whoever she meets nowadays. When Mrs Helliwell come round about Gladys joining the Sunday School class, cook told her you'd been calling. Mrs Helliwell was ever so upset.'

Thoroughly confused as well as alarmed, Henry asked, 'I don't understand. What has Mrs Helliwell to do with – anything?'

'Well, she feels the same way Cook does. She don't want to go on being a widow, neither. She said she was hoping to find a father for Gladys.'

'Oh, good Lord!'

'Then there's Aunt Syb . . . ' Polly insisted inexorably. Henry sat abruptly.

'But Mrs Porrit . . . is – Mrs Porrit. That is to say, your aunt is a *married* woman.'

'She said that don't signify. I was standing by that table when she said it.' Henry looked at her in growing horror.

'What can Mrs Porrit be thinking of?' he whispered. Polly shrugged.

'I don't know. But she's a terrible one when she's set her mind on something. Never gives up.'

'But . . . but . . . ' Henry Durrant made a sorry lover. Anxiety caused him to push both hands through his hair until it stood up in spikes. The remaining potato cake congealed on his plate. 'What am I going to do?' Polly regarded him enigmatically.

'That's for you to decide, Mr Durrant. But you'll have to do something. I shouldn't leave it too much longer neither or you might end up in a pickle.'

He dared not wait even though he'd had no confirmation of his hopes. Summoning up every scrap of courage, Henry cleared his throat and declared himself.

Discretion was essential. Nothing passed between them when anyone else was present. Polly had a quiet word with the mistress, Henry an even quieter one with the vicar. He mumbled so much the cleric asked him to repeat himself.

'Miss Unwin? You mean – our Unwin? Isn't she a little young?' Henry reddened.

'She has been good enough to accept my proposal. I can assure you, sir, there has been no impropriety.'

With Mrs Heyhoe present, the vicar knew there couldn't have been.

'In that case . . . I suppose we'd better publish the bans. I believe Unwin is rising twenty-one, she won't require her aunt's permission.'

'Ah, there is a little difficulty, sir, which I hope we can avoid . . . That is, we do not want our intentions becoming known beforehand.' Henry wiped a handkerchief over his forehead. 'May I enquire what the procedure is . . . that is to say, the *quietest, most discreet*, form of the er – matrimonial service?'

The vicar's wife was equally startled. 'Marry Mr Durrant, Unwin? Surely he's the person Cook claims has been calling on her?'

'Mr Durrant has been calling, madam. Mrs Heyhoe may have been mistaken as to the reason.' The mistress stared at the quiet, contained face.

'Isn't he a little old to be your husband, my dear?'

'I don't want a young man, madam. Mr Durrant will suit very well. His mother left him a tidy sum so we shall be quite comfortable. He has a good job, he'll bring in a regular wage.'

Her mistress said a little awkwardly, 'There's more to marriage than that, Unwin.'

'Yes, madam. I do know.'

I doubt it, thought her mistress.

'What about your aunt,' she asked helplessly. 'What does she have to say?'

'Aunt Syb isn't to be told, madam.'

'Oh, but you must – '

'My aunt wants Mr Durrant for herself, madam. Same as Cook. And widow Helliwell has been hanging about his house – '

'What!'

' 'Tis true. That's why Mr Durrant needs a wife as soon as possible and no one must know of it beforehand.' The mistress reeled from the shock.

'But your aunt is a married woman . . . I realize Mrs Heyhoe is older than Mr Durrant but I assumed . . . ' She and the vicar had assumed, as Durrant continued to call, he must require a motherly, bosomy spouse. 'As for the other person you mentioned . . . ?' Polly nodded sagely.

'Mrs Helliwell. She didn't really stand a chance madam because of her daughter. Mr Durrant can't stand Gladys' snivelling but it's Cook I'm worried about. She's got her heart set on him, I know she has. She keeps saying how she's only forty-nine. But I remember how she was fifty two birthdays ago, madam. She thought I'd forgotten but I hadn't. She keeps insisting Mr Durrant is nigh on fifty but he's only forty-four next birthday and that's the truth.'

And you are only twenty, thought her mistress. She seized at the remaining straw.

'About this Mrs Helliwell . . . ?'

'She's the woman who does the ironing, madam. She come round last week about her little girl going to Sunday School.'

'Oh, that woman!'

She looked much more suitable. The vicar's wife immediately decided Henry Durrant should be pointed in her direction. Meanwhile her kitchen maid must be discouraged.

'Well, Unwin, we won't speak of this any more at present. I shall consult my husband, naturally. I will ask his advice on your behalf – and you must promise me to do whatever he recommends.' Polly considered her request briefly. There didn't seem any harm in it.

'Very well, madam.'

Later, behind their bed-curtains, the mistress was extremely annoyed to hear her husband shout with laughter.

'I am not amused, William. In fact, I cannot think of a more awkward situation.'

'My dear,' he remonstrated, 'only consider. That little mouse, Unwin, whisking Durrant from under their noses while those two termagants vie with one another, and the widow next door tries to lure him . . . As for the man himself – Heavens, he's the meekest, most ordinary fool in Christendom!'

Another paroxysm interrupted. His wife tweaked the last of her curling rags under her nightcap and turned to scold.

'William, I still find it extraordinary that you should laugh. Mrs Porrit, whom you united with her husband, is breaking God's holy laws – she is ignoring her marriage vows.'

'I dare say she is,' he countered briskly, 'so would you if you'd been stupid enough to marry Enoch Porrit – '

'William!'

'I'm sorry, my dear, that was going too far. However, I do have some sympathy for her.'

'William, the woman has lust in her heart!'

'Perhaps she has,' he yawned, 'it's far too late to argue theology. I agree with you though, it's a pity the widow didn't succeed. She sounds nearer Durrant in age – and her child would benefit from his support.'

'Unwin is far too young.'

'Possibly. But now you say Mrs Heyhoe is also love-sick? I must say, I'm concerned at the prospect of losing a good cook. Has Durrant – encouraged – her in any way?' Even as he asked, his face crinkled into yet more laughter. 'That colourless chap . . . setting so many female hearts a-flutter!'

His wife said coldly, 'Far from encouraging anyone, Unwin was adamant Mr Durrant was unaware how the other women felt – which I agree, does make him a fool.'

'Naive, possibly.'

'The point is, William, what are we going to do?'

'Goodness knows . . .' It was on the tip of his tongue to tell her of his conversation with Henry but he decided against it. Instead he said, 'A kitchen maid is easier to replace than a cook.'

'William! Unwin has promised to abide by your decision.'

'Oh, well . . . Tell her she's too young and must wait at least another six months. That gives the widow one more chance. Let us hope she takes advantage of it.'

But Henry Durrant had learned the rules for obtaining a special licence. In mortal dread of Sybilla as well as Mrs Heyhoe, he established residence by booking a hotel room in Ely. He even asked Mrs Helliwell to keep an eye on his cottage while he was away.

He and Polly were married a month and a half later, a week after Polly's twenty-first birthday. Two strangers, willing to escape from the rain and earn sixpence, came into church to bear witness. After the ceremony as it was her half day, Polly went straight back to the vicarage. Her mistress was giving an important dinner party and Polly's conscience smote her. Tomorrow was soon enough to break her promise to the vicar.

Alone at Willow End, Henry lay awake, full of anticipation at the thought of his bride. At the vicarage, Polly ran to keep up with Cook's bidding; she barely had time to think.

Later, in the privacy of the dank game larder, she wrote two letters. The first was difficult; Polly sucked her pen as she considered how best to explain. If only her mistress could begin to comprehend what it felt to be secure at last? In the end Polly simply begged her pardon. The letter to Cook was even shorter.

Dear Mrs Heyhoe,

Mr Durrant and I were married today in Ely. I have put the junket in the pantry as it was beginning to set. Thanking you for all your past kindness in teaching me so many recipes.

Yours faithfully,
Polly Durrant, Mrs.

It was past midnight when she and Lily finished the washing up and crept upstairs. At half past five, Polly rose, dressed, laid the fires, prepared breakfast in the kitchen, took Cook her early morning cup of tea and returned downstairs. She left her two letters on the hall table, tucked a now slightly larger paper parcel under her arm and closed the vicarage door behind her.

Her arrival at Willow End was equally discreet. Henry greeted her with a stutter of welcome. As she hung her coat on the peg, he asked if he might have a kiss. Cool lips rested on his for a brief moment and the new Mrs Durrant gave him a critical look. After a sleepless night her husband wasn't at his best; his eyes were bloodshot, he looked his full age. His hair had, as usual, been pushed into a spikey halo, his cravat was awry and his collar, worse.

'That wasn't clean on this morning?'

'Er, no . . . I haven't managed to find an alternative . . . , my laundry hitherto has been done by Mrs . . . er . . . ' Henry's hand flapped in the general direction of Widow Helliwell's cottage. 'Under the circumstances, I haven't liked to . . . '.

'Best change it,' Polly advised, 'I'll go upstairs and find you a clean one. We can't have you going to work looking like that.' Her lover stared at her abashed.

'I'm to go to the factory today then?'

'Of course.' Polly was surprised. To lose a day's work was to lose money. 'You're not feeling poorly are you?'

'Er, no. No, quite definitely . . . I feel – very fit.'

'That's good. You go and change. I'll make breakfast. And let me have the rest of your washing. I can do it later.'

For the second time that morning, she cooked bacon and eggs. As Henry creaked overhead, Polly bustled about quite satisfied. It was a nice little house, for the time being. Once she'd given it a good spring clean it would be even better. It would suit until they found somewhere larger. Her husband appeared round the awkward bend in the stairs. She gave him an encouraging, approving smile.

'Eat your food while it's hot.'

Sybilla Porrit was annoyed. A cyclist consuming one of her teas had complained that the milk was curdled. Then a note had arrived from a customer whose shirt had been returned minus two buttons. She'd had to be polite to the cyclist but she could vent her anger on Mrs Helliwell. She set out for Willow End.

As she walked along the muddy path, swallows swooped above and a moorhen chased her brood to safety on the river. Sybilla didn't notice. Her mind was occupied with the delightful anticipation of a possible encounter with Henry Durrant.

She'd remembered to wear her greeny-blue glass beads, only twopence second-hand and worth it because they emphasized her hazel eyes. Her hair was in curl, she was looking her best. The idea of the scolding she was

216

about to administer couldn't detract from the pleasure of seeing Henry afterwards. He was bound to notice how well she looked.

Instead of knocking at the end cottage first, Sybilla couldn't resist slipping round the corner to check whether Henry was in his back garden. For once, she couldn't see clearly because a line of washing blocked her view.

One of the garments, longer than the rest, danced tantalizingly so that she had to stoop to peer beneath. As she did so, it occurred to Sybilla that she'd never seen washing hanging here before: Henry was one of their customers. Next door, Mrs Helliwell's lines criss-crossed, sagging under their burden, sheets and tablecloths were draped over every bush, there wasn't a flower to be seen whereas in Henry's garden only plants usually bloomed.

The dangling sleeve waved indolently as though bidding her to be gone; Sybilla's gaze refocussed. That sleeve was familiar; it ended in a mended frill and the cause of the rent had been Enoch. He'd torn it in one of his rages. The garment was hers, or rather it had been before she'd passed it on to Polly years ago – what was her old nightdress doing on Henry Durrant's washing line!

Watching from her bedroom window, Mrs Helliwell knew. She was in hiding. She and Gladys clutched one another in terror as they peeped through a crack in the curtains. So petrified was Mrs Helliwell she'd spent the entire morning up here, ever since Polly first appeared to peg out the clothes, wearing a wedding ring! Afterwards, when she came across to confirm the news of her nuptials, her goggle-eyed neighbour almost fainted.

Having dropped her bombshell, Polly calmly announced she was off to buy a bit of fish for Henry's supper. In her stupefaction, Mrs Helliwell didn't ask questions. Instead the suds grew cold as she wept over the loss of a possible husband. She sought comfort from her damp-nosed daughter, then it occurred to her to wonder whether Mrs Porrit had heard? The fact that her

217

employer might arrive, ignorant of such a shattering event, struck terror into Mrs Helliwell's heart.

Down below a pounding began on her back door. It wasn't tentative, it required an answer. Up in the bedroom the hand holding the curtain shook.

'Mrs Helliwell, I know you're up there. Come down here a minute, there's something I wants to ask you.'

'Go away!' It was feeble, it wouldn't have deterred a mouse let alone Sybilla. Mrs Helliwell recognized that her employer was ignorant. Mrs Porrit also appeared to be in her usual state of temper. Mrs Helliwell listened to the door handle turning against the chair which had been wedged beneath.

Outside, Sybilla was mystified – what was the widow up to? She couldn't be that frightened over two missing buttons? There was a routine in such matters; Sybilla would deliver a scolding, deduct the cost from her wages and consider the matter settled.

She stepped back and gazed up at the tiny back window. From her vantage point, Gladys began to whimper and her mother stuffed the corner of the bedspread into her mouth.

'Don't make a sound,' she implored. 'Heaven knows what Mrs Porrit's going to do next!'

'Have you started doing laundry for my niece?' Sybilla shouted, pointing at the washing line next door, 'because if you have, you can stop such nonsense. The lazy wench can do her own. And why hev you used Mr Durrant's line?'

' 'Tisn't your niece's washing,' Mrs Helliwell said in a quaver.

' 'Course it is,' Sybilla snorted. 'I'd know that nightgown anywhere. 'Tisn't fitting to put it in a gentleman's garden, neither.'

'That line of washing do belong to Mrs Henry Durrant – and she hev put it up!'

Having delivered this in a terrified squeak, Mrs Helliwell sank below the level of the cill. Down below, understanding was slow. Nothing so far made any sense.

Mrs Henry Durrant had hung up the washing?

There was no such person.

218

That was her old nightgown.

She'd given it to Polly.

Had Polly given it to anyone else?

If not . . . ?!

Like a clap of thunder, comprehension reached Sybilla.

Her mouth fell open. Out of it came a sound halfway between a moan and a roar, a mixture of fury and desolation. The volume increased. It was uncontrolled. It was frustration at losing a dream: she knew she was shackled to Enoch Porrit forever.

The sound made Mrs Helliwell shudder and brought neighbours out of their houses. A passing cat fled under a gooseberry bush and several hens clucked anxiously.

Exhausted by screaming, Sybilla was savage. 'Where's my niece? Where's Polly Unwin? She shall answer to me for this!' People looked at her bemused. 'I never give her permission to be married!' she shouted.

One housewife noticed the washing in Henry's garden.

'Oh, look . . . ' she called to a friend, 'Mr Durrant must have got himself a housekeeper.' Upstairs, Mrs Helliwell popped up at her window like a jack-in-the-box.

'No he hasn't. He's been and gone and married Polly Unwin, that's what the fuss is all about,' she cried and bobbed back inside.

Sybilla shouted vehemently, 'He can't have, he's mine, he's not hers, he's mine!'

One or two were beginning to understand. The young housewife laughed.

'Why shouldn't Mr Durrant marry Polly – good for him, I say!'

Humiliation was total. Sybilla rushed away in search of revenge.

The letter fell from Mrs Heyhoe's nerveless fingers. Her imagination had never roved as freely as Sybilla's. Instead, she'd thought only of the benefits. Marriage to Henry meant she would be able to give up work. She would wait on him for the rest of her life, naturally, but she'd no longer have to stand fourteen hours a day in the vicarage kitchen.

She would sleep in a proper bedroom, not an attic three flights up when her legs were bad.

She would regain that sweet status afforded to all married women which disappeared as soon as they were widowed.

Above all, she would lose her fear of old age.

Sybilla might hoard; Cook was profligate, wasting money on gewgaws and clothes. Marriage to Henry Durrant would save her from penury. But as she sat in the kitchen that morning, this worst truth of all dawned slowly: Henry Durrant had never even cared for her.

Lily ran upstairs to discover that the mistress had also read her letter from Polly. Mrs Nibs' reaction was anger mixed with disbelief. How dare Unwin defy both her husband and herself!

Lily was about to describe Cook's emotional state, when a terrible noise reached them. It increased and drew nearer. A voice full of vitriol was mounting the stair. It wasn't one of the furies, it was Sybilla.

She scorched through the kitchen snapping at Cook, 'Don't just sit there, we got to stop 'er! I never give my permission – where's His Nibs?'

Mrs Heyhoe sat, paralysed and Sybilla rushed past on her way to the study.

Years ago, the vicar had established certain rules. After family prayers and breakfast, it was clearly understood he would retire to his study and remain there undisturbed till lunchtime.

It was a period of meditation in his constant search for The Truth. Safe from prying eyes, he conducted it with both feet resting comfortably on a drawer, chair tilted back and his eyes protected by *The Times*.

He ignored the noise outside; whatever the problem was, his wife would deal with it. The turbulence increased and drew near. Suddenly the study door burst open and a virago stood there, baying for justice. Boudicca herself couldn't have been more passionate. The vicar came to with a crash.

'What the devil . . . !'

'You got to stop 'er before it's too late!!'

In the High Street, Polly Durrant was considering supper. Henry had given her a shilling. She'd decided to be lavish and buy him a nice piece of turbot. With caper sauce, that would be a truly celebratory meal. Suddenly, her new husband appeared in front of her.

'Polly . . . '

'Henry? What's wrong?'

'Nothing. Nothing at all.' Embarrassed, he took her arm. 'Hang it all, Polly . . . a chap only gets married once. When I told them down at the factory, they insisted. We've the rest of the day to ourselves.' She stared at him anxiously.

'You'll not lose money by it?'

'No!'

'That's all right then. I was just buying a bit of fish for supper.'

'Very nice . . . you don't fancy going home now, I suppose?'

'Whatever for? I haven't finished shopping yet.'

Alas he couldn't bring himself to tell her. He trailed behind and when the basket was full, suggested half-heartedly, 'I supppose you wouldn't care for a trip on the river? The steamer goes from Thetford at half past two.' For once he'd said the right thing. Polly's eyes shone.

'Can we afford it? I've always wanted to go.' Henry's heart thudded with joy.

'Of course we can! Come, let's have that basket sent home.'

They chugged quietly down stream on the *Pride of the Ouse*. Henry held her hand while Polly thought of her brothers and the time when Albert had disappeared beneath the water lilies. Incoherent with happiness, Henry squeezed her fingers to demonstrate his love.

Sybilla had been ejected. Back outside Willow End she shrieked to any who would listen that the vicar was a spineless creature, not prepared to do his Christian duty, but somehow this marriage would be annulled.

A small crowd gathered. One man, who felt a glimmer

of pity, called, 'You'm making a fool of yourself, woman. Your niece have catched a husband. She's entitled. Go back to your rightful place, alongside your own man.'

Exhausted with emotion, Sybilla opened her mouth to reply but her long dead conscience, Jeremiah's voice, echoed inside her head:

'He's Polly's husband now, Syb. Afore the sight of God.'

It was dusk when the newly-wedded pair returned. Polly was perfectly calm. All her energies were directed towards the caper sauce. To her dismay, her husband gulped it down.

'You'll get indigestion if you don't chew each mouthful.'

'Be hanged to that, Polly. Come over here a minute.'

'When I've washed up.' Henry waited once more.

When the dishes were put away, the grate had to be swept and the wick trimmed. Despite his excellent manners, Henry grew restive.

'I want to take down your hair, Polly.' She looked at him in surprise.

'Why? I can manage it myself.'

'I want to feel it through my fingers, see it resting on your shoulders ...' He grew red-faced. 'I want to undo your bodice, Polly.' Her eyes widened in fear.

' 'ere, you're not going to be like Enoch Porrit!'

'No, no!' the desperate lover cried.

'I wouldn't have married you if I thought you were like that.'

'I love you, Polly!'

'That's all right, then.' She finished sweeping the rug. 'There ... I do like to see a place look tidy, don't you?'

'Can we go to bed now?'

'Yes, if you like.'

Out of habit Polly undressed modestly under her nightgown before jumping into bed. Below, Henry listened to every sound. When he heard the bedsprings creak, he seized the candlestick and clutching his nightshirt close, hurried up the stairs. Polly watched as he blew out the flame.

'You will be gentle?' Her voice sounded quite fierce in

the dark, almost an echo of Sybilla's and added to his nervousness.

'Of course I will!' Feverishly he scrabbled under the bedclothes. 'Wouldn't you like to take off your nightgown?'

'No!' Equally fierce.

'You are fond of me, Polly?' There was a longish pause.

'I like being married, ever so. I really enjoy it when people has to call me "Mrs Durrant".'

But what about me, Henry wanted to cry. Instead he said humbly, 'I love you, Polly.'

'Yes . . .'

The effort to be gentle combined with his first attempt to make love, proved too much. Henry's control gave way. He groaned. As he rolled over onto his back Polly expressed surprise.

'I'm sorry, I'm so sorry!' Henry moaned wretchedly. She didn't know why he should be upset. It was certainly different to her Uncle Porrit's behaviour, perhaps because Henry was a gentleman? If that was all there was to it, that and a bit of kissing, she could manage, Polly decided.

Chapter Sixteen

The North-West Frontier

By the time they reached Nowshera, Pomfret, once more
a private, was full of a deep foreboding. 'If we've come
this far, stands to reason we'll be sent further north
sooner or later . . .'

Albert was too contented at being in a barracks to
worry. Up country and at this height meant the weather
was very different from the heat of the plains. As soon as
the sun sank behind the rim of the mountains, the
temperature plummeted, too. It was the end of the rainy
season, everywhere was lush green and teeming with
insects. To be under a roof, with a bedstead standing in
four saucers of water to deter creepy-crawlies and thus
enjoy uninterrupted slumber, was indeed a luxury.

They would stay here for a week if they were lucky. A
day to put his kit in order and, after that, a chance to
explore.

There had been one change in their circumstances; he,
Pomfret and Chas had been separated by Chas's
promotion. Those months scaring birds on fenland farms
had brought a reward; Chas's aim was found to be
exceptional. He had a natural ability when it came to
assembling and maintaining either the Nordenfelt or
Gardner machine guns and, unlike Albert, he'd learned
the virtue of keeping his thoughts to himself. As a result,
he'd been made a corporal.

While Pomfret rumbled on, Albert lay on his back and
examined their quarters. Brick built just over thirty
years previously, the walls and ceiling were white-

washed and the floor constantly swept. Overhead, a fan stirred the air gently, moved by a string tied to the wrist of a punkah-wallah, who sat in the corner, cross-legged and somnambulant.

Albert hadn't experienced such cleanliness for months. It invigorated him as it did the rest of the regiment. Infantrymen set to with a will. Outside lay a busy garrison town. Eager though they were to see it, soldiers spent hours cleaning and polishing in order to dazzle the ladies of the cantonment when they emerged.

There was a constant clatter of horses and harness. Two regiments were assembled here at present, no one yet knew why. Albert didn't care. He'd reached that stage in service life when one day was very like the next. The occasional train journey broke the monotony, especially like the last, climbing higher and higher until the view from the carriage windows silenced them all. That plus forays to see more of the sights and smells of India helped dissipate boredom, for Albert's curiosity could never be satiated.

Rumours still persisted, of troubles they might have to 'put down' but these so far had proved inaccurate. He was thankful. He would be perfectly content to end his service without being involved in conflict. He'd had plenty of time to assess whether he really enjoyed being in the army. It had been a way of escape and for that he would always be grateful. Now it was time to move on. What to do with the rest of his life? Albert was vague as to the direction he should take, it was sufficient to count the days until his release. Days! that was all.

He must write again to Polly. It was only a guess as to when she might expect them, for none had learned of any travel arrangements, but what a celebration they'd have! He'd been half-hoping for some news from her. The last letter hadn't told him much. In fact Polly's end of the correspondence had dwindled since her marriage. He hoped the dear girl wasn't regretting it. One had to read between the lines to guess what Polly actually meant but, by all accounts, Aunt Syb hadn't been very kind.

Pomfret's grumbling broke through his thoughts.

225

Albert swung himself upright. 'What's the problem, old chap? It's not like you to be so down. You haven't got a touch of the collywobbles by any chance?'

'You ain't come across they Pathans before or you wouldn't ask such a stupid question.' Albert's bright blue gaze rested on him thoughtfully. It was ridiculous to imagine Pomfret frightened but uneasy he most definitely was.

'Good, are they?'

'The best,' said Pomfret emphatically. 'As good as we are and when it comes to night fighting, even better. They've had a lot of practice up here. But it's not that, it's the way they bear grudges.'

'Oh?'

'If you offends them, they'll seek you out, doesn't matter how long it takes, and slit your throat.'

'That's all right then,' Albert said comfortably, 'I ain't never been up here before.'

'No, but I have.'

'Ah . . .'

'These tribes are different from the other fuzzies. Up here they got these rules, see. And they stick by 'em. If they're on your side, they'll share their last biscuit. If you're under fire, they'll come and give a hand but if you offend their sense of honour . . .' Pomfret shook his head gloomily, 'Gawd help you.'

'What happened?'

'I helped a girl pick up the bits of her water jar when she dropped it.' Albert's eyebrows shot up. 'You can laugh,' Pomfret said heatedly, 'but I accidentally touched her hand as well.'

'So?'

'So you don't touch Pathan women, not their hands, their feet, not any little bit. You don't even look at 'em. If any come near, you cross over and walk on the other side of the street. I tell you, Albert, what I did that day was serious. The old Subahdar from the Gurkhas, he come and told me.'

'Told you what?'

'That girl's father would have a bullet with my name on

226

it. Didn't matter how long he'd have to wait, he'd come after me. I'd broken the *Tor* which is one of their strictest rules.'

'For touching her hand accidentally?' Albert was incredulous but it was obvious old Pomf was serious. 'How long ago was this?'

'Seven years. Nearly eight.'

'Oh, well!' Albert laughed with relief, 'he'll have forgotten all about it by now. He might even be dead.'

'If he is, his brother has to do it. Family honour. That's what their blessed code's all about.'

'He won't even remember who you are, all that time ago,' Albert scoffed. 'Remember what they're always telling us – how we all look alike to them.'

'Not those of us who is over six foot two inches tall.'

'No . . . well . . .'

'Besides, the day after it happened – me picking up the pieces an' that – an Afghan wearing one of those funny flat hats come to our camp asking who I was. Wouldn't go until he'd got a bit of paper with my name on it.'

'He was trying to scare you –'

'He succeeded,' Pomfret said tersely. 'The beggar's been on my mind ever since, especially once we come north of Amritsar. They don't think nothing of travelling for miles, these Pathans don't. I'd recognize him all right. He's bound to know who I am. And another thing; one of their other little foibles after a battle is to kill off their own wounded.'

'Go on!'

'They do, so.' Pomfret drew a line with his thumb across his throat. 'That way the wounded can't be captured and tortured and spill the beans about the rest. Now, with a nasty little habit like that with their own brethren, what chance have I got when they catch up with me?' But Albert had been caught by Pomfret's tales before and this one sounded highly unlikely. He reached for his hat.

'I'm not staying indoors, whatever they're like,' he declared, 'I'm off for a walk.' As might have been expected, Pomfret declined to accompany him.

The previous day they had crossed the Kabul river, above

the point where it joins the Indus. On either bank were crumbling forts built by long-dead conquerors, now with the British flag flying proudly. 'Onwards and upwards' was another of Pomfret's sayings; in this district, there was no alternative. Mountains stretched ahead on every side, reaching towards an infinite sky.

'Have we got to climb that lot?' Albert had groaned when he saw them.

'I bloody well hope not,' Pomfret had replied, 'the natives ain't very friendly.' At least the explanation today accounted for that.

Albert stood on the verandah and stared pensively at the parallel lines of barrack roof tops descending the slope. Everywhere was so neat and smart a chap couldn't help straightening his shoulders. There were familiar shrubs like rhododendron growing here, full of chirping sparrows. After the strident, vulgarly coloured birds of the plains these brought a lump to his throat. In fact if it weren't for the mountains, he might be back home already. A wave of nostalgia swept over him and he found himself wiping his eyes. This would never do! Albert blew his nose with great gusto.

The parade ground was busy, he noticed; Sepoy cavalry in formation, practising a full-dress affair for the forthcoming old Queen's birthday. They turned out in spectacular fashion for their Empress, she'd been venerated for well over a decade. Albert felt calmer as he remembered. It was proper for them to rule here and keep the peace, his earlier doubts were forgotten as he saw on every side evidence of Imperial Might.

One of Pomfret's many dispiriting topics had been the different fighting tactics they could expect. 'They don't come out and fight fair and square up here. They ambush. Hide in nooks and crannies among the rocks and then pick you off. Specialists in deliverin' a bullet to the back of the 'ead.'

'Very unsportsmanlike,' Albert said primly, 'but there's been a peace treaty in this area for goodness knows how long.'

'If you ask me they're about to ignore all that. Why

228

d'you think two regiments have been ordered up here? This ain't no peace-keeping force, Albert. Them flat-hatted natives are getting restless.'

From their verandah, Albert gazed across to where Chas was billeted. The sight of bright geraniums in white-washed pots couldn't entirely soothe him, Pomfret's words just refused to go away. Perhaps Chas was free to accompany him on his walk? Most problems shrank to a manageable size once Chas had applied his rational mind.

There was a further delay before they could start. The certificate for marksmanship had arrived from army headquarters in Simla. Albert joined the group admiring the parchment. Chas's promotion had produced another sample of Pomfret's mordant wit.

'Wait till there's a war, then see how far your brother gets. He could end up a general. Why, even you could make corporal, monkey-nut. Lots of vacancies occur when there's a war on, can't think why.'

He couldn't diminish Albert's pride. Wait till Aunt Syb discovered Chas had a stripe. It would be a facer too, for Uncle Porrit. His willowy, handsome brother, the moustachios so flamboyant now – a positive masher compared to scruffier members of the regiment; not as big as Pomfret, of course, but then nobody was.

'Fancy a stroll, old bor?'

'Why not.' Once outside the gate Albert interrupted Chas's informative chatter about what they might expect to find up at Peshawar.

'The women up here are out of bounds, did you know.' His brother stared.

'That's scarcely news, young 'un. They are everywhere in this dem country.'

'No, not like other places. You mustn't even look at them in the street. Their relatives get very upset if you do.' Chas stepped aside to let a sweating oxen team haul a baggage waggon up the slope. Ahead, squatting in the shadow of a wall, sat two of the forbidden fruit, swathed in the *chadar*.

'Can't say I'm tempted,' Chas commented fastidiously.

'Those two women look more like rolls of carpet than specimens of feminine allure. Anyway, there's plenty of our own sort, more than sufficient for my needs, I can assure you.'

It was true. Garrison towns usually had an excess of unattached females whose passage from England had been financed by hopeful relatives and Nowshera was no exception; a marriage market in which young men dabbled at their peril. So far Chas had swaggered and had known himself admired, but had behaved prudently.

However, it was a further cause for pride in Albert that at twenty paces, with eyes half shut, his brother would observe, 'There's a pleasin' little filly, with a good pair of calves unless I'm mistaken.' Albert marvelled. Never once had *he* been able to see more than an inch or so of ankle, yet his brother with half an eye managed to penetrate through flounces and furbelows to the essential framework underneath. Such sophistication!

Not only that; Chas had courage enough to raise his hat to these apparitions. If a female person drew near he would say bold as brass, 'Afternoon, ma'am. Pleasant weather for the time of year.' As like as not, the 'pleasing little filly,' would respond, 'Good afternoon, most pleasant.' A head on a slender neck would incline in their direction. Albert's heart would pound and pound ... but nothing more happened. Chas had as yet no stock of felicitous phrases with which to continue the conversation and they would be forced to walk on.

Nevertheless, his brother's predilection for social intercourse might prove an additional hazard on the North-Western Frontier.

After two weeks in the barracks the Fusiliers were split up. A detachment of twenty-five men under the command of a lieutenant was despatched to the head of the railway and from there on a two day march to the foot of one of the mountain ranges. There was a briskness about their orders this time which had been lacking during the past few months.

'Something's up,' Pomfret predicted. 'It'll be an extra

grog ration next, you'll see.' Albert didn't care. Two more weeks had been crossed off his calendar, two more to go. It didn't occur to him that the army might not notice the date.

They were back under canvas in a rocky landscape with very few trees, where the night winds blew cold with the approach of winter. After the burning heat of the day, Albert and Chas shivered. They tried to convince one another that this was the weather they'd been hoping for ever since leaving England. Chas drew him aside.

'There's a pertic'lar little job we've been sent to do up here,' he murmured conspiratorially. 'I've been detailed to play a part but I shall need a couple of chaps to assist – fancy coming along?'

'Rather!'

'Maybe old Pomf would be interested.'

'What do we have to do?'

'There's been trouble on the caravan route. Up there.' Chas pointed to where the ancient track disappeared over a saddle of rock, silhouetted against the late afternoon sun. 'The local tribe have been bribed for years to keep 'em peaceable but now they've become greedy. They're demanding extra money from the camel drivers before they let them through the pass. We've been ordered to sort 'em out. Show the flag. Ride through as though we own the place for a day or two, you know the sort of thing.'

'Establish a presence.'

'Exactly. Make sure they understand what the money's been paid for. The point is there's one fuzzy who's been pooping off the odd shot to frighten the camel drivers into paying up. *We've* got to flush him out before the rest of the chaps can risk going through the pass. According to the scouts he's up there on his own, in a kind of rocky lair.'

'When do we go after him?'

'Tonight, so that the march can begin at dawn.'

'Why don't we all stick together and do it?' asked Pomfret when he was told.

'There's only one native up there!' Chas said scornfully,

'Besides he's in this hidey-hole. We shall have to flush him out.'

'There's safety in numbers,' Pomfret grumbled.

'Look, are you interested or not?'

' 'Course I'm interested. Why spend the night warm and snug with the rest of the chaps when I could be freezing cold halfway up a mountain?' He gave an exasperated sigh. 'I must be stupid!'

'Right. We leave at eight o'clock. The scouts will lead us to the lair. Our aim is to take him completely by surprise and frighten him into the open by making an absolute hullaballoo. The minute he attempts to escape, that's when we'll pick him off.'

'Hurrah!' cried Albert, ebullient and excited. That was what he'd been missing all these months, why he'd felt so dull. He hadn't had a proper adventure. Thank goodness Chas had come to the rescue. 'Hurrah,' he shouted again, beside himself. This was the thrill of the chase, of catching a fox. 'We'll scare him the way you used to scare the crows, Chas.' Pomfret wasn't so sanguine.

'Never mind bird-scaring, suppose he sits tight? How d'you propose to dislodge him then?'

'We shall close in from three sides. Dammit, Pomf, if three of us can't tackle one lowly native . . .' Chas tweaked the growth on his upper lip. 'But the aim is to be discreet. Officially we're at peace with the tribes in this area.'

'They don't scare that easy up here,' Pomfret insisted.

Later, as pouches of ammunition and firecrackers were shared among the bearers who were to accompany them, Chas sketched out details of the plan.

'We climb up underneath his eyrie. He'll almost certainly be asleep. He can't keep a lookout indefinitely.' This was said defiantly. Pomfret didn't argue. 'However, we shall proceed as if he was wide awake for complete surprise is essential.

'I'm told there's an overhang which will give protection for the last stage. We work our way along to the end of that and then we're out of sight and can sort ourselves out. Plenty of cover for us to climb up and get into

232

position, you two on either side and myself above, I hope. We'll have to assess the terrain once we get there but the scouts were confident. Then, when we're ready, I give the signal and you two make as much racket as you can –

'Like there was twenty-five of us, you mean?' Chas looked at him coldly.

'He may know there are that many of us already, I don't know. We can't be sure how good their intelligence is up here but it won't matter. Either way he'll *assume* he's outnumbered and head back to join up with his chums. Which is when we finish him off.'

'In the dark it won't be obvious there's only us three,' Albert pointed out.

'I hope not,' said Pomfret devoutly. 'I hope the little sod thinks the whole British Army's come after him, it's the only way he *is* likely to feel frightened.'

'After he's run away, we're to burn everything in the lair. Then we come back and join up with the rest to march through the pass. That way the caravan drivers will see that it's safe once more.' Chas stared severely at Pomfret. 'Any questions?'

'No, Corporal.'

By eight o'clock, Albert was bubbling over. This really was fun! He couldn't contain himself, he acted the fool in front of everyone, forcing even Pomfret to laugh. Chas indulged him but once they set off, ordered him to cut the tomfoolery. Pomfret murmured, 'Do as he says, monkey-nut. You're in the real army, now.'

Gradually the climb became very steep. Chas set a steady pace. They left the treeline behind and the wind was colder. Nearer the pass, the rockface was covered in scree which was loose underfoot. Ahead, the two scouts moved confidently but Pomfret fell behind. Chas and Albert had to wait every hundred yards or so.

'He's like a lumbering great elephant. Why can't he keep up? Our packs are heavier,' Chas complained.

'He ain't young any more. I don't suppose we could manage any better at his age.'

Chas was unsympathetic. As Pomfret, puffing, drew

233

alongside, he ordered, 'Move a bit faster. And not so much noise. We're not that far off.'

Ahead they could see an even darker mass against the black mountain face. The two scouts were already there. The three bearers moved up to join them, stealthily. As for noise, Chas was being over-cautious, Albert considered. The wind up here was too strong to let sound carry far.

'No more talking from now on.'

They reached the overhang. The ledge was narrow, they had to move on all fours. Jutting outcrops every so often meant they had to squirm underneath on their bellies. Behind him, Albert heard Pomfret swear softly.

'Chas should've asked one of them bloody Geordie miners for this caper, not me.'

'Ssh!'

They were halfway along when one of the scouts dislodged a rock. It thudded down the mountain face. Albert's heart was in his mouth as they waited for a cry from above. Surely that had woken their quarry?

Silence. They waited several long minutes. Eventually Chas indicated they were to proceed. Albert tugged at Pomfret's sleeve to warn him; infinitely carefully, they inched forward.

At the end of the overhang, Chas joined the scouts for a brief discussion. Hands gesticulated. Albert and Pomfret watched uneasily. The cold had spoiled Albert's enjoyment, making him shiver. He hoped old Pomf wouldn't notice. He wasn't frightened, of course – that was a silly idea! It was just that here he was, halfway up a mountain in the North-West Frontier when he could have been back home with Pol and Aunt Syb. Never mind, only two weeks to go!

The discussion finished the second scout collected one of the ammunition pouches plus a pack of firecrackers. He began to climb away out of sight. Chas rejoined them, looking slightly annoyed.

'There's been a change of plan. We're not where I'd hoped to be. The scouts have brought us up the opposite side, facing the lair rather than on the same side. I don't know why they've done it,' he sighed. 'You can't get any sense out of them sometimes. But it doesn't matter, we can still carry out the original plan.' He brightened. 'The second scout is taking me to a higher ledge, where I can look down even though it means I'll be further away. You two are headed up over there, to a cave. You'll be more or less opposite where our cove's hidden so see you keep your heads down.' Albert felt Pomfret stiffen.

'Doesn't sound very sensible to me.'

'Of course it is! It's black as pitch, he won't be able to see you at all. We'll be able to make just as much noise – it'll echo all round the mountains – sound as if the whole British Army *is* coming at him. It's the best we can do under the circumstances, anyway. When you're both ready, pass the word up and I'll give the signal. That's when you start the din. I'll be covering the lair. The minute he pops up his head . . .' Chas mimed firing a rifle.

Albert stared into the blackness. 'You'd have thought he'd have had a camp fire. It's a cold night.'

'He'll be damn well hidden,' Pomfret murmured with certainty. 'They always are.'

When they reached it, their cave was shallow, across a void and facing the saddle. Albert wriggled to the edge and looked up. There was another perch some twenty feet above the cave. To get to it, Chas would have to scramble across an exposed rock face. There was another serious problem, he realized; the moon was rising, casting a shadow over the col but revealing their side of the mountain in an increasing amount of silvery light. Pomfret saw it too.

'If there were twenty-five of us, we could've sent enough up the other side and sat tight and waited until we'd got him surrounded,' he hissed.

'There's no point in discussing it – we'll manage.' Like Chas, he was becoming impatient. Three to one? Why was old Pomf making such a fuss. The old soldier shrugged and moved away to his end of the cave.

The bearers were unpacking the pouches and loading spare rifles. After hurling the firecrackers, Albert and

235

Pomfret's orders were to fire directly into the lair, to chase the sniper out.

'Scare him silly, so he won't stop and think, he'll come charging straight out,' Chas had predicted confidently.

The fellow must be somewhere beneath that lip, thought Albert, peering into the darkness. If anything, impenetrable shadows opposite had deepened. He looked round for their scout in order to pinpoint the exact target area but he was nowhere to be seen.

Despite the caution, there were metallic clicks as the bearers continued to load. Albert told himself stoutly it didn't matter, they were too far away to be heard. The void might look only ten foot across but that was the effect of the darkness. He must throw each firecracker as hard as he could, to allow for the gusting wind. The bearers had divided the supply into two piles, his were beside his right hand.

He heard Pomfret's tiny whisper of, 'Ready, old chap?' Before Albert replied he wanted to reassure himself Chas was on the ledge. Once more he leaned out and stared up at the dark sky.

Above, the silhouette of the second scout was visible. Albert couldn't make out if Chas was there as well. Best stick to what he'd been told to do, he decided, otherwise he might keep the other two waiting. He flattened himself behind a rock and felt for his rifle before picking up the first firecracker. The signal was to be a whistle from Chas. That's when I can make as much noise as I like, he thought happily. Excitement began to build again, ridiculous and childish, 'I'll huff and I'll puff and I'll blow your house down!' he whispered to the invisible foe opposite.

Further down the cave, he could hear Pomfret ease himself into position nearer the edge. They were both crouched behind what cover there was among fallen slabs of stone. It was thrilling! Albert's heart began to thud once more. Opposite, their target area was still in Stygian blackness. Which reminded him, why hadn't he still seen the first scout?

A movement, slightly below and back along the route

they'd climbed, drew his eye. He could just make out the shape of a man – the Afghan who should have been beside him was actually running away! Or was he? For seconds Albert's thoughts were in chaos then, as he watched, the man appeared to be swerving away towards the opposite side of the mountain. Why?

The answer came as the moon rose another fraction, glinting on metal, not in the area of the supposed lair but several feet above, in an ideal position to fire down into their cave. That same instant, the situation became crystal clear to Albert: betrayal!

Without hesitating, he grabbed his rifle, aimed at where the glint had been, shouted and fired simultaneously.

'Chas! Look out! He's higher up.'

There was an answering volley from the opposite side, not one rifle but several. Astonished, Albert fired a second time automatically. Pomfret seized his weapon, screaming at him, 'Throw a torch, lad! Show us how many there are!'

Please God let it stay alight, thought Albert striking matches in a panic. Behind him he could hear the bearer exchange his empty rifle for a loaded one and the sound calmed him. These bearers had been in battle before, they knew what to do. It was no longer an adventure, he prayed again for his hand to stop shaking. Standing up quickly and at full stretch, he tossed the blazing torch high into the void.

For a frozen moment the blackness was illuminated. Dominating their position from a high ledge opposite was a group of men, wearing the flat *pakol*, now sinister rather than amusing, with rifles trained on their cave. Not one, but six or seven of them. Terror constricted Albert's throat!

The torch passed close enough to the group to dazzle them and two Pathans stepped back in alarm. Pomfret took careful aim. His shot brought an answering cry. The torch flickered and fell into the void. Following its track, Albert caught sight of the treacherous scout once more. He'd paused in his rush to join his comrades, and

237

kneeling, now lifted his rifle to his shoulder. He pointed at a spot above their cave. Chas! It broke the knot of terror and Albert screamed his name. Back from above came a reassuring shout.

'All right, young 'un. I've seen him.' As a bullet spat into the rocks Chas cried cheerfully, 'Missed!' before beginning the scramble down to the cave.

The torch had burnt out. Albert and Pomfret fired up into the blackness. Bullets were bouncing off on all sides now. Albert fired disjointedly. The heat burnt his palms. From his end of the cave, Pomfret kept up a much more accurate rate. Two of the bearers kept his guns reloaded while the third stayed with Albert. Pomfret saw Albert's erratic pattern; he must steady him otherwise ammunition would be wasted.

'Leave off firing and use the firecrackers, lad,' he ordered, 'Chuck 'em hard. Stun the bastards!' Wild with excitement, Albert was on his feet once more, the better to hurl them. Never mind how many there were, he'd scare those fuzzies all right!

Explosions ricochetted. One cracker landed on the ledge itself. It was enough for Pomfret to see a foot lit by the sparkle as one attempted to kick it away. He fired low and hit the target. There was a scream as the man clutched a shattered bone, lost his balance and toppled into the blackness.

A fall of stone and scree told them Chas had arrived, winded but calm. He knelt beside Pomfret, away from Albert's wild capering, and took the same careful aim. There was another choking cry.

'Six to go?'

'Five with luck,' said Pomfret. 'It was six, not seven to begin with, I think.'

'Sorry about this.'

'It's all right. Never trust a fellow in a flat hat, that's what I say.'

Albert's aim was improving, he'd found his length as he bowled across the void. When his own pile of crackers was exhausted, he rushed across and scooped up Pomfret's. He screamed occasionally as he leapt about and drew the opposing fire. He didn't care. He was seized with the lust of battle and nothing could frighten him.

The bearers were loading at full stretch. When the crackers were used up, Albert searched alone among the ammunition pouches for another missile. In the darkness, his fingers closed round a Mills bomb. Glory be – he mustn't muff this chance! Still jigging from foot to foot, he threw far too mightily at the high ledge.

The arc was wide but as the bomb exploded against a high rock, shattered pieces rained down on those below. Two men cried out as they were hit. Chas and Pomfret fired simultaneously at the sounds. Another screeching, a moan which faded as it disappeared into the void.

'Four?'

'Good man.' They had a rhythm now, firing sparingly, alternating their shots. Pomfret was enjoying himself, cursing between each volley. Albert crawled too close and threatened his aim, Pomfret yelled at him to stay clear. A hail of bullets followed but fell short. Chas muttered gleefully, 'I do believe the wind's in our favour at last.' He ordered, 'Hold your fire a moment.' They froze, every ear listening intently whilst from among the ammunition Albert now selected a grenade.

In the silence there came a crackling sound followed by a burst of flame. The enemy had turned the tables. Burning brushwood hurtled near enough to reveal their own positions clearly. Instantly bullets began reaching their mark. The first caught one of the bearers as he crouched to exchange rifles. He screamed and more bullets followed, killing him and injuring the second bearer. Chas and Pomfret jerked to the back of the cave for safety.

Albert stood, pulled the pin and bowled. This time his aim was true. The explosion, amplified by the deep rim of the mountains made them clutch at their ears, the shock wave brought down another rush of stone and rubble.

The silence that followed was profound. Pomfret eased his aching shoulder, red-hot from cradling the butt. Chas fired once, twice and waited. The remaining bearer tried to push a loaded rifle under his arm but he didn't take it, he listened instead.

There was no answering fire. He whispered an order. A flare was put into his hand. He lit it and held it high before flinging it into the air. The ledge appeared empty apart from inert bodies. There was no one living to fire back.

Was it over? In the silence Albert recognized a terrible truth: he'd killed. He'd never wanted to! Let the old queen find someone else to defend her from her enemies. He heard his own, wobbly voice. 'This wasn't a good idea after all, Chas!' From the other end of the cave came a cheerful roar as Pomfret staggered to his feet, his stiff knees creaking but full of delight at what had happened.

'Nonsense, monkey-nut. You've done very well indeed! That last effort – I reckon you saved our bacon ' But from below where the forgotten scout still crouched there came a sharp *crack!* Pomfret tottered forward and fell. The bullet with his name on it had found its mark.

Chas insisted they stay where they were until a relief party could reach them. He despatched the remaining bearer back to camp and kept up a steady rate of fire to keep the scout pinned down. Albert did what he could to make both wounded men comfortable. After that, all they could do was wait.

As the sun rose making an inferno of their shallow cave, flies came from nowhere to settle on the dead bearer. Sheltered by his comrade's body, the wounded man continued to moan softly. Gliding lazily on a rising thermal of air, a vulture circled lazily, watching unblinking, content to wait his turn.

Others on the ledge tore voraciously at dead flesh. Above, a cloud of flies buzzed over the corpse of the loyal scout while in the cave, Pomfret, the blood pumping from the wound in his shoulder, fought off death with bared teeth.

When there was enough light to make out the terrain, they saw that the treacherous scout had slipped away. Chas insisted they keep watch, there was a danger he'd gone for reinforcements.

In a tiny patch of shade, Albert fanned first the bearer

then Pomf. Tears ran unchecked. All the earlier excitement had disappeared. It wasn't like fox-hunting at all, it wasn't even an adventure, watching a friend die slowly. The dead bearer stared in sightless reproach, the death rictus making a gaping hole of his mouth – why now when in two weeks they could all go home?

Pomfret stirred and the pain bit hard. He swore; horrible obscene filth because he knew his life was ebbing. Albert knelt closer. Pomfret saw the tense young face, he tried to rally him. Macabre jokes rattled in his throat. Chas called abruptly for him to be quiet.

'What's the point . . . Not long . . .'

Chas crawled to the edge of the cave. There was no sign either of the enemy or of their relief. Shielding his eyes he forced himself to check the number of bodies on the ledge. Three. Was it two or three who'd fallen into the gorge? It made him dizzy peering over the edge – he couldn't make out any human debris. Maybe the Pathans had already collected their dead?

He risked standing up to stare at the distant plane. No bullet rent the silence but nor was there a trail of dust to indicate a marching column.

He and Albert made a screen with their tunics. They took it in turn to be lookout but at a whispered request from Pomfret, Chas moved further away and left Albert alone with his friend.

'Monkey-nut . . .'

'Yes, Pomf.'

'That girl . . . with the water-jar . . .'

'Yes?'

'There was . . . a bit more to it . . .' Albert thought there must have been. He waited.

'I sort of . . . held onto her hand . . . longer than necessary . . . Gave her a bit of a squeeze.'

'Yes.'

'She was . . . a good looker. I thought of giving her . . . a kiss . . . Never got that far. Pity, really. Lots of girls . . . I should have kissed . . .'

The pad on his shoulder was saturated. Albert had torn up his shirt, there was nothing else he could use. He wiped both hands on his trousers and flapped at the flies. Blood was everywhere now, so slippery underfoot he could scarcely risk moving. Tears splashed into the ever-increasing dark pool.

Pomfret stared upwards, straining to make out the familiar features. 'You still there, monkey-nut...?'

'Yes.' Albert reached for his friend's ice-cold hand. 'Right beside you.' He must keep their spirits up, Pomf was depending on him. 'It won't be long now.'

'No,' Pomfret agreed laconically. 'See you... kiss plenty ...of girls ...'

'Yes, I will.' He'd kiss every girl in the whole blessed world if they'd let him!

'Bye, old chap.'

'Hold on!' begged Albert but Pomfret didn't have the energy. It was too much effort to drag one more shallow breath into his body, too much pain. He closed his eyes against the damn flies; the day had become so dark, it was easier to sleep.

The lieutenant was meticulous over the wording of his report. Chas had to listen as he read each sentence aloud, twisting the words this way and that before committing them to paper, wringing each phrase dry of any misunderstanding. It only dawned very slowly that it wasn't style so much as content which so troubled the officer. How to convince Simla that there had been no lack of judgement.

'I don't think we need describe the exact *size* of the party... No need to detail who was included and who, er, left out.'

'There were three of us, Privates Unwin and Pomfret and myself, that was all,' Chas said stonily, 'accompanied by three bearers and two Afghan scouts, one of whom proved to be an accomplice of the enemy –'

'Precisely!' the lieutenant seized upon that as a pariah might snatch up offal. 'If we had but known we had a traitor in our midst, eh? I don't think we need go beyond that?'

'The enemy was apprised of our plan beforehand –'

'We cannot be certain of that!'

'And was thus in an advantageous position, well armed and awaiting our arrival.'

He couldn't write that! The officer looked at him angrily. Surely the corporal understood how much they both had to lose? The lieutenant's own position was critical.

'The trouble is, Corporal, will they understand? I mean, there they are in headquarters, and here you and I are, in the thick of it as it were ... with inadequate intelligence.' He sighed and shook his head. 'The trouble is, some *might* say the entire detachment should have gone to flush the sniper out.' He glanced up again but could read nothing in Corporal Unwin's expression.

'As far as I was concerned, acting upon the advice we then had ... and with which you agreed at the time, Corporal ... a party of three, well supported, appeared perfectly adequate. Why send twenty-five when three would do?' Chas spoke as if he hadn't heard.

'As soon as the scout had led us into the trap, he attempted to rejoin his comrades but didn't achieve his objective –'

'That's an assumption,' the lieutenant insisted. 'Now I'm not saying he didn't betray you. He must've done.' Even the lieutenant couldn't explain away six or seven well-armed tribesmen but he'd no intention of confessing to Simla that he had been relying on a traitor for intelligence. 'Is it not equally possible that scout might have had a change of heart and have been on his way to seek help when he disappeared?'

'Then why, sir, did he never arrive? The bearer got through but so far there has been no sign of that particular scout.'

'He may still be out there somewhere ... Wounded,' the lieutenant suggested lamely. He fiddled with his pen rather than meet the incredulous face.

'You haven't explained satisfactorily, sir, why the scout continued to fire at *us* rather than the enemy?'

'Don't be impertinent!'

'And why he then fired the bullet which fatally wounded Private Pomfret –'

243

'We cannot be certain it was he who fired it! It could have been one of the enemy.'

It *was* the enemy, Chas wanted to shout. Instead he said quietly, 'Doctor McPhaill has seen the wound, sir. He can verify that it was fired from below and not above.'

Unless he turned out to be a treacherous bastard as well?

He realized that when it came to saving one's own hide, an officer had more expertise than an NCO. In his head he heard a familiar cynical voice: 'Never admit the possibility of a mistake, old son, otherwise you'll end up the scapegoat.' It was Pomfret.

Well this had been a colossal mistake. They'd lost three men and the pass was still under threat.

'Should we not ask for reinforcements, sir?' The lieutenant flung down his pen.

'That's a virtual admission of incompetence – I shall do no such thing! I don't know what you expect to gain, Corporal? It's perfectly obvious to me that with a modicum of care on our part this report will satisfy Simla and we can proceed on our way . . .'

'But the pass is still under threat.'

'If there were to be a fresh outbreak of unrest after we had left it need not be connected with what happened, nor be deemed our fault. I shall claim that we *successfully* killed the sniper plus the natives alongside him – that much nobody can deny. I shall add that *nobody* escaped.' Chas was silent. 'Come on, speak up. What's wrong with that? No one will ever know. You can surely rely on your brother?'

'Private Pomfret was killed, sir.'

'He died, certainly.' That couldn't be denied, the burial party was due to assemble within the hour but to the lieutenant this was an additional advantage: dead men rarely talked.

'My brother and I are applying for our discharge. Sir.' The officer lost his temper.

'One more remark like that, Corporal, and you will be on a charge. You have my word!'

'Yessir.' Chas stood smartly to attention.

244

'A discharge is out of the question while the unrest continues. All such requests are suspended pending the arrival of our relief . . . Look here, surely you and I can put our heads together like sensible fellows? What should have been a straightforward exercise turned out to be a slight mishap.'

'Especially for Private Pomfret and two of the bearers.'

Bearers? The lieutenant turned choleric. What had bearers to do with anything?

'Corporal, you are dismissed!'

'Sir!' Chas saluted and clicked his heels. 'Private Pomfret had a saying . . .' This bastard wasn't going to prevent him repeating it. 'He used to say the British army was made up of idiots ordered about by fools . . . and if ever the idiots realized this, it would be all over for the bloody fools.'

That afternoon as well as completing his report the lieutenant recorded the burial of 60749 Pte S.R. Pomfret whose next of kin had been informed and that Corporal 74487 Unwin C.J. had been reduced to the ranks.

Sadly, no one in Simla was interested. Rumours of unrest now emerging from South Africa were occupying their full attention.

In less than a month, the camel trains were once more held to ransom. The pass needed permanent policing but the regiment was moved back to Amritsar. It all seemed so pointless. Chas's pride in his marksmanship faded. As for Albert, he still grieved. Pomfret had been the tough old oak to whom he'd clung for so long.

He would wake screaming of blood. When a cloud of cockchafers descended, he wanted to run from the sight and smell of the heaving, glistening black insects, for they reminded him far too vividly of those fly-blown bodies on the ledge. He wasn't sure what the future held but he wanted to go home. Eventually the army obliged.

The original detachment decided they would arrange a celebration before they left Delhi, where the regiment was due to split up; a farewell to arms for those returning and a toast to the memory of Pomf. The loveliest creatures from the European community would be persuaded to attend, and Chas and Albert encouraged to drown their sorrows.

Albert became drunk very quickly. He sat peacefully in a corner until some of his colleagues noticed and carried him back with them to the barracks. Chas was left to his own devices. He returned the following morning with minutes to spare before Reveille and it was noticeable in the days that followed that although Albert was once more chirpy Chas continued to be downcast.

On the voyage, he was still moody. Albert couldn't understand it. Why be sad now when they would soon see Polly? This episode was over, he and Chas had survived. 'Onwards and upwards'. Hang the future! They could worry about that later.

In vain did Albert call on Chas to come and watch flying fish, sparkling like jewels, skimming over the waves, leading them back to England. Chas ignored every happy shout and lay in his bunk.

Once ashore they were confined to the barracks at Chatham (where the authorities intended they should use up their pay in the camp stores) but nothing could stifle Albert's spirits nor, apparently, lift Chas's depression.

Four days before their release, a letter arrived. The envelope was scented and the inscription in lavender ink. Chas read it, groaned, and tossed it aside.

'Oh God, she's found me! I thought I was rid of her at last . . .'

'What's up?'

'Don't you understand? This is what's been bothering me. Read it for yourself.' The letter was short.

'My dearest Chas,' Albert began. Dearest? He looked at Chas whose face was thoroughly miserable.

'I took ship the week following our fateful meeting and by enquiry, discovered our arrival was but a few days ahead of your own, at Tilbury. My family welcomed me there as heartily as ever, especially when I told them the Glad Tidings!

'Today Papa has been to London to find out when you

246

are due to be discharged. The military were able to advise him. Imagine our joy when we learned it is to be on Friday next!

'He and Mama will be at the barrier at Waterloo, with their brother Francis and family, together with their baby, all of them eager to meet my dearest boy, as indeed am I! Until then therefore, I remain,

Your loving Connie.'

Albert was dumbfounded. 'Your loving Connie!' Chas reached across, took the letter and said bitterly,

'It'll be my Waterloo, all right. Notice how she's mobilized every single relative? I shall be taken prisoner at the barricade and marched off to begin my life sentence.'

'But who on earth . . .'

'She was the sister of one of the sergeant's wives at Delhi. Constance Sprat.'

A filly? With excellent calves?

'You never said?'

'It was the night of the party when we both got drunk.'

'What happened!' Albert shook him. 'Quick, tell me about it!'

'They took you back because you were incapable. They left me behind and I come over all sleepy. Remember the women who were there?'

Albert only had the vaguest memory. He shook his head.

'Well one of 'em, Connie, she was the oldest,' Chas said callously. 'She asked, why didn't I kip down for a bit? Seemed like a good idea at the time. I could scarcely keep my eyes open. She knew her way around because she was staying there with her sister and brother-in-law. She took me to one of the upstairs rooms – which turned out to be hers only I didn't know that at the time – and helped me into her own bed.'

'Golly!'

'I didn't know! I thought she was being . . . well, helpful. We'd been chatting for a bit. She told me she'd been in Delhi for four months . . . she'd got her passage home booked. I reckon I was her last chance!' Chas burst

247

out. 'Most of the rest of the chaps seemed to know her well enough – I should've known. I reckon she'd been offering herself around the regiment.'

'Chas!' He'd never heard him so bitter.

'I was properly caught, young 'un. You got to swear you'll never let it happen to you for I couldn't bear to think that it might! When I woke up, there she was, beside me. With most of her clothes off.'

Albert's eyes bulged.

'She was calling out, "Not to worry, Annie. This dear boy hev promised to marry me." That's when I saw she was talking to her sister in the doorway. The sergeant was standing right behind her. I tell you, bor, I didn't hev no chance.'

'Then what happened?'

'She and her sister both scarpered. The sergeant made me swear I'd behave honourably before he let me have me trousers. He asked what would happen if Connie had a baby? Honestly Albert, I swear I never touched her. I mean, I didn't even fancy her that much,' he pleaded. Albert was still too shocked to respond. 'She just seemed – kind – and with me head splitting it seemed easier to let her help me off with me tunic – but that was all she took off. The trouble is, I don't remember what happened after. Surely I would've?' Albert couldn't help. He wasn't altogether certain of the performance of nature's mystery.

'What did you tell the sergeant?' Chas looked at him pitifully.

'I agreed to marry her, dammit!'

'Oh, Chas!'

'What else could I do? It was obvious they wasn't going to let me go. They'd been hoping to nab someone for dear Connie ever since she landed. Remember how the captain kept on trying to force me to sign on again?'

'Yes?'

'That was the sergeant's doing. He wants me under his thumb, where he can keep an eye on me. He knows I loathe the sight of her now. When I said I was applying for my discharge, he warned me not to try and "avoid my responsibilities".'

248

'Connie promised to write as soon as she got to London ... which she has ... I was hoping she might have given up.' Chas groaned more miserably than before. 'Some chance! I'm her "dearest boy" and she's hanging on like glue! She's that much older, Albert ... and she's got a mole on the side of her nose.'

'So what are you going to do?'

'Do a bunk.' Albert's eyes widened. They were to be paid the balance of what they were owed on the day of their release, not before.

'It could mean losing our pay!' Chas cried in despair.

'I know but I daren't wait. Can you lend me any? I only need a few quid.'

'Where are you going?'

'America.' Albert gasped. 'Where Irish's sister went, to Iowa. D'you remember how his relatives had found work out there? I shall ask him to write. I should be able to find something, it's farming country.'

'I'll come with you –'

'No, Albert. This time, I'm going on my own.'

The argument went on for hours. In the end they reached a compromise. Albert would not go to America but he would, like Chas, do a bunk.

'I shall have to,' he insisted, 'if I'm to help you to get some cash – you can't go to America without. You'd starve.'

'You'll forfeit your pay – and they might come after you. At least they won't catch up with me.'

' 'Tweren't that much,' Albert said bravely, considering that money was the only prospect he had. 'I shall earn some more soon. How much d'you reckon you'll need?'

'Dunno. I'll ask Irish.'

After consultation it was decided that £15.0.0d was the minimum sum for Chas to reach his chosen destination.

'I know how to get you that much,' Albert said mysteriously.

'You weren't planning on doing anything silly, like stealing?'

' 'Course not, I shall borrow it.' Chas's face fell. They didn't know anyone with that amount.

'I shall ask Aunt Syb.' If he hadn't been so distraught, Chas would have laughed but Albert said solemnly. 'She's got savings.'

'She won't give a penny to either of us!'

'I shall tell her it's a loan.'

'She's too mean.'

'I shall persuade her somehow. Now, if we're bunking off, where d'you suggest we hide?'

Another of their original cabin-mates, the Geordie miner, offered a possible solution: his brother was in London working as an ostler in a mews in Fulham. Maybe he could provide accommodation, over the stables?

Chapter Seventeen

Coming Home

Polly moved her heavy body awkwardly from room to room. She was tired but she had to see over the house and be away again before she and Henry were observed. There would be trouble enough once they decided to take it.

Strange they'd stayed so long at Willow End before finding a permanent home. At first they'd been reluctant to stir, content to let the dust settle after the upheaval of their marriage. Then the sowing season came round and Henry had been fully occupied with his seedlings. Polly declared herself content at being among nice neighbours – why not delay their search until next year?

The truth was they were still shy of gossip. Sybilla had made such a laughing stock of them all; for months, humiliation lingered and rankled. They'd only to walk forth into the town for laughter to begin anew.

After that inertia set in; why move while they had no children? Secretly, Polly was relieved. She wasn't sure she wanted a family. Suppose she had a boy who looked like Henry? With thinning hair and a pinched face on a frosty morning? There was another, deeper worry: Polly couldn't rid herself of the memory of the tiny, skinny dead baby in Sybilla's kitchen. Supposing she had one like that?

She'd summoned up courage to visit Ma Figgis in the early days of her marriage. She wanted confirmation that Henry's was acceptable behaviour. He was forever demanding to touch her body, to see it naked, by

251

candlelight. Naturally, Polly felt embarrassed, any respectable girl would. She consulted her Bible and became ever more worried. Was her new husband misbehaving like the 'beasts of the field'? She'd no idea. Eventually, unquiet in both mind and body, Polly decided she had to find out. It was a measure of her isolation that since her marriage there was no one else she could turn to.

Fortunately the old woman had taken pity on her. Far better Polly came to her now than wait until she became pregnant. The mysteries of procreation were revealed and, after a glance at Polly's set face, a few simple ways of lessening the chance of having a child.

'Don't always work, mind you,' Ma Figgis warned. 'Nature has nasty ways of making you fall when you least wants it. 'Tis her way of ensuring there's a sufficiency. There's only one way to stop babbies coming, my dear, that's to say "No".' She waited in vain for some response from Polly.

'I daresay you'll be wanting a little one though, you and your handsome man?' Polly's reaction this time had been a small, cold sniff. Not a passionate nature, Ma Figgis decided; a contained little maid. It was a wonder she'd been the choice of Henry Durrant who could've taken his pick. Ma Figgis knew very well who'd been after him; it had given the town the best laugh they'd had for ages.

She watched Polly walk away and wondered why a child might be unwelcome. By all accounts the couple were comfortably off. Perhaps the girl was afeared? Some women were and with good reason, birth for them could be a terrifying ordeal. Ma Figgis bit into one of the biscuits Polly had brought. Maybe the new Mrs Durrant took after her aunt? Now there was a woman who couldn't bear the very idea . . . Which was understandable, when you recollected she was married to Enoch Porrit.

As she picked her way along the muddy street, Polly was preoccupied. Henry was within his rights apparently, it was all part of being one flesh. Ma Figgis had even hinted

252

that some women enjoyed love-making. Polly supposed her parents must have done – they'd always appeared so happy. Odd to think of her father behaving like Henry but she'd been assured there was no other way of conceiving or of making love. Polly sighed. Somehow the idea of babies arriving spontaneously in a bag or under a bush had been much more acceptable. She now knew if she were unfortunate enough to become pregnant she'd have to endure an aching back and swollen legs. Ma Figgis had described the disadvantages plainly. And at the end of it, all Polly could expect was a small human being whose demands would be endless. Someone who would dominate every aspect of her life. It wasn't an attractive prospect.

Perhaps, had she known of Polly's fears, Ma Figgis might have tempered her descriptions. As it was, these weighed heavily. If saying 'no' was the only sure way to avoid the disaster of pregnancy, then so be it; Henry would have to do without.

There had been times when they searched for a house. It fell to Henry to take the initiative, which slightly annoyed him. To his way of thinking women should be home-makers, eager to find a nest.

Had he stuck to his original plan, of course, the house would have come first, then the wife. By now he was experiencing the occasional doubt – how different things might have been had he waited. Would he have proposed, for instance, had he known of Polly's frigidity?

His thoughts began to veer towards the unpleasant. Had she 'led him on', deliberately frightening him with talk of Sybilla, Widow Helliwell and Mrs Heyhoe in order to become married herself. Did she care for him at all?

When he reached this point, Henry shied away from any conclusion. Perhaps her feelings would change, given time? If only they could have a child! His yearning for one was deep but he scarcely referred to it, for fear of upsetting her.

Once, determined to know her mind, he had taken her as far as Thetford where new property was being built.

253

Polly agreed the houses looked very nice, but ... They discussed their requirements in desultory fashion; a bit of garden and at least three bedrooms. Polly believed Chas and Albert would return and when they did, they would obviously live with her, although she hadn't confided this to Henry. Finally she declared she would know the right house when she saw it. With that Henry had to be content.

The morning Ma Figgis confirmed the disagreeable news of her pregnancy, Polly's thoughts began to clarify. What she'd wanted all along was to set up in rivalry to her aunt. That was it! A house on the London road offering cream teas, far more delicious than those for which Aunt Syb charged so much. Polly knew she was a superior cook. When word got round as to the excellence of her scones, customers would flock to her tables and desert Sybilla.

It would mean a lot of extra work, especially with a child to care for. At the back of her mind was the wish to be independent once more. Being Mrs Durrant was still nice, but Polly remembered wistfully when everyone had praised her cooking. Henry scarcely noticed what he ate. He was anxious to pet and make a fuss of her person but that, to Polly's mind, wasn't the same. Her body was as God made it and not to be referred to, Cook's magazines had been adamant on that.

However, first things first: Henry held the purse-strings. She would have to tread carefully if she were to persuade him, for she knew he would be against the notion.

It was Ma Figgis who'd first set her thinking of it. 'Now's the time for you to get what you want out of your man,' she'd advised. 'You can twist 'em round your little finger for a week or two. After that ... when the novelty's worn off, don't be surprised if he don't begin to wander. Turn a blind eye, that's my advice. They come running back when the babby's due, 'specially the first one.'

She recollected of whom she spoke. 'Your man being older than some, he might stay loyal, my dear. He probably won't bother you, neither, not while you're carrying. Some of 'em's that selfish, you wouldn't believe!'

Henry had been overwhelmed. He stuttered and beamed his delight and declared they must now find a home. No more living in this pokey one-bedroomed affair. Polly capitulated gracefully and promptly. She said 'Yes, dear,' which fairly bowled him over. For the first time since they'd married, he was truly, blissfully happy.

Over the years Henry's initial eager desires had become dulled, only fanned into gratitude by her occasional kindness. Out of loyalty, he would have denied regretting his one impulsive act, but out of genuine frustration there were times when he sought the consolation of his garden.

With the announcement of her pregnancy, however, everything changed. Regrets, past recriminations were swept aside. He wanted to cheer, he was speechless, he begged Polly to repeat what she'd just said, fearing he'd misheard.

'Three months gone, Ma Figgis reckons.'

'Shouldn't you ... please, will you visit the doctor, Polly. I should like you to have the best advice and attention.' She shrugged.

'If you like. She knows more about babies than he do, though. She's delivered plenty.' Polly busied herself scrubbing the parsnips Henry had dug, hiding her face so he shouldn't see her panic. This came in waves, making her hands shake as she thought of the perils to come. Never mind babies dying, women died having them!

'My dearest love ...' Henry felt her go rigid under his touch. He despaired. Even now, bearing the fruit of his love, she obviously found him repugnant.

Polly wished he would soothe away her fears. She waited for his arms to encircle her tightly and smother every anxiety, it was such a fragile, tenuous thing this business of loving. She was scared of relinquishing her defences, at being swallowed up by Henry yet at the same time she was eager to confess how frightened she was. Behind her, Henry waited, keen for the smallest indication of affection but Polly gave nothing away. He moved, to put a space between them so that she could relax.

'We shall have to find another house right away,' he said formally. 'I want you to have plenty of time to make yourself comfortable there. Perhaps, if you feel up to it my dear, we could begin our search this weekend?'

At the sink, Polly sagged with disappointment. Henry, alert, thought he saw tension begin to fade. He was so dispirited that she should continue feel like this.

'Have you had any further thoughts where we might begin our search?'

'Yes, I've decided exactly where I'd like to live. If we could find a nice little house on the London road.'

'But that would mean . . . We shan't be able to avoid . . . Mr and Mrs Porrit . . .' As usual, embarrassment made him stutter.

'I shan't mind. You never know, Aunt Syb might come round when she hears about the baby.' It was so unlikely he was about to protest but held back, remembering pregnant women had to be humoured.

'Whatever you think best, Polly. I shall be content with whichever you choose . . . A home for – our son!' The wonderful words were uttered at last. 'Oh, Polly, I'm so happy!'

It was true, she could see it. Now was the moment for her to reach out. Instead, she said in a gruff small voice, 'Don't count the chicken afore 'tis hatched, Henry. It could turn out to be a girl – and we might both die.'

'No! Please don't even think of such a thing! Promise me you'll visit the doctor, Polly. Oh no account should Mrs Figgis be relied upon. You must have the best care possible.' His concern warmed her. She smiled briefly.

'If it'll set your mind at rest, Henry.'

'It will, indeed!'

'I shall go to the doctor tomorrow then. And we shall find ourselves a house this weekend.'

It wasn't that easy. Polly was almost into her seventh month before a suitable dwelling became vacant. Now she and Henry were viewing it. He was ecstatic over the sanitary arrangements, calling excitedly, 'The water

closet has the latest scientific movement, The Comet!'
Polly listened absent-mindedly as water flushed through
the pipes. It was the size and scope of the front garden
which interested her. This was nothing but a tangled mass
of brambles at present.

'Henry, could you come a minute.' He hurried downstairs, breathless and anxious.

'What's the matter? Are you unwell? Here . . .' He dusted
the window cill with his handkerchief. 'Do sit and rest,
Polly. As soon as you feel up to it, I shall take you home.'

'That front garden . . . d'you think you could make a
lawn in the middle of it.' His ideas had been entirely
different.

'I was thinking of beds of sweet-smelling flowers, Polly,
so that you'd have fragrance as you walked about . . .'
When you are nursing our child was what he wanted to
say, but he was so anxious not to frighten her.

'I'd rather have a lawn. As big as you can make it.' She
hadn't told him about the cream teas but she wanted an
area big enough for four tables because Aunt Syb only had
three. Henry hid his disappointment.

'Just as you wish, my love.'

'With flowers round the edges.' It had to be pretty
enough to attract customers.

'You are quite sure this is the house you want?' he
asked, again. From the parlour bay window, it was painfully obvious they would be living across from Sybilla and
Enoch Porrit. 'There is another property a little further
out. Not too far to push the perambulator. There are trees,
the air would be purer.' Anxious he shouldn't think she
wasn't pleased, she squeezed his arm and smiled.

'This'll be perfect. There's a lovely bedroom for the
baby . . .' and two boxrooms for when Chas and Albert
come to stay. 'Please Henry, we can afford it, can't we?'
That smile was all it needed to warm every fibre: Henry
glowed.

'Of course we can!' He had earned his reward.

'Give us a kiss, then.'

It took Albert two days to reach the outskirts of Suffolk for he didn't want to waste money on fares. He completed part of the journey in empty farm waggons, travelling north from Covent Garden. After that, he went east, cross-country, sometimes walking, occasionally hitching a lift, savouring the scents and flavours so long denied him. Chas remained in London, seeking information about his passage. They'd decided it needed only one of them to tackle Sybilla.

On the last stage, after alighting in a pink-streaked dawn at Downham Market and bidding his latest benefactor farewell, Albert struck out on the last stage, following the softly flowing Wissey for a mile or two. The landscape changed subtly, becoming increasingly familiar. When the first lonely squat flint cottage appeared almost furtively from behind a clump of alders, it was enough to bring a lump to Albert's throat: he was nearly home!

He inhaled the sharpness of furze and wild thyme until his lungs could take no more. Arriving at a sandy gash in the landscape, he pulled off boots and socks to enjoy the powdery earth seeping between his toes. There was a choice of secret tracks ahead, each one threading mysteriously between ancient gnarled trees, paths wide enough for one man but never two.

Albert was conscious of how unused he was to being alone. There'd always been comrades on either flank. Here was only silence. The isolation threatened his unconscious whistling. He hadn't been on his own for over eight years – it was enough to make anyone nervous.

Thrusting trepidation aside, he began to walk rhythmically, looking neither to left nor right. A superstition arose that the Old 'Uns had formed a ghostly army round about, whooping to warn their loved ones that it had been a successful day's hunting. Would he stumble across a group of thatched huts in a glade with smoke rising through the roof holes? Would the natives here be friendly?

Albert laughed and tried to whoop himself. It turned into a croak as a movement caught his eye. A forester had moved out from the shadows to discover who the noisy fool could be. His face was grim at the thought of a poacher. Albert forced himself to smile and bid the man a cheery good-day before pressing on.

He rested on a bank of ferns, watching a squirrel amass her winter store in the branches above. His future would have to be settled by the time the cold weather arrived. What sort of work should he look for? He could turn his hand to many tasks thanks to the army. He could survive provided he had somewhere warm and snug to live.

Albert wasn't ambitious. If he'd been in a pickle because of a young lady, he might have done a bolt like Chas, but it would never have occurred to him to go to America. He wished Chas wasn't so set on the idea. If only he hadn't been so foolish. Miss Constance Spratt might have turned out to be all right, given half a chance ... It was Albert's nature to think kindly of everyone until they proved unworthy. His eyelids closed and for an hour or two he slept.

When he awoke it was time to smarten himself. He was covered in dust after his march and coming across a reed-fringed lake he stripped and dived in. It was icy cold! He surfaced with a yelp that had resident birds lifting in a frenzy. They circled and spiralled as Albert surged up and down the lake, exhilarating in his renewed vigour.

He shaved with his sliver of a mirror propped up on a fallen tree, watched by returning crossbills. He took care to brush his clothes. The army had made him self-sufficient and neat. It hadn't diminished his perky, enquiring manner. Now, almost back to where he had begun the great adventure, a spring returned to Albert's step. He glanced about keenly and covered the last half-mile at a jaunty speed. He would enter through his aunt's back garden gate, the same way he'd departed.

Sybilla was in the kitchen. She looked up to see a young man emerging from behind her privy. She was about to grab her rolling pin – hawkers and tinkers were never welcome – when something stayed her hand. It wasn't his clothes, they were smart. His boots shone beneath the layer of dust and the confident angle of the cap wasn't that of a beggar, nor the neckerchief – but who the devil was it?

Albert saw her frozen stare and grinned; she didn't recognize him! My word, but she had changed as well! Physically she was the same; a little stouter perhaps but, in his opinion, that was no bad thing. It emphasized the square shape of her face, however, as did the tight bun, which was a pity; Aunt Syb had been almost pretty when the silvery fair hair hung in curls.

Her high-necked blouse glistened fresh and crisp in the morning air. She hadn't lowered her standards, she was smarter than he remembered. A handsome woman his aunt, not to say formidable. That hard tight expression was harsher though? He refused to let even this unease threaten his mood. He moved forward with a smile, confident of a welcome provided Enoch Porrit wasn't at home.

It didn't occur to Sybilla that it could be Albert. He'd been a skinny little boy. This was a wiry young man, not tall but fit and muscular, his face burnt brown by the sun, with an easy-going, assured manner. It disturbed her to think she should know him yet couldn't think of the name when suddenly the man called out, 'It's me, Aunt Syb. I'm home,' and the bright blue eyes were immediately Jeremiah's!

She felt guilty and angry in the same instant. Without stopping to consider, she cried harshly, 'Come back like a bad penny, I see?'

Albert hesitated. 'You're going to make me welcome, I hope?'

'Why should I?'

He refused to be disappointed. Still smiling politely he chided, 'Give over, Aunt Syb. You're pleased to see me after all these years? Where's Polly?'

By way of answer, she spat. A full mouthful of spittle that landed in the earth at his feet, startling him with its ferocity.

'Gone to the devil for all I care!' He covered the last few yards and gripped her arm.

'Don't you ever speak of my sister like that, d'you hear! Don't you dare!' He took a deep breath to calm himself. 'Now, give me a civil answer, woman. Where is she? I know she's married.'

He'd shaken her. In the old days, Albert would never have dared take such liberties. Sybilla looked pointedly at his hand. Slowly, he released it. Still perfectly cool, he repeated, 'I asked you a question, Aunt Syb.'

'What of it.' There was obviously a lingering hatred against Polly, Albert couldn't understand it.

'What's the matter with you? Can't you even tell me where they live?'

'Where they've always lived. Down Willow End.'

'That's all right then.' It had been a long time since Polly's last letter. Even though he didn't understand Syb's attitude, he decided to leave the sensitive subject. After all, he'd come here to ask a favour, for Chas's sake, he had to succeed. 'It's you I come to see. Ain't you going to ask me inside?'

Hostile, guilty over remembered wrong-doing, above all nervous because of his unruffled demeanour, Sybilla Porrit stood back to let him enter. Whistling to himself, Albert examined the kitchen, measuring it against his memory.

'I always thought of this as such a big room . . . it ain't though, it's tiddly. Table's still in the same place, I see. That ceiling's so low though!'

She wanted to reach out to him in some way. Instead, she said flatly, 'You've grown.'

'Very true. Is *he* in?' He could see by her expression Enoch wasn't. Good. Without waiting to be invited, Albert sat and stretched out his legs. 'It's good to be back, Aunt Syb. Ain't you missed me and Chas?' He'd given her another opportunity but again Sybilla didn't take it.

'Where is Chas? Didn't he come with you?'

'Stayed behind in London. On business.' Albert was deliberately vague. 'I come on me own.' He might as well get on with it. 'I got a request to make.' Already? Sybilla's chin went up and good intentions were ignored.

'You got a nerve,' she sneered. 'Just because you've

been away I suppose you expects me to make you welcome now, feed you, give you a room –'

'No, no, nothing like that. I know you has to earn your crust. I don't suppose *he's* supporting you any better? And I ain't planning to stay, nor burden you. Besides, this is too small for me. I has to make my way in the world. London's the place for that.' Albert didn't notice the effect these words had. 'We've done with the army, Chas and me. We've seen a bit of the world . . . India's a big place . . . and we've had our share of trouble. I've come home. Chas though, he wants to see some more before he settles down. He needs a bit of financial assistance.'

He glanced up for the first time since he'd begun. His cheerfulness vanished; was his appeal going to fail? He said with careful emphasis, 'We've learned how to be business-like, Chas and me . . . We'll sign a bit of paper . . . pay interest, do things properly –'

'How much?'

'Fifteen pounds.'

'Seven per cent.' It was worse than unreasonable, it was outrageous. Albert controlled his temper.

'You're a hard woman, Aunt Syb.'

'Take it or leave it, it makes no difference to me.' He'd have to take it, there was no one else. He nodded, reluctantly.

'When d'you want it?'

'Tomorrow.'

'I shall have to go to Thetford. Come back about noon. Use the garden gate, no reason the neighbours should know you're here.'

And that was it. No invitation to stay, no enquiry as to his well-being, no suggestion he might like a meal. She was treating him like a fugitive! If he'd come out of prison that morning, she couldn't have been more unwelcoming. His aunt wasn't just hard, she was damned mean! Albert squared up to her.

'I'll not trouble you further, I'll be off to see Polly. She's a married woman now.'

This was said pleasantly enough but the very mention

of Polly's name brought the same response as previously. Sybilla's face contorted. She muttered through clenched teeth. 'Much good may it do her.' Albert slipped the strap onto his shoulder and hefted his pack onto his back.

'What's up?' he demanded. 'You never used to take against her so. She was the only one of us you treated decent. Gawd knows she worked hard enough to please you . . .' The face opposite was rigid. He asked again, 'Has Polly done summat to upset you then?' Again there was no reply. He waited a moment longer. Finally he spoke his mind openly.

'You've become too hard, Aunt Syb. It don't become you. Father would have been sad to see it, truly he would. I don't know whether 'tis Porrit's doing . . . if so, he'll have to answer for it. But I'll have no quarrel with you, so don't act bitter with me, if you please. I respects you and always shall, till you give me cause to do otherwise. I asks that you do the same. Chas and me, we took ourselves off, like you wanted. Took me a while to realize you must have been encouraging us all along.'

Sybilla opened her mouth to deny it but he jumped in quickly. 'You'd no business to let a mere boy go on such a mad caper . . . Thank your lucky stars no harm come of it.' He made a leisurely business of putting his cap back on and adjusting the angle.

'If you think we ought to be grateful that you took us in, think again. I reckon you got more'n your pound of flesh in return. I ain't feared of you no more, Aunt Syb. Nor of Enoch Porrit. Neither is Chas. We've killed men out in India . . . We didn't enjoy it. 'Twas army orders. But just you remember that next time you wants to say summat hurtful. You can tell Uncle Porrit too if he imagines he can still take off his belt an' leather us. There was two frightened boys left this house . . . there's two grown men come back. Men who is peaceable unless they're provoked.

'I shall come back tomorrow and sign the paper. For Chas's sake, I thank you for agreeing to lend him the money. I'm sorry to have to ask you for it but 'tis business and you'll not suffer by it; you'll gain all that interest. As

263

Chas is going away, I shall see you gets the money and he can repay me when he comes back.'

Albert paused, wondering if she might soften and suggest a lower rate. Sybilla remained silent. 'You shall have all the money back as fast as I can earn it, you have my word.' He swung off down the garden path, stopping only to inhale the fragrance of a rose. Sybilla stood staring after him.

She'd been too harsh; her sluggish conscience roused itself for once and pricked her self-esteem. But Albert didn't understand how much she had suffered, her mind blustered! Losing Henry Durrant like that – Polly was nothing but a sly little minx . . . Over and over, the same conviction churned – Henry was still hers – Sybilla refused to let go of the notion. It was what kept her going when Enoch was at his most hateful, or when he stole from her purse. If only Henry Durrant had waited; sooner or later she might have been free to become his wife. That same obstinate streak that helped her survive and kept her daydreams alive was active once more. Unfortunately, it was also selective. Sybilla chose to forget how she'd made a fool of herself. Polly had stolen her best hope; she should be made to pay.

Albert was more than a little shaken. It had been his habit, if not Chas's, to embrace and enlarge the few happy childhood memories he had retained. In eight years he'd had plenty of time to think and had infused each recollection with a roseate glow: surely Syb hadn't been *that* unkind? Oh, but she had! Now he stripped away sentimentality and anger filled the vacuum.

It must have been burdensome for a young bride faced with three unwanted children but they had tried very hard to please her. He recalled the anxious conferences as he, Chas and Polly sought courage from one another to face the cruelty of Enoch. Perhaps that was the explanation; living with Porrit had coarsened Syb.

Sustaining anger wasn't part of Albert's nature. His natural optimism rose as he walked about the town, marvelling at the changes. There were plenty of new houses, most with a neat panel set into the flint and brick containing the name and date. He took a particular fancy to 'Lime Tree Villa 1896' which was so new the builder hadn't yet planted any lime trees, he noticed.

It came to him suddenly, he'd like a house like that. With a dear little wife eager to welcome him. My word! Laughter bubbled inside. Imagine such extravagance – Albert Unwin, esquire – it was ridiculous, he'd never be able to afford it. Nevertheless the idea left him elated. No doubt about it, the town was flourishing. His town! Forget India, this was the best spot in the world! Wildly happy now, Albert looked into each passing face, searching for childhood friends. Any he recognized were treated to a joyous reunion.

By the time he arrived at Willow End, he was in a mood of high expectancy, the sour taste of Sybilla clean forgotten. He knocked boldly. There was no need, the door wasn't locked but he waited until he heard Polly's slow step. He couldn't wait for her to undo the latch. 'It's me, Pol – I'm back!' The door creaked as she pulled it open. He saw how shadowy her eyes were, then how swollen her body.

'Albert!' Polly's face was ecstatic. She looked over his shoulder at the empty garden path. 'Is Chas with you?'

'No, I'm on my own but he's all right. He's in London ... Pol – are you going to have a baby?' He stared excitedly at her face. Immediately he saw the fear.

'Me and Mr Durrant are expecting a little stranger,' she said, awkwardly formal, as though distancing herself from the inevitability. Then happiness obliterated everything else. Polly clung to him tightly. 'Oh, Albert, I'm so glad to see you again!'

When Henry returned, it was to find his wife ecstatic and a healthy, bronzed young stranger occupying his chair. The room was full of contented tobacco smoke. Polly, laughing at some joke, was moving between kitchen and living room carrying a heavy tray.

'Polly – put that down at once!' Henry hadn't meant to sound abrupt. It was jealousy although he didn't recognize it. 'You know you shouldn't do such a thing,' he ordered. 'Please, my love, let me take that tray –' She cut across his next words.

'You remember my brother, Albert?' The handsome ex-soldier was on his feet, beaming at him. All Henry could remember was a ragged unprepossessing little lad.

'Pleased, I'm sure.' Henry tried to be more friendly. 'You've been in India, I believe . . . When d'you go back?' That popped out before he could stop himself. Albert laughed.

'I've left the army for good.'

Henry had been full of news. He'd been planning all day how to tell Polly the glad tidings, anticipating her delighted reaction. She'd be so pleased she'd fall into his arms . . . Instead, he was expected to exchange politenesses with an unwanted relative.

'I've managed to secure the house, Polly.'

'Oh, Henry, I am glad!' She sparkled but it was to Albert that she spoke. 'This place is too small. We've found a much nicer house. We shall be moving as soon as Henry can arrange it.'

'Quite a decent little property,' Henry thrust himself back into the conversation. 'Three bedrooms. Latest in er – water closet fitments. On the London road.'

'But that's where –' Albert glanced from husband to wife. Polly went pink.

' 'Tis where I want to live.' Albert looked back at Henry.

'It's what Polly wants,' he said fondly.

Yes, thought Albert, I can see that, but how unwise. Why move to where Sybilla could show open hatred? He hadn't mentioned their aunt's strange behaviour before but here was a further puzzle. Polly and Henry must be aware how Sybilla felt! There were altogether too many unexplained mysteries and Albert felt fazed. To change the subject, he indicated Polly's belly.

'Splendid news to come home to, Henry. Fancy Chas and me becoming uncles all of a sudden.' The expectant father pursed his lips and waited until Polly had disappeared into the kitchen.

'Please don't speak of it,' he hissed. 'I try not to refer to it

266

for fear of upsetting her!' Albert was astonished.

'But it must be nearly due, with her as big as that?'

'Two more months. To be precise, one month and approximately three to four weeks. With a first child, one cannot be certain, I'm told. I keep in touch with our physician, privately. Polly does not know, nor must she be told.' Henry laid an expressive finger to his lips and whispered, 'The slightest strain and your sister is inclined to nervous prostration.'

What nonsense! Pol's got him twisted round her little finger, thought Albert. Nervous prostration indeed! He and Chas would have teased her out of such behaviour. What a dried up old stick Henry Durrant was, to be sure. A lot older than even Albert remembered. Hair, what there was of it, sticking up in every direction, complexion pale as milk and wearing an old-fashioned high collar that might have belonged to his father.

What a pity Pol couldn't have found herself a younger chap, someone with a bit more *fun* about him. In the small crowded room, he could sense Henry's hostility and felt a twinge of guilty sympathy.

'I daresay you're wondering how long I'll be staying,' he volunteered cheerfully. 'Truth is, I got to start back to London tomorrow. Chas is expecting me.' The relief on Henry's face nearly made him laugh.

'You must stay as long as you wish, of course,' Henry began. Albert shook his head.

'Not this time, thank you, Henry. I shall leave in the morning after I've finished some business here.'

'What a pity.' His expression belied his words. 'Is your er brother . . . Is Chas . . .?'

'He won't be coming this time. Between you and me . . .' Albert checked that Polly was out of earshot, 'Chas is planning on going to America. I ain't told Polly yet. Didn't want to upset her.'

'No, indeed.' Henry was grave. 'She talks of him often. In fact she's been over-excited knowing your arrival must be imminent,' he sighed, because Polly had talked of little else. 'This news of Chas must be kept from her, she'll be most upset.'

267

'The truth is, Henry, Chas has had to leave – in a bit of a hurry. Because of a little bit of bother,' Albert hinted. 'Nothing serious, you understand. But it's better if he disappears for a while. Now I don't suppose anyone'll come asking questions but if they do, you just let 'em know, private like, that Chas has gone to 'merica. No need for Pol to hear.'

'I – see.' Henry's previous doubts about his wife's family had been confirmed. Albert continued cheerfully.

'I've taken french leave myself, as a matter of fact. I hope to go back and sign off.' That way it might be possible to rescue a morsel of his back pay. Henry looked even more severe.

'I see,' he said again.

'So you won't be seeing much of either of us in future, what with Chas in 'merica and me needing to earn a living.' Henry could afford to be expansive.

'For Polly's sake, I'm sorry to hear it.'

'Yes.' Pity the chap's got such an honest face, thought Albert wryly, he can't wait to see the back of me. 'I'd have liked to visit Pol a bit more often.' He offered his tobacco pouch; Henry declined.

'No, thank you. Do you think your sister is looking well?'

Albert considered. 'Peaky,' he said, eventually. 'Too thin about the face.'

'Polly always did have that shadowy look,' Henry was immediately on the defensive.

'Ye-es.' Henry ran worried fingers through his hair.

'I can confess to you, Albert, that I'm worried about her. She lies awake, imagining the worst that can happen. When I question her, she denies it but I know it's so. She's terrified of the actual birth. I blame Mrs Figgis and her old wives' tales – I have tried to convince Polly that it's a woman's natural function, bestowed on her by nature as on females of every other of God's creatures.' Which wouldn't cut much ice with Pol, Albert knew. You had to bully her out of it when she was in a mood.

'Would you like me to have a talk to her?'

'No, indeed!' cried her husband, stung. Polly must

268

never know they'd been discussing her behind her back. 'When the time is right . . . I shall – speak to her again.'

If you wait much longer, it'll be too late, thought Albert.

Over supper he exerted himself with travellers' tales, to make Polly smile. Henry hid his jealousy behind the lamp. Only when they rose to go to bed did Albert broach the taboo subject.

'Not long now, eh, Polly?' He delved into his pack. 'If I'd have known, I'd have brought something for the baby. As it is . . . this is for you. From Chas and me.' The length of shot silk shimmered orange and gold. Under the Indian sun the vivid colours looked natural. Here, they were disturbing.

'Albert – how beautiful!' Polly held the exotic length against her dark hair and pale skin. 'I shall make such a lovely bodice and skirt.'

'I can't see you wearing that colour, dearest.' Henry's tone expressed the conviction that his wife shouldn't be seen in anything so vulgar.

'P'raps when Pol's up and about again,' Albert suggested, 'when she's got her figure back and you want to take her out and show her off. That's when you can wear it, Pol. Like a ripe peach, you'll be, in that.'

To Henry's fastidious mind, his brother-in-law had an unfortunate turn of phrase. Thank heaven he would be leaving in the morning. Henry could hardly risk introducing him to colleagues at Lingwoods, he had his reputation to consider.

Albert produced another package like a rabbit out of a hat.

'This is for you as well, Pol. Chas and me planned to surprise you on one of your birthdays. It was the second time we camped at Delhi – years ago that was. Old Pomf – remember I told you about him – he was still alive then. We used to talk about you, tell him how pretty you must've grown. He was always saying he'd like to come and see for himself, poor old chap.'

Chattering easily, Albert fastened the bracelet on her

269

wrist. Polly gasped at the gold and jewels, twisting her arm under the light.

'Oh, Henry, did you ever see anything so beautiful!' Beside it, her engagement ring appeared insipid.

'It come from a market seller in old Delhi,' Albert told her. 'We'd just been to see this lovely marble tomb . . . They told us the chap had built in memory of his wife. That's when Chas said – "Bet she wasn't nearly as pretty as our Pol".' He smiled fondly and Polly blushed. 'Chas was right, eh, Henry?' Henry didn't reply. Jealousy rose like bile. Polly turned the bracelet round and round with delicate fingers.

'I shall treasure it as long as I live, Albert.' Her eyes were solemn with the knowledge that her brothers cared for her as much as they always did.

'It's certainly most charming,' Henry said curtly, 'but overly rich considering our circumstances.'

Enoch Porrit slouched at the kitchen table. He kept out of the way most evenings, waiting until the lodgers had been fed and any callers had departed before returning home. Once a week he varied his habit, with sly intent. On Friday nights, he hung about outside the gate, attempting to waylay one or other of Syb's lodgers, demanding, 'If you let me hev the rent, I shall see my wife gets it.' The young men knew this wasn't true. Both had endured Syb's wrath as a result but neither felt like arguing with Mr Porrit. He was large; he had a short temper plus an inclination to use his fists. One young man had already handed in his notice and was searching for less tempestuous accommodation.

Tonight Enoch had been unlucky. As Syb set food in front of him, the memory made him want to hit out. Thrusting hands into empty pockets, he said scornfully, 'I heard them two nephews of yourn hev come crawling back.'

'Only Albert . . . he ain't staying. Chas is still in London.'

'Good riddance!' Enoch seized a knife and fork. Sybilla had surprised him, he'd imagined she would deny it. 'Tell

270

'em they ain't wanted!' he shouted belligerently, 'Neither of them. D'you hear me?'

Sybilla moved nearer the lamp as she searched among the bobbins in her workbasket.

'Thought tha' would be an end of it once they'd joined the army,' Enoch grumbled, shovelling food into his mouth. 'After all we done for 'em, they got a cheek, coming back. If I catch either of 'em hanging round here –'

'If you do, you'll be civil for a change.' She bit the frayed end off a length of thread. 'They both killed people while they was in India. Albert said it was army orders . . . but he intended you should know about it. He ain't above doing it again. He's grown, too. You'll never take your belt off to him no more, Enoch Porrit. If you did . . . you'd get bested.' Having demonished her husband's pride in his own strength, she stared unwaveringly. 'Albert's a man now.' Her nostrils flared at the flabby, beer-swollen features opposite. 'Fit and strong,' she repeated. 'He ain't afeared of you.'

Enoch pushed his plate away. He'd never thought of the boys being fully grown. Somehow he'd convinced himself he'd never see them again. And now they'd come back fighting men. For all his bragging Enoch had only ever slaughtered rabbits down the warren. Albert and Chas were in a different class altogether. If they came back boasting of what they'd done, Enoch would lose what little status he had. Food lost all savour as he thought of it.

'Tell 'em they're not wanted,' he muttered passionately, 'not wanted at all.'

Seeing his reactions, Sybilla felt a sudden revulsion at the way she'd behaved. She knew if she'd made one gesture today, that's all it would have needed. Albert looked as open and tender-hearted as his father but with an overlaying toughness acquired in the army.

There was still tomorrow, an opportunity for her to offer the money as a gift. Even as she thought of this, Sybilla vacillated. Money was different. Why should she become soft and silly all of a sudden – didn't she need every penny for that wonderful moment when she'd be free to go to London? Hadn't she got to make up what she'd lost through Enoch's thieving ways?

Albert with his careless chatter, off to make his fortune wherever he liked. She was tied to this millstone . . . Her mood changed, self-pity obliterating all else. Albert and Chas could do what they pleased whereas she was cursed.

On the floor of the cottage at Willow End Albert settled himself for sleep with his pack for a pillow, satisfied he'd sent Polly to bed happy. It occurred to him that he could haved asked Henry for the loan. Hadn't Polly once written of a 'tidy sum?' Henry didn't look the sort to demand seven per cent per annum. Ah, well . . . Another time, perhaps. You lived and with a bit of luck you learned not to make the same mistake twice.

The silk and the bracelet still lay on a chair. Dying embers flickered over the vivid colours. What a shame old Henry didn't care for the choice, they'd been to Polly's liking all right, but then he and Chas knew her so well whereas Henry . . . Albert yawned. A mite old-fashioned perhaps.

A baby! Albert broke off from yawning with a grin. How would Henry cope when it came to a squealing, damp bundle? He chuckled then scolded himself. Even if Pol wasn't looking forward to it, Henry was. Albert had seen his face when he whispered of a son. He wasn't such a bad old stick! 'Better had be a boy, though,' Albert murmured as he snuggled down under the blanket. 'Don't go letting Henry down, Pol old girl.'

Upstairs, they whispered, conscious of their visitor below. Henry had never seen Polly so happy. Her eyes were shining. Tonight she should have shown him her gratitude for having secured the house of her dreams. Instead all she wanted to talk about was Albert.

She sang the following morning. Taking a turn round the garden, Henry shut his ears to the sound. Thank heaven he would soon have a son to console him. As it was . . .

Henry wrestled with his jealousy; decency and hospitality prevailed.

As Albert approached he burst forth, 'You and Chas must look on our future home as your own.' It was out and he felt noble.

'That's very kind. Don't worry about us, though. Chas'll be far away and I have my living to make. I shall come back to see the baby but apart from that . . .' Albert shrugged, 'this is too far from London.'

'You might want to come back here one day.'

'It's a lovely spot,' he agreed. 'And it is home. I suppose it might turn out to be where I end up – but not yet.'

'You've got a lot more living to do first, I suppose,' Henry said heavily. Albert laughed.

'That's it! You put your finger on it, old man. That's just what Chas and me have got to do before we can become a couple of old codgers.'

It only occurred to him later why Henry hadn't smiled.

At midday, he entered as bidden through Sybilla's wicket gate. She was waiting. Albert made one protest before signing his name on the paper the bank had prepared.

'Seven per cent is worse than moneylenders charge, Aunt Syb.'

'Take it or leave it.' She refused to meet his eye, he noticed.

'Ain't you interested in how Chas and me got on?' he asked, baffled. 'Don't you want to know what happened to your own kith and kin no more?' She didn't reply. He picked up the three banknotes and tucked them carefully away. 'I asked Polly last night, afore Henry come home . . . I said, why's Aunt Syb took such a scunner to you all of a sudden? D'you know what she told me?'

Sybilla was suddenly scarlet.

'Pol had some tale that you didn't want her marrying Mr Durrant because you'd taken a fancy to him yourself.'

'Get out!'

'Which I told her was stupid,' Albert stood his ground. 'She said Mrs Heyhoe and Widow Helliwell was after him – that was understandable, both of them needing

273

husbands – but you're a married woman, Aunt Syb –'

'Get out of my sight!' He picked up his pack.

'I'm off. You'll get the money care of the post office, as arranged.' At the door he waited for some sign of farewell. She kept her back to him.

'I told Polly she must have been imagining things,' he said quietly, 'I said you was shrivelled inside with no decent feelings left because of Enoch Porrit. But I was sure you wasn't as wicked as to lust after Mr Durrant 'specially now he's your nephew, so to speak.' He was ridiculing her!

'Get – out!' But she was mistaken; Albert didn't see any humour at all. He shook his head sadly as he walked away.

Sybilla had never felt so exposed. She twisted her hands together until they hurt. How dare he, how dare anyone criticize!

Slowly she gathered herself together. This was the morning when she did her shopping, she wouldn't let Albert upset her routine. In the first shop she visited, the butcher was waiting, eager to know her reaction to today's most important piece of news.

'Have you heard, Mrs Porrit? Mr and Mrs Durrant are to be your neighbours. They've taken "Holly Villa" opposite from the first of next month.'

And, as he told every other customer that morning, Mrs Porrit's face was a picture.

'Her was dumbfounded. Her eyes did bulge. Flashed, too. Thunder'n lightnin' you might say.' Housewives nodded sagely. Storms were brewing and no mistake. Goodness knows what Mr Durrant was thinking of, with his wife in an interesting condition? The next few months promised to be very lively indeed.

'So tell me first about Polly?' Chas and Albert faced one another across one of the scrubbed tables in The Coachman's, the best value in the area according to Chas who'd been lying low in the mews. 'You reckon she's happy?'

'I think so . . . I still don't know why she married Henry . . . She didn't want to talk about the baby neither, but I think she's happy.' Albert obviously wasn't convinced.

274

Chas said worriedly, 'If only I didn't have to go to America!'

'Oh, but you do, old bor.' Albert had returned from his second expedition that day and now looked very solemn indeed. 'Miss Constance Spratt is threatening to sue you for breach of promise.' Chas shuddered.

'She turned up at the camp?'

'In company with the sergeant and his wife,' Albert began to chuckle. 'Following your h'inexplicable disappearance off the London train where she'd been waiting at the barrier together with her family.' Chas groaned. 'According to the chaps, when she found you'd done a bunk, she was most put out. She made a lotta suggestions as to what her relative, the sergeant, should do once he caught up with you.'

'My God, I hope he doesn't!' Albert looked at him, full of sympathy.

'You'll have to go, Chas. She sounds like a woman who don't give up easily.'

'She's a woman scorned. I was her last chance,' Chas said mournfully. 'Mind you watch your step, young 'un.'

'I will,' Albert nodded. He looked round but both the waitresses were busy. Mother and daughter, they rushed to serve noisy cabbies. 'Cor, I'm hungry!'

Outside, rain poured down. Albert was subdued at the thought of what was now inevitable. 'Let me go with you as far as Liverpool.'

'No. It's my fault you couldn't collect your pay today.'

'Didn't seem a good idea to show my face in camp. I met the chaps in Chatham. They told me about Miss Spratt.'

'There's no point going to Liverpool. Stay in London like you planned.'

'Best place to find work,' Albert agreed stoutly.

'We'll be living so far away from one another . . . I do wish I could have seen Pol. Mind you keep an eye on her for me.'

'I will. Ah . . .' The girl was hovering, tray in hand. She was a pretty little thing with a mass of black curls and lively dark eyes.

'Yes, gentlemen? We've got pigs trotters, lovely for

275

keeping the cold out, they are. Or stewed cowheel. Both with bubble and squeak.'

'We need filling up,' Albert told her solemnly, 'We're hollow all the way down inside.' She grinned.

'Best have a plateful of bread and dripping then.'

'Cowheel,' Chas said, 'and a glass of porter.'

'Same for me.' Albert watched her skip back to the serving hatch. At the back of the cafe, her mother sat with a hand pressed against her side. He heard the proprietor ask, 'Is your Ma poorly?'

'It's all right, Mr Bennett, I can manage. Two cowheel and two glasses of porter.'

'Chas, how are we going to keep in touch?' His brother looked at him blankly. 'We can't send letters care of Pol, I shan't be going there that often. You'll be on the move. I haven't an address.' Chas pondered.

'What we need is a post restante. What about here?'

'Pardon?'

'This place. We could ask. You can call when you're passing.' Albert was reluctant.

'I've heard there's work down Billingsgate. I might be living over there.'

'Nip over on an omnibus then!' They roared with laughter; as if Albert could afford that luxury!

'Don't forget to let me know your address when you reach Iowa.' Albert suddenly felt bleak: it sounded like the far side of the moon.

When Esther arrived with the food, they put their proposition to her; any letters to be kept and Albert would call when he could. 'There won't be that many,' Chas confided, 'I ain't much of a hand with a pen.'

'They'll have an American stamp,' Albert boasted.

'I shall have to ask Mr Bennett.'

The elderly proprietor wasn't one to turn down business. 'Ha'penny a letter an' 'e 'as to buy hisself supper whenever 'e comes. What's up with your Ma?'

'She's got a stitch, Mr Bennet.' Esther hurried back to Albert.

'Done,' he said when she'd told him.

When Esther cleared away their plates and the time for parting had come, Chas said awkwardly, 'I never did thank you for being so quick with that grenade.'

'I hadn't thought what it might mean . . . all those flies. An' the vultures –'

'If you hadn't thrown it, they'd have finished us off.'

'I wish they hadn't got old Pomf!'

'You can't save the whole world, Albert. You did your best. You saved me.' Albert's face clouded.

'It's the last time I kill anyone, Chas.'

'So I should bloomin' well hope, now you're not in the army! Now don't waste your life, old Pomf wouldn't have wanted you to, neither do I.' He'd embarrassed Albert.

'I shall find summat, I expect.'

'Do the best you can, young 'un. Look after Polly and remember what a fine chap father was.' He'd thoroughly alarmed him this time.

'Here, Chas, you are coming back?'

'Of course,' but he avoided the anxious face.

'Wish I'd had time to write to Aunt Syb.'

'Why?' Albert had forgotten his lie. Chas looked at him narrowly.

'To thank her for giving me that money. She did *give* it, I suppose? You weren't telling a fib?'

'Of course she did,' said Albert, telling a second, 'she wanted to help you get started.' Chas marvelled.

'I always had her down as such a mean old skinflint. I ought to try and thank her –'

'Don't bother. I'll make sure she knows.' He watched Chas pick up the small canvas bag. 'Stay a bit longer,' he begged. Chas shook his head. He wanted to say so much but it was impossible. He put fourpence on the table for his supper and walked out swiftly into the rain.

Alone at the table, to his horror and shame, Albert promptly burst into tears.

Chapter Eighteen

Dark Days

Winter came early, with thick frosts followed by heavy snow. It blanketed the forests, chapped the skin and froze the blood. The wind tore across the Fens with an icy contempt for every fragile living thing in its path; birds died in the hedgerows and deer, rarely seen, wandered up to the houses in search of food. People complained unceasingly.

Old men told one another there never had been such times. Superstitions resurfaced. This weather wasn't natural, it was the result of strange comets sent by other worlds or it might be those ungodly followers of Darwin who were responsible. Opinion finally settled on the younger generation, lacking as they did any respect for their elders.

Those still warm-blooded enough to enjoy dangerous games skated recklessly on meres and rivers, circling great barges now held fast by the ice. And at dawn one dark December morning, into a silent muffled world, Polly's baby was born.

The doctor had tried to banish her fears. He'd succeeded with her husband but then it wasn't Henry who was enduring labour, hour after hour of it. Eventually the medical man went home, promising to return when needed. Ma Figgis waited until he'd disappeared before producing her hidden bottle. She mixed a hefty measure in a tumbler of hot water. 'Get that inside you, Mrs Durrant. 'Twill do you the world of good.'

The restorative was trickling down Polly's throat as Henry re-entered. 'Is that more medicine?'

'It's what she needs to give her strength, Mr Durrant, not like that nasty physic.' He wanted to take the glass away but Polly refused.

'Ma Figgis knows what's best, Henry –' Another spasm interrupted. He watched, wringing his hands. When it was over she whispered hoarsely, 'Go away, please . . .'

'But, dearest . . .'

'Best do as she says, Mr Durrant. You'll only upset yourself staying here.'

He tried to stand his ground but after she'd settled Polly against the pillows Ma Figgis led him outside.

'I know what I'm about, Mr Durrant. Your dear wife is worn out. A stimulant will help her regain a little strength.'

'Had it been necessary, the doctor would have prescribed it.'

'When they're that young they stick to what they've learned at medical school,' she retorted. 'He's still wet behind the ears. Me, I've birthed half this town. Three generations in some families, that's why he left me in charge.' It was true although Henry preferred to rely on science.

'The doctor assures me there's no danger. I depend on you to inform me when I must fetch him again.' Ma Figgis sighed.

'It's going to be a long night. This babby's not wanting to be born.' His confidence began to fade.

'Surely there is a due time and season for all things to come to fruition? The latest scientific thinking confirms it.' She snorted.

'I never had no schooling, Mr Durrant. 'Tis nature I knows about.' Another cry and she made to return inside the bedroom.

'Please,' Henry begged urgently, 'I'll do anything . . .'

'I know, I know . . .' They always said that, especially the first time, 'but there's nothing more we can do except wait.'

*

As the night wore on Ma Figgis was worried that the baby might not survive. Polly was young enough to have another but she didn't want to be the one to break the news to Henry.

She sat by the fire as her patient writhed on the bed, marvelling how Henry had aged during the past few hours. His was an important position at Lingwood's by all accounts. Now, with unbrushed clothes and dishevelled hair, he cut a pitiful figure. Perhaps she should drop a hint that he should smarten himself before setting off for work tomorrow?

'Ah!' The cry was fiercer and broke through her musings. Back at the bedside, Ma Figgis decided she no longer wanted the responsibility.

'Not long now, dear,' she murmured automatically and slipped away to send Henry for help.

After the agony, the silence was a benison. Henry paced the living room floor to warm stiffened limbs. The second expedition through the snow had affected his temper. He considered requesting Polly not to be so loud. It must be over thirty hours by now – supposing the neighbours complained? Henry had a horror of being thought a nuisance. What was happening was woman's natural function – the beasts of the field managed it more quietly so why not Polly?

He mustn't scold; it was the first occasion and she had been deeply apprehensive. For that Ma Figgis was too blame – if only Henry could have prevented her from poisoning Polly's mind. His thoughts took another turn; what was happening up in the bedroom was the miracle of life itself. Excitement overcame fear. Christmas was almost upon them. They'd planned a quiet celebration because of Polly's condition, but now it would be a truly joyful thanksgiving.

Albert had intended to come but a letter arrived instead; the journey was too risky in this weather (it was also too expensive although he didn't mention that), he would visit in the New Year. He'd had no news yet from Chas. Privately, Henry was relieved. This first Christmas in their new home with their son would be too solemn an occasion to share.

Was it unnaturally quiet upstairs? He recalled sentimentally that the Christ child's had been a silent birth. Did that mean his baby had already slipped into the world? Even the creaking floorboards overhead were mute.

He recalled the soft hush of a summer garden. His baby son would be like one of the flowers, the tiny head poised on the stalk of a neck as his mother hummed him a lullaby.

Outside dawn was beginning. Fresh snow glistened like crystal. The first day of a new life! He must demonstrate his deep gratitude to Polly. A pair of earrings perhaps? Something dainty, not like that gaudy Indian trinket.

'Mr Durrant . . .' Henry hadn't heard the door open. At the sight of the doctor's face his pulse began to race. 'We've done what we can. I'm thankful to tell you your wife has pulled through.'

Pulled through? What a ridiculous remark when there'd been no danger!

'And . . .? He couldn't go on.

'The child is alive. I regret to say, not for much longer, it's only a matter of time. There were breathing difficulties during the birth. Difficulties which could not – cannot – be remedied. A malfunctioning of the lungs.' He waited for understanding to reach Henry. When it did the doctor couldn't meet his eyes. 'I'm very sorry,' he repeated.

'My son!'

'It's a girl, Mr Durrant. I'd like you to come upstairs so that we can say a prayer.' There was no point in sending for the vicar, the snow was too deep, the man would never reach here in time. 'We'll be as quiet as we can so as not to disturb your dear wife. She's been very plucky, you know.'

In the end Polly had overcome her terror, to the doctor's admiration. There'd been no hysterics. She had produced an inner strength which he hadn't anticipated.

281

When Ma Figgis had whispered that the infant could not live, she'd been fatalistic. She'd refused to look at it and had resolutely closed her eyes as they wrapped it in a shawl.

But the worst piece of news had yet to be told. 'I fear Mrs Durrant cannot be exposed to further trials. Another such birth could kill her. Hers is a delicate constitution.'

'No!' Behind him, Henry clutched at the banister for support.

'I'm extremely sorry to have to tell you that, Mr Durrant.' Words seemed inadequate faced with such naked despair.

'My wife doesn't care for me, she never did. A child of my own, doctor – a son . . .' Henry pleaded with both hands. The words came frenziedly from an overwrought brain, the medical man didn't want to hear them.

'Mrs Durrant has escaped death tonight, sir. She is bearing her grief with fortitude,' he admonished. 'Do you do the same if you please, for her sake.'

Henry followed in a daze. The baby was dead and the truth had finally been admitted to another human being: Polly didn't care for him. The double loss left him numb.

Inside the room Ma Figgis stood by the fire, crooning to a white-swathed bundle. Polly lay exhausted. She didn't move when Henry entered, even her eyelids were too heavy. It distressed him that she should sprawl like that – legs wide apart under the sheet like some loose woman. A wife of his should show decorum.

He realized both the doctor and Ma Figgis were waiting for him to react. What was he expected to do? The doctor gestured. Oh no, he couldn't kiss her! There was no shred of gratitude or affection. Polly had failed him; it wasn't only the infant who was dying here, it was love itself. As he looked at the exhausted, sweaty face, Henry felt no compassion. He detached himself from what was happening. He had pinned all his hopes on the infant; it was expecting too much of him to show sympathy to his wife.

The doctor decided Durrant was still suffering from shock. Ma Figgis indicated her bundle: the tiny mouth had slackened – had it ceased to take in air? He whispered urgently, 'Have they mentioned a name?'

'Not as I've heard, sir.'

'Mr Durrant?' Henry looked at him with haggard eyes. 'What did you intend your daughter should be called, Mr Durrant?' He hadn't a notion. He stared helplessly at the bed. 'Don't disturb your wife . . . Is that your Bible?' It lay ready on the tallboy together with pen and ink, to enter the name of his son. That choice had been mulled over for weeks; Ernest Henry Albert.

The doctor opened the Old Testament at random, ran his finger down the page and nodded at Ma Figgis. She moved closer and he moistened his fingers in the water jug.

'We will baptise this infant, Mr Durrant, that she lose all sin and be received by our Blessed Lord to dwell among his spotless white lambs forever.' Raising his hand, the doctor sprinkled a few drops of water. 'Milcah, I baptise thee In the Name of the Father, and of the Son, and of the Holy Ghost. Amen.'

Milcah? Poor little thing! thought Ma Figgis indignantly.

Despite the weather, the sad news spread fast. In each shop Ma Figgis visited, customers gathered to shake their heads. Most reacted predictably; Mrs Durrant was young and would have another child but that had Ma Figgis pursing her lips. It wasn't for her to betray medical secrets her audience were informed, and everyone understood. It was a sad day for Mr Durrant, neighbours said to neighbour, especially when you remembered he'd inherited a tidy sum.

Sybilla still hadn't heard when Ma Figgis accosted her in the ironmongers.

''Tis mournful tidings for your family, Mrs Porrit, as doubtless you know?'

Sybilla noticed how every other customer was pretending not to look in her direction. She asked slowly, 'I don't know as I takes your meaning, Ma Figgis?' The small familiar dog came waddling across to sniff at her skirts. Sybilla twitched them angrily away. 'Go on with you, shoo!' Unperturbed, Ma Figgis replied.

'Your niece have had her baby. A terrible bad time 'twas for her. 'Tis all over now, though.' To the amazement of those watching, Sybilla became quite excited.

'Do you mean that Polly . . .? Is she . . .?'

'Mrs Durrant survived, thanks be . . . 'twas the babby died. A little girl it was. Doctor was there but he couldn't save it. Summat wrong with its lungs, he said.'

Without pausing to think, Sybilla said callously, 'Serve her right.'

'Oh!'

She never noticed the effect of her words. Her mind was full of suppurating hatred that had festered since Polly's marriage, she was incapable of rational thought. The move to Holly Villa had only been for spite so that Polly could flaunt her pregnancy. Sybilla had been forced to watch from behind her Venetian blinds as Henry's child swelled inside her niece's womb.

And now that child was dead. Sybilla said even more defiantly, 'Serve Polly Unwin right, I say.'

In that instant she became aware of their horror. Everyone stared openly: customers, the ironmonger behind his counter, his wife coming through with a warming drink, all were frozen in condemnation.

Self-preservation snapped back into place. Sybilla fumbled for phrases, fulsome insincerities she could heap on Polly when Ma Figgis came at her.

'You wicked woman! You cruel, heartless wicked woman! You've gone too far this time. There's your poor niece – her who did *want* her babby . . .' She glittered, full of menace as to what she could reveal if she chose. Sybilla's throat went dry. 'You're not fit for decent company. This town don't need women like you, Sybilla Porrit,' Ma Figgis declared vehemently, 'I shan't never speak to you again.'

She'd unlocked their tongues. The shop clamoured with the dislike: women who'd been short-changed for their laundry, those who'd felt the sharp edge of Mrs Porrit's temper now told her how much they'd resented it.

The shop-keeper struggled to restore calm. He ran from one end of the counter to the other, penned in and helpless.

'Ladies ... ladies, please!' Some of his stock was precariously balanced and with so much emotion bouncing to and fro – 'Pray do not upset yourselves.'

Serge skirts and flounces, umbrellas and capes, swished dangerously. Tallow candles rolled across the linoleum, firelighters overturned and two dozen mousetraps came crashing down. Scarcely anyone noticed.

With her back to one of the displays, Sybilla Porrit faced them. Everyone in that shop had known her since childhood. Early in her marriage they used to greet her with a sympathetic smile, a squeeze of the hand. Now, one and all declared her to be a leper. They fell in with Ma Figgis's suggestion; henceforth, they too would ignore her. One old man shouted triumphantly, 'Us'll not talk to 'ee. Tha' shall be ignored throughout this town, Sybilla Porrit.'

At the back of the shop, overcome by the excitement, Ma Figgis's old dog relieved himself against a can of paraffin.

Snow that was so white in the countryside had turned to slush in the mews. The temperature fell and everywhere was coated with ice. Ostlers and coachmen swore as they chipped away at drinking troughs. Horses skidded and fell on the increasingly dangerous slide children had fashioned over the cobbles.

The frost bit hard. Mews front doors no longer stood open, they were snatched shut as inhabitants scurried inside, eyes red-raw from the wind. Broken windows had paper stuffed into every cranny. Beyond the arch, the poor huddled together and begged with frantic terror in this, the season of goodwill, against what January might bring.

The approach of Christmas brought conflicting emotions for Vida Meaney. In the mews everyone made an effort to be festive. For Esther's sake she must try – if only Lem could bring in a bit of money! His resolve over work had weakened further. For months they had been dependent on Kezia with never a farthing to spare. Vida had the energy, the will-power, but with so little sight, she was marooned in their upper room.

'Hallo ... anyone home!' Esther was climbing the ladder. 'Did you think I'd forgotten you?'

'Course I did,' Vida was fiercely determined to be cheerful. 'I've been lying here, feeling lonely. Clean forgotten I'd got this lovely girl coming to see me. Where are you then? Give your Aunty Vee a kiss.' The rough scarred skin pressed against Esther's smooth one. 'Where's your mother?'

'She'd told me to come on ahead ...' Esther sounded anxious. 'That stitch has come back again, Vee. She said a rest would make it better.' Her voice trembled, 'I do wish we could afford a doctor.'

'Has Bridie seen her?' The mews relied heavily on Bridie's expertise.

'Mother said I wasn't to bother her on Christmas Eve.'

'Now listen to me, Esther. Go straight round and tell her your Ma's sick. They'll be off to Mass later so hurry up. Don't matter what day it is – Bridie wouldn't forgive us if we didn't tell her your Ma was poorly.'

'Here ...' Esther held the food to distract her, 'guess what we're going to have tomorrow. Mr Bennett gave us half the leftovers and twopence extra. We shan't starve, that's for certain.'

'Any jellied eels?' said with longing but no real hope, it was Vida's idea of heaven.

'Sorry ... Plenty of potatoes, enough for all of us. Onions. Half a pound of sausages – pork not beef. Faggots, cabbage, a bit of cheese and a loaf. Egg and a drop of milk for the ferrets – we shall have a feast, Vee. And a proper boiled pudding – I made that myself.'

'Bless you!' Plum pudding was the next best thing to jellied eels, of course it was. 'Leave the basket, I'll put everything away.' She knew every corner of her kingdom blindfold, 'You nip round to Bridie's.'

Esther stepped outside, tying her scarf tightly. There were

286

squeals from the children on their slide. She was still young enough to be invited to join them but declined. What confused her more was to be old enough to attract those young men lounging under the street lamp near The Musketeer.

The Macguires' front window had a crude homemade crib illuminated with a candle. Even a tiny pool of warmth was welcome on a bitter evening. The door was on the latch, Esther slipped inside.

Downstairs was used for storing hay and straw. Upstairs, the two small rooms exploded with children and happiness. At its centre, controlling with a brawny arm or a shout was Bridie herself, supremely content.

'Esther! The prettiest baby I ever delivered – come on in! Where's your Mam?'

Esther scooped up a child who demanded a kiss. It only needed a few words of explanation before Bridie began issuing orders.

'Alberta, take over for me. Don't let any of 'em burn themselves or go looking for their presents.' She grabbed her worn jacket. 'I'll be back to take you all to church so keep yourselves clean, d'you hear?' She lowered her bulk perilously down the ladder asking, 'Is the pain worse this time?'

'It must be. Mother doesn't complain of course.'

'Naturally ... when did Kezia Morgan ever do that?' Outside the icy gusts made them duck. 'Blast this weather ... it freezes the drop on the end of me nose!' Clutching one another to stay upright the two of them slithered under the arch. Crowds bustled past outside, laden with holly and mistletoe. By contrast, the empty cafe looked bleak.

'Ain't Bennett staying open tonight?'

'He's feeling his age, Auntie Bridie. He said he was treating himself to Christmas Eve at his own fireside. His wife wants him to sell up, you know.' Esther reached through the letterbox and opened the lock with familiar ease. 'That makes Mother feel even more poorly, worrying about what's going to happen.'

Bridie found herself wondering caustically if Lemuel

Meaney understood the significance. Kezia's earnings kept the Meaneys afloat yet still he made no real effort to find work. If that supply of money dried up . . . Mustn't think ill of him tonight though, she scolded herself, not on Christmas Eve. How could one ask forgiveness for trespasses otherwise?

Inside, she heaved herself up the three flights. The worst thing about being poor, she thought philosophically, was where you ended up. Either a dank cellar, a mews reeking of horse dung or a draughty old attic.

Once she'd gained the landing she needed time to catch her breath and looked about. There was the wash-stand, half hidden behind the screen. Kezia and Esther hung their washing here as well. Kezia's mania for being clean! Bridie shook her head. The walls were running with damp.

Inside the spotless room, Esther had made an effort to brighten it with pictures cut from magazines. One showed a view of a mountain in Wales. Did it make Kezia homesick? Forever pining for hills, she was.

'Hallo there . . .' The figure in the chair stirred slightly. Esther knelt beside her and whispered, 'Mother?' She took the hand and kissed it. 'Auntie Bridie's come to see how you are. Is the pain any easier?' Kezia pressed her hand against the hot nagging ache and tried to smile.

'I'm bound to feel better now that you're both here . . . How are you, Bridie? It's good of you when you're so busy.'

'Any excuse to escape the bedlam.' Bridie Macguire touched the hot forehead and saw the strain in the big expressive eyes. With a slight shock she noticed Kezia's hair was mostly grey now.

'If only you'd taken my advice, Kezia Morgan,' she said sadly, 'when those young cab-drivers were queuing up to marry you at the beginning. Living in comfort you'd have been by now, not like this.'

Her gesture encompassed the small pieces of coal beside the dead fire, carefully hoarded against tomorrow. The wind whistled through the ill-fitting dormer. A forlorn effort to add cheer with a few holly sprigs only served to emphasize the rest.

There was a candle in the saucer but Bridie didn't suggest it should be lit, it too would be rationed. And this frail woman continued to support that lazy, good-for-nothing Lemuel . . .

As if reading her thoughts, Kezia murmured, 'You mustn't condemn. Esther and I owe Vida everything. If she can't earn any longer . . .'

The other woman replied far more gently than she felt, 'It wasn't her I was thinking of . . . Here, just let me have a feel . . .' As she pressed it against the hard swollen stomach, Kezia gasped.

'How long has it been like that?'

'A day or two, I can't remember. The pain's moved about. It started here . . . now – it seems to be everywhere.'

'Hmm . . .' Bridie drew Esther aside. 'Don't argue with what I'm going to suggest. We've got sixpence to spare at home – I'm sending our John for the doctor.'

'Why?' Esther was startled rather than apprehensive.

'It might be appendicitis.'

It was the same Poor Law ward Vida had been in years before. Bridie wondered if Kezia would remember that, provided she recovered from the anaesthetic. When they'd wheeled her past on the way back from the operating theatre, her pallor had been ghastly.

Mercifully, Esther had been asleep. Her head still rested heavily against Bridie's shoulder.

A door opened at the end of the passage and a surgeon, pulling on his frock coat, bustled past in search of seasonal festivity. His natural superiority made her nervous. She waited for one of the nurses to appear instead. There were fewer on duty tonight, because of Christmas.

She saw the clock above the ward door and sighed. Ten minutes to midnight. She hoped Alberta had taken the family to church. The Holy Mother would surely forgive, you just couldn't be in two places at once.

The ward door opened and a nurse came out. Bridie put a finger to her lips and indicated the sleeping Esther. She

289

eased the girl onto the bench and tip-toed across. 'How is she?'

'Are you the next of kin?'

'No, that's her daughter over there. I'm Mrs Morgan's friend.' Bridie couldn't find the words. 'Is she . . .?' The nurse's natural pity was mixed with frustration. This was such a depressing ward. Despite their care so few patients had the stamina to survive an operation.

'She hasn't recovered consciousness. We're not sure if she will. It was too late to save her, you realize that? If only she'd visited the doctor before the appendix burst . . .'

I mustn't weep, I mustn't think of what is bound to happen, Bridie told herself; Esther needs me to be strong.

'I'll wake the girl.' She returned to the bench. 'Esther, dear.' It nearly broke her resolve to see the warm smile as Esther yawned and stretched.

'Goodness, I was fast asleep!' The smile faded as she remembered where they were. 'How's Mother?'

'We're going to sit beside her bed, dear. She's still not come round. They're not quite sure if she's . . . if she will. Be brave, now. Be my best girl, for her sake.' Bridie gripped her arm tightly as they followed the nurse down the dimly lit ward.

It was the same when Vida was here, Bridie thought, the same bed behind the same screens. The same hopeless eyes watching us. Dear God if Kezia has to die, don't let her regain consciousness and find herself here. Take her quickly please Lord, if it be Thy Will . . .

Esther stood beside her mother, her hands clamped together to hide their trembling. Bridie moved to the opposite side and bowed her head.

'I'm going to talk to her, lovey. There's a chance she might hear. It could help her feel happy.' Esther nodded, tears flowing. Bridie stroked the worn inert fingers on the regulation coverlet.

'It's been a good few years now, Kezia . . . I'd never been in such a smart house. Kensington too — never been there again, that's for sure. What a night that was. You so brave — and scared. I remember Rose's face when I told her how babies were born ... I don't think she's ever recovered from the shock! Remember how fierce you were after, standing up to those Massinghams?'

The warm Irish voice continued, faltering occasionally. Towards morning, the sunken features on the pillow moved for the first time. Esther bent close.

'What is it, tell me?' she whispered. There was a faint murmur. Esther caught the word and looked up. 'Just – "bluebells".'

'That's all right then,' Bridie said simply. 'Her boy Adam was waiting for her. We've no need to worry. He'll take her by the hand and show her the way.' She lowered herself onto tired knees and clasped her rosary.

In the lodging room he shared in Shadwell, Albert crouched under his blanket to read Ma Figgis's letter. Barrack room life and the heat of India had been replaced by cold and filth. His boast that he would find work had been made before Albert realized how many others were in the same position, even more desperate than himself. An increasing use of machinery had driven more people from the land in the last ten years than ever before.

It had been exciting when he'd found his first job. He'd walked past the Tower of London every morning on his way to Billingsgate market but, once there, his task was to sweep away offal as fast as screaming cockney women could gut the fish. Every night he would scrape fish scales from his hair and skin. Then a boy turned up who was willing to accept a lower wage and Albert was dismissed.

He'd tried the docks after that. Crowds clamoured for work every morning and were selected for their strength, like beasts. Albert knew his own body might fail without regular food and exercise. The first time he wasn't picked, he knew real fear: he might not survive!

It wasn't just his muscles, his general appearance worried him. A chap needed to be smart and confident to succeed. The second-hand suit bought when he'd first done a bunk was now very shabby. In the crowded dirty room he shared, Albert sat cross-legged in his corner,

291

constantly mending and patching. His possessions which fitted into a biscuit tin comprised shaving kit and towel, cobbling tools, sewing things, pen and ink. These, his blanket and a spare set of underwear were all he possessed. What was to happen? This existence couldn't continue – what would old Pomf have done?

He'd earned enough at the beginning to feed himself properly but once a week, every penny he could spare – and some that he couldn't – was despatched to Sybilla. She never acknowledged these remittances, he hadn't given her this address, he was always hoping to move on. By Christmas it began to dawn on Albert that he might not and his situation was desperate.

He'd few friends. There were none in the lodgings he could trust. On Christmas night he stood at the back of a church to listen to the eternal message, but slipped outside in shame before the collection was taken. It was a choice between that or a proper meal: the flesh needed succour. For a treat he would walk to Fulham to see whether there'd been any news from Chas. Afterwards . . . his mouth was already watering at the prospect – he would have a hot meal.

When he finally arrived, the cafe was closed. Albert glared at the sign. At the back of his mind had been the thought he might see the pretty girl again. He kicked the wall in futile anger then, thrusting his hands in his pockets, began the weary tramp back to Shadwell.

The letter from Ma Figgis, written at Polly's behest, was waiting for him. He wasn't to be an uncle after all. Pol had been very ill but was now beginning to mend. 'Poor old girl,' he murmured.

'Wha'?' It was one of those who shared the room, a man who had given up the fight to keep himself decent. Verminous clothes stank and Albert could see that as usual he'd managed to stupify himself with drink. 'Wha' d'you say?'

'I said – there's always someone worse off than yourself.'

'Nah!'

But Sybilla Porrit would have agreed.

The lodgers had returned to the bosom of their families;

Mr and Mrs Porrit were therefore alone to celebrate Christmas Day. Husband and wife sat on either side of the kitchen table. They'd eaten their dinner. Sybilla had cleared away the dishes – in silence. Enoch now decided it was as good an evening as any to mend a rat trap.

Apart from the rasp of metal, the occasional rush of sparks from the fire, the only sound was the clock ticking. It was measuring out her life. It weighed down Sybilla as she sat with nothing to do except think. She'd spent weeks trying to circumvent the town's edict; it was too late. Every single acquaintance cut her dead.

She'd knocked at the vicarage back door but Cook was deaf to her appeal. The new kitchen maid had returned to say, 'Mrs Heyhoe was not at home.'

Sybilla knew better than to try at the front. Mrs Nibs wasn't likely to receive her. Head high to conceal despair, she returned home. Even Widow Helliwell took advantage of her plight; she demanded a rise in her hourly rate which Sybilla was forced to pay – what else could she do?

She'd stopped attending church. Not to hear the glad tidings had hurt more than she'd expected. She'd opened her Bible but Enoch continued to jeer until she closed it again.

At the beginning Sybilla had wondered whether now was the time to go to London but her daydreams, exposed to reality, had withered rapidly. Difficulties emerged that she'd never considered previously. How could she go alone? In her dreams, Henry Durrant had been at her side. Where would she live? How could she support herself? It was bitter to lose hope but worst of all was the knowledge that she lacked sufficient courage to venture from the place of her birth.

Albert's postal orders continued to arrive. Was he likely to return? If so, she told herself firmly, she wouldn't turn him away next time. She would invite him in and make him welcome. Albert wasn't one to bear a grudge, he would forgive – or would he?

Sybilla had a wild notion of writing to Albert and asking if she could join him but he'd never included an address. Polly would know. Here, Sybilla's courage failed entirely; she couldn't bring herself to cross the London road to ask. She examined the postmarks. Where was Shadwell? Here there was no one she could ask for none would reply.

It was warm in the kitchen but Sybilla felt cold. Was she to be an outcast for the rest of her life!

'Tea?' She jerked back to the present.

'Pardon?'

'Get me a cuppa tea.'

She'd half a mind to argue but what was the point? Enoch watched her put the kettle on the hob, take down cups and saucers from the dresser and smiled, satisfied.

'How about behavin' dutiful, Syb?' Her face was in shadow, waiting for him to continue. 'You ain't got no other choice, hev you? There's only me willin' to speak to you now. How about behavin' like a wife should an' doin' what I wants in future, eh?'

He leered, overjoyed that he'd regained power over her. Deep inside an emotion stirred in Sybilla that she'd never experienced before: outrage. Her hands shook and the crockery rattled. She was shackled to this dreadful creature who was proposing to treat her abominably forever more.

Sybilla couldn't breathe. Her life was at rock-bottom – all through her own stupidity, she acknowledged that now. If she was to go on living, she would have to fight her way back otherwise she might as well be dead. There was nowhere she could hide. However long it took, whatever the humiliation, the only way forward would be through her own efforts. Most important was to keep a sense of self-esteem.

'How dare you order me about – you thief!'

'Wha?' The tool fell from Enoch's startled hand.

'How many times have you taken the rent off my lodgers. One of 'em's spread the word about what it's like here on a Friday night when you're drunk –'

'Doan' you start calling me names –'

'Lord knows how I'm going to let that room now because of you. But it won't stop you thieving, will it? Taking the laundry and the tea money, what Widow

294

Helliwell and me hev earned with our sweat. How many years since you give me a penny?' Inflamed, Enoch began unbuckling his belt. Sybilla's contempt filled the room.

'Is that the only answer you can give? Threaten to mark me again?' Her bitter tone stayed his hand. 'The day I does what you wants, Enoch Porrit, I be going soft in the head. God willin', I ain't never going to be that stupid. From now on you make your own bloody tea.'

Chas hadn't reached Iowa. He'd lost most of his fifteen pounds, stolen on board the boat to America. After that he'd had to take whatever work he could find and now, in the mid-west, was the hired hand on a lonely farm.

It was a rough hewn cabin on a windy plateau but the welcome had been warm. The owner, Mrs Ramsey, was grey-haired and quietly spoken. She had been working the land ever since she and her husband first came here. His grave was in a corner of the plot.

Chas slept in a bunk house along with the widow's young nephew. It was arduous work; there were logs to split, cattle to tend and sloping fields to plough and harrow. He'd been here for nearly a year.

On a day in late March, a travelling preacher arrived with a letter. Mrs Ramsey read it with a satisfied smile. As she served supper she announced, 'I'm aiming to get married come the Fall, Mr Unwin. I shall be putting this farm up for sale.' Chas stammered his congratulations. He'd assumed the widow was too old for such frivolity.

She explained, softly, 'My intended's dear wife died the same time as my husband. We've been waiting till it was seemly for us to marry. It's been a full three years now.' Still embarrassed, Chas bent over his stew. 'I shan't be sorry. Farming is a tough life for a woman on her own.'

'I'm sure it is.' The leathery face was as weather-beaten as his own. To Chas's mind, marriagable women were pink-skinned creatures with soft dimpled hands. He examined Mrs Ramsey's, brown and sinewy, like the rest of her.

'This could be the place for you, Mr Unwin. Find yourself a wife. Give me a down payment. I know you can work hard. Me and my intended would trust you for the rest.'

She'd startled him. Buy a farm? He'd certainly not considered that.

The following morning, Chas climbed the hill behind the cabin. There was more land to be cleared, stretching down on either side. Trees grew thickly, protecting the cabin from the worst of the weather. Below on narrow terraces, spring corn was showing. A man could do better than scrape a living here; eventually, he could have a comfortable life.

A wife? Chas hadn't given that serious thought for a long time, not since escaping from Miss Spratt.

But as he gazed westwards and sniffed the wind, full of the sappy aroma of spring, he was filled with a desire to see beyond the horizon.

'You're not ready to settle,' the widow was sympathetic rather than disappointed. 'When you find the right woman, travelling won't seem so special. You can leave whenever you're ready. Me and the boy can manage.'

In the bunk house that night, Chas thought as he so often did, of Albert. He'd avoided writing so far because of a sense of failure. Now, after Mrs Ramsey's offer, Chas's self-esteem rose a notch. If she was willing to trust him, maybe others would too.

'Dear Albert,' he began, and stopped. It wouldn't cheer his brother to hear of the loss of that precious money. Dollar coins he'd earned since coming to America glinted under the lamp. It wasn't riches but enough for his passage westwards.

His clothes were ready for the morning. The patched old suit he'd bought in London and a coarse shirt Mrs Ramsey had made from flour bags. Fewer possessions than when he left England but a man travelled light over here.

The moustachios had been recurled and the nephew had helped him trim his hair. He was fit, he was still young, what more could a man ask? Spring was here. Tomorrow he'd be on his way and maybe find a filly with a neat pair of calves? Optimism flowed through Chas's veins.

'Dear Albert,' he wrote with a flourish, 'greetings from the land of opportunity!'

Chapter Nineteen

Spring, 1901

The old queen was dead. No one alive could remember a time when she hadn't reigned over them. Crowned heads of Europe followed the gun-carriage, Albert was one of thousands lining the pavements. The sonorous *Death March* made hearts overflow as they marvelled at the small coffin. Surely only a giant could have ruled over them for so long? 'Not much of her, was there?' Albert agreed with the one who spoke. Another conclusion was that Victoria's passing signalled an end of an era.

Not that there was much improvement in his life at the docks. Pessimists this particular morning were predicting that 'things' were bound to go in threes. Albert wasn't having it. Not when the first event had been an overhead cradle spewing its load. The netted packing-cases began to spin. In the split second before the cable gave way, Albert's sixth sense warned him. He shoved the next man aside and cannoned into the smartly dressed youth beyond shouting, 'Look out!'

Wooden boxes split as they fell, disgorging heavy farming machinery. A curved steel cutting tool embedded itself in the side of the hold making Albert's stomach churn. The man beside him grasped his hand in speechless, terrified gratitude but the smart youth pretended there hadn't been any danger.

'I can take care of myself!'

Albert recognized the younger son of the dock owner, a spoiled sprig sent to "learn the ropes". 'Keep your hands off in future!' Albert walked away, too faint to argue.

He sat on a bollard until his heartbeat became less

erratic. He hated this place; grey granite stones with metal rings set into them. Turgid water lapping against the dockside, leaving a perpetual oily smear with each falling tide. Behind him, storage wharves were black with soot and above, a permanent pall of smoke concealed any sign of spring.

Early rain had made the granite slippery. It brought no sense of freshness but emphasized the impenetrable greyness of his world, not a scrap of colour anywhere – but something glittered, trapped beneath a pile of rotting wood. Albert got to his feet.

It was a man's wallet, sodden at the exposed corner but an item of quality. Exquisite leather, designed to fit the inside breast pocket of a well-cut coat. Gold initials had caught the light: A.L. O'D. Mr O'Donovan, the dock owner! He'd visited two days previously when he'd first introduced his younger son.

The wallet fell open it was so thickly stuffed with notes. Albert trembled; here was more money than he'd ever seen in his life!

He remembered his outstanding debt to Sybilla; eleven pounds yet to pay; if he took twelve no one would know. Temptation was so strong it shook his starved frame. For a moment, Albert dithered. It was the gang-leader's shout that brought him back to earth. How could he live with the knowledge that he'd stolen? Memories of his gentle parents' strictures shamed him.

He was about to hand over his find when he had second thoughts. This man was a bully who demanded the price of a drink from every docker he selected. Albert tucked the wallet into his pocket; he would deliver it himself, intact.

'You're finished for today, Unwin.'

'What?'

'Young O'Donovan claims you injured him, pushing him like that.'

'I saved his life!'

'No one else saw it.' No, Albert thought savagely, they'd lick young O'Donovan's boots rather than contradict him or the gang leader.

'What about my money?' The man was indifferent.

298

'You'll lose half a day. Come back tomorrow. Not that I'm promising to take you on, mind. Trouble-makers aren't welcome,' he sneered.

Albert marched away in a rage. Outside the gate, he examined the address on an engraved visiting card. St John's Wood! That was miles away. Could he – dare he – use some of the money to get there? Of course he couldn't! There was nothing smaller than a pound note, he'd be accused of being a thief if he tendered that. Instead he began to walk.

His strength had diminished. He wasn't eating enough nowadays, he was constantly cold and wet. Now, with only half a day's pay he'd no prospect of a hot meal this evening. Hunger gnawed at him. Honesty demanded a steeper price than he'd bargained for, but surely he'd be offered something for his pains?

'I mustn't expect nuthin',' Albert told himself doggedly, ' 'tis only doing what's right, giving back the money.' All the same, he continued to hope.

The houses were larger and surrounded by gardens, and the streets became wider the further north he went. Trees were plentiful too but their branches and trunks were winter-bare. A policeman directed him to Carlton Hill. Albert stared at the imposing wrought iron gates. He could see the house clearly now, grey and yellow London brick with a handsome portico – he'd never been close to elegance before. Soaked to the skin, he climbed the steps and hauled on the bell pull. The footman summed him up in a glance. 'Push off.'

'I ain't going till I've seen Mr O'Donovan,' Albert stuck out a foot to prevent the door being slammed. 'I have information which concerns him personally. See you tell him that.'

The footman ostentatiously fastened the chain before departing. On the step, Albert grew increasingly chilly. The butler stared with even greater contempt and began a harangue.

'It's no use carrying on,' Albert interrupted. 'I've come all the way from the docks and I'm not leaving till I sees Mr O'Donovan.'

'What's it about?'

'A personal matter.'

Next came the elder son who was informed, civilly, he wouldn't do. Edward O'Donovan suggested they at least admit the vagrant – he didn't appear violent – and get the matter cleared up. He told Albert pointedly not to move off the tiles. 'Don't want you ruining the carpets.' Albert gazed longingly at the distant hall fire. Two dogs were sprawled in front of it, on rugs.

'Just as you wish, sir.'

When Edward O'Donovan returned with his father, there was another spectator; the younger son had now arrived home and leaned over the banister. Albert ignored him.

'Thank you for agreeing to see me, sir –' He was stopped by a shout.

'Hey, that's the chap who almost knocked me under that load, pater. He's got a nerve coming here!' What a liar! Albert kept his voice steady.

'I've come to return your property, Mr O'Donovan,' and produced the wallet. 'It was under some rubbish on number two dock, sir. Sorry it's so wet.' He shivered and coughed. Mr O'Donovan frowned.

'I thought I'd lost this for ever.'

'What absolute cheek! That's papa's – what do you mean by keeping it?' The younger son had bounded down the stairs.

'I didn't keep it,' Albert turned on him furiously, 'I brought it straight round. It took me half a day to get here, that's all.'

'You could've given it to me.'

'Oh, no.' Out of habit, he slipped into imitating the same arrogant tones as he replied, 'I don't trust you, young fella-me-lad, nor the foreman neither. You tell fibs and he demands a cut from every man-jack of us.'

Oh, gawd! he cursed, why can't you think before you speak, Albert Unwin! O'Donovan senior regarded him coldly.

'It was in my mind to reward you. As it is, you have insulted my family. How do I know you didn't filch the

300

wallet in the first place?' The younger son thrust forward eagerly.

'I'll say! I believe he was actually trying to push me overboard.'

'What?'

'That's another lie!' Albert's temper exploded inside his shivering body. 'I saved your son's life. The overhead cable snapped, I pushed him clear. There's a ton of machinery at the bottom of the hold says I did. I wish I hadn't, though –' he cried passionately.

'How dare you!'

'Accusing me of stealing – my parents taught me right from wrong, which is more than you've done for your family, Mr O'Donovan!'

'I shall have you thrown out! As for work, don't you dare show your face at my dock again.'

'Quite right, pater!' The son's eyes were vindictive, 'I'll fetch Bates, he can chuck the fellow down the steps.' He ran toward the baize door, shouting for the butler. Mr O'Donovan walked away without a backward glance.

When they were both out of earshot, a voice from the shadows said quietly, 'Well done . . .' Albert spun round. 'Ssh!' Edward O'Donovan moved into the light and pressed a guinea into his hand. 'Come and see me at my chambers tomorrow, 15a Albemarle Street.' Albert was bewildered.

'Why?'

'I'm impressed . . . and I'd like to help. I doubt if there'll be much of a future for you now at the docks. Word gets about, you know. My father's is a powerful voice.' Albert's mouth tightened.

'If I'd kept the money he'd never have known.' Edward O'Donovan stared at him.

'Could you have lived with that?' Albert shivered then shook his head reluctantly. 'Good man. You won't regret it. Ten o'clock tomorrow. Don't be late.'

Once outside Albert hesitated. He was so cold all he wanted to do was use his guinea to travel home and crawl under his blanket. But having come this far out of his way, suppose there was a letter from Chas? He could afford a good hot meal. No one would remark on his damp shabby clothes in that cafe. Perhaps that pretty little waitress would be there to serve him? With a lighter heart, Albert set off down Maida Vale.

She'd lost her sparkle. There was no sign of her mother and she wore dark clothes; Albert put two and two together. There weren't many customers tonight but as the girl headed towards his table, there was an urgent tap on the window.

Albert turned. The ugliest man he'd ever seen was peering through the steamy glass. The girl obviously recognized him. She opened the door and the man sidled in, cringing. Albert couldn't hear the conversation but she spoke in an angry pleading whisper. He watched her take out a small purse. She emptied the contents into her palm and offered them to the man. He hunched his shoulders as if declining to make a choice but the girl insisted. Eventually he snatched up sixpence, leaving a few coppers in her hand, and disappeared as quickly as he'd come.

Albert was shocked. Was it a beggar? The girl shouldn't give away her money like that. Or perhaps the man was her father? Even so, those few coppers were obviously all she had. He was still disturbed when she arrived at his table.

'I'm sorry to keep you waiting, sir.'

'That's no matter.' He wanted to smooth away her anxiety. 'Cheer up,' he said gently, 'things is bound to get better!'

'I hope so!' The sign was heartfelt. 'What would you like tonight? There's mutton broth or beef stew with dumplings.'

'Both,' it was extravagant but he could afford it, 'hang the expense. Got a letter for me?' She immediately recalled who he was; her face lit up at the thought of his pleasure.

'Yes we have! Mr Unwin, isn't it? With an American stamp. It come a few weeks ago –'

'Quick! Where is it?' Esther ran to the serving hatch and spoke rapidly to the sullen-faced man behind it. He appeared to argue before handing over the precious envelope but the girl stood her ground. She was flushed when she reached his table again.

'It's the new manager. I told him Mr Bennett only asked a ha'penny.'

'By the look of him, this man wants more?'

'Threepence,' she admitted, 'but I told him a ha'penny was what was agreed.' She sighed. 'It's been dreadful since Mr Bennett retired. Here's your letter. I'm afraid he'll want threepence next time.' Albert was examining the familiar writing greedily. 'I said you'd ordered both dinners so you shouldn't have to pay more.' She was anxious, 'You have, haven't you?' Albert nodded.

'I won't deny that I'm starving tonight.' He wanted to repay her kindness and see her happy. 'Have you had your supper yet?' She shook her head. 'How about joining me?'

'Oh, I couldn't!'

'Go on! I'll ask permission.' He was on his feet but she grabbed his arm.

'It's not that – I has to pay for anything I eats these days.'

'What?' Albert stared through the serving hatch. The swarthy burly man was scolding another girl who struggled with a heavy cooking pot.

'That's Mary Macguire,' the waitress whispered. 'She's my friend. She's only been here a week but she's already given in her notice. I wish I could do the same,' her voice quavered, 'but I live here, you see. This is my home.'

'Leave it to me.' Albert went up to the hatch as she watched, fearfully.

'I've invited the young lady to join me in supper,' he'd switched to an authoritative tone, 'that'll be mutton broth and beef stew twice, with plenty of bread and butter – spread thick.' The new owner looked him over. The voice was smart but the clothes were poverty stricken.

'Where's your money.' Albert held up his guinea between finger and thumb then leaned forward aggressively.

'I likes my food with a touch more politeness and less sauce. An' be quick about it. The young lady and me are both hungry.' He rejoined Esther, sweeping off his cap. 'Right, miss, that's settled. I shall be honoured if you will join me, when convenient.' She relaxed and giggled, her bright-eyed self once more.

'Thank you kindly, sir.' Dropping one of the mock bobs he remembered, she scurried to attend to the remaining customers leaving him to enjoy this precious first link with Chas.

It wasn't a long letter; one sheet of paper written in pencil. The opening phrase leapt out at him: 'The land of opportunity'. Oh yes! Chas must have succeeded. This idea took root and coloured every word Albert read.

Gradually reviving in the steamy warmth, he considered his own lack of fortune. He'd lost his job, the cocky O'Donovan son would see to that. He almost regretted his impulsive invitation to the girl as he remembered – the guinea was all he had. Work still wasn't plentiful despite the new era. Rich folk were numerous but the poor seemed worse off than before. Would Edward O'Donovan prove as good as his word?

The last few customers were leaving. The girl returned to the hatch carrying two bowls of broth and put one in front of him. She hesitated.

'Are you sure you can afford . . .?'

' 'Course!' Albert was indignant. 'When I invites someone, I means it.' She still appeared reluctant. 'Look, apart from the letter from Chas I've had a bit of luck today.' Her expression puzzled him then he realized. 'I wants to share it, that's all. A bit of company makes food taste better.' A touch indignantly, 'I hope I knows how to treat a lady.' Esther's face cleared.

'Thank you very much.' She sat opposite, shyly. 'My name's Esther Morgan.' Albert stuck out a paw.

'Pleased to meet you I'm sure. Albert Unwin.' She was even prettier close to, especially now she'd gone pink. He picked up his spoon and Esther did the same. Eating was a serious business for both of them. When the bowls were empty, Albert sat back full of the glorious if seldom-realized sensation of a well-fed belly. 'My that was tasty. Do you work here on your own now Miss Morgan?' He read the answer in her face and said gently, 'Your mother's dead, I think?'

'Yes.'

'I'm sorry to hear it.'

'They operated but she didn't recover. I wish she could have, just long enough to go back to Wales.'

'Wales?'

'She was born there.'

'Ah . . . I come from Suffolk, that's a long way from Wales, too. Where were you born may I ask?' Some of the curls had escaped from the black ribbon. Esther smiled.

'You'll find it hard to believe, Mr Unwin, but I was born in ever such an elegant house in Kensington.' The famous story was retold. Albert scarcely heard any of it, he was so beguiled by those animated, lively eyes.

When it was done and she waited for his reaction, he asked cautiously, 'Was that your Pa who came in just now?'

Esther frowned, then laughed. 'Oh, you must mean Uncle Lemuel?'

'Helping him out, were you? I couldn't help noticing.' She sighed.

'Times are bad, they usually are for him. He and Aunt Vida looked after Mother and me . . . Mother did what she could, now it's up to me.' Esther had lost all trace of happiness; she looked careworn. 'It frightens me sometimes, Mr Unwin. When Mr Bennett was here, it wasn't so bad. But now . . .' She glanced nervously at the hatch.

To distract her, Albert told her of Chas and Aunt Syb, mentioning the millstone of his own debt without revealing its magnitude. Over beef stew they commiserated with each other's plight but Albert refused to let her be gloomy.

'Look on the bright side, Miss Morgan. Who knows, your Uncle Lemuel might find work tomorrow. I'm hoping to do so myself as a matter of fact. This afternoon, I lost my place. But would you believe it, no sooner had

305

that happened than a guardian angel stepped in and give me this guinea. It's him I'm to see tomorrow and I have high hopes. Of course I'll never be as clever as my brother Chas. You remember the night when he set off for America?' He produced the envelope with a flourish. 'Well, I'd like to read you the good news I had from him today. My brother, Miss Morgan, has found his feet in America. Why, bless my soul, he might even be rich by now! See how he begins: "Greetings from the land of opportunity!" Well now, what d'you think of that, eh?'

The face was so bright and happy above the frayed neckerchief. The jacket was streaked and stained with wear – he was so shabby, this kind man! Even the cap was patched. Esther was immensely touched that someone so poor would insist on sharing his luck.

'I'm so glad your brother has been successful, Mr Unwin. Perhaps he could afford to repay your aunt himself?' Albert attempted insouciance.

'Oh, that doesn't matter. See here; Chas explains how he found work in New York but gave it up in order to travel. Restless, he is; always was. He's been helping out on a farm these last twelve months, now he's ready to move on once more. With him being so busy I don't hardly like to bother him over a trifling fifteen pounds.' Albert omitted to add that Chas hadn't included an address. Esther didn't notice, such an enormous sum filled her mind.

'I'm sure your brother would be glad to help ... especially as you've relieved him of the worry of it till now.' Her young face was filled with anxiety. 'Sometimes I wonder if I'll ever be free of caring for Uncle Lemuel.'

'Now then, Miss Morgan ... Every cloud has a silver lining, so they say.' She managed a watery smile.

'It's very rude of me, you having been so kind.'

'Nonsense! I tell you what – there's yet another treat in store for me tonight. When we've had a cup of tea and I've paid the bill – I'm going to ride home in an omnibus! There now, what d'you think of that?' His beaming excitement made Esther want to applaud.

'I've never been on one either, Mr Unwin. I wonder what it's like?'

In Albemarle Street, Albert examined the nameplate: Mr Edward O'Donovan was a solicitor in a joint practice. He climbed the stairs and was shown into a study with a crackling fire. Edward bade him welcome.

'Were you ever in the army, Mr Unwin?'

'Yessir.' The shoulders had straightened automatically. Edward smiled.

'At ease. I guessed at it by your boots.'

'Did you, sir?' Albert was amazed. There was more patch than boot these days and it grieved him to have to be so sparing with the polish. 'I does what I can . . .'

'I'm sure you do. You weren't in the engineers by chance?'

'Northumberland Fusiliers, sir. Private. My brother was made a corporal but I never learned the knack of holding my tongue.' Edward O'Donovan chuckled.

'So I noticed, Mr Unwin. Last night, it gladdened my heart to hear so much truth spoken under my father's roof. I can assure you discussion of your visit continued long after you'd gone.' Albert felt a spurt of pride. 'I resolved then that you shouldn't lose either by your honesty or frankness. However, to business. A client of mine is developing a new form of transport which he hopes will transform all our lives. He needs one more employee from whom he requires the highest standard of integrity. Training will be given but a certain degree of mechanical aptitude is necessary. I imagine the army trained you sufficiently?'

Albert's mind was in a whirl. Last night an omnibus had been a new experience. Now if he'd understood correctly, he was about to learn some of the mystery of how it worked. All in twenty-four hours!

His silence caused Edward to enquire, 'Is something bothering you, Mr Unwin. Perhaps you feel your army experience wasn't relevant?'

'Oh, I worked on the transport side, Mr O'Donovan,' Albert said hastily, 'with elephants, actually. They can be very fussy animals, sir.' Edward tried to keep his mouth from twitching.

'I'll take your word for it.' He pushed an envelope

across. 'That's the name and address. I'm afraid I can't guarantee Captain Inskip will offer employment for it's up to him to decide, of course.' Immediately the shoulders opposite began to droop. It had all been too easy, Albert thought bitterly, he should have known better! Edward noticed the change.

'The note I've written recommends you most strongly, Mr Unwin. Chin up, man. And, good luck.'

'Thank you, sir.' Edward O'Donovan showed his human side.

'Anyone who tells my brother to his face that he is a liar, is my friend. Would that my father could see it. However . . .' Albert got to his feet.

'Families can be a disappointment, Mr O'Donovan. I have an aunt the like of which I wouldn't wish on my worst enemy.' Edward chuckled.

'I trust I never encounter her!'

'Yes . . . an' should I be in a position to save your brother again, you have my word I wouldn't lift a finger.' Edward O'Donovan inclined his head and pushed a folded banknote across.

'Oh no, Mr O'Donovan, you already give me a guinea –'

'Honesty deserves a proper reward.' To Edward's surprise he found his hand being gripped vigorously.

'Thank you very much indeed!' Albert's eyes were brimful; it startled Edward to realize five pounds could mean so much.

He watched Albert cross the street from behind his window. 'Poor beggar,' he said aloud. Daylight had revealed much more poverty despite exhaustive efforts on Albert's part to tidy his clothes. 'What must it be like to be so near destitute?'

Albert floated on air. To have so much money was intoxicating. He must act quickly before disaster struck. At the post office he despatched £4.0.0d. to Aunt Syb. With a bit of luck, he might manage to pay the rest of the debt off quickly now that he had prospects.

Next, there was his appearance. He couldn't afford to appear at Captain Inskip's door in his present state. He walked back to Shadwell where his knowledge of pawn shops was comprehensive. He haggled hard and long. After last night's feed, he felt ready to tackle the world. He even treated himself to a proper haircut and shave.

That afternoon, trim and smart, he knocked at the address in Kensington. This time, the footman enquired as to his business instead of turning him away. Albert's confidence increased. He had the sense to stand to attention in Captain Inskip's presence. Questions were barked in quick succession. Albert replied briefly and precisely. He was asked to recount his finding of the wallet.

'Heard about it at my club last night,' the captain explained, 'thought it pretty rum. O'Donovan admitted he'd never expected to see the money again.'

'I nearly regretted handing it over,' Albert said evenly. 'If'n Mr Edward O'Donovan hadn't been so kind, it could've turned out differently.' The captain looked at him closely.

'You mean – you might have been tempted to turn dishonest?'

'I might, sir, yes, after the way I was treated. A man deserves to be dealt with fairly.'

'He will whilst in my employ, provided he is honest and reliable. I demand integrity otherwise the engagement will be terminated immediately. Is that clearly understood?' Albert realized he was being offered – a proper job! Terms were suggested which startled him.

'Believe in encouraging staff,' the Captain said simply. 'Annual rises, provided he learns all that is needful, gives a man incentive.' Albert agreed fervently. To have a regular weekly wage was enough encouragement for him and to start at £30.0.0d. per annum with a possibility of £50.0.0d. in five years' time, Glory be! He wanted to pinch himself.

'Tomorrow morning, 7.30 sharp,' the captain ordered, 'can't abide unpunctuality. Got anywhere to live?'

'I shall have to find myself new lodgings, sir.' Captain Inskip produced one of his cards.

'Give this to my batman, Cadwallader. Not married, are you?'

'No, sir.'

'Good. Cadwallader may be able to offer you a billet himself. And take this pamphlet with you. Electrical phaetons, tramcars, trains . . . I tell you Unwin, steam and horses, the petrol combustion engine, they're all obsolete.' He had a fanatic's enthusiasm. 'Electricity. It's as powerful as the life force itself. It's bound to change every aspect of our lives.'

My word! thought Albert.

He condescended to travel back in one of the obsolete horse-drawn omnibuses. Last night he'd been struck by how marvellous they were. He'd travelled cheaply on the open upper deck and pulled the tarpaulin apron close to keep dry. Last night, he'd marvelled at the speed and convenience, he'd even toyed with the idea of inviting Miss Esther Morgan to accompany him one day. This morning he had nothing but criticism for their shortcomings. It was incredible how quickly a chap's outlook could change.

At Shadwell, he collected his rolled up blanket and small tin box from the defeated man who guarded personal belongings inside a dingy cubicle by the main entrance.

'I shan't be coming back, Fred.'

'They allus says that . . .' The voice echoed after him as Albert hurried away, 'They allus says they'll never come back here again but they does . . . if they haven't died on the pavement by then.'

The address was in Chelsea. Albert lingered over the words: Inskip and Parkinson, manufacturers of 'The Inskip Electrical Phaeton' . . . This small visiting card was his ticket to the future!

Cadwallader was a tall lean man whose demeanour gave nothing away. 'Yes?'

'The Captain sent me.'

'Captain?'

'Inskip.' Albert looked pointedly at the sign above the workshop. Inside he could hear men whistling as they worked. Soon he would be whistling alongside! 'This is where they make the phaeton?'

'It might be.'

'I've been taken on. The name's Unwin, Albert Unwin. I've been eight years in India and five miserable ones down the docks. This is the first proper chance I've had of a decent job so you'll be seeing a lotta me in future, Mr Cadwallader.'

It was difficult to judge whether this news pleased the batman or not.

'Captain Inskip said as you might know of a decent billet.' Would the man unbend?

Cadwallader admitted grudgingly, 'I might know of somewhere.' He eyed the biscuit box and rolled-up blanket. 'That all you've got?'

'Yes.'

'Follow me.'

It was the third bedroom up a narrow flight in a terrace near the river. Albert was enchanted. 'I've never had such a lovely room, ma'am. It's very considerate of you to take me in.' Mrs Cadwallader was diminutive and round. She spoke in such a tiny breathless squeak Albert had to strain to hear.

'I never know who he's going to bring home . . . He's such a one!' She gazed at her skeletal spouse in wonder. 'He once brought an Indian gentleman but he didn't stay . . . He didn't take to our food. What time do you like your eggs and bacon, Mr Unwin? We has ours at a quarter to seven.' Albert's body trembled in anticipation; for five years now he'd faced each day on nothing more than bread and weak tea.

His new landlady told him her terms, which included his washing. It meant he'd have to buy another shirt. She left him to 'settle in' and Albert set out his worldly possessions, spreading them in a line to fill one whole shelf.

There was an old three-legged stool. He dragged it to the window and began reading his pamphlet: *Electricity – a force for good in our Universe – by Captain G.C.P. Inskip, retd.*

For some reason, Albert found it difficult to concentrate; his thoughts would keep wandering back to Miss Esther

Morgan's bright, vivacious eyes. After a while he scolded himself. 'It's no use, Albert Unwin . . . you ain't got the means, not until you've paid off Aunt Syb. An' as for that poor gel . . . she's got that ugly bloke to support.'

Despite everyone's gloomy predictions, Polly recovered speedily. It was as though, with the threat of pregnancy removed, she was able to relax. Henry saw to it that she was well cared for by a succession of neighbours under the supervision of Ma Figgis. It was Ma Figgis who confided that Henry had been 'spoken to' by the doctor and warned not to pester.

'Your husband's the sort who'll take note, Mrs Durrant. Not all of 'em does. I've known some poor souls fall pregnant within weeks of a lying-in even though their man knew another babby could kill 'em.' Polly shuddered.

'I couldn't bear all that pain again.'

'Don't fret yourself, you won't have to, I'm sure. Let's hope it won't upset your husband too much, knowing he won't ever be a father.' She half guessed that it would, however, but neither she nor any of Henry's acquaintance realized how deeply he grieved over his loss.

When Polly first ventured downstairs, eager to take up the reigns of housewifery again, Henry intervened. Despite the diminution of his affection, he would never neglect his duty towards her. 'Not yet, Polly. Conserve your strength until you are completely recovered.'

Ma Figgis was most impressed. 'A true gentleman . . . not many as would be so thoughtful.'

Polly didn't fully comprehend the extent of Henry's grief. She was concerned to draw a veil between herself and her experience. What had happened was sad but it was over. She'd never been quite certain she wanted children and now that her body was beginning to recover she could enjoy her fine new house instead, polishing it a little more every day. She became obsessed with the furniture; she began to embroider and filled the parlour with cushions. Best of all, she made plans for the summer

312

when chairs and tables would be out there in the garden, enticing customers away from Aunt Syb.

She watched dreamily as Henry toiled in all weathers, to create a lawn and fill the flower borders. For him, it was a distraction both from what had happened and the empty future which lay ahead.

Ma Figgis kept Polly abreast of the gossip. Sybilla's efforts at rehabilitation had attracted a certain amount of attention. The town sat up and took notice. Gradually her actions became the opening topic of almost every conversation. What would Mrs Porrit do next? Polly found herself impatient to hear each new installment.

'The vicar's wife agreed to see your aunt las' week. That's the third time Mrs Porrit hev called, humble like, asking if she might be admitted. She do keep trying an' no mistake. She starts by asking Mrs Nibs if'n they could say a prayer together . . .' Ma Figgis lowered her voice to indicate what came next had been overheard and was confidential. 'She goes on her knees an' asks forgiveness for all her past sins . . . All of 'em, Mrs Durrant. Your aunt didn't leave nothing out.'

'What did Mrs Nibs have to say?'

'Oh, she asked the Lord in his infinite mercy to look kindly on his poor servant in her distress.' Polly wondered silently if any God could be so naive as to believe her aunt sincere.

'Then what happened?'

'Your aunt told Mrs Nibs she had come with a contrite heart, to make amends. She said from now on she had turned over a New Leaf. She said she knew we had been put on this earth to help one other . . . and that it was time she took her turn.' Ma Figgis was slightly shocked by Polly's cynical smile. 'Your aunt hev backed up her words with deeds, Mrs Durrant. She asked the vicar's wife if she could be of assistance at the Sunday School Anniversary, helping serve the children's teas.'

'Poor little things!'

Some days later, Ma Figgis reported, 'They was as good as

313

gold at that Anniversary, Mrs Durrant. His Nibs said he'd never been so impressed. The children never made a sound – and they washed the dishes and scrubbed the floor afore they left. Vicar's wife said she'd never seen the hall look so spotless.'

'Aunt Syb must've threatened 'em with the devil, the way she did me and Albert. Used to scare us half to death, she did.'

'Vicar's wife was ever so pleased,' Ma Figgis said with reproof. 'She keeps repeating how Mrs Porrit do hev a natural authority with children. Some folk do hev a change of heart and 'tis up to us to be Christian-like towards 'em. I might find it in me to nod, should Mrs Porrit happen to pass by in the street,' she finished defiantly.

Which in this town would mean two or three times a week, Polly reflected.

That night she demanded to know from Henry when she might expect to see blooms and tested the quality of newly sown grass with impatient feet. The wind held a promise of warmth, she must be ready by the time summer came. She brought a touch of happiness to her husband by demanding he take her arm as she walked up and down – in full view of the house opposite. It gave Polly satisfaction to see the lace curtains twitch. Let Sybilla wonder as to why her niece was examining the garden so intently, it made Polly happy to think she might begin to worry.

Two tables to begin with; she could expand to four next year. Once she did that, another pair of hands would be needed and Polly knew exactly where to find them; she would offer Widow Helliwell the position. That surely would annoy Aunt Syb most of all.

314

Chapter Twenty

Of Love and Death, 1903

It was a little over a year since Albert had found the wallet on number two dock. Even so he found it difficult to believe the passage of time; that period of his life was a fading dream. Nowadays he woke eager to be at work with colleagues he respected, all of them striving to perfect the *Inskip Phaeton*.

Unfortunately, it was taking longer to develop than the captain had anticipated, all of them knew that. Albert frowned as he brushed his teeth. His understanding of electricity was still limited – the problem was how to store enough power. The captain spent his days in an increasingly urgent search for ways of improving the batteries while the rest of the workforce cut and shaped metal, turned wooden spokes for wheels, painted and varnished, building up stocks of parts in anticipation of the fifty or more phaetons which would go on sale once the problem had been conquered.

'Breakfast's ready, Mr Unwin.' Mrs Cadwallader's voice, floating upwards, mingled with odours of bacon and egg. Albert emptied the contents of his basin into the slop bucket, lined his shaving things precisely on the shelf and examined himself in the glass.

He was almost thirty. That thought worried him too if he allowed himself to dwell on it. So much of life behind him yet what had he achieved? He hadn't even begun to fulfil his promise to Pomfret. He'd *intended* to kiss every girl in the world but somehow the opportunity hadn't arisen. Once or twice in his fish market days the women there had screamed and poked fun at his masculinity. One Christmas a cheerful, fat girl had even kissed him under the mistletoe but it hadn't been romantic. All Albert could remember was the slimy fish scales and hot sour breath upon his cheek.

After his first encounter with Miss Esther Morgan, his feelings became confused. She'd been too young to kiss, only a schoolgirl in those days but even so ... Albert found himself remembering her now, the way she'd skipped about the cafe, full of laughter.

Yes, when it came to kissing he'd rather begin with Miss Morgan; it was simply a question of waiting for the right moment. Provided she agreed, of course. He'd no intention of forcing his attentions on anyone. He was a little uncertain how to ask permission. If only Chas were here to advise! but it couldn't be helped, he would just have to manage as best he could.

The face reflected in the mirror had a healthy glow. He'd regained the strength he'd developed during his army life. All trace of the gaunt-faced labourer had been erased thanks to good food and steady employment. His life had taken on an orderly pattern which pleased him. Six days a week before work began, Captain Inskip led his small workforce in prayers because he believed it encouraged a proper frame of mind. After that, once tasks had been allotted, each man was trusted to pursue his work diligently with only minimal supervision.

At lunchtime they were encouraged to take regular exercise. Albert and Cadwallader swam three times a week. They took turns on an old bicycle Cadwallader had picked up cheaply, a 'bone-shaker' which lived up to its name on cobbled Fulham streets.

Once or twice, Albert thought longingly of using it to visit Polly – particularly after she'd written describing the many cyclists who now visited Brandon and Thetford. Proper mashers some of them sounded, while the rest sported old-fashioned Penny-farthings. Henry had considered taking up the sport but sadly, once he'd purchased a machine, discovered he couldn't stay upright. Poor old chap ... Albert shook his head.

Somehow, he could've have prophesied that might happen.

He couldn't make the journey to Suffolk without asking for more time off. Captain Inskip had allowed each employee one long weekend during the summer, to ask for more would be greedy. Instead, Albert contented himself with writing letters. Polly's tardy replies contained enough to make him marvel – fancy setting up in rivalry to Aunt Syb! And reading between the lines the dear girl was making a success of the venture.

Albert spared another thought for Henry. What had his reaction been? Serving afternoon teas must have been Polly's idea. And imagine enticing Mrs Helliwell away from Aunt Syb to cook scones and biscuits, not to mention employing Gladys to wait at table. Polly must have plenty of customers to afford their wages but the nerve of it, the positive sauce! Battle lines drawn up across the London road; Albert chuckled every time he thought of it.

Captain Inskip had made good his promise; Albert's wages had risen to £33.0.0d. per annum. He continued to pay off his debt and had managed to save a little. Twice he'd treated himself to a visit to The Coachman's. An hour or two feasting his eyes on Miss Esther Morgan was enough to make the sun shine. Now, with the end of his debt in sight, Albert dared to begin making plans.

He would dine at the cafe tonight. This time he would drop a hint to the dear girl that, provided he wasn't reckless, another year should see the beginning of a small degree of security. He wouldn't ask for her promise – that wouldn't be fair, not yet – but Albert intended Esther should know how he felt. Only another twelve-month and he might risk – a kiss!

Such a reward was worth waiting for, even Pomfret would have agreed. Did Miss Morgan treasure a spark of affection towards him? If he'd been Chas he could have kindled that spark into passion, but at least when Albert asked for a double portion of cowheel, it was done with such emphasis, he knew Miss Morgan must have understood. Those beautiful dark-blue eyes were intelligent. Once she'd given him one of her pert bobs, that had kept him happy for weeks.

Suppose when he arrived at The Coachman's tonight there'd been two miracles: not only a letter from Chas but the news that Lemuel Meaney had found work. Albert's spirits soared. Perhaps he would call on Mrs Meaney and ask that she encourage her spouse to greater efforts? There was no end to Albert's ambition this morning. Whistling happily, he ran downstairs.

Esther had been awake since dawn, reliving the terrors of yesterday evening. Her torment had begun when the new owner returned from The Musketeer. The last of the customers had left and the clash of the door startled her.

'We're closed – oh, it's you. I've nearly finished –'

'Come here!' She was immediately frightened. Mary Macguire's replacement had long since gone home and she was alone. Never before had the new owner returned so late. 'I said – come here.' Even as she hesitated, he pulled down the blinds, sealing them off from the world outside. Then, slowly and deliberately, he pushed home the bolt.

Esther watched, her heart thudding. What was he up to now, this cruel man. Something had happened. There was a look in his eyes she hadn't seen before. He was gloating over her fear.

As he moved towards her, she cried, 'Don't! I shall scream.'

'Who'd listen?' he jeered, 'who'd come to the aid of – a bastard!' She gasped. 'Fancy you not mentioning a little detail like that to your employer? Want to know who told me? Dear old Lemuel Meaney. Let the cat out of the bag properly, did Lem. Boasted tonight how he was there when you were born. And your mother nothing but a skivvy. She got chucked out for being a whore.'

'She never did!'

'Don't you argue with me!' The swarthy sweaty face loomed over her. 'You tried to keep it a secret – didn't want me to know, did you? Knew I'd chuck you out, too. Well, you can pay for deceiving me, miss.'

'No!' Esther screamed as he pinioned her arms and

318

buried his face in her neck, tearing at her blouse. Her back was pressed against the sink and her restricted fingers scrabbled among the utensils on the draining board. They found a ladle. As his grip eased slightly, Esther wrenched her arm free and, bending back even further, swung it across his face with all her strength, clipping the edge of his brow.

'Aah – you bitch!' The man let go as blood spurted and Esther dodged beneath his arm. 'Oh, no you don't!' He clutched at the wound with one hand and with the other attempted to stop her flight, catching a handful of her skirt. Esther fought to release herself. Stitching gave way with a sharp rip. She tugged, sobbing, gathering the rest of the garment tightly. When she broke free this time, he flung the bloody rag at her, catching her full in the mouth. The hot salty wetness made her retch as she raced up the stairs to the attic.

She turned the key and jammed a chair under the handle. Outside, her frustrated tormentor kicked and swore, shouting that she could never leave his employ. A bastard had no rights – she would pay for this evening. From now on, however much she fought against it, she must become his creature and do his bidding.

Esther's sobs dwindled finally. The attic door still held and on the other side she heard her employer's final muttered threat. Perhaps it was the realization that it was his own property he was destroying which stopped him. He gave a last frustrated kick, a last threat of retribution and headed back down the stairs. Esther heard the street door slam, and sank to the floor, every ounce of courage gone, filled with despair. How could she go on? Far better finish it now. Tomorrow would be the end of her. Her strength could not withstand another onslaught, she would end up giving in to him for she had nowhere else to go. Hysterical weeping overcame her.

Never could the stain of her birth be washed away but she needed to be clean. Esther reacted just as Kezia would have done. She returned to the landing and filled the bowl. Where his hands had touched, she scrubbed herself almost raw before she felt wholesome again.

She couldn't seek refuge with Vida, not after what Lem had done. Could she ask Bridie to take her in? Thanks to Lemuel she hadn't more than fourpence in her purse and Tom Macguire had no work at present. The entire Macguire family were existing on Alberta's earnings and those couldn't support another mouth.

As hopelessness threatened, Esther suddenly remembered the Mission ladies. If all else fails, Kezia once told her, go to them for help. But, she'd added shame-facedly, never tell them your father and I weren't married. Esther had been too young to understand. Now she had no illusions.

But as the morning sky lightened, so did her bruised heart. The owner would never attack her in front of customers. As soon as the lunch trade was over she would slip away to Kensington and beg those women for succour. Out of Christian charity they would understand. They would protect her, maybe even find her another position. Comforted at last, Esther slept.

In the workshop in Fulham, Cadwallader was particularly sombre. It puzzled Albert in his sunny mood. 'What's the matter, old chap? Lost a shilling an' found sixpence?'

'No.'

More time passed. Albert finished sanding a piece of wood and squinted along its length. The phaetons were fitted out in good quality leather and walnut veneer. This particular facia was ready for varnishing.

'So what is the problem?'

'Nothing to do with us . . . not really.' In an unexpected burst of candour, Cadwallader added, 'Thank your stars you ain't married, Unwin,' and that was all.

It was tantalizing but it didn't do to ask more questions. His words didn't make sense, though. The Cadwalladers were the happiest couple Albert knew. Mrs Cadwallader always amazed that her husband was such 'a one'. Love did that, he decided, blinded a woman to the ordinariness in a chap and transformed him into a hero.

Would Miss Esther Morgan ever hold him in high regard? The possibility sent a shiver of delight. He put

320

worry aside and concentrated on the evening ahead. Anticipation almost spoiled the featherlight brush strokes. He whistled so hard, his throat became sore, but dreaming of Miss Morgan meant the day passed very pleasantly indeed.

At seven-thirty, Albert sluiced himself at the pump in the yard and told Cadwallader he would be dining at The Coachman's. Setting his cap at its jauntiest angle, he set off.

To add to his delight, one of the new Foden traction engines trundled past at a crossroads! This was a rare sight. Tomorrow he would describe it to his colleagues but tonight, Miss Esther Morgan should be the first to hear. How fascinated she would be!

It was a terrible let-down; there was only one other customer and no waitress. The owner was surly. No, there was no letter from America, what did Albert want to eat? Albert sniffed; nothing enticed him tonight, most of the smells were stale. Tripe and onions sounded safe but not when he saw it on the plate.

'That's not fresh!' The plate was banged down so hard, milky gravy splashed the front of his jacket.

'It's what you ordered!' Albert folded his arms.

'Try giving it to the cat. See if she'll have it.' The grim face leaned closer.

'I don't care whether you eats it or not. You pay me for it now.'

It was on the tip of his tongue to be sarcastic but he needed to know what had happened to Esther. He started to speak but was interrupted by the sound of the door opening. The owner's face darkened to an even uglier shade.

'Where the hell have you been!' Esther was standing there, tear-stained and trembling. 'Get your apron and start work. I'll deal with you later.' She scurried past, shrinking away as if afraid of being hit. Albert was on his feet.

'Here! That's no way to speak to a –'

'Mind your own damn business!' The thick finger jabbed Albert painfully. 'The girl's mine to deal with how I please.' Albert heard Esther's terrified whimper.

'I said – that's no way to speak to a lady – just you apologize to Miss Morgan.'

The swarthy chin jutted within inches of his own.

'Apologize? She's the daughter of a whore!' Albert hadn't much choice of weapon so used what came to hand. Rancid tripe hit the man squarely in the face and the gravy half-blinded him. It gave Albert a breathing space and he grabbed a chair. As the man came for him, he brought it down with a crash on the thickset skull.

It was no contest. The cafe owner was large and far more muscular. He shook himself at the impact but that was all. As he gathered himself for a charge Albert recognized the inevitable outcome.

'Hop it!' he shouted at Esther, 'quick as you like!' and turned to face his assailant. There were no reinforcements. The only other customer had seized the opportunity to leave without paying. Albert began dodging and feinting, all he had in his favour was lightness and speed. As soon as Miss Morgan had made her escape he would follow as fast as he could. He prayed she would be quick! The big man came with a rush. Oh, gawd! thought Albert, this was insane!

He was kicked outside. His lip bled from a deep cut, his ear was already beginning to swell and his brains throbbed in his skull. Esther tugged at his sleeve, pulling him away into an alley. Through jumbled woolly-headedness, Albert made out her words.

'What am I going to do? That's my home ... all my things are in there ... Upstairs.' His heart sank: she wasn't asking him to go back but that's what it meant. If Albert Unwin hadn't known what it was to be destitute perhaps he wouldn't have been so foolhardy, but he understood only too well. Miss Morgan needed every one of her belongings.

He breathed deeply and held onto the wall until it was safe to let go. It still felt as though glass was splintering inside his head and his eyes wouldn't focus. Esther suddenly realized how desperate the situation was and dabbed at his bloody mouth with her handkerchief. 'Oh, please, no, don't go back. It doesn't matter, really it doesn't, Mr Unwin, I shouldn't have told you,' but he put her aside gently.

'Ssh, of course it matters. It's all you've got. I'll do my best.'

A small crowd had gathered. They murmured as he reappeared. He wasn't coming back for more? Yes, he was! They couldn't believe their eyes. They watched, some silent, some telling him not to be an idiot as Albert advanced, wavering slightly to where the triumphant bully filled the cafe doorway.

Through stiffening lips, Albert announced, 'I've come to collect Miss Morgan's things.'

He wasn't quick enough. The contemptuous fist caught him squarely on the nose. He heard the bone crack. His legs buckled and two of the bystanders saved him from falling. All around, voices urged him to leave now, not to be stupid.

Albert brushed the helping arms aside. He couldn't breathe, it was difficult to form the words. 'Biss Borgan's things,' he repeated, 'she won'd be cubing back.'

It wasn't foolhardy now, it was suicidal. The cafe owner swelled into a vast sinister being. Albert blinked. He put up his fists but something blotted out the light completely.

He was on the pavement. A circle of faces stared down. One voice called out above the rest, 'He ain't dead then?' He tried to stand but the message didn't get through to his legs. People pulled him upright – he cried out; every part of his body hurt. He gripped hands convulsively and bit his injured lip as he tried not to blub.

The cafe was a blur. Albert glared to force his eyes to stay open. He staggered forward, arms flailing, despite shouts urging him to quit. He was within inches of annihilation when from further off an authoritative voice called out, 'What's all this then?'

The policeman held his lantern high. Immediately the crowd began to melt into the night. Albert saw Esther on the edge of the pavement, her hands beseeching him to give up. He wobbled but stayed on his feet. 'All we want

... are Miss Morgan's things.' Behind him there was a roar of defiance. Albert closed his eyes and waited for death but blackness intervened and he sagged at the constable's feet.

They lugged him round to the mews, to the Meaneys', and laid him on the floor beside the ferrets' cage. Bridie was summoned and sent her children running to bring salve, disinfectant and hot water. Vida stood at the top of the stairs straining to hear what had happened.

Esther arrived, sobbing, on the constable's arm, her precious belongings for which Albert had paid such a price, hastily stuffed into a basket. On top was the picture of a Welsh mountain that had once made her mother so homesick. Vida listened to the incoherent tale and began, finally, to understand.

As Bridie tended the battered unconscious face, Esther spoke of the Mission Ladies. 'They asked who I was ... about mother and her Adam. Then they told me I was wicked ... The offspring of Sin! One of them told me I was damned.'

'God forgive her,' Bridie spat out. 'You shouldn't have answered their questions but take no notice what they said. Here ...' she demanded of the constable, 'help me lift his head, will you. I want to make him comfortable.'

As she cleaned away blood and dirt the policeman issued his orders. 'No more trouble. And whatever you do, don't let this silly beggar near that cafe again. He could get his head knocked off next time.'

'Who is he, does anyone know?' Bridie demanded.

'Mr Unwin,' Esther sobbed, 'he comes to the cafe to see if there's letters from his brother in America.'

'Not any more he doesn't,' the constable said firmly. Bridie looked at Esther keenly. It wasn't just a brother's letters had induced a man to face such punishment.

It was past midnight before Vida Meaney went to bed. She remained in the dark on the topmost stair long after the others had gone.

Down below Esther cradled Albert's head in her lap.

324

Her tears bathed his unconscious face. There was nothing more to be done, Bridie declared. It was up to nature to take its course. Either the poor chap would recover, or ... She shook her head. Albert Unwin had gone a nasty colour and his breathing was erratic. Esther wept and whispered how brave he was, how it was all her fault, she should never have asked him to go back. Bridie consoled her as best she could. When she had gone and Esther believed herself alone, she whispered the first soft words of love to her unconscious hero.

All this Vida heard from her stair. She'd also caught Esther's earlier passionate remark, 'If only we could send for the doctor but I haven't got more than fourpence. Uncle Lem's had the rest of my money.'

'I know, love, I know,' Bridie had sighed. 'You're as daft as your mother ever was.'

'Uncle Lem let out my secret. That's what the fight was about. Mr Unwin was trying to stop that man ... he called me a bastard and said I was his creature,' Esther sobbed. 'He said I had to do what he wanted. Mr Unwin tried to stop him hurting me.'

'Lem did that? Told him? The stupid ...!' Words failed Bridie Macguire. 'After all you've done for him.'

Vida felt sick with shame; not just the betrayal but the fact the girl had continued to support them since Kezia's death. Yet hadn't she guessed all along and hidden from the knowledge?

Lemuel always denied he'd been begging, claiming he'd earned every penny and she had allowed herself to be blinded a second time because it was easier. Now she faced up to what they had done: she and Lemuel were parasites, living off this poor child.

Down below, Esther continued to hold Albert's hand while above, Vida endured agony of mind. Albert's laboured breathing gradually took a normal, regular rhythm. Bridie had done her work well. The broken nose had been eased into a proper shape and straws inserted to enable him to breathe. The flesh was dreadfully swollen but it would heal, given time. Sufficient money had been collected to buy a dose of laudanum which

Bridie had administered sparingly, enough to ease the pain.

There was a slight sound; Vida stayed perfectly still. Albert had regained consciousness and was trying to speak. He peered up at Esther's face, so close to his own that her hair brushed his skin. He saw gladness and joy in her eyes.

'Are you feeling a bit better, Mr Unwin?'

'Your things . . . did you get them?'

'Yes, yes. The policeman helped me fetch them down. Don't try and speak.' She could see how much each ragged breath hurt.

'You've lost your place . . . That chap won't have you back.'

She assured him it didn't matter, she was anxious he shouldn't struggle. She offered him the rest of the medicine but Albert had made a momentous decision. He needed to know her answer now.

'You don't have anywhere to live.'

'Maybe Bridie can squeeze me in somewhere.' She couldn't bear to ask Vida after what Lem had done.

He wanted to touch the lovely hair. Instead, he asked simply, 'Will you let me look after you, Esther?'

'I . . . I . . .' She was confused but he made everything plain through thickened battered lips.

'I've loved you ever since you were a little thing, helping your mother. I've always wanted to marry you. Please say yes.'

The mass of hair masked her weeping. Her arms still cradled him. Bending her head she whispered, 'I love you too but I can't marry you! I made a promise to Mam to look after Lem and Vee. They can't manage without me.' It was true and he shared her despair.

'But how can you do that now?'

'I don't know!' Esther wailed. 'I shall have to try and find another place . . .'

'Hush, hush . . .' he did his best to comfort. 'Look on the bright side, Miss Morgan. You've got your things back . . . maybe tomorrow something will turn up.' Pain came back with a vengeance, aggravated by hopelessness.

Albert gave up the struggle and begged for enough laudanum to give him oblivion. Drop by drop, Esther dribbled it onto his tongue until his eyes glazed and his body relaxed.

Above, Vida listened to her stifled sobs until after a final, exhausted, 'I do love you, Mr Unwin,' Esther too fell asleep, arms still cradling him. Watching over them, the ferrets sat upright in their cage, ruby eyes glittering.

That last whisper was the knife in Vida's heart as memories flooded back.

She remembered the day when a beautiful Welsh girl appeared from nowhere and begged to be taken in. It hurt to recall just how much rent she and Lem had charged that girl over the years. Kezia's health and strength had been expended on their behalf.

It had been no true kindness either, looking back. Vida had always behaved grudgingly towards her. And after the accident, how harshly she'd treated her then, because Kezia remained beautiful and she was disfigured.

Did beauty matter in the end? What joy had it brought Kezia? Vida remembered Bridie's account of that sad Christmas night at the hospital and the final murmur of 'bluebells'. Kezia had shown love to everyone and, above all, true faithfulness to Adam. For most of her life Vida had known only bitterness.

It hurt to remember Esther's whisper after the funeral, 'I'll look after you now', and her own brusque rebuttal that it wouldn't be necessary because Lem would change.

Lemuel would never change; he couldn't. She had married him knowing him to be weak. How could he be blamed for the loss of the compensation money? He couldn't have acted differently, it wasn't in his nature. For Lemuel Meaney to provide, it needed all Vida's strength to keep him up to the mark.

Blindness was no excuse but it had made it easier to pretend rather than question Lem closely about money. If she had loved him more would their lives have turned out differently?

It was too late. Vida was weighed down by the thought of so many things left undone, so many thanks unsaid.

She listened to the regular breathing below. They were deeply asleep, it was safe to move. She rose, cold and stiff, and went back to her room.

Esther must have her chance. She couldn't begin married life encumbered by that promise; the time had come for the debt to be discharged.

Vida remembered the toddler who'd played beside her chair during those summers long ago, gurgling with joy at being alive, giving out love unstintingly. How long was it now since she'd known Esther to be truly happy?

Thank God the accursed accident hadn't deprived her of her strength. Vida had railed against it often enough, out of frustration. Now, finally, she had a use for it. She made her preparations carefully. By the time Lemuel returned from The Musketeer she was ready for what had to be done.

When Mrs Cadwallader opened her front door the following morning, she clutched at her heart and cried, 'Mr Unwin! What has happened?' Albert's beam was lop-sided and his swollen mouth worked with difficulty.

'A small altercation,' he admitted modestly, 'with a rather large chap. Is Cad about?' She was solemn.

'We was worried when you didn't come home last night, we wondered whether we ought to tell the police. But this morning there was a summons from the captain, not to go to the workshop but to visit him at his home.'

'Perhaps he's found how to store electricity after all,' Albert said, attempting a cheerful smile, 'if he has, our troubles are over. I've got some really splendid news, I want you and Cad to be the first to know: I've met the most marvellous girl in the world and I've asked her to marry me.'

'Oh, Mr Unwin!' She gazed doubtfully at the ravaged face, the bloodied torn jacket and bandages, 'I hope you'll be very happy.'

'Don't let appearances deceive you, Mrs Cad. This come about because my girl's employer turned out to be a very wicked person indeed. However, I'm glad to say steps are being taken to deal with that. However . . .' his happiness began to evaporate, 'that's as far as it goes for the present. It'll be years before me and Miss Morgan can get married.' He pushed away the bleak thought – 'if ever'. 'She has given me her promise and from now on, I'm her chap. I'll tell you all about it after I've had a wash.'

'I'll bring hot water. Let me have that jacket, I'll try and get some of the blood off. Have you had breakfast?'

He'd had a slice of bread with Bridie Macguire but Albert acknowledged now that he was starving. It was love did that to a bloke, he declared.

The stairs winded him, the bruised ribs were playing up and his head ached dreadfully but three sausages were a restorative. He wondered if his dear Esther was being looked after as well.

In the mews, news of the altercation – and more importantly, the cause – had spread fast. As a result, Tom Macguire and several of his friends were due to visit The Coachman's to settle accounts on behalf of Esther, but Albert had been ordered to stay clear.

He caught sight of himself in the mirror. Would his face ever get back to normal? Would Esther continue to love him? His nose was twice its size, he touched it apprehensively – hot as fire – and so tender! As for those bloodshot eyes... When Mrs Cadwallader appeared with the jug he dipped in his flannel in the water, applied it gingerly – and yelped.

'Arnica, that's what you need Mr Unwin, an' not just a little jar. Barrels of it. I'll get you some when I'm out.'

At the workshop in Fulham, his workmates declared the sight of him would curdle the milk. Albert didn't care, he was in love! His whole vision was filled with the image of Miss Esther Morgan. He began to describe her but was persuaded to desist. Angels dwelt in heaven, not on earth, he was told and such a one as he spoke of couldn't be a mere mortal. Several demanded how an angel could be responsible for his present condition? Albert began to grin but immediately regretted it. For the present it was essential to remain poker-faced.

329

The happy atmosphere continued because it was the day for testing another vehicle. The battery, a heavy lead box, was unplugged with the usual crackle. No one handled it without thick gloves ever since one of their number had been knocked down, his hands and ankles rendered useless from shock.

There were splashes of acid before the box was strapped into position on the running board. The stench played havoc with Albert's tender nostrils, he covered his face with a handkerchief. The brake was released and the fifth prototype moved in a stately silent circle round the yard to a burst of applause. Half an hour and the power would be exhausted but once the battery life could be extended indefinitely, nothing was impossible. Men could glide over the earth for ever in these beautiful machines. No more noisy combustion engines, no more fumes. Such men would have to be wealthy, naturally; the sort who wouldn't want to soil their hands and might require a chauffeur! Albert immediately saw himself in peaked hat and gloves, high on the driving seat, with Esther waving him off in rapt adoration.

Cadwallader arrived and he returned to his varnishing. He would work late tonight to make up for the time he'd missed. Esther Morgan's name had now been added to the list of those whose future depended on the success of the phaeton.

'You all right?' Cadwallader was regarding him critically. 'Heard you been in the wars.'

'As well as can be expected, considering,' Albert replied cheerfully. 'Sorry I couldn't send word. How's the captain this morning?'

'He's coming down here later.' It happened once or twice every week and Albert was bursting with his own news.

'I've got a young lady, Miss Esther Morgan.' He waited for Cadwallader's congratulations. Instead the ex-batman looked at him oddly.

'I wouldn't make too many plans if I were you.'

'Plans isn't exactly made,' Albert replied grandly, 'but Miss Morgan has done me the honour of accepting my

330

proposition that we might get married one day. When circumstances permit.'

Again Cadwallader didn't comment. Instead he remarked, 'Wait until you've heard what the Captain has to say,' and that was all.

Albert was philosophical. Cad wasn't the sort to be over-enthusiastic. Of course he'd be completely bowled over once he actually *met* Miss Morgan. Albert worked away at the beautiful walnut, his mind playing with delightful fantasies.

Supposing the Captain had solved the problem of the batteries? Hundreds of phaetons would take to the roads – maybe thousands. It would make their fortune and wages were bound to rise. Perhaps *he* could undertake to support Mr and Mrs Meaney and then he and his dearest girl . . .

Albert's spirits reached the sky; nothing was impossible, not now he'd gained the heart of the most wonderful creature on earth. He'd write to Polly. He might suggest taking Esther on a visit for their honeymoon, and once Aunt Syb met her . . . why she might even let him off the rest of the debt!

It all depended on Captain Inskip.

'It is with the utmost regret that I have to tell you . . . work on the Inskip Phaeton must cease immediately. The lack of success is no fault of yours. I hope you will believe me when I say I too, have done my best. Until we solve the problem of how to store sufficient power, this machine cannot travel for more than half an hour. That, as you all realize, is insufficient.'

They stood in a silent circle round the latest vehicle, sunlight glinting on lovingly polished brasswork. At first, none could believe it except Cadwallader who already knew. When the captain spoke again they began finally, to comprehend.

'I am confident there will be a solution one day . . . but until that time comes . . .' He stared at them directly. 'There's no more money left. I have pledged all I dare risk

331

in the hope that we would achieve a solution . . .' His soldierly bearing sagged despite his resolution. 'The time has come to call a halt. Each of you will be paid one month's salary and given the best possible reference for you have all served me well. From tomorrow, however, I must urge you to seek work elsewhere. I wish you good fortune. Good day to you.'

In the small kitchen, Albert found himself comforting Mrs Cadwallader. 'Don't take on . . . Cad's bound to be all right.'

'The captain's offered him his old job back as valet,' his landlady snuffled into her handkerchief, 'he'll take it if nothing else turns up . . . he and the captain have been together too long to go their separate ways. But his heart won't be in it, Mr Unwin. He took a real pride being in charge of that workshop.'

'He's a grand chap to work for,' Albert agreed heartily, 'very fair.'

'He's a one, isn't he? It'll mean less money in future,' Mrs Cadwallader looked at him nervously. 'I shall have to take in more lodgers . . . just as I was looking forward to having a bit of peace.'

'I wish I could help –' Albert began. She immediately became practical.

'Don't be silly, Mr Unwin. You'll have to save every penny now you have a young lady. You must find a cheaper place. I hopes I shall have the pleasure of meeting Miss Morgan before you leaves us . . .'

It was later than he'd promised before Albert reached the mews. The letter to Polly would have to wait. First he'd gone enquiring for a smaller room but even the meanest rent made him nervous. It was one thing to have a regular wage, but now . . . He felt the renewed panic of his Shadwell days and scanned advertisements in tobacconists' windows.

Should he apply again to Edward O'Donovan? Not unless he was desperate, Albert decided; he didn't want to appear a beggar. What was important was to appear

332

cheerful in front of his dearest girl. She too would have been searching for work.

Esther was on the look-out for him at Bridie's upper window.

'What it is to have such a 'andsome young man!' Alberta Macguire rolled her eyes, 'with his nose spread from ear to ear!'

'An both 'is eyes, black as velvet!' John shouted.

''ow d'you manage to kiss him with his lip split in half?' another brother wanted to know.

'Leave Esther alone, she's had enough,' Bridie scolded. 'Have you introduced Mr Unwin to Vida and Lem yet?' she asked.

'They wasn't up,' Esther replied. 'Uncle Lem came back after we was asleep and this morning Albert wanted to get back to work as soon as ever he could.'

'Bless him,' Bridie sighed. 'How he managed it I shall never know. He should have stayed where he was another day at least. No doubt Lem was too drunk to notice the two of you last night,' she added significantly, 'which is the pity. It might have come as a warning to see you with a young man.'

She was still indignant at what Esther had endured. 'Fancy a decent girl having to put up with that beast in The Coachman's! And Lem being partly responsible for what happened. Why you never come round straight away and told your Aunty Bridie, I do not know . . .' Esther reddened and muttered something about being a burden. Bridie sighed. 'I know, my precious. We're still living on what Alberta brings in . . . Tom still hasn't found anything.' Her thoughts returned to the cafe. 'I should have listened to our Mary when she give in her notice, she said he was a horrible man. He deserves a thrashing and with luck, that's exactly what he'll get tonight.'

'I don't know how Aunt Vida will pay the rent this week.'

'Now don't start that again,' Bridie chided. 'I've told you, same as I used to tell your Ma – not that she ever listened – from now on you've got Mr Unwin to think

333

about. Lem can find the rent himself for a change. Your young man's going to need a lot of looking after if he gets into scrapes that easily. A proper hero he might be, tackling that bully, but he ain't built for fighting.'

There were conspiratorial looks between the younger male Macguires. Bridie noticed. 'Whatever's planned for tonight, you two are to stay out of trouble. Is that understood?'

'Yes, Ma.'

'Eugene?'

'Yes, Ma.'

'He's here! Albert's arrived!' From the window she saw a familiar figure turn in under the arch. For Esther he was crowned in silver and gold. She was outside in an instant, arms held wide, face alight with love as she ran towards him, 'Albert!'

It wasn't the proper thing, it wasn't done at all but why should they worry what anyone thought? Albert caught her in his arms. Under the lamp he kissed her for only the second time in his life. He'd never make good his promise to Pomfret now but he knew it didn't matter. There was no more pain as long as he held Esther close. He could feel the pounding of her heart resting so close upon his own. She was his and he hers; there wasn't a richer man upon earth.

He hadn't realized he was a hero. To his amazement, people came out of their houses to shake him by the hand. He might have been beaten last night but in what a noble cause! And Esther would be avenged, every mother with a daughter assured him of it and their menfolk confirmed it. Tom Macguire enquired of the assembly, 'Eight o'clock, lads?'

Growls of agreement all round. One demanded, 'Does Lem know?'

'I'll remind him when I see him.'

'Mr Unwin, it's time those bandages were changed,' called Bridie and Albert went inside obediently.

Tonight he'd not come empty-handed. Three pennorth of pigs trotters went a long way among the young

Macguires. Amid the euphoria, the thought troubled him that he hadn't yet broken the bad news of his lack of employment. Twice he tried, but Esther's happiness was such a shining presence, he couldn't bring himself to shatter it.

After Bridie had finished tending him, Albert rested on the battered old sofa. Esther knelt, clasping his hand. 'When you've recovered, can we go round to Aunt Vida's? She doesn't know about us – I do want her to meet you. Next to Bridie, she's my greatest friend.'

'Of course we can.' No, he wouldn't tell Esther he'd lost his situation, not yet; one problem at a time was enough.

The conspirators gathered in small groups. Tom was ringleader. 'We goes in and orders a meal . . . we all ask for something different . . . that means he'll have his hands full. He'll start cooking everything. We want to cost him as much money as we can.'

'Ain't we going to eat what we orders then?' one demanded plaintively.

Tom Macguire said simply, 'Can you afford to pay?'

'No.'

'Well, then. None of us can. That's not what this is about. What we want is to distract him as well as *waste* a lot of food. Now, when I gives the signal, I want you all to come at him at once.'

'What signal?' Tom produced a pepperpot out of his pocket.

'It's what my old gran used to use, God bless her. Pepper in their eyes, she'd say, a hatpin up their bum, you'll never have any trouble after that. I'll chuck the lot to give us time to knock him flat.'

Amid the enthusiasm another said anxiously, 'Let's hope so, Tom. He's a big chap and when you remember what he did to Unwin –'

'That ain't going to happen to us,' Tom said firmly. 'Eugene? Is my Eugene here?' The boy pushed his way to the front.

'Yes, Dad?'

'You're to keep cavey, understand.'

'Oh, but Dad!'

'It's very, very important. If that copper comes back an' gets a whiff of what's going on, we're all for it. Right, lads? Hear that, Eugene? You're responsible. Right, then. Off we go. Not all together, mind. Don't want him to be suspicious. Eugene, we're relying on you so keep your eyes peeled.'

Attempting nonchalance, affecting bravado, they disappeared through the archway. Bridie watched them go.

'Alberta, put the kettle on and get the medicine chest out.'

'Yes, Ma.'

'You two love-birds better go for a walk. I shall have my hands full soon.'

'Do you feel well enough, Albert?' Esther asked tenderly. 'We could go and make Aunt Vida a cup of tea.'

But in the darkness at the foot of the ladder, they lingered. More kisses were exchanged and lovers' whispers. Albert had to tell her again how he adored her and Esther express her delight. They dawdled past the remaining houses until they reached the last narrow front door.

'Uncle Lem's forgotten to leave the gas on tonight,' she said, surprised. 'We'll light it for her. Aunt Vida likes the glow in the passage, it helps her find the banister rail. Perhaps Uncle Lem hasn't gone with the rest of them.' She pushed open the door.

In the Coachman's, plans had gone awry. The owner hadn't been fooled when so many unexpected customers arrived, unable to conceal their excitement. These weren't regulars – he demanded to see the colour of their money before he began cooking so many orders.

Tom Macguire went into action. An extremely rude remark brought the owner snarling out of his kitchen. When he was near enough, Tom flung the pepper in his face.

'That's for what you did to Esther,' he shouted. 'Come on, lads!' They hurled themselves at him, a mass of

336

scrawny men punching, kicking and hanging on grimly to this maddened bull. Outside, Eugene heard crockery smash with a sense of deprivation. He wanted to be in there, fighting!

A small figure suddenly burst out of the mews and sped along the pavement towards him, shoving pedestrians aside and screaming at the top of his voice. 'Eugene, quick! We've got to find a policeman!' It was his younger brother, Michael. Eugene stared in disbelief.

'Keep your voice down an' don't be bloody daft!'

'Ma says we have. Find a copper quick as you like, she said. It's Vida and Lem,' Michael clutched Eugene's arm, unsure of what had happened but knowing from adult behaviour it must be something dreadful. 'Please, 'Gene, we must!'

Albert stood grey-faced in front of the tableau. Outside he heard Esther's distressed cries grow fainter as Bridie led her away. Through the open bedroom door Lemuel Meaney's body lay where Vida had left it, on the double bed. She'd managed to strangle him, despite his frantic struggle. The marks of that were clearly discernible on her arms and on her grey-black mottled face, livid among the scars.

Albert had flung open the window and a breeze stirred her body hanging from the rope. If only he'd had the strength, he would have righted the stove she'd kicked over, climbed up and cut her down. Lethargy born of panic had drained him completely. That and the knowledge it was all far too late. Vida must have strangled Lem as he slept but she'd waited to kill herself until after he and Esther had left this morning, otherwise the noise would have alerted them. Imagine sitting there all night, with a stiffening corpse for company, waiting, knowing all the while what you were going to do. A shivering wave of nausea swept over him.

Was that what happened when despair became too great? After the lifelong fight was it the only answer for Vida Meaney? Albert felt shame that he'd regarded the Meaneys as a millstone, dragging Esther down. The man

337

had been ugly, therefore he'd been shunned. Perhaps all he'd needed was the occasional encouraging word, just as Albert did.

He was expecting Esther to face just as uncertain a future. Would his lovely girl end up a body on a rope? He groaned, his head in his hands. Only minutes before the prospects had seemed so bright.

A breeze lifted the scrap of paper. Vida's wedding ring kept it anchored to the table. Using a ruler to guide her pencil, she had printed beside the ring:
TO PAY FOR BURIAL.
And beneath,
LOVE TO ESTHER.

It was love, too, thought Albert through his tears; the greatest love on earth. Vida must have discovered their plans, that's what made her do such a terrible thing. Out of love she'd killed first Lemuel then herself in order to set them free.

The minister had seen the birth certificates; he eyed the wedding party with extreme distaste. The space for the bride's father's name had been left blank, yet the woman standing in front of him showed no shame. She smiled. Clad in cheap finery, her hair a mass of dark curls — not one jot of penitence!

Indignation began to simmer. He was being called on to perform a marriage ceremony for – a Daughter of Sin. It was absolutely disgraceful!

Among the witnesses he recognized one or two who'd demanded some weeks previously that he should inter a suicide and her murdered husband – in his church's burial ground! The minister's blood pressure rose even higher.

He'd weighed in with all the authority of his office on that occasion. Those bodies had been despatched to a graveyard outside his parish where, thank God, some impoverished cleric had been persuaded to do the committal.

Beside the bride was an older woman, quite stylishly dressed, her hair the same shade of auburn as Queen

338

Alexandra's. The minister's second glance reassured him; only another maid, obviously in her mistress's cast-offs. Nevertheless, she looked a cut above this motley crowd.

Rose returned his stare coolly. She'd come to give Kezia's daughter away, as was appropriate. She noted the mean, tucked-in mouth and hostile stare. The rectory staff must have a difficult time of it.

'How old are you?' the minister asked Esther.

'Seventeen.'

'Date of birth entered on the form, as per instructions.' The groom was too cocky by half.

'We are gathered here on *solemn* business,' he admonished, 'Where is the written permission of parents or guardian?' It was their turn to stare and their ignorance was an added irritant. 'This marriage cannot go ahead without permission where a minor is involved.' To his astonishment, the bride herself spoke up.

'If you means family, I haven't a single relative in the world. Only my friends, and they're all here. If you won't marry us, sir, then Mr Unwin and me will have to find someone who will.'

That a woman from the lowest class – nothing better than a skivvy – should dare to speak thus, was appalling! The minister had scarcely recovered when the groom began insulting him.

'We shan't leave till you've given us our money back, mind.' He turned to a fat raddled woman beside him. 'How about your priest chap, Bridie, will he do it?' The minister gasped.

'A priest? There are *Catholics* here?'

The groom replied impertinently, 'Why not? Even lepers was invited into church in Jesus' time. Since he was crucified, things have gone from bad to worse in my opinion.' The minister clung to the matter in hand.

'You cannot seriously consider marriage using a Catholic rite –'

'Look,' the groom interrupted reasonably, 'me and Miss Morgan want to be wed. Are you going to do it or not? We could always manage without . . . only we'd prefer to be pukka.'

339

Such wickedness . . . he felt faint. If only God would answer his prayers these people would be smitten with his Almighty Fire. There was a cough; he opened his eyes. They were all still there, waiting for his answer.

He rallied. It was his Christian duty to show them The Way. After that, this sacred edifice would have to be purified. He began to gabble.

'Dearly beloved we are gathered together in the sight of God . . .' when the groom held up a hand. 'What now?' he cried, exasperated.

'Do it properly, nice and slow,' Albert Unwin demanded. 'Ain't we paid the same as everybody else?'

The wedding breakfast was courtesy of Bridie Macguire. Cushions had been surreptitiously stripped from various carriages in the mews to provide seats, and children ran to and fro refilling the beer jugs. There were plates of bread and butter and Rose had thoughtfully supplied a cake. It was less than a month since every neighbour had pledged all they could to give Vida and Lemuel a good send off. Black plumed horses and an elaborate wreath had been expensive; today money was scarce.

Many apologized. Albert assured them it didn't matter; he and Esther were honoured to have their company.

'The vicar won't forget your wedding in a hurry,' one declared. 'He did a proper job after you scolded him. Reckon you evened it for Vida and Lem.'

'I hope so,' Albert said simply. He felt Esther squeeze his hand in loving pride.

'You did right, Albert. Aunty Vida would've been proud of you.'

'Never feared nobody, did Vida,' one called loudly.

Albert said judiciously, 'From what I've heard, Mrs Vida Meaney must've been the biggest hearted woman there ever was, next to Esther's mother.' He picked up his glass. 'Absent friends.' There were approving growls on every side.

'To Vida . . . not forgetting that lazy old bastard, Lem . . .'

'An' to Kezia . . . not forgetting her lovely daughter.'

340

' 'Ere, 'ere!'

Rose felt tears pricking and blew her nose. Salt water left stains and this was her best silk blouse. She lifted her veil and dabbed carefully. Albert's best man, a most lugubrious gentleman's gentleman in her opinion, appeared in front of her with a cup of tea.

'A wedding can be most trying to a lady's nerves.'

'Thank you, Mr Cadwallader. I was recalling the night dear Esther was born,' Rose raised her little finger, and sipped.

'H'indeed?' Mr Cadwallader was impressed. 'I would not have thought that possible, h' if I may be so bold. Would you, Mrs Cad? With the greatest respect of course, madam.' Rose preened.

'Oh, yes . . . Kezia and I shared a room in those days. The night she told me she was having a baby . . . Well!' She gave Mrs Cadwallader an expressive look, 'I shall never forget it as long as I live.'

'I can imagine!' Mrs Cadwallader had been nervous of this elegant woman but now ventured to ask, 'Were you and Kezia in service together?'

'Nursery maid and house maid. That was a long time ago. I have been in my present position for several years. Personal maid to Lady Fordham, very considerate. Never questions a single bill – leaves the paying of them to me. "I cannot bear the sight of tradespeople," she says, "relieve me of the anxiety". So I do. With ten per cent discount for prompt settlement.'

Mr Cadwallader said enviously, 'A very *beneficial* arrangement.'

'Very . . .' Rose became pensive. 'Mr Meaney was there that night, keeping watch outside the door.' She shook her head. 'He, Mrs Macguire and myself saw that girl come into this world. This is a sad day as well as a happy one.'

'It is.'

When guests had gone, when Rose had been seen off with respectful adieux as befitted her status, the Cadwalladers prepared to take their leave.

'That's a fine girl you've found,' Cadwallader told him.

341

'Stood up for herself in church. I like to see a bit of spunk in a woman.'

'She's had to defend herself before,' Albert said darkly.

'Never mind, she's got you now,' Cadwallader was almost tempted into a joke. 'Fight off lions you would, Unwin.' These words stopped Albert in his tracks.

'D'you know, I once promised to do that for my brother.' He sighed. 'I wish I could have written, to let Chas know. He never did send an address.'

'Found a situation?' Cadwallader enquired delicately.

'Not yet. There's plenty of labouring to be had, at a pittance . . . The thought of doing that again frightens me, Cad. You feel your strength slipping away – and I've got Esther to think of now. She's found a situation, bless her. It's only skivvying but she insisted on taking it.' Cadwallader produced an envelope furtively.

'I didn't want to give you this in front of everyone. There's a wedding present in here. Ten pound: five from the captain and five from his friend, Mr Edward O'Donovan.'

It was a life-saver. Albert's gratitude was such that he could scarcely speak.

'The captain said to make it last . . . Well, you know that as well as anyone, doncha.' Albert nodded. 'Sorry I can't contribute. Mrs Cadwallader and me wanted to –'

'No, no. It's not necessary.'

'Well we wanted to do something,' Cadwallader insisted, 'and the wife remembered how fond you were of that flowery washbasin and jug, so that's what's in that parcel by the door.'

'It's very generous of you, Cad.' The lugubrious face looked even sadder.

'There's something else, from the captain. He's given one to everyone at the workshop. His last communication, he said: in other words, your reference. It's with the money in the envelope, you can read it later. Good luck.'

'Same to you old chap.'

Albert had found them a room in a tenement block, built to house families who sublet to make ends meet. There was plenty of noise and very little privacy. He was apologetic. 'It's not much.'

'It's our home!' Esther's eyes shone. 'Can we put my picture up?'

'Of course we can.' He unfolded his collection of tools and began hammering in a nail. Abuse came from the other side but he ignored it. Standing back, as far as ten square foot would allow, Mr and Mrs Unwin viewed the Welsh mountainside with satisfaction.

'Maybe we'll go there when we can afford the fare.' Esther shook her head, determined not to hurt his feelings.

'I'd just like to keep the picture where I can see it. Mam never had her photo taken, you see. It always reminds me of her.' Albert kissed her tenderly.

'Wherever we go, we'll take it with us. Oh, here . . . We got a wedding present.' He gave her the envelope. 'You're to take charge of our money from now on.' Esther's eyes widened.

'Ten pounds! Oh, Albert!'

'It means we don't have to worry about the rent till I find summat.' He lowered his voice, conscious of listeners on all sides. 'Where will you hide it?'

'Never you mind,' she said primly. 'There's a letter inside addressed to you.' Albert read;

'Dear Unwin,

I enclose a reference which I trust will enable you to succeed with any application you may make.

Yours sincerely,

Geo. Inskip.'

The enclosure made Esther marvel.

'He thought a lot of you, then?'

'He probably said the same about the rest. We were all part of a team, you know.' She wasn't allowing her hero to escape that easily.

'Look, it says "highest possible regard". He wouldn't have written that unless he meant it?' Albert tried not to look pleased.

'We'd best unpack. You've got to be up at half past five.'

It didn't take long to unwrap and put away two cups

343

and saucers, two plates, a knife, spoons and forks. Esther used the newspaper to line the rickety chest of drawers, while Albert wrestled with a contraption he'd been sold cheap down the market.

'It's for sitting on during the day . . . and sleeping at night . . . only I don't quite see how . . .' Ancient springs twanged, showering him with rust. 'Oh, that's how!' He stared at the uneven surface. 'Doesn't look much like a bed to me. What d'you think?'

'Should it tip like that?'

'No.' Albert bent down to examine it. 'Blow me, there's a leg missing!'

'Here.' Esther tugged out the brick from the grate. 'This should do.'

'We can't use that. How we're going to make a fire?'

'I shall get us a paraffin stove tomorrow. And a folding table.'

'That ten pounds might have to last a long time, love.'

She smiled reassuringly. 'I shall be ever so economical, Albert. Just you wait and see.'

He went outside so that she could undress. Esther swept the floor clean of cockroaches, hung up her clothes, pulled on her nightgown and slipped beneath Albert's greatcoat covering the uneven springs. Tomorrow, as well as a table, she would look for a pair of sheets.

She lay back against her folded shawl and surveyed her domain. Albert had whitewashed the walls and she had polished the small sash window panes. The floorboards were freshly scrubbed. Tomorrow she would renew the trickle of Keating powder along the skirting boards to protect them from ants. This tenement wasn't too bad. Esther knew of some which were infested with vermin.

The gaslight had been turned down. Moonlight shone on the rounded shape of her clothes hanging behind the door. The box containing Albert's belongings was against the wall, beyond it stood one of their two chairs. Washbasin and jug had his shaving things beside them.

On a shelf was a loaf and some scraps of bacon ready

344

for breakfast. Once they had a stove they could begin the day with hot tea, that way they could be warm without spending money on coals. Oh, there were so many ways in which she intended to be a good housewife! Esther stretched out with a happy sigh.

She would be providing ten shillings a week until Albert found a position. She'd always promised Kezia she wouldn't go cleaning but she'd had no choice; she was a married woman now, with responsibilities.

Clouds rippled across the moon casting shadows over the Welsh mountain landscape. Esther heard a soft tap on the door and Albert's murmured, 'May I come in?'

She could scarcely breathe. Her heart pounded and her body throbbed with the rush of excited blood. One arm, tucked behind her head, was enmeshed by the shawl. The greatcoat rested heavily, she felt as if she couldn't move. When she spoke, she almost choked. 'Yes, Albert . . . please do.'

High above, the moon shone on the discontented in their Kensington mansions, it silvered the hopeless, sleeping in doorways and through the uncurtained window of this small room in Chelsea it illuminated the glorious love in Esther's eyes. Albert folded her in his arms. How far had he travelled only to find the answer to all things here. Esther welcomed him joyfully. In his ecstasy Albert knew he'd found the Grail for which Pomf had been searching. Whatever happened from now on, he must never fail this glorious, magical girl.

Chapter Twenty-One

Circumstances, 1908

Sybilla pulled down the slat and peered across the road, to fuel her daily dose of hatred. Thanks to Henry, Polly's tea-garden was a positive bower, the entrance to it via an arch laden with roses. She imagined she could almost smell them from where she stood. An overpowering stench, she muttered, far too sickly sweet. Fingers twitched with the uncontrollable desire to rip up every plant by its roots.

If she cared to climb the stairs, she could stare through her bedroom window at the tables. Five this summer, with four chairs apiece and rarely an empty one during weekends.

Occasionally a potential customer would detach himself from the queue, walk across and examine her own bill of fare. Sybilla had learned to ignore overheard adverse comparisons about peeling paintwork and the unkempt garden – for Enoch could no longer be cajoled into maintaining them. No matter what she tried, she couldn't tip the balance of the tea-garden business; Polly was the outright winner.

It was a serious matter. Her income had dwindled whereas opposite, what with Henry's wage as well as the teas, Mr and Mrs Durrant were comfortably off. That too, didn't improve Sybilla's temper. As for lodgers, she was hard put to cajole any to stay after one of Enoch's drinking bouts. Altogether, Mrs Porrit felt justified in feeling aggrieved.

Long ago she'd become fully rehabilitated. What was

past had been atoned for – at considerable cost. Sybilla gritted her teeth as she remembered abasing herself to all and sundry. No matter; she was the equal now of anyone in Brandon. As such, she was entitled to complain that Polly was sly and Henry Durrant a man to be pitied. For in imagination Sybilla had deftly transferred her role from that of Henry's intended wife to being his particular friend.

'My niece hasn't given him any children. A woman can't call herself a wife until she does that,' she would observe.

No matter that Ma Figgis had explained plainly enough: 'It's not that your niece *can't* have any more, Mrs Porrit, it was the doctor's recommendation that she don't try. On account of her feeble constitution. An' Mr Durrant being a gentleman, he won't have any *forced* on her, if you see what I mean.'

Sybilla snorted. Henry Durrant deserved a son, every man did. Except Enoch Porrit of course. She gazed angrily at Enoch's efforts to liven their flower beds. Plenty of colour she'd told him. All he'd done was plant a few dejected bushes and some nasty marigolds. Covered in black fly they were.

She saw Gladys emerge across the road, smart in her frilly apron and cap, and set up the folding sign:

AFTERNOON TEAS.
Home-made cakes.
Cyclists welcome.

On a bright green background, the cream lettering enticed passers-by. Polly's neighbours had even been known to patronize, for the sake of one of her buttery biscuits. Sybilla had watched sourly.

Gladys . . . and Widow Helliwell. That woman had dared to desert, without giving proper notice, leaving Sybilla in the lurch! All due to that treacherous minx, Polly. A thought distracted her; she'd heard a rumour that Albert intended visiting his sister this summer, with his wife and new baby son.

347

Immediately, Sybilla's rage was diverted. That cheat! He'd never finished repaying – she'd have the law on him, she'd sworn it. She'd already visited the bank manager to ask his advice, which she promptly ignored.

'I would suggest you let matters be, Mrs Porrit. Mr Unwin has paid in full the original sum – when people learn the rate of interest you were charging –'

' 'Tis my concern, not theirs. Anyway Albert agreed to pay so 'tis his own fault.'

Albert had sent a letter, which Sybilla had immediately torn up, begging to be let off the rest of it. As if she would! Her nephew must think she'd gone soft in the head. Instead, she'd found a solicitor willing to do her bidding. She wanted a summons to be sent off straight away but discovered the guilty party was entitled to a warning first.

She'd warn Albert to his face. In front of whatever stupid girl had been giddy enough to marry him. As for their baby, Edwin, the child could starve for all its great-aunt cared.

Polly came into her kitchen. Mrs Helliwell saw her pale complexion and tut-tutted. 'Still feeling billious, are we? What a good thing Mr Durrant returns tonight, madam. That'll be just the tonic you need.' Polly smiled mechanically.

'I expect it will, yes. Can you manage without me today?' She felt stifled by the heat.

'Of course we can. My Gladys can do the tables. There shouldn't be much of a rush this afternoon.' Mrs Helliwell enjoyed working for Polly. This kitchen was so much more superior to her own, to be in charge was a pleasure. She began scooping flour into the mixing bowl. 'A few more scones, just in case. You go and lie down, madam. Mr Durrant will expect to see the roses back in your cheeks by this evening.'

In her room, the door tightly shut, Polly sat and wept. She couldn't seem to do anything else these days. It had all happened so quickly! An emotion stronger than any she'd experienced had swept aside every scruple. It scarcely seemed possible that she should be in such a fix. Yet she'd broken the commandments and connived to deceive Henry – it was a judgment on what she'd done. All for the sake of a man Polly had known less than four months: Philip Ottram.

He'd arrived with other members of his cycling club on a Saturday in April, so unexpectedly warm, it had brought newly-hatched flies buzzing over the tea-tables. The sun sparkled with the first dazzle of spring. Leaves were vivid green, bicycle spokes flashed silver and flushed with their first successful ride of the season, the men from the Norwich fraternity sprawled in her garden chairs.

Mrs Helliwell had been away. Polly and Gladys flew among the tables with plates of sandwiches and more hot water. Even so, Polly had time to take note of one particular cyclist; young, blond and very tall. He'd flung himself on the grass declaring the ride had been exhausting, yet when Gladys staggered out with a heavy tray, he'd been the first to rise and help. Afterwards, with the sun glinting on the fine blond hair, he looked up suddenly and caught Polly's stare. She flushed. Closely fitting breeches showed her limbs which were well-muscled and automatically she compared them to Henry's thinning shanks. The young man's shoulders were broad and when he held open the kitchen door for her to pass through, Polly found his brown eyes were far too perceptive.

He saw me staring at him, she reddened again at the memory; he looks as if he knows what I'm thinking.

'Can I give you a hand?'

'Oh, no. No, thank you.' Customers were not encouraged to come inside the house.

'We must have seemed like an army, arriving like that. We should have written beforehand.'

'It's not necessary . . .' Absently, she noticed a blackbird land on one of the tables and begin attacking a sugar lump. 'That dratted bird!'

'Here, let me.' He flapped his arms at the sinner with enough energy to scare off an eagle. Polly burst out

349

laughing. He returned quickly to stand beneath the kitchen window, his face on a level with her own.

'That's better.'

'What is?'

'You'd such a solemn look. I prefer it when you laugh.'

Bother the man! Would he never stop making her blush?

He was the club's cashier and when he came to pay the bill, he added a handsome tip. 'For your daughter.'

'Gladys? She's not mine – but she'll be well pleased with this.' He bowed.

'Thank you again for our excellent tea. We shall be here next Saturday se'nnight, if convenient.'

'Why, yes . . .'

He was a solicitor, she discovered, articled to his father and still young enough to enjoy using quirky words. There was more besides, about his love of sport and cycling.

The following fortnight the weather turned cold; fewer members came but Polly was ready for them. As well as tea she had hot soup and they trouped into her kitchen to drink it – it seemed only polite to allow them in for that. Henry was away, admiring a colleague's French lupin seedlings.

The cycling club declared they'd seen enough of the Brecklands, so on the next visit Philip Ottram was alone. It was a Wednesday afternoon, half-day closing; he was the only customer. Henry was at work, Mrs Helliwell nursing Gladys through an attack of measles and Polly on her own. As it was raining, she naturally invited him inside. This time Philip consumed his cream tea in the parlour.

He made her laugh with outrageous descriptions of his father's elderly clients. 'You'll never meet them, Polly. It can't harm anyone if I tell you about them.' That was another thing; they were on first name terms already without having been properly introduced, yet it seemed only natural.

It was as he was leaving, expressing mock horror at the prospect of a lonely ride back in the rain, that Philip's hand brushed against hers. The contact startled her.

350

Polly drew back. Philip said quietly, 'You know how I feel, don't you?' The intelligent brown eyes demanded an honest answer. She whispered fearfully.

'Yes, I do.'

'I'm awfully sorry . . . it's caddish of me. I should never have returned after that first visit.'

'Was that when you . . . did you feel the same?' Astonishment robbed Polly of caution. Philip Ottram recognized he was making love to a very naive woman. He stifled his scruples. She was married after all, not that much of an innocent. He nodded vigorously.

'The very first time. When I saw you standing there in the garden, in your print dress. You looked like a picture from my mother's embroidery frame.' He moved forward impetuously and kissed her cheek. 'You're no tapestry girl though, are you, Polly? You're real.'

'Don't! Please!'

'Shall I come back?' He was so close, his breath mingled with hers. 'It's up to you to say, Polly.'

'I can't! We mustn't!'

'I will if you want me to. I love you, Polly . . . dearest girl, with the big, scared eyes. Don't be frightened. Please let me come.' He was so beautiful, his arms wrapped round her tightly in a way Henry had wanted to but never quite dared attempt. Instead of holding herself stiffly, Polly's body responded with a will of its own; she felt herself go weak and clung to Philip for support.

'It'll have to be on a Wednesday afternoon . . .'

She felt wicked when she lied to Mrs Helliwell.

'It's the weather,' she said glibly. 'It's still so cold. Folks don't want to take their tea outdoors this weather. We'll close at one o'clock on Wednesdays, same as the rest of the town. I shan't dock any from your wages.'

Mrs Helliwell could afford to relax. 'Once the season gets busy doubtless you will wish to reconsider, madam. When there's only a handful, I agree, there seems very little point.' Henry made Polly feel much worse.

'I'm so glad, dear. You work too hard and there's really no need – on Wednesdays or any other afternoon for that

351

matter.' He sighed. He'd always imagined Polly would relinquish her tea garden once she'd established her supremacy over Sybilla but so far she'd refused.

Polly guessed his thoughts. She turned away so that he should not read her face. She was behaving as no decent woman ought . . . but Philip Ottram's face came between her and everything in the world. She listened only to the beating of heart. Six more days and then she would see him again!

He was no furtive lover. Not for him any fumbling in the dark. Philip stripped off his clothes and stood where sunshine through lace curtains dappled his body. He urged her to do the same, the downy blond hairs on his arms mesmerizing her as he undid her clothes. Bodice, skirt, petticoats and chemise fell to the floor and she stood before him naked. Strangely, Polly felt not a vestige of shyness, but she still shuddered.

'You're trembling. Are you cold?'

'No!'

'My dear love!'

In the large double bed which was Henry's by right, Philip took possession of her as though he'd never let go. Breathless, ecstatic, Polly cried aloud with the joy of discovery.

'I never knew that it could be like this . . . Oh, Philip, I do love you so!'

'Polly! Dear, dear Polly!'

He came every Wednesday, arriving the back way discreetly and at different times. They made love as yellow spring flowers gave way to the pink and blue shades of early summer. If Mrs Helliwell was surprised that the tea garden remained closed half a day each week she made no mention of it. Why worry? Her wages weren't affected and she and Gladys could enjoy their free afternoons.

With the onset of late July rain, Philip's visits became less frequent. Watching from her window, Polly prayed that he would come just once more. She had wonderful, terrible news. Over and over the feverish thought

352

churned that it would be all right once Philip knew: he would decide what to do for the best. Without him she felt helpless with no will of her own.

On the mantlepiece, the letter from Albert remained unanswered: could he, Esther and their new baby come for a visit in September? Henry had reminded her again this morning. He was looking forward to seeing them, he told her. He thought he'd better say so, Polly had become very moody; a few days in Albert's company would restore her spirits. Something he could never achieve, he acknowledged privately.

He was curious to meet Albert's wife. He tried not to feel envy over their son. Perhaps it was the thought of a baby in the house which was upsetting Polly? As usual Henry felt too diffident to ask. Instead he busied himself manufacturing a cradle for the child.

Esther heard the familiar step bounding up the final flight of stairs. 'I'm home!' She hurried to put away clothes that had been airing in front of the stove. In one room and with a baby, it took all her efforts to be tidy.

'It's Daddy,' she cried. 'Daddy's coming!' There was a contented gurgling sound from the bed. She knew Edwin had understood. He was so intelligent, this son of theirs!

Albert swept in. 'Where's my lovely girl . . . and my boy!' He had an arm round each of them. Only when he was satisfied nothing had changed since his departure that morning could he be persuaded to let go. The water was ready in the bowl for his wash and Esther put the kettle on for tea. 'Any letter from Pol?' She shook her head. 'Ah, well . . . no doubt the dear girl's been busy with all her customers. Here we are then. All for you, Mrs Unwin.'

It was the weekly ceremony: the wage packet being handed over intact. Albert could do so with pride nowadays. Esther had pencil poised and used the envelope for her sums.

'There's half a crown rent . . . eightpence for gas this week. A bit extra for milk for Edwin.' The neat column of figures was checked and adjusted. As usual, she managed to squeeze a few pence over and declared, 'A shirt, Albert. I insist. You'll want to look smart when we do go to Brandon. Put this in the jar for me, will you, dear.'

The same weekly ritual applied to their savings bank, which had a hole in the lid big enough to take a florin but was normally only fed with coppers. Albert assessed the weight. 'Five bob?'

'Nearly.' Esther knew to a farthing but refused to spoil it for him. 'We'll have enough, I promise.' She would beg or borrow the balance somehow, so that Albert could have his treat.

'As soon as Polly gives the word, eh?' She smiled.

'I am looking forward to it. Our first real holiday!'

Sybilla stood on the vicarage back doorstep, jaw thrust forward, all traces of her once pretty hair tucked beneath her felt hat. Mrs Heyhoe, remembering the fresh-faced kitchen maid, marvelled at the changes. A swift calculation; Sybilla must be about forty-one or two, that was all; she looked nearer fifty.

She'd put on weight, too. Indeed, if one were being unkind, one would declare Mrs Porrit had become quite stout. Unfortunately, she was also dowdy and for that, the Salvationists were to blame. Sybilla had forsaken the Baptists as well as the Church of England. She'd given up, too, those small touches of finery. It was a pity, dark tones didn't suit her, but religion was her shield against any who dared criticize.

Every Sunday she was frequently heard praying aloud for those who trespassed against her. Her voice was shrill when she 'Washed in the blood of the lamb' but it was in the Sunday School she came into her element.

Not a child dared giggle, not a whisper was heard when Mrs Porrit described eternal flames and perpetual torment. Despite their tears, white-faced children were forced to return week after week for more. Their parents were delighted with their offsprings' subdued behaviour. Any nightmares were simply put down to indigestion.

As for Sybilla, she declared she never felt better than when doing the work of The Lord.

Today, impatient at being kept waiting, she rattled her collecting tin.

'For the orphans' Christmas treat.' Cook sniffed.

'Why should I pay for your orphans? Ain't we got enough Church of England ones?'

'God forgive you for your narrow spirit an' lack of charity, Mrs Heyhoe.' Sybilla lowered pious eyes and threatened, 'What about your immortal soul, hev you considered that lately? At your age, which of us can say when the Dark Reaper will strike? St Peter keeps a reckoning, don't forget, in his Terrible Book.'

'What if he do? What have I got to be afeared of?'

'We are all sinners, Mrs Heyhoe. None of us hev such a clean slate, we cannot but be afeared of the Dreadful Abyss.'

Cook folded her arms and faced the former kitchen maid coolly.

'You make your own peace with the Almighty, Sybilla Porrit, I ain't got nothing to worry about. I shall face Him with a clear conscience and St Peter can keep that terrible book of his tight shut. Now, if you've done with begging would you care to come inside for a cup of tea?'

The invitation was so unexpected, Sybilla was over the threshold before it could be withdrawn.

' 'Tis so cold, tea would go down nicely,' she admitted. As she followed Cook into the kitchen, she added conversationally, 'Hev you heard about Emily Tally? Her what was keeping company with Uppsy Biggs? Four months gone and Uppsy can't be the father, he's been working in Lowestoft since las' December.'

But it wasn't Emily Tally that interested Cook.

'Is it true your nephew Albert's coming on a visit?'

Sybilla's mouth tightened. 'If he is, 'tis nothing to do with me, as well you know, Mrs Heyhoe. If my niece Polly is foolish enough to impose on poor Mr Durrant's good nature by entertaining someone what owes me money –' but Mrs Heyhoe wasn't interested in that, either. In a roundabout way, Sybilla had satisfied her curiosity. She obviously hadn't heard the gossip about Polly. When she did . . . Mrs Heyhoe half-regretted she might not be there to see the reaction first-hand.

'It'll be nice for your niece to meet her new sister-in-law,' she said absently, biting into a custard tart. The pastry stuck to her denture. 'Underdone in the middle,' she pronounced ominously, 'and that new girl so wasteful of butter, you would not believe.'

She rid herself of her visitor as soon as she decently could and sat gazing into the fire. Sybilla Porrit might not yet know but Polly's secret couldn't remain hidden. Ma Figgis had been the one to spot it, as might be expected, and had told Cook in confidence, believing Mrs Heyhoe still to be a friend of Mrs Durrant.

If Ma was right, the little stranger would be due round about next March. Poor Mr Durrant indeed, as Cook thought of him now. Serve him right for marrying Polly when he could have had a wife of solid worth.

'Serve him right,' she whispered to the flames. Burn they ever so brightly, they could not consume the last vestige of her dislike. A girl who'd captured Cook's Last Chance didn't deserve pity. Let Henry not be fool enough to think the child his for she wanted Polly to suffer.

But suppose the child was Henry's after all, and not that handsome young blond fellow's? Like others in the town, Mrs Heyhoe had heard about him, cycling in every week. With his smart breeches and cap, he was as conspicuous as a peacock, even if Sybilla Porrit obviously hadn't seen him. No doubt Mrs Durrant took good care that particular visitor wasn't visible from the other side of the London road.

Despite the gossip, Ma Figgis saw matters differently. She assured Mrs Heyhoe that Polly's condition was the result of Henry asserting his right to an heir. She admitted she was surprised, knowing the risk.

'But every man wants a son, 'tis only natural. Mebbe she'll have a better time of it after so long.'

Cook brooded. Even if the child were Henry's, surely some kind neighbour was bound to whisper of the handsome stranger's visits and sow the seed of doubt. Mrs Heyhoe couldn't bear to think Polly might escape unscathed!

Her breasts heaved with indignation until common-sense reasserted itself. Of course someone would tell Henry; one of the God-fearing among whom righteous-ness was strong – why, it might even be Sybilla Porrit herself once she learned about it.

And of all men, Henry Durrant would be the most sensitive to misdemeanours committed by his wife: he would suffer all right. Satisfied that, whatever happened, Henry and Polly's happiness would be destroyed, Mrs Heyhoe helped herself to the last custard tart.

Had Albert's long-delayed visit any connection with Polly's pregnancy, she wondered? Maybe Polly had invited him to give her support with her husband? Cook hoped not; she bore no grudge against Albert. By all accounts, he hadn't had an easy time of it in London.

Gladys bustled into Polly's kitchen. 'Four cream teas, two with lemon and a plate of fairy cakes. And the couple on table two have asked for their bill.' Her mother folded it and placed it on a saucer on Gladys's tray.

'Be very respectful. They're not cyclists, they're gentry.'

'They come on the excursion train, not in a motor car, mother,' Gladys had her own ideas on class, 'they're just ordinary.' She whisked off with the bill and her mother tut-tutted.

'I put it down to the lack of a father, Mrs Durrant. Gladys never used to answer back.'

'It doesn't matter, provided she's polite to the customers.' Polly sounded strained. She'd come down-stairs again but sat staring listlessly out of the window. Mrs Helliwell was concerned.

'That rest doesn't seem to have done you much good, madam. You're still looking pale.' Polly shrugged.

'I don't suppose Henry will notice.'

'Oh, but he will. Mr Durrant notices every little thing, you'd be surprised.'

I hope not, thought Polly wildly. Dear God, don't let him suspect, not until I've seen Philip. She rose. 'I think I will go and lie down again.'

'There are only two tables left.' Mrs Helliwell began

stacking plates and cups in the sink. 'Gladys and I will clear away before we go.'

Half an hour later, she called up the stairs, 'Everyone's gone, Mrs Durrant. We've taken the sign in. Usual time tomorrow?'

'Thank you, yes.'

'We'll say tiddly bye then.' Mrs Helliwell could be arch.

Polly heard the door close, followed by the gate, but continued to stare out of the window. Inertia gripped her. No visit from Philip nor any way of contacting him. She was very near desperate. There would soon be no way of concealing the news from Henry. Once he discovered the truth, how would he react? Panic began to well up inside.

Philip! Polly's gaze fell on Albert's unanswered letter. That was the way! She would write to her lover.

Later, after supper, Henry said pleased, 'Letting Albert know we'll be glad to see him?'

'Er, yes . . .'

'Perhaps I should add a line? I'd like him to feel he's doubly welcome.'

'It's not necessary, Henry, really it isn't. He is my brother, I'll send this myself.'

'Just as you like, my love.' Hurt, he retreated into his shell.

In an elegant Georgian office in Norwich, Philip Ottram faced his father. 'I'm sorry to trouble you, sir . . . I need your advice . . . On a personal matter. I've been awake all night trying to think what to do for the best.' His father smiled genially.

'I'm flattered you still come to me for that. No doubt two heads are better than one. Do we send for tea, or is it serious enough to warrant sherry?'

'I'd rather we didn't. It's best if you see this . . . it came yesterday. I can explain, once you've read it.'

Mr Ottram took the notepaper.

'Dearest Philip,
Hoping that you are well. I write because I am three months overdue.

358

When you didn't come I could not think what else to do so put pen to paper.

I am troubled in my mind. Mr Durrant does not know.

Your loving friend,

Polly Durrant'

The paper fluttered onto the desk. 'Good God . . .'

'I'm extremely sorry, father.'

'Your mother must not be told!'

'No, of course not.'

'What an irresponsible way to behave!'

'Father, I am truly sorry –'

'So I should damn well hope! Why does she write? Does she want money?' Philip went scarlet.

'It is as she says – I haven't seen her for weeks. But she's not that kind of person, father, you must believe me.'

'They're always "that kind of person". This man Durrant, presumably he's her protector?'

'He's her husband,' Philip cried indignantly.

'Then why can't she pretend it's his?'

'I don't suppose she and he . . . He is a good deal older. She was very young when they married. Please don't think badly of her . . .' Philip clenched his fists, 'Polly is such a decent girl, that's why the idea of telling her husband hasn't occurred to her. I hate to think of her in such a fix.'

'What the devil did you expect!' His father was exasperated. 'She must convince her husband, and quick. Otherwise it'll be extremely serious. These things cost a great deal of money.' Philip looked at him aghast.

'You don't mean . . . that Polly should get rid of it?'

'Of course I do. Haven't you learned anything since you came down? This is the real world, not cloud cuckoo land. And *decent* married women, Philip, do not commit adultery.' His son winced.

'It's as much my fault as hers –'

'Don't let me hear you say that outside this office!' His father had lost all patience now. 'Do you suppose this elderly cuckold will permit his wife a divorce? Have you any intention of declaring your paternity, or of marrying the woman if she were free? Of course you haven't! What is more I can assure you, Philip, if you don't sever your connection with Mrs Durrant immediately, it's the end of our future partnership.'

'I – I . . .'

'Quite.' Mr Ottram let misery take hold for a moment. 'I repeat my original question. Is this . . .' he indicated Polly's letter, 'likely to be followed by a demand for money? Think before you speak. Try and be detached.' Philip swallowed.

'I don't believe so. Mrs Durrant runs a small business which brings in a little money. Her husband is also in employment. They are not wealthy but neither are they poor.'

There was silence while Mr Ottram considered. Eventually he said, 'My advice is that we arrange a meeting and persuade the woman to accept the alternatives: either she must convince her husband the child is his, or arrange for its disposal. We shall pay any expenses – through a third party, of course.'

'Father, let me at least write to her – Polly must be frantic –'

'You will not commit one word to paper, I expressly forbid it.'

'But to be so heartless!' Philip's eyes fell when faced with his father's stare.

'You should have thought of that before. I trust you will never forget you have been the cause of this woman's predicament.'

'I love her, father –' It was weak.

Mr Ottram said coldly, 'When you eventually fall in love, Philip, it will be with a suitable girl such as those your mother invites to the house, or with whom you play croquet. After her father and I have had the opportunity to approve the match, you may announce your engagement. After a decent interval, the marriage will then take place. I trust that during that time you will restrain the animal side of your nature –'

360

'Father!'

'Meanwhile, we must get this business attended to as soon as possible. My secretary will write and arrange a meeting.'

Philip said wretchedly, 'I think it might be difficult for Polly to come as far as Norwich.' His father nodded with faint approval.

'A moot point.' He looked at the address. 'Brandon. No doubt she can travel to Thetford. I'm acquainted with the bank manager, we'll request the use of his chambers. You must give me your word not to contact Mrs Durrant yourself, is that understood?'

'Yes, sir.' Dejected, Philip moved to the door. His father's sarcasm followed him.

'I presume this accounts for the various 'sporting activities' on Wednesday afternoons? From now on, there will be no more half days, Philip.'

It was the day before Albert and Esther were due. The tea-garden was closed for the season and Polly announced she was going to Thetford to do her shopping. Henry nodded approval.

'Don't overtire yourself, my dear. You're looking far from well these days. I want you to enjoy Albert's visit.'

His concern added to her guilt; she managed to murmur, 'I shall be back by suppertime.'

She arrived at the bank ten minutes early. Clerks glanced curiously, making her feel hot; why had Philip asked her to come here? The letter had been strange too, not written by him but sent by someone in his office. Polly was bewildered.

A clerk led the way into a large room overlooking grounds at the back. A tall man stood by the window and Polly cried out instinctively, 'Philip!' but as he turned, she saw he was much older.

The clerk announced formerly 'Mrs Durrant, sir,' and withdrew. Mr Ottram moved across. He saw a slender woman, not pretty but with huge shadowy eyes. She was extremely nervous and clasped her bag tightly.

361

As he approached she said with quiet dignity, 'I beg pardon, sir. I thought you were someone else.'

'I am Philip's father, Mrs Durrant.' Her eyes widened in fear, he almost felt sorry for her. 'Pray be seated. My son will be joining us but there are matters to be dealt with first.' Polly clutched the edge of her chair.

'Please, where is Philip? Why isn't he here?'

'I arranged this appointment on behalf of my son, Mrs Durrant.' He waited then added deliberately, 'Philip showed me your letter.'

'Oh!' He thought she was about to faint and moved as if to support her but she cried out, 'No!' She took a deep shuddering breath to steady herself. 'Please, please tell Philip I'm here.' Her beseeching eyes would have melted a harder heart. Mr Ottram turned away to study the paper in his hand.

'Bear with me, madam, he will be with us directly. First there are questions I must put to you. I shall be as brief as possible.'

She listened in a daze and appeared not to hear. Eventually, to jolt her out of her apathy, Mr Ottram said emphatically: 'or an – abortion'. Polly started up.

'How could Philip want such a thing!'

'That is not for my son to say, madam. However, if you do not wish your husband to discover your infidelity, there are only two courses of action . . .' Mr Ottram paused but Polly was too confused to understand. His first suggestion still shocked her.

'If that is what Philip wants, he must tell me so himself.' But even as she said the words their meaning hit her hard. 'No, I cannot do it. I couldn't kill this baby, it's a part of our love.' Mr Ottram thought this sentimental and unseemly. He began again in a businesslike manner but she realized he was offering money, Polly called out again, 'No, no. I never said I wanted any.'

'There may come a time, nonetheless –'

'Never!' She wouldn't allow him the satisfaction. 'The child is mine . . . if Philip doesn't want it, if he really thinks the only way is to kill it, I shall manage.'

'During the period of Philip's visits to you . . . Have you and Mr Durrant ever . . .' This time his meaning was unmistakable. She went deep crimson.

'You're telling me I shall have to convince Henry it's his?' It was impossible for Polly to imagine such a conversation having a satisfactory conclusion but she tried to persuade herself. 'Perhaps he won't question it. He's always wanted a son.'

Mr Ottram decided the woman wasn't as frail as he'd first imagined; she'd grasped the point soon enough.

'I have prepared a paper for you to sign.'

'Why? What reason is there . . .?' Polly read through it slowly.

As understanding reached her, Mr Ottram saw the terrible hurt. In a remarkably steady voice, she said, 'You must send for Philip now.'

'Wouldn't it be better –'

'I shall not sign until I've seen him.' He tugged the bell-pull. When the clerk reappeared, Mr Ottram nodded curtly.

Polly heard the man leave and after an interval, the door reopened. Footsteps advanced towards her. It took every ounce of will-power not to turn her head.

'Polly – I . . . I'm sorry . . .'

Without looking at either of them, Polly rose, picked up the pen, dipped it in the inkwell and with one great stroke, slashed the paper through from top to bottom. The steel nib ripped the blotter beneath. Mr Ottram jerked back as though he'd been stabbed.

Polly stared at her handiwork a moment. When she spoke, she sounded very tired.

'I should've known what would happen, right from the beginning. I never even thought it would be like this. You must take my word that I shan't ask for money for I shall never sign my name to any such paper . . . You never intended it any other way, did you, Philip? It was all part of a summer's day for you.' Without looking at him for fear of losing her courage, she whispered into a void, 'You was the whole world to me, and you knew it. Don't you ever come near me again.'

That was all. Without looking back, Polly walked out of the room leaving father and son together. After she'd gone, neither spoke. Between them on the desk, the trickle of ink spread like blood from a wound.

Albert was supremely happy. His belly was full, his lovely Esther was on one side, Pol on the other – they'd taken to each other immediately, much to his satisfaction. The baby slept peacefully in a corner, tucked in the new cradle. Henry sat at the head of the table – it had been a splendid evening altogether and Albert was positively replete with good news.

'The reason why me and Esther could *afford* this little holiday ... I've got a new job. Thanks to old Cap'n Inskip's recommendation – me having worked before with electrics in a manner of speaking – as from last Thursday week, I've become a qualified tram driver! There ... what d'you think of that?'

Esther had been both amazed and delighted. Polly was subdued.

'That's nice.'

'Nice! It's more than that, Pol, it's bloomin' marvellous! We've had a bad few years, I don't mind telling you now. I never put the worst of it in my letters, but it was only thanks to this lovely girl of mine that we survived.'

'Albert, there's no need –' Albert reached across and took Esther's hand.

'I want them to know, love. I'm proud of you.' He went on quietly, 'Yes, all I could get once was street sweeping, two filthy months of it. Esther went office cleaning to help out. An' she used to scold if I got depressed. Kept me going, she did. Then I got a job as a warehouseman but there wasn't enough money, we had to flit.'

'Flit?' Henry's life had been more sheltered.

'I come home skint and Esther realized we haven't got a hope of paying the rent, so first thing she does is puts on her best hat.'

'Bailiffs can be ever so mean,' she explained, 'but if you've got it skewered to your head – what can they do?'

'What indeed?' said Henry gravely.

364

'Then she goes round to Bridie Macguire and asks for a loan of Lem's old cart. He was the one who . . .' Henry nodded. He and Polly had heard that sad story. 'We parks it round the back in the yard, piles everything on it and scarpers. Hid up for a couple of days in the mews after that. Then we finds this new place in Fulham. Trouble was it had a parrot.'

'A parrot!'

'Not in our room, you understand; the one next door. Only the parrot's fleas don't know they're supposed to stay *in situ*, as it were; they spreads themselves around. We complained to the landlord, of course.'

'Dear me!'

'He said, like it or lump it. So we decided to lump it – we could've paid the rent before we left –'

'It was a matter of principle,' Esther said firmly. She didn't want to give a bad impression, she was rather in awe of her brother-in-law. 'We left a note saying if he was prepared to fumigate the place and get rid of the bird, we'd come back and pay what we owed.'

'Only he wouldn't so we didn't,' Albert said comfortably. 'And now we've got this nice little room. All found and a view of the tree-tops. A pleasant class of neighbourhood, the drains don't stink however hot it gets and baby's thriving.'

'And now Albert has this splendid situation . . .' Esther gazed at him proudly, she'd never imagined he'd become a member of the professional class, 'Ever such responsible work.'

'My lovely girl was on the front seat first day I drove my tramcar down Oxford Street. It cost a ha'penny but what did that matter? An' as soon as we'd got five bob together I told her, we're blowing the lot on a visit to Pol so she an' Henry can meet Edwin.' He beamed round the table, 'In fact, things is so bloomin' marvellous, we're keeping our fingers crossed it won't all disappear. I trust we find present company as satisfactorily situated?'

'We have very little news, I fear. At least, nothing so momentous. Our lives progress in orderly fashion from day to day,' Henry offered diffidently.

'There is one item,' Polly's voice sounded odd, 'I've been waiting to tell you, Henry.' She transferred her gaze quickly to Albert. 'We shall be a family the next time you visit.' Esther understood immediately and clapped her hands.

'That's lovely, Polly! I'm so happy for you.'

'I don't understand?'

There was a spot of colour in Polly's cheeks as she said brightly, 'Early in March, the doctor thinks. I saw him this morning. And you mustn't worry about me, Henry. I'm much stronger than I used to be.' He stared in disbelief as Albert thumped him on the back.

'Well done, old man. A cousin for Edwin, eh!' They looked at him expectantly but Henry still didn't speak. Polly rushed on. 'Doctor thinks I'm well enough. I thought you'd be pleased. Do say you are, dearest.'

'I am, yes. Of course.' It was mechanical; he remained in his chair as Albert rushed to hug and kiss his sister. Despite her pounding heart, Polly managed to keep her voice level.

'I know the doctor said I shouldn't try again but that was years ago. I'm much stronger now.' It was Esther's turn to embrace her.

'You must take the greatest care, Polly dear, and Henry will look after you, I know he will. Oh, it's so wonderful, holding a child in your arms! I hope you'll let Albert and me visit often.'

'Of course they will,' Albert said heartily. 'You don't mind, do you, old chap. Now that I've got reg'lar employment, we can afford the train fare, you see. I'd like to think your kiddie and ours could get acquainted. It'll be like Chas and me when we were nippers. Couldn't have managed without Chas, could I, Pol?' He went to where the cradle stood and rocked it gently.

'Looks like this'll come in handy, Henry . . . what about young Edwin then, ain't he a picture? Got his mother's eyes, his grandmother's nose but I dunno – he ain't a bit like me. You didn't get up to nothing, did you, Esther? Not while I was tramping the streets trying to find work?' And at this incredibly funny suggestion, Albert roared with laughter. Esther joined in, so after a pause did Polly; Henry remained mute.

Later, in their bedroom, Polly brushed her hair with a trembling hand. She daren't admit to herself that she hadn't convinced him – she had to carry on as if she had. Henry sat up in bed, she could see him in the mirror – in the bed where she and Philip . . . He watched steadily, he'd scarcely taken his eyes off her all evening. Polly's nerves were tightly stretched.

She asked, apparently carelessly, 'You are pleased, aren't you? You haven't really said. The doctor was surprised. I told him we'd been careful but these things happen, he told me. I felt really happy. Deep down inside I've always wanted to give you a child. I never said so, it seemed pointless before. Now it's as if it was meant to be . . . An' it's true what I said, I do feel much better.'

Henry knew he had to speak. He was still utterly confused. How could Polly be expecting a child? One dreadful possibility loomed and he spoke rather than let it take root in his mind. To think the unthinkable might lead to madness.

'To me you've seemed rather pale lately.'

'That's because I'm pregnant.' She was gabbling and tried to slow herself – if only he'd stop staring! 'I've been doing extra because of their visit but I shall take my time after they've gone. The doctor said you weren't to worry.' She begged his reflection in the mirror, 'Tell me you're pleased, Henry, otherwise I shall think you don't want it.' Her heart was in her mouth when she said that.

After a pause, he asked simply, 'What will you do about the tea-garden?'

'I might re-open. Not if you didn't want me to, of course. I might ask Mrs Helliwell if she'd like to take it over. Or I could close it altogether.' Polly turned to find Henry had pulled up the sheets, as if for sleep. Almost pleading now, she asked, 'Whatever you think best, dearest?' He didn't reply.

On her side of the bed, Polly bit the sheet to conceal her sobs. Henry hadn't kissed her, he always did before they

367

slept. In the past she'd often pretended not to hear his request. Tonight he'd made no move at all.

Instead, Henry stared into an infinite darkness, his thoughts confused and one enormous, terrible doubt looming over him. He refused to consider it at first. But Polly had never loved him as he had once adored her. His dead love made her transparent now. He knew every nuance, every fleeting change of expression. It had to be faced: was the child his?

In the darkness he wrestled to control his thoughts for he would never be comfortable until he knew the truth yet, as usual, he kept silent rather than risk confronting her.

He could hear her weeping. If only he could respond to her entreaties with a glad heart! He knew he couldn't, not yet. If his suspicions were correct he was condemned to spend the rest of his life with the evidence of her lies.

After church on Sunday, while their wives hurried home to prepare lunch, Albert and Henry dallied at The Ram. In the bar, Albert was greeted by Enoch Porrit.

'Her wants to know when you're comin' round . . . to pay what you owes. She'll have the law on you, else.'

There were sniggers from his cronies. Albert nodded but held his tongue. Once he and Henry were out of earshot, he confided the story of the debt. Henry was shocked.

'Seven per cent is too much!'

'It beat me into the ground. I wasn't earning more than eight an' six a week sometimes. I give her back fifteen pound. It took me years to do it and it's all I'm willing to pay. She's had her pound of flesh,' he said stubbornly then sighed. 'I will admit, I ain't looking forward to the visit this afternoon.'

'A pity Chas could not repay the money himself.'

'He had enough on his plate. He'd only got the fare and a little bit extra. He must be rich by now – I expect he uses pound notes to light his cigars – but I shall never ask him for the money. Did I ever show you his letter?'

The creases were so worn, Albert recited the contents

rather than unfold the paper. Henry said suddenly, 'You're both fond of Polly aren't you, you and Chas?' Albert looked at him in amazement.

'Of course we are! She's the best sister a chap could have. We went through thick and thin together when we was living with Aunt Syb. Why, me and Chas — we didn't feel right unless Pol was with us. We didn't half miss her in India.' This testimonial didn't bring any reaction. Albert was uneasy. He and Esther had been puzzled by Henry's apparent indifference to Polly's news.

Eventually, Henry said, 'She shouldn't be having another baby.' Albert was relieved; if it was concern for her health — maybe he could reason with him.

'She wants one though, don't she? She told Esther whatever the risk she was really pleased to be giving you a son. So if she's willing . . .' But Henry's expression didn't soften. ' 'Course there's no guarantee, but I don't suppose you'll mind if it's a girl? Especially if it looks like Pol, eh? Next to Esther, she's the prettiest girl I know. She cooks well, an' all.' Nothing, it seemed, would rouse Henry to enthusiasm. Albert became anxious.

'You are all right, you and Pol?' he asked awkwardly. 'I mean — she keeps the house nice. You can smell the linseed the minute you walks in, she uses so much polish. Always was a tidy little soul.'

'I'm too old to have a son.'

'Nonsense!' Albert could reassure him. 'I was nervous about it but I never shall forget the night Edwin was born. Bridie come round, Esther wouldn't have no one else. We had a job getting her upstairs — she's so fat nowadays. Anyway after I'd heaved her as far as our landing, she told me to disappear but I couldn't leave my lovely girl, could I? I sat on the stairs. I wanted to run away. The neighbours grumbled about the noise but once they knew the reason, they was really kind. It was daylight before it was over. It went quiet — my heart nearly stopped. I banged on the door and said to let me in. Bridie opened it a crack, said keep your voice down and make us a cuppa tea for Gawd's sake. You have to go downstairs to fill the kettle at our place but there's a gas ring on the landing, ever so convenient.

'When I went in with the teapot, you could've knocked me over.' Albert was rapt with happiness, 'There weren't two people in that room, Henry, there was three! First was my girl, pleased as punch, and beside her was this little perisher, his face all squashed. He started to cry and Bridie gives him summat to suck while we has our tea. She said two generations was enough and to send for someone else when it was baby's turn to be a Dad. That was when I realized it must be a boy – I was that excited, I'd forgotten to ask!

'That cuppa was the best I've ever tasted ... sitting there, cuddling my own little son. I know you must be worried because of what happened last time but Polly's game to try again, so why not? I see the way she watches you – she's worried sick you're not happy, she said so to Esther. I hope you can see your way to telling her you're pleased, and put her mind at rest.'

Emotional, embarrassed, Albert drained his pint, wiped his moustaches, blew his nose and sat back. After a long pause Henry cleared his throat.

'Polly must give up the tea-garden. It's too much for her.'

'That's a good idea,' Albert agreed heartily. 'Why not close it down altogether and let old Syb have her customers back. Live and let live, that's what I say.'

Esther insisted on accompanying him on the visit to Sybilla; Albert was secretly thankful. She was adamant about taking Edwin, too. 'How could anyone resist that smile? The dear little chap ... Is he ready to charm his great-aunt then?' Albert kept his doubts to himself. Maybe Sybilla had changed? Maybe the moon really was made of green cheese?

As they crossed the London road, he was aware of being observed. 'Look at her, peeping at us through the blind slats!'

'Behave, Albert! Watch the traffic,' Esther scolded, 'Me and Edwin don't want to be run over.' It was nonsense after London streets but she wanted to distract him; Albert was jittery.

370

'You mustn't let her upset you –' he began again as they walked past the neglected lavender bushes.

'You've already told me a hundred times –'

'Yes, but Aunt Syb's different. She could upset the Angel Gabriel hisself –'

'Sssh!' He knocked and Esther thought – that brass handle could do with a bit of a clean . . . not to mention her top step.

The front door opened and Sybilla Porrit stared at them. A glance at Esther and her lip curled. He'd married a mouse, with a mass of dark hair – and so young! She looked more like a schoolgirl than a wife.

'Oh, it's you?' Albert smiled.

'You knows it is, Aunt Syb. You've been watching us all the way across.' Not the way to begin, thought Esther; Sybilla stiffened.

'Who's this?'

'I'd like to introduce my wife Esther, and our son Edwin, six months old next Thursday.' Esther put out a hand which Sybilla ignored. Perhaps it hadn't been such a good idea to bring the baby?

'So you're the one stupid enough to marry him.' Sybilla didn't wait to see Esther's reaction. 'Come inside, both of you. What I've got to say won't take long.' Albert tried to give a reassuring wink and failed. They followed, not into the parlour, but the kitchen.

'I shan't ask you to sit. Now . . .' Sybilla folded her arms. 'Where's the rest of my money?'

'You've had fifteen pound, Aunt Syb. I sweated to earn every penny, even went without my victuals. I know I agreed to pay seven per cent on top, but that was unfair. You took advantage.' Sybilla's expression changed. Esther recognized hatred with dismay.

'You signed the piece of paper!'

'I'd no choice.' Sybilla changed tactics.

'Who's to say you've paid me a penny?' she demanded with a cunning smile.

'What?'

'Where's your receipts? You ain't got any, have you? Because I never sent any and you was too stupid to ask.

371

So now you can start paying me all over again, Albert. That'll teach you to try'n cheat me. Twenty-two pound seven an six, that's compound interest over all this time – let's see how long it takes you, eh?' Albert was speechless, not so Esther.

'Why, you dreadful old woman – I never heard such wickedness.' She swiftly deposited Edwin in a chair, the better to deal with her opponent. 'Now you just listen to me . . .' She was shorter and squared up as Gyp might have done. 'You're not only wicked, you're a bully, Mrs Porrit. Stop tormenting my Albert, d'you hear. I won't have it.'

'Ah!' It was a gargle rather than a word; it made Albert quake but had no apparent effect on Esther.

'Don't you call me no names!'

'Albert paid that fifteen pounds, as well you know.' She was so angry she wagged her finger. 'He sent postal orders and the stubs are all in his tin box at home. He would've remembered them if he hadn't been so shocked.' Taken aback by her astuteness, Sybilla nevertheless began to rally.

'What if he has, he still owes me the interest. I shall have the law on him for that!'

'No . . .' Esther shook her head vehemently. 'I know what it's like to have a debt – it drains your life blood. You can't do that to Albert and me. He borrowed that money so that Chas could have his chance –'

'What's Chas got to do with it?'

'He needed the money to go to America. To get away from you, I expect.' This made Sybilla really angry: Chas in America and she not even in London? 'As for the interest, we can't afford to pay now there's Edwin to think of.'

'That's your fault,' sneered Sybilla. 'What do I care if you starve.' Esther clenched her fists tight, she was shaking with anger.

'I shall tell everyone in Brandon about your cruel seven per cent. You'll not be able to hold your head up outside these four walls, Mrs Porrit. I shall go straight round and tell the minister of your church – and Albert shall tell

Mrs Heyhoe and all your other friends.' She scooped up Edwin. 'Come on, Albert, let's leave this house for ever.'

'I'm entitled,' Sybilla cried wildly, 'that money's what I need for my savings!'

'Rubbish. You're just a miserable old miser! Trying to force your own kith and kin into the gutter.' Esther swept towards the front door, the baby clutched to her breast.

'Go on, get out! Go back to that whoring sister of yours.' Albert whipped round.

'Don't you speak ill of Polly –' but Sybilla had heard the gossip now, 'That's not Henry Durrant's child. Ask her yourself. That cyclist, he's the father. He come sneaking round when Henry was out. Now she's carrying his bastard. We must all pray this one dies as well, for Henry's sake.'

'Oh!' Esther protected Edwin as though the poison might defile him. She spoke in a low fierce whisper, 'I was born a bastard, Mrs Porrit –'

'What!'

'All through my life people who call themselves Christians have shown me nothing but evil. When you were in church this morning did you promise to love your neighbour? Not to trespass? God forgive you for being such a damned old hypocrite!'

She'd reached the road before she realized her whole body was trembling. Albert caught her by the arm. 'Let's walk for a bit. We can't go back, not in this state.' He took the baby from her. 'Still asleep, bless him.'

Alone on her step, Sybilla was dumbfounded: how dare that chit speak to her like that! Old? She was only forty-two.

'What a wicked, cruel woman . . .' Despite her resolution, Esther burst into tears. 'Saying such things about Polly!'

'Ye-es.' His doubt appalled her.

'Albert, you don't believe . . . It can't possibly be true!' He looked at her helplessly.

'Of course not.' But Sybilla had sounded so sure. Another aspect troubled him. 'Suppose Henry's heard? It would explain why he's been so quiet. You and me was over the moon when Polly told us but he just sat in his chair. This could be the answer.'

'Will you tell him it's nonsense?' Albert was evasive.

'It's not up to us, Esther. It's between Pol and her husband.' He caught sight of her troubled face. 'Here . . . don't take on.'

'You always said Polly and Henry weren't terribly fond of one another.'

'Not that exactly. Henry was fond, very fond indeed. With Pol it was different.'

'Yes.'

'I don't think she realized how deep it went with Henry.'

Esther said in a small voice, 'If the gossip were true . . . about the cyclist . . . it would mean she'd broken her marriage vows.'

'Yes, well . . . maybe it was only gossip. Old Syb's jealousy. But you stood up to her. Who's my lovely girl then!' Determined to cheer as well as divert her, Albert hugged her hard. 'My word but Syb was surprised – I could see her face. Defy the world, you would, Mrs Unwin. Give us a kiss.' Such affection in public made Esther shy.

'When she spoke of money I was remembering Vida and Lem . . . What they sacrificed!'

'I know, love. Don't cry. You'll upset baby – an' me as well, come to that.'

'D'you think she will try and force you to pay?'

'I dunno. Let's put it out of our minds and enjoy the rest of the day.'

Calm once more, they walked arm in arm as far as the river. The leaves had fallen and were wet underfoot. Albert showed her where he had nearly drowned among the water lilies and they watched as the bright lights came on one by one in the big house opposite. Elegantly clad occupants wandered up to stare at them from inside the French windows. As the sun began to set, a cold mist rolled across the fields.

'Best go back, dear. It's nearly time to feed Edwin.'

'Yes, of course. He's been such a good little chap today.'

Albert looked at her hopefully. 'Maybe it was only gossip?'

'We must believe so, for both their sakes.'

'Yes.' But the seed of doubt was well and truly sown.

At the station Polly clung to Albert. 'You will come back?'

' 'Course we will.'

'As soon as you can? As soon as the baby's born?'

'I can't promise exactly when,' Albert began. Esther leaned out of the carriage window to kiss her.

'I shall save in the jar and as soon as it's full, we'll buy another excursion ticket.' The bright cheerful face made Polly smile.

'I'm glad Albert found you, Esther. You're just the girl he needed.'

'He looks after me, I look after him and we both look after Edwin,' Esther said simply. 'Goodbye, Henry. Goodbye dear, dear Polly. I shall be thinking of you.'

Albert unwrapped her arms and murmured gently, 'Be a good girl now, Pol. Look after Henry.' He climbed on board. As the train began to move he waved, and waved again. His last sight was of Henry already walking away but Polly still stood, watching them go.

Chapter Twenty-Two

Momentous Events, 1909

In Albert's new situation, life had become almost too exciting. The daily battle between horse-drawn cabs, automobiles, omnibuses and trams to occupy the stretch of road that was Oxford Street, taxed his nerves to the limit.

Skill and concentration apart, there was also a need for tact. A small, bowler-hatted inspector named Pentwhistle had been given responsibility for Albert's particular section of tramline; he'd also become a thorn in Albert's flesh.

Esther grew to hate the very name of Inspector Pentwhistle. Each day there was some battle to report. Thanks to a regular wage, they had moved into two rooms in Lillie Road – it was her nicest home so far – but for how long was a constant anxiety.

Nowadays when she heard Albert's footstep, Edwin would be admonished to silence, 'Until we see what sort of mood your father's in.' Always she would greet Albert with a smile and, if the signs were propitious, risk teasing him into laughter. If they were not she would serve up tea and listen sympathetically, in silence.

The problem for Albert was Pentwhistle's desire to be seen as general of his small army, especially when there was a crowd. During the rush hour orders would ring out. 'Be quick with that pole . . . At the double! Mustn't keep the public waiting.' Albert seldom saw the owner of the voice due to his small stature, but Pentwhistle's roar made up for this deficiency.

'The phantom was there again today, love,' Albert sighed and stirred sugar into his tea. 'I did the change-over within the time – Pentwhistle knows the schedule – I can't start back before the halfhour, can I? People relies on us to be *on time* not five minutes ahead.'

'I think baby's cutting a tooth . . . He's been a bit miserable.'

Albert brightened. 'Let's have a look.'

She put Edwin on Albert's lap and prayed he wouldn't grizzle. Albert pushed a finger inside the rosebud mouth. Immediately petty irritations were forgotten. 'You're right, I can feel it coming through the gum.' He looked at her excitedly, 'How about a nice bit of beef? Edwin can learn to chew properly on that.'

In Suffolk, Sybilla continued to brood too. Albert's wife had insulted her – only a schoolgirl, it was ridiculous him marrying someone so young – and her no better than she ought to be. How dare she speak so to a God-fearing woman! Nor was Sybilla prepared to give up the fight for her money. She told the solicitor to issue the summons. For some reason, the man delayed. Weeks passed. Sybilla complained to everyone who would listen including Mrs Heyhoe but Cook answered tartly.

'You leave your nephew alone. He's got a nice little family, he deserves a bit of peace.'

'What about my interest?' Mrs Heyhoe glanced up from poking the fire.

'What about it? He paid what he owed, didn't he? You was too greedy for your own good.'

'I shall pray for him . . . and that slut he's married . . . and that whore of a sister of his, who's betrayed her husband.'

'Seems to me . . .' Mrs Heyhoe struggled upright, 'you're asking the Almighty to overlook one little item, Mrs Porrit. Does you beg His forgiveness for your sharp tongue and mean spirit? In case the Great Reaper comes to call?'

February was dank and miserable; rain fell persistently, filling undulations in the lawn, soaking the stacked chairs

377

and tables, covering the white paintwork with a residue of slimey green mould. It seemed to Polly as if all her past achievements were being washed away in the mud.

In previous years the furniture had been carefully stored at the end of the season. This year, Henry announced he needed the garden shed for his plants and Polly felt nervous of defying him.

She grew despondent; wood could rot without adequate protection. Her pretty chairs were beginning to disintegrate under the onslaught of so much rain. But as her belly swelled she became lethargic. Perhaps it didn't matter anyway; Henry had never wanted her to have the tea-garden.

'And I shan't have time for it, shall I?' she murmured to the child inside, 'not once you're here.'

Albert's letters were a solace. She found herself looking out for the postman. She laughed at Albert's threat to frizzle Pentwhistle to a cinder with a bolt of electricity from his tram-pole. Henry hadn't seen the joke; he'd been shocked.

In the desolate winter silence, Polly tried to rid herself of despair. She recalled how she'd laughed aloud during Albert's visit, something she hadn't done for ages. Esther was such a dear girl too, always thoughtful.

Timid though she was of Henry nowadays, Polly read aloud snippets from Esther concerning Edwin's progress. His attitude didn't soften. Nor did he admire the lovingly embroidered baby clothes sent at Christmas. On her darkest days, Polly would open the drawer and stroke the fine handiwork in search of comfort.

It wasn't the birth that frightened her now so much as the future. As her pregnancy increased, Polly's mind slowed to a calmer rhythm but the worry remained: would Henry change?

When warmth returned to the sun, maybe their life together would revive? Were they intertwined with the cycle slumbering beneath the soil? Polly linked her hands beneath her belly to cuddle the child. 'We shall have such times, you and me. I shan't feel lonely with you beside me. And he'll come round, he'll enjoy being your papa.'

But she wasn't sure and she'd no one to turn to. She'd been so busy with her tea-garden, she hadn't cultivated many friends and Mrs Helliwell could never be a confidante. There was only Albert, and he so far away. Esther was too young. Polly couldn't bring herself to describe her worries in a letter.

Perhaps this uncertainty was her punishment. That brief glorious feeling of being loved was bitter as gall now it had turned out to be nothing but betrayal.

She couldn't seem to reach Henry. Yet how could they continue to live in this intolerable limbo? 'There ain't been much fun since we were married,' Polly sighed, 'I know I've been wicked but it won't ever happen again. We can't go on like this . . . I do wish Albert was here.'

There was a broken piece of guttering through which the rain splashed against the window cill. She spent much of her time listening to the hypnotic sound, looking out on the sodden tea-garden. That had been a success, no one could deny it. Henry had been surprised. He'd also been nervous of reprisals by Sybilla but these hadn't happened.

Polly had even managed to put by a little money. It meant she could give Esther a ten pound note when they left. The girl had thanked her with tears in her eyes. It would be an insurance against the future she'd told Polly, in case Albert found tram-driving too arduous.

If only Albert and Esther could be here when the baby arrived, or wonder of wonders – Chas return. Between them they would coax Henry into a better frame of mind. These thoughts grew more urgent as days lengthened and Polly's time drew near.

Henry struggled grimly through the slush. The bitter wind made his eyes water. He'd been bidden to come to the surgery and once there, the doctor didn't waste time. 'It's about your wife, Mr Durrant.'

'Yes.' Henry showed no curiosity. The doctor wondered why after all these years this grey-faced man should want a child.

'Although Mrs Durrant is unwilling, I wish to arrange her to come into hospital for her confinement.'

379

'She appears to be well.'

'Nevertheless she is – mature – to be undertaking another pregnancy.' The doctor also considered Polly anaemic and melancholic, not to mention the problem of a narrow pelvic brim. 'I don't want to worry you, Mr Durrant...' He glanced up; Henry remained expressionless. Yes, dammit, I do want to worry you, he thought irritated. He went on briskly, 'I would have preferred you and Mrs Durrant to have taken my earlier advice. As it is, we must take every precaution. With your permission, I will arrange to admit her for her lying-in.' Henry bowed.

The doctor wondered whether he should mention the possibility of a Caesarian section? Better not. Henry might react to that by fainting. 'I trust Mrs Durrant is taking care? Plenty of rest?'

'As far as I am aware.'

That evening Henry told her of the decision. Polly said nervously, 'I don't want to put you to unnecessary expense, Henry.'

'You know there's a risk. You must do as he suggests.' He sounded so cold and indifferent, her fears were revived. Polly tried to stay calm.

'Shall I arrange for Mrs Helliwell to cook while I'm away?'

'I can manage. I did so before we were married.' She bit her lip.

'Is there anything I can do to make you more comfortable?' There was a pause. Polly felt the blood rise in her cheeks.

Eventually Henry replied, 'If the house is orderly with sufficient food in the pantry, that is all I require. The coal shed is empty, by the way. We must send for another five hundred-weight. This raw weather looks set to continue.'

Polly served his meal in silence, sat while he ate and read his newspaper. As she began clearing away the dishes, he forced himself to ask, 'When precisely is your child due? I believe you told me March originally?' Aloof and nervous, he was careless of his choice of words but Polly imagined them deliberate.

'I think it could be the end of this month.' She was

trembling. 'Your child!' He'd never referred to it thus before. He'd revealed that he knew about Philip Ottram, or so she concluded.

Frightened though she was, she came to a decision: they must discuss the future here and now – they couldn't continue like this. She would confess and beg his mercy. It would take all her courage. But even as Polly prepared to speak there was a rustle of newsprint from his end of the table. Henry held up the paper like a shield signifying an end to conversation.

During winter months, Mrs Helliwell supplemented her income by helping Polly and others with their cleaning. It was on her next Thursday morning visit that she arrived breathless with excitement.

'I shall have to give notice, madam. I'm really not sure whether I'm coming or going, it's happened so suddenly – I shall shortly be leaving the district – I'm to be married!' From her place by the window Polly thought, I mustn't scoff, why shouldn't she find happiness?

The middle-aged angular woman stood in front of her, simpering like a schoolgirl. The permanent drop of moisture at the end of her nose quivered and fell, to be replaced immediately by another which was dashed impatiently away.

'You must be surprised, madam?' It was almost an accusation as Polly hadn't uttered a word.

'Yes, of course. My felicitations, Mrs Helliwell. Do I know your fiancé?' The widow reacted archly to the word.

'You might have seen him,' she said, 'if you happened to be at the butcher's when he called. Mr Walker travels in shop-fittings. He's deputy manager really. We don't mention that in front of people, it's a private agreement between him and his superior, not public knowledge.' Polly acknowledged the confidence. Mrs Helliwell waited expectantly for more congratulations which Polly felt unable to give. Why encourage matrimony, it could only bring grief.

'Have you known Mr Walker long?' Mrs Helliwell went pink.

'Long enough, madam, I do assure you. He's a little older but similarly placed; he lost his first partner many years ago.'

'I didn't mean – '

'We met in the High Street. My umbrella had blown inside out and Mr Walker and I collided. Fate, I call it,' she finished defiantly.

Polly replied dutifully, 'It must have been.'

'And Gladys will have a father. What I've always intended she should have.' Polly wondered if Gladys would agree now she'd had a taste of independence. 'Mrs Durrant must be told first thing I said to Mr Walker when we were discussing our arrangements, so that she can advertise for my replacement.'

'That's most considerate. Have you decided when the happy day will be?'

'The twenty-second of March. We may have to delay our honeymoon, business is so brisk at present, but Mr Walker wouldn't hear of deferring the er – nuptials.' The future bride blushed. 'I shall be moving to Birmingham almost immediately afterwards. Mr Walker has – a villa.'

Polly asked tiredly, 'Will you still be able to see to Mr Durrant? The arrangements have been altered. I now have to go into hospital tomorrow.'

'But I thought . . . ' Mrs Helliwell frowned. 'That is to say – I understood . . .?'

'The child may be due earlier than we first thought.'

'Oh . . . I see.' To Polly's oversensitive eye Mrs Helliwell appeared to give a knowing smile. She knows, she thought! Mrs Helliwell must have seen Philip on one of his visits . . . Her imagination began to race: if Mrs Helliwell knew then so did the rest of the town, her secret must be common knowledge. How could she face walking down the street! Mrs Helliwell interrupted her distress with a discreet cough.

'Have you any idea how long you'll be away, madam?'

'None,' Polly said evenly. 'Mr Durrant and I will discuss the problem this evening. We will not trespass on your kindness.'

'Thank you. A week, perhaps? I could manage that.'

Mrs Helliwell began to tie her apron strings. 'I should be happy to oblige Mr Durrant for a week but after that ...' She was coy. 'There's very little time and my trousseau to prepare.'

'Yes, of course.' The idea was macabre. Would those sharp features and dewdrop nose be shrouded in lace and veiling? Polly remembered her manners. 'Please accept the best wishes of Mr Durrant and myself for your future happiness.'

'Thank you, madam.' Satisfied, Mrs Helliwell confided boldly, 'Between you and me there was a time – before you and Mr Durrant were married of course – when I thought *he* might have become Gladys's new papa.' How much more happy Henry would have been, her words implied! Then, recalling she was no longer dependent on Polly and remembering her anguish on the day of the marriage, Mrs Helliwell went one step further. 'Looking back, I know I made the right decision, by not encouraging Mr Durrant's hopes. Mr Walker is a much more masterful person.'

'How nice,' said Polly.

Ma Figgis didn't normally worry about moral issues but Polly Durrant's situation troubled her. Hadn't Mrs Durrant first come to her for advice, lacking a mother to turn to? Then there was the sad business of the dead child. Now with all this gossip, and Sybilla Porrit's voice especially loud, Polly's social standing was precarious. She was entitled to the benefit of the doubt, which was why Ma was on the lookout for Henry that morning.

'Not long now, eh, Mr Durrant?' Henry came out of his reverie reluctantly and raised his hat.

'Good morning.'

'We must pray your wife has it easier this time.' Discussion of gynaecological matters in the street was enough to embarrass Henry deeply.

'I, er ... yes. Indeed.'

'She's so pleased to be giving you a son at last. She told me so herself.'

'I'm afraid I really must ...' He tried to escape.

'She's lonely in that fine house, you know. Not many come visiting. I expect that's why she started selling teas. To see a few friendly faces.'

'Possibly.' It was an aspect Henry hadn't considered.

'Made a success of it, too.'

'That is true.' His breast swelled a fraction.

'But I expect you'll be glad to see her give it up. I thought of telling her myself. You must want your babby to have *all* his mother's love and care?' For the first time, Henry actually began to warm to the woman.

'Most certainly. There's no need for Polly –'

'Of course there isn't. Not now. She won't be lonely when she has your babby. Everybody pops in when there's a child in the house. You won't know yourself once you're a father, Mr Durrant; it changes your whole life.' Henry's spirits rose. Why had he always despised this wise old biddy previously?

'I'd take it as a favour, Mrs Figgis, if you would convey your views to Mrs Durrant. She is extremely melancholy at present.' Ma took the bull by the horns.

'I'd be glad to. Especially after that jealous old aunt of hers has been spreading such lies. It's being married to Porrit what does it. I shall tell her next time I sees her. Good day to you, Mr Durrant.'

Her hints took root. Henry walked with a lighter step. Of course the child was his! No one else had visited Polly. Those who consumed her scones were served by Gladys or Mrs Helliwell and were merely transient. He must learn not to condemn so quickly. That old woman might not be prepossessing – the smelly cur was partly to blame – but there was wisdom as well as goodness in her.

'Don't disturb yourself. I'll put the kettle on, shall I?' Polly rocked her heavy body to and fro nervously.

'It's kind of you to call, Mrs Figgis.'

'I see'd your man this morning. He wants you to give up that tea-garden, my dear.'

'I shan't re-open next season.'

'That's right. Them cycling clubs can find refreshment somewhere else.' Ma had placed herself deliberately with her back to Polly. 'I told him you'd been lonely . . . how you were looking forward to loving *his* babby.' The emphasis was faint; so was Polly's reply.

'Thank you.'

'He's a kind man. He'll come round, whether 'tis a boy or a girl.' She turned to face her. 'Let's hope it has its mother's dark eyes, eh? Now, where d'you keep your sugar?'

That night, Polly finally wrote to Albert.

'Dearest Albert,

I hope you and Esther are well and Edwin is . . .' She was about to add 'over his cold' but realized that had been weeks ago.

' . . . and Edwin too' she amended.

'I wish you could have visited at Christmas. The doctor has arranged for the baby to be born in the hospital. I go there tomorrow.' Polly hesitated, unable even now to express her fears. Finally she wrote,

'It is for the best. Henry is the kindest of men. I pray that I shall be strong enough and that he will come to love the baby . . .' She crossed this out. ' . . . that he will have a son to love.' Tears fell, smearing the ink. She'd intended it to be full of news but instead ended abruptly.

'If anything happens, tell Chas God bless. Kiss Edwin for me. Thank Esther for her cheerfulness.

Yr loving sister,
Polly Durrant, Mrs.'

'Smell the flowers, Mrs Durrant . . . You're going to sleep now . . .' A gag was in her mouth, a heavy rubber mask clamped to her face, she was being stifled! Polly struggled but strong arms pinned her down. 'Deep breaths,' commanded the voice and she lost consciousness.

Faces swam in and out of the mist. The doctor appeared. There were sounds coming from his mouth, but she couldn't understand. A starched frill and a nurse's gentler features, the voice was more soothing but nothing made sense. Polly wanted to move but her body was tightly sheeted to the bed. Throughout two days and nights faces appeared, some ordering her to do things, some cajoling. She retreated, refusing to listen; all she wanted to do was sleep.

She thought she heard Henry. When eventually his voice became insistent, Polly opened her eyes. He stood some distance away, the nurse beside him.

'Move nearer, Mr Durrant. She's very weak today, she cannot hear you unless you're close to her.' Henry moved reluctantly.

'How are you?' Polly's mouth and lips were dry. Her eyelids drooped. 'Can you hear me?'

'Yes . . .' It was the tiniest sound because everything hurt. Henry leaned nearer.

'I've engaged a wet-nurse for the baby as you are unable to feed her.' Slowly, Polly's eyes widened and she stared. Henry turned to the nurse.

'Does she understand or have her wits been affected?'

'Have patience, Mr Durrant. Your wife's very, very weak. We're quite worried. She's not picking up because of the fever.' He tried again.

'You've not been well, Polly. But you must try and improve for the sake of the child.' The nurse moved to whisper in her ear.

'We had to engage a wet-nurse because of the risk of infection but as soon as you're over the worst, you can care for baby yourself. Maybe you can even have a peek at her soon.' Polly was confused.

'Baby?'

'Your little girl, Mrs Durrant. So pretty. Have you chosen a name?'

A girl; Polly understood at last. A girl! Had it been a boy she would always have thought of it as Philip's but a girl would be hers alone. A sudden fear broke through the haze and stabbed, needle-sharp. She whispered, 'No name . . . not yet.'

The last time they had baptised a child, she had died. Polly beseeched, 'Is she . . .?'

'She's a very healthy baby, Mrs Durrant. Not large, a dainty little thing. She's begun taking milk and sleeps

386

soundly. You've no need to worry.' Gaunt shadowy eyes searched the nurse's face and found nothing but the truth, her baby was safe. The nurse was pleased to see her patient taking notice at last. 'We've called her Primrose. She's like a spring flower with all that blonde hair.'

With her words, the faint hope that had arisen following Ma Figgis's assurances, shrivelled in Henry's breast; how could a fair-haired child be his?

But Polly felt an explosion of love inside. It was *her* baby. If only she could live to see it grow! The mists were descending again, muddling her reason. She must make Henry understand what was to happen – she felt so weak! He was already retreating further from the bed.

'Baby . . . Albert and Esther.'

She saw a glimmer of understanding followed by a refusal to accept the implication.

'You must do all they tell you to, Polly, then you will grow strong and can come home.' He wanted to avoid all such dangerous discussion and gathered up his hat and scarf.

'Please,' she begged but he affected not to hear.

The doctor called at the house later and interrupted Henry's supper.

'The crisis will come tonight unless I'm mistaken. I've given instructions for a couch to be made ready, although I imagine you would prefer to remain at your wife's bedside.'

'If you think it necessary.'

'Sir, Mrs Durrant is extremely ill.' The doctor didn't hide his disgust at what he saw as callousness. Henry looked away. He knew what the man was thinking, but the very thought of returning to that room reeking of sickness and antiseptic made him ill; he was too diffident to explain.

'I don't know that my presence will be of any use – '

'Mr Durrant, the fever is not responding to sulphonamide. Unless your wife can bring herself to fight, I fear she may sink beyond our powers to save her.'

The gaslight was dim. Henry waited in the shadows. The door of the room was ajar. Outside a nurse sat at her desk writing notes. Occasionally there was a faint mew from one of the row of bassinettes. Henry wondered which one contained Polly's child. They'd offered to show him yesterday but he'd declined. The sister had been sympathetic, believing him to be more concerned for his wife; Henry felt guilty over that.

In the last few months, since distancing himself from Polly, she'd lost her familiarity. He'd forgotten various details of his wife's face. It lay on the pillow defenceless against his scrutiny, the mousy hair cut short because of the fever, in spikey tendrils. He couldn't bring himself to look too closely for the grey skin was covered in sweat. Every so often the nurse would enter, wring out a flannel and wipe the unconscious features. She didn't ask Henry to help; he was thankful. They asked nothing of him except that he sit there and watch Polly suffer.

Was she aware of him? He'd touched her hand tonight. Her eyes hadn't opened but her fingers had curled round his. Was she dying? As that thought finally forced itself into his consciousness, Henry stifled a cry of protest. He didn't want that to happen.

Bit by bit he began to examine his feelings. He'd never love Polly as he had at the beginning but she was a part of his life; the house was empty without her. Despite Ma Figgis's assurance he still worried over her possible infidelity – it had occupied his thoughts for months, it couldn't be banished at a stroke – was the child in the bassinette his? He was almost convinced he was the father. If only the nurses hadn't told him of the blonde hair!

The night sister entered the ward and murmured to the nurse. Together they came and stood either side of the bed. Henry averted his eyes but they pulled the screens across so that he shouldn't be disturbed.

He heard the soft sounds as they tended Polly and the ugly retching moan in consequence. The smell of blood made him shudder. Their tasks complete, the nurses folded back the screens revealing Polly once more.

Henry acknowledged his own feeble nature; he hadn't had the courage to ask his wife if she'd deceived him. He wondered vaguely what the possibilities were if she had?

He wanted Polly home – she wouldn't return without her baby – so that meant . . . His thoughts shifting and vacillating, Henry yawned. One thing was certain, he'd been sitting here the devil of a long time.

Polly was dreaming. She, Chas and Albert were on the river bank, it was a lovely sunny day and Chas had agreed to teach her to swim. 'All right, come on. Pol. I'll show you. Give us your hand.'

The water was cool and clean. She wanted more of it and plunged down beneath the surface. Down, down, bubbles bursting about her ears.

The sudden sussuration of skirts and aprons startled Henry. Shadows made by the starched caps danced on the ceiling as they bent over the bed. The doctor came hurrying in, pulling on his jacket. Henry wished he could disappear. They tugged away the bedclothes – he was appalled that his wife's nakedness should be so exposed. No one made any attempt to cover her as a nurse mopped frantically at the blood. 'Haemorrhaging badly . . .' Henry tried to remember what that word meant. On either side of the bed, the nurses moved swiftly.

One rubbed Polly's hand, calling her name urgently. A syringe appeared, the doctor flicked away excess liquid and plunged it into a vein. Henry turned away, swallowing hard.

Albert was making her laugh. He stood on the bank, the tail of his shirt clinging to his skinny little legs. He was doing one of their favourite imitations: Sybilla scolding Enoch. Polly laughed and laughed . . . Chas was tugging her hand, trying to attract her attention.

'Polly, look who's here.'

It was a girl she'd never seen before, very pretty with blonde hair and large grey eyes. Instantly Polly knew who it was. There was something she had to do for her.

'Don't go away!' she cried. 'Stay there, don't be frightened.'

389

She swam back to the surface, forcing her way through waves of pain. Albert's voice was loud.

'Go on, Pol. We'll look after her but we'll need a bit of help. Make Henry believe she's his.'

The nurse urged, 'She's asking for you, Mr Durrant.' He wanted to stay where he was, he could see the shape of the skull beneath the tight skin. Polly's mouth was tight and wide. He stumbled to the bedside. Her eyes searched and found him.

'Baby – Albert and Esther,' she cried hoarsely. She burned with the last flicker of life.

'She said that yesterday,' murmured the nurse.

'Tell her what it is she wants to know,' the doctor ordered, 'quickly now.' Henry had only rushed one decision before and had lived to regret it. He would've remained silent but for that intense look. The nurse's grip was fierce.

'Hurry!' she hissed. Henry stared at the distraught face.

'Yes, all right, Polly,' he said, 'I understand. You want Albert and Esther to care for the child – but I must know if she's mine!'

Polly cast aside all care for her immortal soul. Her mind was fading but he must not reject her baby. A solution came to her, even *in extremis* she managed to chuckle because the idea was naughty and Albert would think it funny. To the listeners, the sound was ghastly.

'She's to be called Henrietta,' said Polly, and died.

Esther heard the familiar footstep and her heart contracted. 'No noise,' she begged Edwin softly. 'Don't grizzle tonight. Try and sleep.' She had such dreadful news to impart.

'I'm home!' But she didn't rush into his arms. 'What's the matter?' The telegram was on the mantlepiece. Unable to speak, Esther pointed to it.

From his cot Edwin watched as his father began to cry like a child and, hugging him to her bosom, his mother rocked to and fro in a fruitless effort to console him.

Darkness filled the small room; for the first time in his

life neither parent took notice of him and Edwin began to whimper.

The night before the funeral, Sybilla made her move. The idea had come to her within minutes of hearing that Polly was dead. She didn't waste time grieving, why should she? Jeremiah's voice might have halted her once but she'd stopped listening years ago. She'd never liked Polly, she decided; even as a child she'd always had a deceitful streak.

Besides, the beauty of her idea was its simplicity; such an obvious solution. With a bit of luck, she'd make her fortune by it; at the very least, she'd recover her seven per cent.

'Which is mine by right,' she repeated as she did, constantly. 'Why shouldn't Polly be the one to repay me, she was his sister.' Thus convinced, Sybilla could hardly wait for a decent interval before crossing the London road and knocking on Henry's door. It annoyed her that Mrs Helliwell should be the one to open it.

'What are you doing here?'

'I might ask you the same!' the widow retorted. The advent of Mr Walker in her life had brought poise as well as courage. 'I suppose you've come to offer your condolences. Better late than never. I shall pass them on. Mr Durrant cannot be intruded upon in his hour of grief.'

'You mind your own business,' Sybilla answered rudely. 'What I've come to say is private. Where is he?'

Mrs Helliwell flounced ahead and flung open the parlour door. To Henry, it seemed as though the wheel had come full circle. Here were the three who'd changed the course of his life: Mrs Heyhoe occupied his armchair, Mrs Helliwell stood in the doorway with Sybilla behind her, and the one he'd married by the way of escape lay in her coffin in the dining room.

'Mrs Porrit,' Mrs Helliwell announced, 'come to pay her last respects.'

'I hev not. I ain't so hypocritical as some. What if my niece is in her shroud, I don't suppose she'd welcome the sight of me, nor do I pretend to be sorry. Afternoon teas

391

was always my idea, she'd no business starting up over here and 'ticing my customers away!' That burst out because it had festered so long.

'There's no law says there should be only one cuppa on offer,' Mrs Heyhoe said darkly, ' 'Specially when that partic'lar one is overpriced – '

'Mrs Heyhoe, this is hardly the time to quarrel – '

'I hev come round on a private matter,' Sybilla said loudly, repeating with emphasis, '*Private*, as between you and me, Henry Durrant.'

He moved so that the black armband was conspicuous.

'I have nothing whatever to say to you, Mrs Porrit. If you have not come to bid my dear wife farewell then kindly take your leave.'

'I shall bid her farewell all right; tomorrow, in church,' Sybilla announced ominously. ' 'Tis her tea-garden I hev come to discuss.' Realizing he didn't intend granting an interview, she added with slight discomforture, 'I hev come with an offer, if you wants to know. I'm agreeable to taking the business off your hands.'

'What – business?'

'Polly's tea-garden, of course. You won't be wanting to keep it on, not now. I shall close mine down.'

'What!' squeaked Mrs Helliwell. Mrs Heyhoe stared.

'Do my ears deceive me?'

'You always was a bit deaf,' Sybilla sneered nastily, 'I expec' age hev reeked more havoc, or else 'tis wax.'

'How dare you!'

'Ladies, ladies!'

'Give credit where it's due; my niece always was light-handed with her scones and pastry, not like some.' Sybilla glanced at the others contemptuously. 'I taught Polly all she knew, of course. She was *fully trained* by the time she went to the vicarage kitchen.'

'She was not!'

Henry was in a cold sweat at the warring factions on either hand. 'Mrs Porrit, I have not yet considered the future – '

'I hev. I come to tell you what I've decided an' all,' Sybilla told him firmly. 'For a start I ain't looking after that bastard of Polly's, no matter what.'

'Mrs Porrit!'

'You wicked woman – you should wash your mouth out with soap!'

'Well, someone's got to and it won't be him, will it, considering it's not his,' Sybilla retorted, pointing at Henry. 'No, I done my duty once,' she continued unperturbed, 'looking after those three unwanted children, an' I lost money by it. Once is enough.'

'Mrs Porrit, I must insist you leave this house.'

'I did without so they could hev their victuals, I ain't going through that a second time.'

'No one has asked you to –'

'But I'm quite willing to take the business off've your hands, Henry Durrant. I got it all worked out: you an' me shall change houses.' Henry's mouth fell open. It didn't occur to her that he was utterly shocked. She hurried to describe the advantages. 'That way, you gets a brand new garden to occupy your lonely hours and I shall take the burden of Polly's customers off've your shoulders. With an adjustment on your part for my goodwill, of course.' He gasped at the effrontery but before he could respond, Mrs Heyhoe jumped in.

'If you think anyone nibbling your bakewell tarts won't notice the difference, Sybilla Porrit, you need your brains examined!'

'You can certainly count without my help,' Mrs Helliwell cried, 'I shall not set foot inside this house again –'

'Once and for all, ladies – I AM NOT LEAVING HERE!' Henry was exhausted with the effort of asserting himself. 'Now go, all of you. I wish to be alone.'

He stood, hands clenched, shaking with anger as the gate slammed behind them but in the dimly lit hall his imagination played him a dreadful trick; beyond the dining room door, he thought he could hear laughter.

The new Mrs Walker stared at him doubtfully. Henry sat in the one downstairs room of her cottage, uncomfortably warm in his overcoat. He hoped it didn't show.

393

'Surely this abode is no longer a suitable dwelling, Mr Durrant?' Her gesture indicted that he had long ago risen above such surroundings. 'Besides ... I understood you had decided to stay where you were.'

'I've changed my mind.' A few weeks in the echoing empty rooms, the double bed a constant reminder of his marriage, had been sufficient. 'My house is now up for sale.'

'My word!' Mrs Walker knew the tea-garden had been closed permanently, to Sybilla Porrit's chagrin, but this was news.

'I have already purchased the cottage next door, where we used to live. I now wish to buy this.'

'And live in both d'you mean? Return to your former home and add to it?' It seemed a very odd notion to her. 'As you know, Mr Durrant, I only rent this property.'

'I have already spoken to your landlord. Provided you are willing, I will take over the remainder of the lease. When that falls due, I shall negotiate the purchase.'

As the future chatelaine of a brand-new villa in Birmingham, Mrs Walker was disparaging.

'I fear there is a certain amount of *damp* here. Even Mr Walker cannot suggest a cure.' By implication, the problem was therefore insoluble but Henry didn't care; it was the garden he was after. The two plots at Willow End would be made into one. He would spend the rest of his days with an adequately sized piece of ground, much of which he already knew had desirable, friable soil.

Mrs Walker gave one of her discreet coughs. 'How is dear little Henrietta, may I ask?'

'She continues to thrive. She and her nurse will occupy one cottage and I the other.'

'Oh, I see!' She hadn't guessed correctly but how very proper. Mrs Walker nodded in approval. Another thought struck her. 'Is it not likely ... We have known one another a long time, Mr Durrant, and you are still a young man ...'

Mrs Walker had discovered like so many before and since, that with the onset of middle-age, the perspective changes: Henry understood.

394

'I shall not remarry.' She became flustered.

'Pardon me! I was thinking of your child, Mr Durrant. Now that she no longer has – a mother.' Mrs Walker buried her moist red nose in a handkerchief.

'She has her nurse,' Henry replied.

He had not fulfilled his promise for Polly had placed him in a dilemma. If the child truly was his, ought he not to bring her up himself? Reluctant though he was, he regarded that as his duty.

He also felt relief over Polly's death – which added to his guilt. For with her passing, Henry discovered a burden had been lifted; his dead love had been buried with the coffin. Never again would he risk affection for another human being, he'd been drained of all he had to give. The child, however, remained a problem.

Despite Sybilla Porrit's vicious words, he risked believing the infant his. Ma Figgis had assured him and Polly had given the baby his name.

Vacillating yet again, Henry was forced to recall the infrequency of his love-making. Polly's attitude had always distressed him: she'd endured rather than enjoyed and never succeeded in concealing the fact.

Henry could only admit his persistent worry to one other person, and then haltingly. After the funeral, when Ma Figgis approached to express her condolence, he ventured a muttered, 'I cannot believe my wife really wanted . . . She found affection – difficult.'

Ma Figgis said shrewdly, 'Consider how she was brought up, sir. Watching the way her Uncle Porrit treated *his* wife. Mrs Durrant never got over that.'

Henry's embarrassment grew. 'Polly had no cause to fear as far as I was concerned.'

Ma put a sympathetic hand on his arm. 'It was too deep by then, d' you see. That's what made it so brave, her having another child. She knew of the risk but it was her way of trying to show her love.' It was also nature's way of demonstrating an adulterous liaison but this was no occasion for cynicism. When Henry looked at her, Ma Figgis's gaze was steady. 'She loved you as much as she was able, sir.' That was surely an honest epitaph.

Henry had nodded, too near tears for words.

But as for asking Esther and Albert to care for Henrietta, he couldn't add to their burdens, not yet. He would wait, he decided. The infant was well looked after and the nurse agreeable to living next door. For the present it was as satisfactory an arrangement as he could devise.

He stood for the last time in the front parlour on the London road. The window was bare; he wondered if Sybilla was watching from behind her slats. She would be cursing him if she were. She'd ranted when he'd finally made her understand that Polly's tea-garden was not for sale! Henry had torn down the sign and disposed of the sodden furniture. Some in the town were astonished at the haste but told one another he couldn't bear to be reminded of his dear wife; in one way this was also true.

As for Sybilla, she'd made good her threat. At the funeral she'd begun offering up loud prayers for the expiation of Polly's sins, but was ordered to be silent by indignant mourners. Hadn't Polly Durrant paid for any wrong-doing with her life?

The familiar cottage door at Willow End wasn't locked; Henry lifted the latch and walked inside. To his delight, the nail on which he used to hang his hat was still there. After an interval of several years, he hung his hat on it once more.

There were sounds from next door. The nurse must be preparing the night time feed.

They had agreed a schedule; she was to bring the child round twice a day for his inspection. Two half hour periods during which Henry could contemplate the yellow downy head and wonder for the umpteenth time whether he had played any part in her conception.

'How am I ever going to tell Chas about Polly?' Albert demanded. They'd called at The Coachman's but the new owners had had no letter. Late spring winds were icy and Esther reached up to tuck in his scarf. Suddenly she had an idea.

'Why don't you start the letter now?'

'Begin . . . then post it when we have an address, you mean?'

'That's right. There's been so much you wanted to tell him. About us and the fight you had. Then there's Edwin, especially now he's taken his first step. There's even Inspector Pentwhistle – '

'Hang on, old girl! Not in my first letter.'

'All right, we'll leave him out for a bit. But why don't you sit down the minute you get back.'

'Esther, you're a marvel! You're the best pal a chap ever had.' Albert kissed her hard.

The pile of paper grew; there would be enough for a parcel once they knew where Chas lived. At first the pages were blotchy from tears but as the summer progressed Albert's optimism returned. After one particularly exciting day, he wrote:

'An amazing experience! Esther and I read in the newspaper that the Frenchie, Blériot, was to attempt a flight across the mighty English Channel and the dear girl suggested we should go and see. The three of us were up at *4.00 a.m.* and took an excursion. We were too late to meet the hero. There was a photograph showing him with the four or five luckier ones. The marvel was that his machine was still there, pegged to the ground and guarded by the police! The AEROPLANE is in my opinion a fine invention, the equal of the INSKIP PHAETON.'

Later, in bed, he wondered aloud if Henry had taken his infant to Dover today.

'I doubt it,' Esther smiled fondly, 'it's not the sort of thing that would interest him.'

'No . . .' Albert snuggled up. 'I wonder how he's coping with Pol's little girl?' Not very well, she thought privately.

'I wouldn't mind another visit to Brandon. It's time Edwin met his little cousin.'

'Only if Inspector Pentwhistle agrees,' she warned. 'You said he was a bit put out about taking the day off.'

'Bother old Pentwhistle!' Albert promptly began to roar

in the same mighty tones. 'Another day of leave? What nonsense, Unwin!'

'Sssh.' Pentwhistle, however, harboured grudges, and when Albert arrived late the following Monday, due to oversleeping, the inspector was waiting, bristling with anticipation: 'You've missed taking out the first tram, Unwin. You have defaulted on your schedule!' Albert considered this as plain as the nose on his face; unfortunately he replied in Pentwhistle's own tones:

'Why, bless my soul – so I have!' In the tram-shed there were snickers of laughter. Men stopped to watch. It had the wrong effect; Albert was encouraged to continue. Thumb in braces, whirling an imaginary whistle, he announced, 'Not here on time to take out a tram? That's a capital offence – off with his head!'

The diminutive Pentwhistle, red with anger, pointed to another vehicle.

'That one's due out now and you're driving it.'

'I haven't clocked in yet,' Albert protested.

'There's no need. You'll get no pay for today, Unwin.'

'What!'

Pentwhistle, blustering, pretended to examine his watch. 'Get started, d'you hear me. I'm within my rights. You have deliberately insulted my authority –'

'You ain't got no authority,' Albert was too incensed to care, 'you're just a bag of wind!' He swung himself into the driving seat. The overhead pole was connected but to the wrong cable, the tram having just arrived from its outward journey. Albert began to climb down again, to make the change-over, only to find Pentwhistle barring his way.

'You will apologize for that remark, Unwin.'

'Get out of my way,' Albert cried, exasperated, 'or you'll make this one late an' all.' Pentwhistle bounced up and down with fury. Albert pretended to be deaf but found he was still prevented from reaching the pole.

By now everyone was watching. Conscious of it, frustrated, Albert paused. Sensing victory Pentwhistle stood almost under his nose.

'Apologize!' The shout echoed round the tram shed.

Albert retreated back into the driving seat and folded his arms. Then he noticed something: Pentwhistle was standing between the rails, directly in front of the tram. Albert released the brake.

At the last minute, the inspector realized but instead of jumping aside, began to run, still between the tracks. Albert followed, heading down the Up line.

Along Oxford Street they went, a pompous red-faced man screaming for his life followed by an empty tram, the driver grinning wildly.

It couldn't last. For Albert's sake, it was as well that it didn't. Pentwhistle was finally dragged aside by an alert-eyed constable who then leaped onto the platform and bellowed at Albert to stop.

That evening, Esther was listening out anxiously. There was no need to tell her he was in trouble, his footsteps did that.

'What happened?'

'Got a cup of tea, love?' He sat to take off his boots. When he took the cup he was half-laughing, half defiant. 'Inspector Pentwhistle an' me . . . had a bit of a h'altercation.'

'Oh, Albert . . .'

'As a result of which . . . I drove my tram the wrong way down Oxford Street.' She looked at him aghast.

'There might have been an accident!'

'There very nearly was. I nearly got him in the backside. We was doing twelve miles per hour when we reached Selfridges.'

'Oh . . . Albert!'

'Provocation,' he insisted defiantly, 'that's what I told the superintendent. But I'm not a driver no more.'

'No.' That much was obvious.

'As from tomorrow, I'm a conductor, collecting fares and helping old ladies up the step. I'm sorry, old girl, the money ain't so special. Why are you putting on your hat?'

'I'm going round to borrow Lem's old cart.'

'We don't need to flit tonight!'

'I know, dearest.' But there would be no more outings on excursion trains, no more rooms in Lillie Road. Esther

399

pushed the hatpins in place. 'We'll have to leave by Friday though, we can't afford to stay on here.'

She didn't scold, she loved him too much. Besides, what had happened was inevitable given the nature of those involved. This time they moved into two ground floor rooms in a cramped terrace in Chelsea. Albert was determined to make amends.

'We've the whole of the backyard to ourselves!' He gazed at six by ten foot of blackened earth bordered by dirty brick walls and the w.c.

'We could use those bits of old wood for firewood,' she said, thankfully. It would save on fuel.

'That timber,' Albert announced, 'is what I shall use to house the ducks.'

'Ducks!'

'I shall buy a couple of eggs, hatch 'em, feed 'em, fatten 'em up. You shall have a proper Christmas lunch, my girl.'

'Oh, Albert!' It was midnight before he'd finished the ramshackle construction, but by the end of the week, Esther was emptying a fireside cupboard to take the eggs . . . and to her amazement, these hatched.

'The thing is, Edwin, with birds, you have to trim their pinion feathers. Birds is natural fliers, my boy. Like Monsieur Blériot. An' if we was to let these two out, they'd be off. Over the mighty English Channel if they happened to take the right direction . . . but we shall have to restrict their natural inclinations . . . once we find which of these here feathers are pinions and lop off a couple of inches. Hold that for me, would you?'

Albert propped the library book on top of the pramcover, adjusted his spectacles and picked up Esther's scissors.

' "The pinion feather . . . is located . . . in the bird's wing. To render the bird incapable of flight . . . remove that part of the wing." Here . . .' Albert was horrified, 'I can't chop off a piece of wing, Edwin. I might give 'em a mortal wound.' He glanced at the kitchen window to see if Esther was watching, and heaved a relieved sigh that she wasn't.

'Tell you what, son, I shall trim a feather or two, to discourage them. Come on Little Tich, let's be having you then.' But neither Little Tich nor Marie Lloyd were agreeable and when Albert re-entered the house he had to hide bleeding fingers in his trouser pocket.

'Did you manage?'

'Yes, love. Best keep the cage door shut though, we don't want 'em *waddling* into someone else's back yard.'

The birds became an obsession. At the end of each day, Albert would visit the hut to estimate how much weight each had gained. He collected scraps and potato peelings, he searched the library for information on various breeds – anything to distract him from the travail of ticket collecting. Best of all, he could talk to the ducks about Polly. He feared Esther might think that he grieved too much.

Christmas approached. Could they really be sure of having roast duck, Esther wondered? Their neighbours upstairs were scornful.

'When's the execution to be?'

'It's not like that at all. It'll be a scientific operation, I read it in a book,' Albert said loftily. 'A sharp knife – quick as a flash – they won't feel a thing.'

'They'll run round for hours. 'Eadless. An' their little beaks go on squawkin' even though they're not attached. Try strangling 'em instead.'

In their kitchen Esther asked nervously, 'Is that right, what he said?'

' 'Course not! What does Bridewell know about it? He's a painter and decorator. Lend us your sharpening stone.'

That evening and the next, Albert honed every knife they possessed. He slashed at pieces of paper, he sliced at a candle on the mantlepiece (and accidentally smashed a jar). Eventually he declared himself satisfied.

'Tomorrow night, that's when I'll do it. Christmas is on Saturday, that gives three days for them to hang in the shed. You has to hang game. You'll watch out for any cats?'

'You know, I've grown quite fond of Marie Lloyd.'

'None of that,' Albert told her sharply, 'they're not household pets, they're food.'

'But I've been helping to feed them. Edwin talks to them when he's in his pram, he can nearly manage their names. Maybe if we was just to eat Little Tich – '

'Both,' Albert was adamant. 'You got to think of it from the ducks' point of view, love. If one goes, the other would know what was coming. She'd wake up every morning . . . in the Condemned Cell.' He was so overcome he had to resort to his handkerchief. That night, neither of them slept.

Heavy eyed, he went to work. Doom-laden, he returned. Bridewell and his wife were at the upstairs window when Albert, clad in Esther's old apron, carrying a selection of knives, marched into the yard.

'I should use a chopping block.'

'Watch out they don't peck your 'and off, Mr Unwin.'

Esther also watched, tears rolling down her cheeks.

Both ducks were waiting amiably. Albert faltered. Normally one or other would be roosting but tonight they were curious, uttering chirpy greetings.

'Marie Lloyd, inside,' Albert ordered. She cocked her head and squatted, confident of a titbit. 'Little Tich, get in that box,' but he too settled beside his mate. At the upstairs window the decorator and his wife became excited.

'You'd best slash 'is head off – he's looking nasty!'

'You watch out the second one don't go for you, Mr Unwin. You could get gangrene.'

Albert drew a knife from his belt and ran his thumb down the blade. Instantly, blood spurted. 'Damn and blast!'

'Albert! Are you hurt?'

'Esther, go back inside. Please.' She was crying openly now. 'They won't feel a thing, promise.' Both birds were squawking with excitement. Albert slipped inside and fastened the door behind him.

It was worse than the army. He crouched and pleaded. 'One of you disappear inside that box,' but neither bird moved; he was their friend, father and mother to both of them since birth.

Albert was savage, he'd been looking forward to this dinner for the last six months! From the kitchen, he heard a wild shriek. Had Edwin divined his murderous intent? Simultaneously, Marie Lloyd advanced, extended her neck and rested her head on the toe of his boot; it was the final straw.

'When I gives the word use them damn pinions of yours . . . Now!' He shoved open the mesh door. Little Tich was unwilling. Albert kicked the bird's posterior. There was a flurry as both ducks emerged. One flexed its wings, the other stayed put. Albert wiggled his arms to demonstrate. 'Go on, fly!'

'Oy!' The warning came from upstairs. 'Look out, Unwin, they're getting away.'

'Oh dear, so they are.' Albert made a feint, slithered on bird lime and fell on his face. This startled them. There was a sudden flap of wings followed by feet pounding across the yard.

'Use my bike, they can't get far!' Albert was forced to mount, 'Bridewell for Clean and Efficient Service'.

'Look, there they go, heading north.' Pedalling reluctantly, Albert began to zig-zag through Chelsea.

The ducks swooped low, calling to him. Albert sent up frantic instructions: 'Keep going! Don't come any closer!' Small boys joined in the pursuit. One had a catapult. Albert had to ride over him to spoil his aim. Bicycle, rider, boy and catapult slid onto the cobbles. Bridewell arrived.

'Now look what you've done. The chain's come off my machine.'

'Oh, dear, so it has.'

Eventually, standing on the bridge which bore his name, Albert watched the birds head up river towards Putney. Bridewell was despondent. 'We'll never catch up with them now.'

'No, I don't believe we will.'

They had sausage and mash with a plum pudding to follow. In lieu of brandy, Albert set fire to the sprig of holly, which resulted in a smaller helping than usual.

'I wonder if those two got as far as Greenland?' Esther squeezed his hand. 'And I wonder what Chas is doing right now?'

'Same as you, probably. Leaning back in his chair because he's eaten too much.'

He wasn't deceived by the exaggeration but hugged her all the same. The room began to feel chilly. 'Have we any more coal?'

'I'm afraid not.'

'Oh, Esther – I'm sorry.' He hadn't a penny to give her until the New Year.

'Albert, why don't we burn the hut! There won't be any more ducks. We could have such a lovely blaze with all that straw bedding.'

'I was thinking of fattening a pig for next Christmas.'

'No, Albert, no pigs.' When she wanted to, Esther could be very firm indeed. 'Pigs can't fly. Now you go and chop a bit of kindling and I'll put the kettle on. We'll soon be warm again.'

Chapter Twenty-Three

One Promise Fulfilled, 1914–18

Following the first wave of enthusiasm, the effect of newspaper reports of the war had been to slow down recruitment from the London tram shed. By the end of the first six months, a fifth of the workforce had volunteered but after twelve, men were no longer rushing to answer the call – casualty lists were being studied seriously by then.

Albert had been frantic to 'do his bit'. As might be expected he wanted to head for France immediately. Esther had to use all her wiles to prevent him. She didn't worry much at the beginning for he was over recruitment age but as losses increased, regulations began to be relaxed.

Nor was the war over by Christmas. The next prophesy was that fighting would cease by the following summer. It became obvious this too was unlikely. Albert continued to be restless so Esther went to consult Bridie Macguire. For once, her old friend had pressing troubles of her own.

'John, my eldest boy – stupid since the day he was born – has got involved back home.' Esther had only the vaguest notion of the events occurring in Ireland.

'When will he be back?'

'God knows,' Bridie exploded. 'Maybe never the way he sticks his neck out. As for joining the British army – he's sworn to fight them.'

'Oh, Bridie!'

'I know, I know. The arguments that go on in our house nowadays . . . It's cruel, Esther. His father swears John can't set foot in here, his sisters have vowed never to speak to him again but I can't turn my back on him, can I? I'm his mother. Meantime, it's not the place to bring your Albert. I don't want any trouble from "patriotic talk" – no disrespect, my dear.'

'D'you think I should encourage Albert to volunteer?'

'Now don't be silly. What would Kezia have said, eh? Or your dear dead father? Of course you mustn't let Albert go. A pity that brother of his doesn't come back and make him see sense.'

'Sometimes I wonder if Chas is still alive. There's only ever been that one letter.'

'Never give up hope,' Bridie admonished sternly, 'but don't let Albert out of your sight. I thought he'd had his fill of the army?'

'He says this time it's different.'

'Yes . . . this time he could get killed,' she said heavily.

But before Albert could do anything rash, his fate was decided for him.

Those in uniform were allowed free passage on public transport. Albert took it into his head to be more generous. He had his own personal scale of priorities: women in mourning never had to pay. Those who were shabby were only charged a nominal amount and if a wornout purse appeared with scarcely anything inside, Albert would wave the ha'pence away.

Such benevolence couldn't last, his ticket sales were suspiciously meagre. He was interrogated, threatened and finally an inspector came aboard to check precisely what was happening. Albert unfortunately lost his temper.

Outside the tram depot, stripped of his uniform, with nothing but his dismissal notice, desolation set in. How to explain to Esther this time? Colleagues had had a whip round. A ten shilling note had been added to his final wage packet. It was all he had until he found another job.

Albert dallied, trying to put off the inevitable. Eventually, he mounted his old bike and set off for home.

Every recruitment poster served to goad him tonight.

Maybe that was the answer? Esther's face appeared in his imagination; he'd given his word not to enlist. But how to support her and Edwin? At least she would be assured of a widow's pension if the worst happened.

The lack of concentration was his undoing, that and by a strange irony, the tram lines themselves. The front wheel of the bike jammed into one, jerking him over the handlebars. Albert landed heavily and broke his leg.

The ward sister at Hammersmith hospital was fuming. 'I'm sorry to have to tell you, Mrs Unwin, but our surgeon has been called up. His deputy went last week, and since then the standard in this ward is a disgrace!' Esther trembled.

'I don't understand?'

'Your poor dear man – so brave. Kept asking for you. Didn't want to take anything for the pain but we insisted, of course. They operated at five o'clock – if you can call it "operating" when there's only a student in charge.' She snorted. 'One or two of my nurses could set a leg better than that. Mr Unwin is in the third bed on the left-hand side. You won't find him making any sense, he hasn't come round properly from the anaesthetic.' Esther was petrified; the only other time she'd visited a hospital was when Kezia had died.

'Albert will get better!'

'Of course he will, my dear. Even if that plaster cast is the worst I've ever seen. I say to everyone who comes into my ward nowadays, is your operation really necessary, I ask? If not, stick it out until a real surgeon returns from the Front. Your hubby had no choice, of course. Third on the left, Mrs Unwin. There's a bowl if he wants to be sick.'

The curtains were drawn. Esther slipped inside, tried not to shudder at the huge metal frame, picked up his hand and kissed it.

'Is that . . . my lovely girl?'

'Yes, dearest.' She tried to keep her voice steady. Agony and worry had transformed him – Albert looked so old!

'Know what I've gone and done?'

'You've broken your leg but try not to worry – '

407

'No, it's not that. Listen, love, I've lost my job. They sacked me – it happened *before* I fell off my bike. There won't be any money while I'm sick.'

'It doesn't matter.'

' 'Course it matters! Where's the rent coming from with me stuck in here?' She wiped away his tears. Deep down she could feel nothing but relief; her dear love was alive, his leg would mend but, whatever else, he'd never have to go to war.

'I'll manage. You just concentrate on getting better,' she soothed.

'If only I knew where Chas was. I could write and ask if he'd lend us something.'

'Lie still . . . and try and sleep.' But he started retching. When it was over she asked, 'Shall I bring you some paper. You could write an account for Chas?'

Albert was white-lipped. 'Leave it a day or two, love. Until I feel a bit more perky.'

That took several weeks. The ward sister had been right; the plaster cast was a disgrace, it had to be removed. Once the damaged leg was revealed, it was obvious that it would have to be re-set; another operation was necessary. By the end of nine months, Albert was declared fit enough to leave provided he had a long period of convalescence.

He'd lost over a stone in weight, he had also lost an inch of bone from his left leg and would be lame for the rest of his life.

Esther had concealed her own situation. Despite her care she hadn't been able to eke out the money more than a month. Without telling Albert she'd given up the Chelsea rooms, moved in with Bridie and had taken up cleaning work once more.

The ward sister told her that her husband would need plenty of rest and good food if he were to recover. Esther was at her wits' end. The only person who might be able to help them was Henry Durrant. Summoning up courage she wrote and asked for a loan of five pounds.

To her amazement, his reply contained ten and an invitation to Suffolk.

'Isn't that marvellous, Albert. He doesn't say how long – it'll be just the place to make you well again.'

'We can't impose. It was different when Polly was alive but we're not rightly Henry's responsibility now. And don't forget he's moved back into that little cottage.' Without money or the prospect of earning sufficient, Esther had fewer scruples.

'He's taken the one next door, remember. I'm sure we could all squeeze in – Edwin won't be any trouble. Besides . . .' Too tired to pretend, she confessed, 'I gave up our rooms. We've been with Bridie ever since your accident. I've had to borrow a bit as well. I've repaid that out of Henry's money and I've given Bridie £3.0.0d for letting Edwin and me stay. She's storing our things until we find a place. I don't want to impose on *her* any longer.'

Weak though he was, Albert acknowledged Suffolk was their only option.

'No letter from Chas, I suppose . . .?' She shook her head. 'Just imagine, Esther, he doesn't know even now that Polly's dead.'

'No, love.' Esther spoke more briskly. 'Now, I want to see you shaved and ready to leave first thing tomorrow. I shall buy our tickets tonight and Edwin and I will bring your clothes by eight o'clock. Mind you eats every scrap of breakfast. I'll send a telegram and ask Henry to meet us.'

'A telegram! He might think it's from the war office. Don't frighten him too much.'

'We shall take a cab,' Esther was reckless on behalf of her loved ones. 'You and Edwin can travel in comfort for once.'

It was a nightmare journey nonetheless. The station was packed with the wounded now being ferried home in search of British hospitals. Esther clung to Albert as the enormity of what was happening in France became plain.

She was still tearful from her parting with Bridie. When her old friend had kissed her farewell, she had said, 'I won't be seeing you and Albert for a while?'

'It's not just John and his Irish friends, Bridie. Albert will need time to recover . . . he's so thin and weak.' His hair had gone grey too but Esther couldn't bear to mention that.

'Thank God you know someone with money,' Bridie was practical. 'If you keep house for Mr Durrant, that'll repay his kindness.'

'He's a shy man,' Esther sighed. 'I hope he means us to stay, otherwise I don't know what we'll do.'

'Chin up,' Bridie ordered. 'See that you charm him so that you can, for Edwin's sake.'

In the carriage Esther closed her eyes to suffering humanity. Her husband was entitled to all the care she could give. He sat opposite, as ashen-faced as those in uniform. One or two soldiers, misunderstanding the situation, congratulated him on having caught 'a Blighty one'. When Esther explained, to her astonishment they still assured her Albert was fortunate.

The train was crowded, she had to have Edwin on her knee. Her back ached with every jolt – no wonder Albert looked so pale.

She had to persuade Henry to let them stay, she'd manage it somehow. In her basket was the picture of the Welsh mountain. It was Esther's way of convincing herself they were moving. And as Bridie pointed out, there was nowhere else to go.

Edwin struggled and she bid him be still, 'For dadda's sake.' We're homeless, she thought, suddenly bitter. All those years of hard work and Albert and I have ended up with nothing. She wanted to cry out at the injustice. The sound of coughing brought her to her senses: here she was, surrounded by those who'd given so much more. Looking at their haggard young faces, she felt ashamed. She remembered Bridie's rebel son John – at least she'd been spared that agony.

The walking stick was on the overhead rack – would Albert ever manage without it? The ward sister had shaken her head.

I shall work, Esther declared to herself. Hadn't her mother done the same? I have my health and strength, we shall manage. That decision taken, she began to doze and fell to wondering about Polly's little girl.

It took the combined efforts of Henry and the cab driver to manoeuvre Albert into the cottage. He was too exhausted to climb the stairs. Esther settled him beside the fire, wrapped him in blankets and turned her attention to Edwin. She wondered if Henry had been dismayed by the sight of their baggage. He'd still made no mention of the length of their stay.

Henrietta was in her cot. Edwin was to have the nurse's bed. 'Nurse has had to return home to care for her father. He's had a stroke,' Henry explained. 'I was so thankful when your letter arrived, Esther.'

'I – see.' Guilt began to lessen.

'When you're ready . . . I have prepared supper in my cottage next door.'

'We'll let Albert sleep,' she decided. 'I'll join you shortly, Henry.'

He'd done his best: the potatoes were underdone but there were flowers. Esther sat across from him and smiled very prettily. 'You've been our saviour,' she told him. 'I'm so grateful. You can see for yourself Albert needs somewhere peaceful to build up his strength.'

Henry said awkwardly, 'I responded not for Albert's benefit but for my own. I have decided to carry out Polly's final request. Before I tell you about it, I would like to fetch the child.'

'Henrietta?' Esther was startled. 'She'll be asleep.'

'She normally joins me at this time,' Henry assured her, 'for half an hour or so. It's been a habit since babyhood. She goes to sleep immediately once nurse takes her back upstairs.'

Esther followed him back to the other cottage. Albert still slept soundly. She waited as Henry went upstairs. He returned leading a somnolent child with grey shadowy eyes and finespun flaxen hair. Instinctively, Esther held out her arms. The girl hesitated then slowly moved towards her. Esther cuddled and kissed until she felt the fair head relax against her shoulder. Henry admired the contrast of black curls mingling with the fair silkiness.

411

'She's so pretty, Henry ... she must be a comfort to you.'

'No,' Henry said quietly, 'I fear she'll never be that. She is another man's child, Esther. You can surely see that?' Esther went red as fire. To hide her feelings she buried her face and murmured soft words to Henrietta.

They already knew, Henry realized sadly. Esther and Albert must have heard the rumours or maybe Polly told them the truth herself?

'I fear that little girl is living proof of her parentage, despite her name.' Esther clutched the child fiercely.

'You're surely not going to reject her! What does any of that matter, Henry? Can't you love her for herself? My mother had to leave home because of me – you can't turn Henrietta away!'

They were dependent on him, she remembered quickly, she mustn't upset him.

'I'm sorry, it's not my place to speak out,' she said to placate him, 'but please don't reject this little girl.'

'Don't worry, Esther, I'd never do that. I loved her mother once. I wish I could have spoken to Polly ... maybe assuaged her fears. I knew in my heart before Henrietta was born ... if only I hadn't been such a coward.'

Esther put out a hand. 'Henry, I can't believe you were ever unkind.' He reddened.

'I fear I was. However,' he stroked Henrietta's hair, 'the knowledge hasn't made me a monster, I trust. Since your letter arrived, I've considered carefully what I must do. Shall I take the child back to bed first?'

'I'll do it.' Esther made her way up the stairs, glad of the respite. She gazed at the innocent sleeping face. Every aspect of it reminded her of Polly, there was no trace of Henry, yet at the same time the unknown father had put his stamp on her, too. 'He must've been such a handsome chap,' she whispered. Tall too, for the child was the same height as Edwin, and Polly had been short.

Feeling more composed, she tucked Edwin's arms under the coverlet and joined Henry in the room next door.

He poured them both wine. 'It is to give me courage,' he admitted, and drank for a while in silence. 'I must begin by telling you of our marriage and what I have to say doesn't reflect well on either Polly or myself. I loved her . . . she was unable to requite that love. I cannot complain for it wasn't her fault, nor do I blame her. I was far too old to be her husband. She loved me as far as she was able.'

Esther looked at the table, the fire, at the contents of her glass – anywhere but at the sad face. Henry Durrant wasn't fashioned by fate to be a tragic figure, yet he was baring his feelings and she could feel nothing but pity.

'No, I cannot blame her,' he murmured again. 'I hope Polly found happiness. I think she did for a time. From what I've since learned, he was a very pleasant young man. From Norwich.' Henry took another sip of wine. 'She paid such a dreadful price.'

'Albert was distraught.' Henry acknowledged a sorrow far greater than his own.

'Once she knew she was dying . . . and realized I was bound to discover the truth . . . I think that's why she gave the child my name.'

'You said you'd decided what to do?'

'Yes,' he sighed. 'I intend to leave Brandon for good. It'll be quite a wrench. I've spent my entire life in this town. I had hoped, coming back to Willow End where Polly and I spent the first years of our marriage, I might find peace. All I remember is how miserable *she* was. So . . . I've decided to go. Which brings me to Henrietta. I want her to stay.' Esther was bewildered.

'You're not taking her with you?'

'I want to rid myself of ghosts. Besides, Polly's last wish was that you and Albert should care for the child.'

'Us? But . . . ' How to explain that they were penniless. 'I'd love to, Henry. Albert would too, I know that. He'd always cherish her because of Polly. But . . . '

'You're worried about Albert's recovery?'

'No, that's just a matter of time. It's his employment. He's lost his situation with the tram car company.' It felt like treachery to say so.

'Ah.'

413

'It's not his fault, Henry, he's worked so hard. And at the end of it all, we've ended up with nothing but what's in that trunk – oh, and a few pots and pans I had to leave behind at Bridie Macguire's.'

Henry said diffidently, 'There are sufficient utensils in that cupboard, I think.'

She didn't understand.

'I want you and Albert to have these two cottages in return for caring for Henrietta. Albert's handy enough to turn them into a proper home. I've never got round to it, I'm such a lazy fellow but the garden has been tended; it should provide you with sufficient vegetables. Once Albert is well enough, I'm sure he can find employment locally, enough to provide a little income. I propose to give you a hundred pounds to carry you through. Part of that is money from Polly's tea-garden. The rest of her savings I've invested and added to, to provide a pound a week for Henrietta's support until she marries. Thereafter, she is to have the capital.' Esther gaped: so much money!

'But what about you?'

'I've retired. I have a gratuity from the factory and enough in the bank to buy a small property near the coast. The ground is much more of a problem nearer the sea. I intend to create a tropical garden.' For the first time, Esther saw enthusiasm in his eyes. 'That should provide employment for the rest of my life, not to say – a challenge!'

'Will you have enough to live on?' Esther asked plainly. Men and their enthusiasms were all very well, but women had to be practical.

'My gratuity will be sufficient. I've never been a spendthrift.' He risked a small joke. 'This is the first bottle of wine I've purchased in many years, apart from port at Christmas.'

'Albert likes a glass of port then,' she said absently. So much to consider!

'Do you think he will be – agreeable?' Esther was helpless confronted by so much generosity. It sounded as if her worries were at an end. She could scarcely believe it possible.

414

'When your letter arrived, all I thought was, Thank God, somewhere to nurse Albert back to health. After what you've told me . . . Polly wanting us to care for that dear little girl – and your kindness – my mind's in a whirl.'

'There's no hurry,' Henry replied quietly. 'We can talk again when you both feel rested. I've prepared the bed upstairs for you and Albert. I shall sleep down here as I used to when my parents were alive.'

Such selflessness and exposing his feelings like that, how lonely he must be! Esther leaned across and kissed him impulsively.

'Bless you, Henry Durrant. See that you make that lovely tropical garden, for Albert and I will bring the children to visit often. And you must always look on us as your family.' Vulnerable to kindness, Henry turned away so that she could not see his tears.

Albert managed the stairs and fell asleep again immediately. Esther lay awake in the old-fashioned feather bed. The prospect of a totally different way of life made sleep impossible. She was a London creature, the countryside was unknown territory. It was so full of noise! Not starlings and pigeons and trams but lots of strange birds; Albert had told her about bats and owls, there were others roosting in the trees, she couldn't identify a single one. She couldn't hear traffic either, only the chuckle of the river and a distant train.

Moonlight shone on a wedding photograph on the tallboy. Polly had been so pretty, smiling too. Henry hadn't changed much: older and greyer but still the same stiff figure with a diffident expression.

What it must have cost to tell her their history tonight. She thought of their own ecstatic union. How she'd missed Albert's loving these last few months and he hers! He used to whisper as much when she visited the hospital, trying to distract her from the dreadful pulleys and weights attached to his leg. It was wonderful to have him back, she snuggled up a little closer and spared a thought for Henry, in his single chilly bed.

These cottages weren't large but full of nooks and crannies – and so clean. The garden was one where children
could play . . . Edwin – and Henrietta. The prospect of
another child made her rejoice. Albert would be
enchanted, he wouldn't hesitate, it might even cure his
desolation over Polly.

The window was open. She listened to the wind in the
trees. Here, she felt so much safer than in London. There
were no drunken shouts from men in the corner pub,
nothing but sweet peacefulness. And such a soft, soft bed
. . . Esther fell asleep at last.

Sybilla had been tempted by the devil and had succumbed.
That, at any rate, was to be her excuse. When the large
silver-coloured motorcar pulled up opposite, she peered
through her blinds. If that tall grey-haired man didn't
know the new owners were away – and his chauffeur was
returning even now to tell him there'd been no reply to his
knocking – he must be a stranger.

Sybilla Porrit was curious about strangers. Particularly
those who called at that address. She saw the chauffeur
begin looking round. Quick as a flash, she doffed her
apron, seized a basket and scissors and appeared in her
front garden as if in search of blooms.

'Excuse me, madam?'

'Yes?'

'My master was wondering when Mrs Polly Durrant
would be at home?' Sybilla stared.

'Polly's dead.'

'Oh, dear . . . When did that sad event occur, please?'
Sybilla did a hasty calculation.

'Near enough eight years ago. 'Twas a judgement on
what she done, if you ask me.' The chauffeur looked at her
coolly and Sybilla swallowed the rest of her remarks. If
she wanted to discover what this was about, she'd need to
be discreet.

'Polly was my niece as a matter of fact. Would your
master care for a cup of tea? This here is the tea-garden
but he could have it in the front parlour as it's drizzling.'

'I'll ask.'

416

The master was even more distinguished close-to, and tall. Sybilla noticed the black armband as he approached. She prayed Enoch wouldn't return early from the Five Bells and interfere.

'I hev put a match to the fire, sir. 'Twill be warm and snug in a moment. This tea's freshly brewed, would you care for a scone with it?'

'Just the tea, thank you. I come in search of information, madam. I understand you are related to the late Mrs Durrant?'

'H'aunt, sir. What did bring her up, her and her two brothers, ever since her poor dear father, what was my brother, died.' The solicitor was accustomed to disentangling relationships.

'Is Mr Durrant still alive?'

'Oh, yes. Henry's . . .' but she hesitated, cautious at divulging too much too soon. ''e was upset, naturally, at what Polly'd done, but who wouldn't be? That's why he sold up and left that house.'

'Why was he so distressed?' Sybilla pursed her lips.

'May I h'ask to whom I am addressing?'

'Certainly. My card, madam.' It was embossed and Sybilla smelled money. She saw the same name as that murmured by gossips eight years previously: Philip Ottram. The address was a business one in Norwich. It wasn't difficult to guess what Philip Ottram's father, now wearing a black armband, might be doing here. With a bit of luck she could earn herself a nice little sum this afternoon. Sybilla inclined her head graciously.

'My name's Porrit. Sybilla Porrit. Mrs. I don't hev any cards on me, I've used 'em all up,' she improvised. He concealed a smile.

'You were about to describe an event concerning your niece?' he prompted.

'Not until you tells me why you're asking, I'm not. After all, it was private. To do with the family.'

'Eight years ago, you say . . .'

'Ye-es.' Sybilla could see her visitor was equally adept at making deductions.

'What was the cause of her death?'

417

'I can't hardly remember, being so long ago.'

'Come, come, Mrs Porrit. Mrs Durrant lived across the street – and you a relative – you must have some idea?' Sybilla was affronted and refused to answer.

'Did the late Mrs Durrant give birth to a child before she died?' He was too clever by half; Sybilla stuck out her chin.

'What if she did?'

'Did the child survive?'

'It might have done.' Philip Ottram towered over her suddenly. 'Why should I tell you for nothing – ' Sybilla began to whine.

'Oh, that's it, is it?' he said with distaste. 'Pray excuse me, madam. I fear I shall have to pursue enquiries elsewhere, where a reward is not the first consideration.'

'Polly died owin' me money, her and that wretched brother of hers who's as stubborn as a mule. I'm entitled to a consideration,' Sybilla cried wildly. 'Albert agreed seven per cent.'

Philip Ottram paused, changed his mind and produced his wallet. From it he extracted a ten shilling note.

'I am not responsible for anyone's debts, Mrs Porrit, but from experience I can understand how an unresolved grievance might colour your remembrance. This will be yours once you have told me everything.'

Ten shillings! It was an insult. He wasn't getting much for that. But Sybilla didn't argue; instead, she gave the appearance of capitulating.

'Poor, dear little Polly . . . '

'The facts, if you please, Mrs Porrit. Nothing more.'

'It was your son who was the father,' she said suddenly, and saw the pain in his eyes. 'Is that why . . .?' she indicated the armband. Mr Ottram struggled to maintain his poise.

'Philip died of his wounds in France. My wife . . . Mrs Ottram has been severely affected. He was our only child.'

'Tut-tut-tut. Wicked, this war.'

'The whereabouts of this child of his are what interest me now, Mrs Porrit. I have come to repair past wrong-doing and provide for the future. Was it a boy or a girl?'

'A girl . . . ' Jealousy that he might be offering the child money made her indignant but Sybilla gave no outward sign. Polly's bastard inherit a fortune? Never! Instead, she gave an exaggerated sigh and gazed at the ceiling, murmuring, 'Poor little thing . . . she was so pretty.'

'Was! You're not telling me . . .? Not the child as well!' Sybilla was tempted; she teetered between greed and indifference. Supposing this rich man could be persuaded to increase his offer of ten shillings? If so, that was when she'd reveal Henrietta was alive. If not . . . 'She was baptised,' she said to encourage hope but this gave Mr Ottram the opposite impression.

'Was that because she wasn't expected to live?' Sybilla picked up the note and fingered it so that it crackled. He was too upset to notice the hint. 'Did she die at birth? Was she buried with her mother?' She couldn't think of an evasive answer quickly enough; he took her silence as an affirmation. He rose.

'I must bid you good-day, madam.'

'Polly's buried in the churchyard. I can show you her grave if you like.' She wanted to delay him but at the same time couldn't think how without admitting the truth. Mr Ottram picked up his hat.

'It was against all hope that I came here. I deserve no less for acting harshly years ago.' Sybilla was taken by surprise.

'Just a minute – ' but he was already on his way through her front door, 'I never said she was dead.'

She'd made no attempt to raise her voice and Mr Ottram didn't hear. Alone in her front parlour Sybilla watched him climb into the silver automobile.

'Ten shillin' and her little bastard stands to gain a fortune! Such a man could've afforded ten pounds mind ten shillings. And he never paid for his tea.'

She was still holding his visiting card. ' 'Twas the devil tempting me an' I succumbed,' she announced to no one in particular. Then, gradually, a solution occurred to her. When the time was right, she would confess her sin. Once

419

she'd worked out a way of persuading Albert to pay her a share of Henrietta's fortune, she would sell him this card. It would then be up to him to visit Norwich and explain. The chap would be so overcome to find he had got an heir, he'd wouldn't care about what had happened here today. All the same, she'd leave it for quite a while. And when the time came for him to be told, Sybilla Porrit would become invisible.

'I might visit London for a spell,' she announced optimistically.

It was three a.m. in a discreetly elegant brownstone house in a quiet New York street. The last client had left and Chas Unwin had seen the staff off the premises. He made his usual checks, locking up and tidying empty glasses and papers for servants to clear away in the morning. When that was done he returned to the drawing room cum office, sank back in his favourite chair and rested his feet on the fender.

He'd come a long way. All across America in pursuit of a dream. He hadn't found it out west. In despair he'd headed back east, intending to return to England as penniless as when he first arrived. Down to his last dollar, fate took a hand. A woman alighting from a cab dropped her purse. Chas ran after her to return it. Sizing him up, with a most unladylike, 'You by any chance looking for work?' Bella Miller had settled his future.

There was only one house rule: no questions to be asked. Chas knew as little about Bella as when they'd first met, but as for her person and the needs of her body, there was nothing concealed between them.

She sat, checking the books at her desk. She'd exchanged her stays for a loose robe and had put on her spectacles. After more than eight years theirs was a well-established routine. When she'd finished, he would lock the money in the safe and pour them each a drink. Then they would go to bed. Chas yawned.

The newspapers were full of the retribution to be exacted from Germany now that the war was over. He glanced at them carelessly but didn't bother to read;

420

Europe seemed a long, long way away.

'It's time you and I began to make plans, Chas.'

'Hmm?' He jerked awake. Bella was replacing the books in the drawer. Automatically, he rose and went to the tantalus. 'We've had a busy week. I shall need you to go to the bank tomorrow.' That too was part of the routine; Bella never kept much money in the house. 'There are important matters to discuss.' She accepted the brandy. 'Thank you. As I said, it's time we thought about the future.'

'How d'you mean?'

'Set a date for when we intend to sell up.'

'What?' He was wide awake now, 'What d'you mean — sell? Why on earth do that?' She took off her spectacles.

'Because I've made enough money.' She looked round. 'This house should round it off with a nice big sum. We'll call in the decorators before we put it on the market.'

'But — why do anything at all?' Bella shook her head at him and smiled.

'The good times are at an end, Chas, that's why. The war's over. Business is bound to decline. There won't be any young men wanting to spend their last night before embarkation in the arms of a beautiful woman. Besides, I never planned to stay — this was always a means to an end. So, you can start planning as well. Didn't you always say there was a piece of property you intended to buy in England? There's no reason why you can't travel there now.'

'I thought ... I had hoped ...' She looked at him shrewdly.

'No, Chas. That was never part of our arrangement. You and I suited one another, for a time. Now that time's over. Pour me another brandy and please don't sulk.'

He did her bidding automatically, moving from the big leather chair to the mahogany tantalus. Lights were dim but shone on heavy, handsome furnishing that Bella favoured as providing a club-like atmosphere for their wealthy clients. The tumblers he refilled were lead crystal, there was nothing cheap. Chas's role in the establishment was that of male protector. Bella Miller

421

had picked him up from a New York street but neither had ever regretted it. And she rightly said, they suited one another.

'But what d'you intend to do?' he demanded. 'And what about the girls?'

'They'll each get a dowry out of the proceeds. You'll have your share, never fear. As for me . . . I shall choose a new name, invent a new past, and set up as a rich widow in a new town. Don't ask where because I shan't tell you. It's the parting of the ways, Chas. I intend becoming respectable.'

'You?!' She wasn't offended, she chuckled.

'Why not? I'm wealthy now. I might even marry provided I can find a widower who can match me, cent for cent. It always helps to have a man about the house.'

'That's unkind!' She leaned forward.

'My dear, it was meant to stir you out of your apathy. You've become too comfortable, your waistline's started to thicken. Start thinking about the future in – where was it?'

'Suffolk.'

'Go book your passage. Six months or so, at a guess.' She looked him up and down complacently. 'Finishing school's over, Chas.'

It was his turn to smile for the mirror reflected a very different figure nowadays. Bella had insisted he shave off his whiskers – 'You're hiding behind them,' she'd scolded. 'Besides, they're old-fashioned nowadays. Learn to do without and become confident.'

She'd exposed and rid him of his inhibitions, one by one. 'That aunt, the farmer's wife – the army! You've been touching your forelock for far too long, Chas. In America, we don't do that.'

He'd broadened out and stood tall thanks to good food and an increasing sum in the bank. He'd had to think fast, he'd had one or too very awkward situations but he'd coped; he'd lost the last of his innocence – and now he was being dismissed.

No, that's not what it was. Chas rejected the thought as unworthy. Their partnership was being dissolved, that was it. As usual, Bella had been the one honest enough to find the right words.

She rose and joined him in front of the mirror, taking his arm, friendly-fashion; they gazed at their joint reflection.

'You haven't changed,' he said.

'I should hope not! It damn well costs me enough to keep the status quo.' She pulled a wry face. 'I'm planning to let that side slip a little. I want to be comfortable in my old age.'

'You'll never be old, Bella.'

'That's stupid and sentimental,' she chided, 'But I certainly intend that you shall never see me that way.'

'In six months' time, you said?'

'About that. Could be longer. Depends on the sale of this place. Meanwhile . . . ' He needed no second invitation and kissed her hard.

'I shall miss you, Bella Miller,' Chas muttered passionately.

Later, he murmured something which she didn't quite catch.

'I said, I must write a letter to Albert.'

'When did you last do that?' He thought about it.

'About 1897 . . . March, I reckon.' Bella was up on one elbow, staring at him.

'You haven't written to your own brother – in over twenty years?' He was defensive.

'There wasn't much point . . . I was a failure. I'd lost the little money I had and was working as a farm hand. I didn't want Polly and Albert to think badly of me. I hadn't met you then.' But there was no getting round Bella that way.

'First thing tomorrow you send them a proper letter and you enclose a ten dollar bill each, by way of apology. Otherwise I'll deduct twenty from your wages.'

There was an ancient scrawl on the yellowing kitchen plaster at The Coachman's in Fulham; the waitress obeyed the instruction. She delivered the envelope into the hands of two of Bridie's grandchildren. The old lady was upstairs in bed, paralysed, following the news of her son's arrest in Ireland. The two children moved into a quieter part of the mews.

'It's from America. D'you think there could be money in it?'

'Open it anyway. Who's Albert Unwin, esquire?'

'Never heard of him.'

' "My dear Albert, This is to let you and Polly know that I am on my way home – " '

'Hey, look at this!' There were furtive glances to see if they'd been overheard. The dollar bills were examined then, in a whisper, 'Let's see what uncle'll give us for 'em.'

The two boys shared the spoils. Paper and envelope were disposed of down the nearest drain.

Chapter Twenty-Four

Flesh and Blood, 1920

'Your aunt's coming this way.' Esther shaded her eyes, 'Wonder what she wants today?'

'Blast!' No matter how many times Sybilla was sent off with a flea in her ear she still came bouncing back. Albert dug harder than necessary, splattering soil over Edwin.

'Blast!'

'Edwin! You mustn't use that word.' Edwin looked at her soulfully.

'Daddy did. Look what he's done to my *clean* jersey.'

His father scolded, 'You shouldn't be wearing that in the garden.'

He was smug. 'Mother's washed the other one.'

'Well, you run along for a bit. Great-Aunt Syb's coming.'

The boy didn't need a second bidding; he disappeared like lightning.

Albert waited until he heard the click of the gate before straightening up. 'You know you're not welcome.'

'I come to do you a favour an' what I come to say is private, not for the rest of the street.'

'Once and for all, I ain't giving you any more money.'

'I shall remind you of that some other time. I come about summat else: a sin I committed 'gainst you and yours.'

'You've committed hundreds and I'm not interested in any of 'em.' Albert plunged his spade back into the soil and cursed when he saw an ants' nest. 'Esther! Bring me a kettleful of boiling water, please love.'

Sybilla stood, lips compressed. Esther came out with the kettle and was about to go back, ignoring her completely, when Sybilla announced, 'I got something to say 'bout Polly's bastard.' At this, Albert heaved his spade up so violently, Esther cried out, 'No, Albert!' He brought it down hard.

'I wasn't going to touch her . . . even though she deserves it.' He eased the weight off his bad leg. 'Go on, then. Spit it out, then we can all have a bit of peace.'

'Ain't you going to invite me in?'

'No.'

'No,' Esther confirmed. Sybilla raised her eyes.

'When I remember what I done for you Albert, an' your miserable brother and sister – ' Esther lost her temper.

'All you've ever done is malign Polly's memory and tell the world that my parents weren't married.'

' 'Tisn't my fault if you an' that unfortunate child of hers were born out of wedlock.' Albert's expression brought her up short. ' 'Tis for her sake I come round this afternoon.'

'You've got nothing but evil in your heart for that child.'

Sybilla dearly wanted to quarrel but recalled the delicate negotiation that lay ahead. 'I ain't saying what it's about out here. 'Tis too important.'

Esther and Albert looked at one another. Albert shrugged. He indicated the wooden bench. 'Over there. I'm not inviting you into our home because you're not welcome.'

' 'Taint yours, 'tis Henry Durrant's . . . he must've been soft in the head letting you two have it . . .' Sybilla settled herself and looked pointedly at Esther, 'I wouldn't say no to a cup of tea.'

'I daresay you wouldn't but I'm not offering,' Esther answered coolly.

'Well, you needn't wait. Albert's the one I want.'

'Esther stays,' Albert said firmly, 'so what's this about?' Sybilla sniffed. It wasn't going as she had planned.

'A while back, this man come calling at Polly's house, looking for her. Out of the kindness of my heart, I invited

426

him in to my place and give him a cup of tea . . . for which he never paid.'

'He must've supped it quick,' Albert observed, ' 'ope he didn't scald his tongue.'

'He was from Norwich. Come to find his dead son's child.'

'Oh?' Albert's blue eyes were very steady now. 'And what did you tell him?'

'The devil tempted me . . . an' I succumbed.'

'What's that supposed to mean?'

'I think it means she fibbed, Albert.' Sybilla flared.

'That's a wicked thing to say – I'm a God-fearing woman!'

'The only thing you're a-feared of, Aunt Syb, is losing sixpence and finding a penny. Now, what did you say to this man? I assume he might've been Henrietta's grandfather?'

'He might've. He said he come to make amends. But you an' me hev got to come to an arrangement afore I tells you anything more.' Esther stared in disbelief.

'What?!'

'You old varmint!' Albert was on his feet, spade in hand. 'You're trying to sell that child's birthright!'

'Don't you threaten me! Help! Murder!' He flung the spade away in disgust.

'You ain't worth hanging for. Get out of my garden, go on, 'fore I forgets and does for you like I did for them ants.'

'I come here of the goodness of my heart, to do you an' that bastard a kindness – '

'You come here because you thinks there's a chance of getting hold of money.'

'That child don't need it,' Sybilla cried indignantly, 'look at all what Henry Durrant settled on her, an' she wasn't his.'

'If you really meant to do Henrietta a good turn, you'd tell us this man's name, Mrs Porrit.'

'You get nothing for nothing in this world!' Sybilla replied. 'You can whistle for his name for all I care.' She flounced down the path to the gate, 'An' I shall sue you for what you owes, you see if I don't!'

When the children were in bed Esther raised the matter again. They were in the living room. Albert had long ago knocked an archway through and built a porch to replace the two front doors. He and Esther had recovered old chairs and revarnished cast-off furniture, transforming the former pair of cottages into a comfortable, shabby home which fitted them like a glove.

A black kitten stretched her claws experimentally and Esther bent to detach her from a chair-leg. 'That tale this afternoon, Albert . . .?' He grunted. 'D'you reckon your aunt was telling the truth?'

'A man must've come looking for Polly's kiddie. Syb couldn't have made that up.'

'If the man's son was dead, I suppose *he* might've been killed in the war?' Esther squinted to thread a needle. 'Henry mentioned Norwich when he talked about – Polly's friend. He was younger than she was by all accounts, so he'd be of an age to go and fight.' The whole subject was one which made Albert uneasy.

'Best leave things be, eh?'

'I was just wondering if we ought to try and find him . . . for Henrietta's sake. If he does want to do something for her.' It was awkward. They were scrupulous in keeping Henry and Polly's money for the child and managing themselves on what Albert could earn. He got to his feet and began poking the fire irritably.

'Trouble is . . . supposing it was true. If the man was looking, in order to give her money, Henrietta could end up with far more than Edwin.'

'Edwin wouldn't mind. He's so proud of her. He doesn't care if she has more.'

'He will as he gets older. He wanted a football last week. I couldn't afford ten and six for one but he knew we'd spent more than that on Henrietta's new slippers.'

'Don't you go buying footballs without telling me, Albert Unwin!'

'You know what I mean.'

'Yes. But we've got to be fair to Polly's memory. This man might be genuine in wanting to make amends. We shan't know unless we meet him.'

428

'I'm not going round to ask Syb for his name!' Albert burst out.

'I don't think you need do that. What about Polly's box? There might be some reference in there?' He shook his head, close to tears.

'I can't. I only looked through it the once, when we moved here. There's all sorts, diaries, everything. Bits from when we were children mixed up with letters. She even kept the ones I sent her from India . . . It makes me too sad to go through 'em again.'

'I know. I'll do it for you.' The kitten was romping round the carpet with a piece of wool. Esther scooped it up and threatened, mock-fierce.

'As for you, you little terror!' The kitten began to spit and fume. It wriggled and bit her finger. 'Ow!' She sucked away the blood. 'I've just thought of a name for this scrap: Old Syb. How about that?'

'Perfick!' He kissed the wound better. 'Make us a cuppa, shall I?'

'How much are you charging?' Albert laughed more than the joke warranted. As he wiped his eyes, he said, 'He must be smart, this chap from Norwich. He's the only one who ever got away from Syb without paying.'

'You did even better,' Esther grinned, 'you still owe her that seven per cent.'

It had taken almost a year before Bella Miller had settled her affairs to her satisfaction. She took it for granted that Chas was also arranging his. Pride prevented him admitting he'd had no reply to his letter. Eventually when she asked, he had to tell her.

'Serve you right.'

'I beg your pardon?' He'd been feeling sorry for himself, as Bella had surmised.

'Next time, don't leave it twenty years between buying stamps.'

'Suppose Albert was stupid enough to get himself killed in the war?'

'If he was, you still have a sister.'

'Yes. But I don't know where she lives. She could be

anywhere by now. I don't even know her married name.' Bella gave him a little shake.

'You're talking of England, Chas, not the United States. She can't have gone far. Perhaps you should start at that cafe in London. Maybe they might know something.'

'Supposing Albert had my letter – and didn't want to reply. He could be offended because I didn't write.' Bella reached up and kissed him.

'From what you've told me, he doesn't sound the sort to bear grudges. Write to him again, you can give him a definite date now. Make sure he understands you're coming home for good. And go book a passage. Tomorrow we're shopping for galoshes.'

'What on earth for?'

'It's always raining in England, haven't you heard?'

She stopped on the quayside and turned to face him. Around them was the bustle of a ship about to depart. 'This is as far as we go, Chas. I've no wish to go on board.' They'd been the last to leave the brownstone house that morning, walking through empty rooms, finally handing over the key to the new owners. Chas had been more affected than he'd expected. He'd felt uprooted and now all the old uncertainties of his youth came flooding back. Bella gripped both his hands. 'Look at me.' He blinked to dislodge unwanted moisture. 'It's a new beginning. No going back, remember.'

'That's just what I *am* doing, dammit!' Chas gave up an attempt to laugh.

'But you're not the same person,' she urged.

'Thanks to you. Will I never see you again?'

'No!' It was sharp. Chas stood a little straighter.

'Sorry, Bella. I shouldn't have asked, I know.' Sunlight was harsh and the wind whipped the veiling into her face. He could see she'd been resolute; her hair already showed signs of grey. He touched it with gentle fingers. 'This won't attract a rich widower.'

'Then I shall have to manage without.' Her voice was steady but he could feel the tension through her fingers.

'Shall I find you a cab?'

'No, thank you. I've no intention you should discover my destination.'

'It must be via the railroad station,' Chas protested. She gave a tight smile.

'Maybe.'

'You will be all right?'

'Of course!' This was so scathing he almost grinned as he raised his hat.

'A foolish question to ask Bella Miller.'

'Not even that any more.'

'No?' He raised her hand to his lips. 'Whoever you are . . . thank you for the best years of my life. Good luck, my dear.'

She walked away without a backward glance, as he'd known she would.

It wasn't Sybilla's nature to give up, not where money was involved. She reasoned herself into the position where whatever Philip Ottram had intended to bequeath to Henrietta, he should first give *her* a proportion, to square the account. Once she'd revealed to him that Henrietta was still alive, of course. Sybilla brushed aside memories of her past deception. It had been Mr Ottram's fault for walking out like that. Now that Albert had proved so uncooperative she would go to Norwich alone. She rehearsed the various arguments in front of her mirror as she decided which hat to wear.

'It wasn't as though I was making but a bare living from my afternoon teas . . . an' how many years since Enoch Porrit gave me a penny for housekeeping? I gets but a pittance from letting them upstairs rooms. At this rate, I shan't have enough for decent lodgings in London, what a woman in my position is entitled to.

'But if'n I was to have what's *rightfully* mine, what Albert – or Polly should've paid me years ago – seven per cent at compound interest – then I might just manage. Not forgetting that cup of tea.' On second thoughts she decided to be magnanimous and overlook refreshments.

'Before little Henrietta enjoys a penny of that money, she would want her dear great-aunt to be comfortably situated, as I'm sure you'll agree,' she finished triumphantly. There: who would dare argue with that?

The expedition to Norwich was an occasion for secrecy and high excitement. Sybilla remembered how she'd felt years ago, with two new five pound notes tucked in her petticoat pocket to tempt widow Helliwell into selling her this house.

Feeling confident, she teased one or two strands out of the tight silvery grey bun. Perhaps she should use the curling tongs? But when she found them at the bottom of the wardrobe, they were rusty. She would try squeezing her hair into waves with her fingers; styles had changed nowadays.

She even considered buying a new jacket. Her best one was old and smelled of camphor. But spending money even on herself was so alien to Sybilla's nature she quickly rejected the idea. Her best would do for a few more years yet. She would wind beads round her throat, the way Queen Mary did with her pearls. That would make her fashionable. She'd never dream of going to Thetford dressed like that but Norwich was different.

'Have you an appointment, Mrs Porrit?'

'Mr Ottram will see me. Just tell him it's about his son's child.' The elderly clerk coughed.

'The late Mr Philip, would that be?'

'Him what commited adultery with my niece,' Sybilla explained affably. She wasn't bearing grudges this morning, she knew it was important to establish identity in matters of law.

The clerk returned and bid her follow. Mr Ottram sat stoney-faced behind his desk.

'I can give you five minutes, madam.' Sybilla brushed this aside.

'If'n you hadn't been in such a hurry las' time, you would hev learned something to your advantage. You rushed off before I'd finished telling you.' She paused, to allow him to offer a financial inducement but his silence wasn't encouraging.

'Polly's little girl's alive. The one your son give her.' Mr

432

Ottram's stare was frightening. Sybilla pressed on, now slightly flustered. 'Anyone can see it's not Henry Durrant's. Blonde hair straight down her back.'

'You – allowed me to leave, believing that the child had died!'

' 'Twas your own fault,' Sybilla said defensively. 'If'n you'd stayed long enough to pay for your tea, I could've finished what I'd been about to say.' Philip Ottram was on his feet, towering over her. She suddenly remembered how big he was.

'How dare you deceive – Where's the child now? What is her name?'

'Now just a minute, you haven't heard what Polly owed me. She made plenty, 'ticing all my customers away, undercutting my prices. Henry Durrant never give me a penny from her estate even though I was entitled . . . '

She was talking to empty air. Ottram was at the door of his office, shouting orders into the room beyond, for his clerk to alert his chauffeur. 'Here,' she called plaintively, 'you've done it again. I ain't finished.'

He was back, stern and authoratitive, followed by the clerk. 'The child's name is Durrant, I presume. Where are she and Mr Durrant living now? I take it they are no longer at the same address?'

'Henry Durrant hev moved,' Sybilla confirmed but stuck out her chin defiantly, 'I'm not saying no more at present.'

'Madam . . . ' It had a dangerous edge.

'Not until I tells you what Albert did, on account of Chas, and why one of 'em must be made responsible. Them Unwins hev cost me dear.' Ottram turned his back on her and spoke to his clerk.

'Let Mrs Ottram know I shall be late and cancel the rest of my appointments. I shall conduct this search myself – I must find the child. There are bound to be those in the town who know of her whereabouts. I shall enquire directions when I get to Brandon.' They were outside his office now and he shut the door on Sybilla's outraged shouting.

'Excuse me, sir. Mrs Porrit mentioned the name

"Unwin" a moment ago ... We received a letter signed with that same name this morning. I have it on my desk.' The clerk retrieved it from the pile. 'Here we are ... I was about to bring it to your attention. The contents puzzled me at first.'

He waited until Philip Ottram had finished reading the brief note. 'The female child referred to is described as the daughter of the late Mrs Polly Durrant ... and the address where the child is living now is on the letter.'

Philip Ottram whispered, 'Thank you! It's a gift from heaven! Let Mrs Ottram know I shall be late ... but that I may have good news!'

The elderly clerk's eyes were sympathetic. 'I understand, sir. My best wishes for a successful outcome – '

'Here! I haven't finished what I come to say.' Sybilla was in the doorway.

'Get rid of that woman!'

'Yes, sir.'

'Mummy, mummy! Come and see!' Edwin was speechless. The huge silver machine filled the rutted lane outside Willow End. 'It's stopped outside. It's a ROLLS ROYCE!'

'All right, dear. I expect they've made a mistake. You and Henrietta wash your hands, tea's nearly ready.' There was a tap at the door.

'There you are, you see.' Edwin was triumphant.

'They're probably lost and need directions.' Esther took off her apron and patted her curls. When she opened the door it was the chauffeur.

'Mrs Unwin?'

'Yes ... ' She looked beyond him at the occupant of the car and knew immediately. 'Edwin, go and find your father. He's probably on his way home. Ask him to come straight here.'

This was in a tone which Edwin had learned to obey. Mystified, reluctant, he asked, 'Can't I look at the motor car first?'

'Later. Run along.' Halfway down the path, the boy stood aside politely to let the tall, grey-haired man walk past, before dashing off down the lane. The man's eyes scanned the cottage windows, eager for his first glimpse.

'Mrs Unwin, I'm Philip Ottram.'

Esther nodded, slightly nervous.

'Please come in.'

'The letter from you and your husband arrived this morning.' He stooped under the lintel. His presence seemed to fill the small shabby room. 'Is the girl – my grand-daughter, is she here?' He was so eager, Esther was suddenly apprehensive at what she and Albert had set in motion.

The Coachman's was so much smaller than Chas remembered; the smells weren't such as to tempt his appetite these days, his body no longer yearned for nourishment and his taste was far more sophisticated. He ordered a meal but left most of it. On his last visit he would've licked the plate clean. The waitress wasn't a pert, dark-haired girl either, nothing was the same. With little hope of success, he enquired the fate of his letter. To his surprise, the waitress remembered.

'From America, wasn't it. Did you send it?' He was too exotic to be an ordinary stranger. The well-fitting broadcloth was light-coloured and the hat had a wide brim. 'I took it to Bridie Macguire's, like it said on the wall.' She insisted on showing him the instruction scribbled on the plaster.

'Then my brother never came here to collect the letter himself?'

'No. Bridie's grandchildren said they'd give it to her. She would've passed it on, I think.'

'Maybe she knows where Albert is. Her address, that's round the corner in the mews?'

'Yes but I shouldn't go there today if I were you . . . not after . . . ' The waitress hesitated then said awkwardly, 'Bridie's son John . . . there was some kind of accident in Ireland. A soldier was killed. John was hanged for it yesterday morning.'

He remembered the mews. Small dark houses, overshadowed and snubbed by their superior neighbours. The atmosphere was tense today, almost palpable as he walked along. This community had banded together in support of one of their own and a stranger wasn't welcome. Eugene Macguire eyed him coldly.

'Yes?'

'My name is Unwin. I believe your mother may know the whereabouts of my brother, Albert.'

'We haven't seen Albert for a long time, since before his accident.' Chas felt a great burst of excitement.

'He is alive then?' He'd been torn between hope and despair ever since leaving New York.

'Albert's alive. Some aren't.'

'No. I've come at the worst possible time and I'm sorry. Do you think your mother would agree to see me? I've come a long way to find Albert.'

'She's half out of her mind. The priest and my sisters are praying with her.'

'I'll not trouble her long.'

Upstairs, black-clad figures were gathered round the bed; soft voices offering what balm they could. The woman lying against the pillows had once been fat. Chas could see the bones beneath the slack skin. She stared unseeing at first then gradually recognition dawned.

'It's not Albert, is it?'

'No, I'm his brother, Chas.'

'You finally come back from America then?'

'Yes.'

'He was always asking for a letter, hoping you'd write.'

'Yes . . . I've neglected him shamefully.'

'You can make up for it, now you're back. Esther took him to Suffolk so's he could get better. They decided to stay there. She wrote again last week, when she heard – there wasn't going to be no reprieve . . . She was always as dear to me as my own . . . ' Sobs interrupted.

Chas dearly wanted to know more but asked, 'Did they go to Brandon?' Alberta Macguire pushed him out of the way, anxious to comfort her mother.

'Where your sister used to live,' she told him impatiently, 'now leave us in peace.'

436

The rhythm of his feet pounding along the pavements: 'Used to live, used to live, used to live . . . ' Had something happened to Polly? Perhaps she'd moved away? Was Albert still ill, was that why he hadn't replied? And who on earth was Esther?

Albert was tired and his limp was more pronounced. Edwin frisked at his heels. Ahead of them they could see the impressive motor car but Albert refused to be dazzled. 'Did I ever tell you about the Inskip Phaeton, lad?'

'Yes, daddy, thousands of times.' At twelve, Edwin had no use for tact.

'It was still a remarkable machine for all that.' The famous day trip to see Mr Blériot had long been overshadowed now that the Royal Air Force were established at Snarehill, but Albert refused to believe the phaeton had been surpassed. 'Ahead of its time, that was the problem.'

They were alongside the Rolls now. Albert could see the chauffeur had on a uniform smarter than anything he possessed. The man didn't bother to look up from his newspaper as he and Edwin turned in at the gate. 'Where's Etta?'

'Upstairs, I think.'

She'd remained hidden from the stranger, refusing to come down, but at the sound of this beloved voice and step, she rushed downstairs into his arms.

'Uncle Albert!' She was too tall for him to whirl round as he used to; instead they hugged one another and she peeped out shyly. The stranger looked fierce. Aunt Esther didn't like him either, she could tell.

'Albert, this is Mr Ottram. Come from Norwich.' Ottram ignored him, gazing at Henrietta with hungry eyes.

'Edwin, take Etta outside and show her the motor car. Ask the chauffeur if you may, first.' The boy grabbed her hand and they ran back down the path.

'It's a Rolls Royce, Etta, the best car in all the world!' Philip Ottram followed as far as the doorway to see them go.

'She's Philip's child all right,' he said with satisfaction. He was supremely confident now. The woman had

437

answered his questions. She'd been reluctant to speak of Polly Durrant but he'd insisted; he knew the whole history now. Unwin was obviously of the same simple mould as his wife and unlikely to prove troublesome. He gave Albert a benign smile. The man's clothes and face were covered in a greyish powder after a day at Mount's whiting mill. He was lame, too, which must hamper his earning capability.

Perhaps his first instinct, to offer twenty guineas, should be revised? Ottram almost laughed; whatever the increase, it was hardly a fortune in exchange for a truly beautiful grandchild.

'That's Polly's daughter you're looking at, Mr Ottram. Our niece.' The voice behind him was firm. Ottram swung round and found himself facing an extremely wary gaze.

'You and Mrs Durrant were close,' he said smoothly.

'When we were children, we were. After Chas and me enlisted we didn't see much of her, but she was the best sister a chap could have. Her last wish was for Esther and me to care for Henrietta.'

'So I understand. Forgive me if I speak plainly, Unwin. My wife and I can offer so much more.'

'Money, you mean. To buy things.' Ottram stiffened.

'And provide a home. We would give that child everything in our power.'

They would give a new name, too: Philippa. All trace of her unfortunate beginnings would be erased so that she could take her rightful place in their lives.

'This is Henrietta's home, always has been. She and her father lived here till she was eight when we took over. Thanks to his generosity, this will continue to be her home as long as she needs it.'

'I've explained our circumstances, Albert.'

'I daresay it don't look much of a place,' Albert surveyed his kingdom with a swelling heart, 'but it's paradise to me 'cause of Esther here, our son Edwin, and Henrietta who can remind us all of Polly.'

There was silence for a moment. Esther broke it saying gently, 'Mr Ottram has made his offer, Albert. He wants us to think it over.'

'I want to take the girl to live with us in Norwich. We

have a fine house with a splendid garden. She would have her own maid – '

'Where's that paper you found in Polly's box, love?' As Esther handed it to him, Philip Ottram thought he recognized office notepaper. 'It was a long time ago when you sent my sister this letter . . . I think she must've kept the appointment, Mr Ottram?' Albert had confounded him: that letter!

'I believe she did, yes. Before the child's birth. My son and I arranged to see Mrs Durrant in Thetford – '

'It was obviously important seeing as Polly hung on to it.' Albert's gaze was unwavering as he held out the paper. 'There's marks on it though, as if she'd been crying?'

Ottram answered stiffly, 'At that meeting I made an offer of financial assistance which Mrs Durrant saw fit to decline.' For some reason he made no mention of what his other suggestion had been that day. Albert was thoughtful.

'I can understand why Polly refused. It would hurt her pride to have to beg. Besides, she'd saved quite a bit from her tea-garden. What else upset her – was it something you said?'

'No!'

'But why was she crying? Was she hoping for a kind word?'

Ottram was angry now. 'Mrs Durrant seemed to think that by seeing Philip her problems could be resolved. I advised her otherwise.'

'What exactly was your advice, Mr Ottram?'

'To convince her husband the child was his, naturally. It was the obvious solution.'

'Not for Polly, she wasn't given to telling fibs. She'd cheated Henry already. Must have been heavy on her conscience, what she'd done. Henry knew. I think he guessed the night she told him she was expecting.' Albert stared at the letter once more. 'Poor lonely old Pol . . . And what might have happened to the kiddie if Henry hadn't behaved like a gentleman?' The choice of word was deliberate; their visitor flushed. When Albert looked up this time, Philip Ottram avoided those blue eyes.

439

'We'll consider your offer, Mr Ottram. It's only fair to Henrietta to do that. We'll talk it over with Henry because he was prepared to care for her for the rest of his life, so it's only right we seek his opinion.'

It had seemed so simple at the beginning; now Philip Ottram was anxious as well as angry. 'I can provide so much more – ' he began.

'I don't doubt you can, Mr Ottram; there's no argument but that you have plenty of money. It's your reasons for coming after all this time which bother me. Especially since finding this letter. Something tells me you'd never have bothered if your son hadn't been killed. I'm sorry for you . . . loving Edwin as I do, I can understand what that must mean. But Pol was a grand girl too, loving and gentle. What she did was wrong but I don't think she deserved to shed all these tears.' Albert tucked the letter away. 'Henrietta takes after her mother, being so sweet-natured. That's why we treasure her so.'

Esther added innocently, 'And she is well looked after, Mr Ottram. We have a pound a week to spend on her, given to us by Henry.'

A pound! His incredulity made her shrink.

'That child needs a first-class governess to rid her of country bumpkin ways before she can enter polite society. Look at her now, for heavens' sake, romping like some hoyden!' They watched the antics in the garden.

'Edwin taught her to play leap-frog.'

'Young ladies do not behave in that fashion. Consider my offer very carefully, Unwin. And remember, I do not intend to give up now that I've found my grandchild.'

They watched him try and speak to Henrietta as he walked back to the car. She immediately retreated behind Edwin and when the tall stranger attempted to give her guineas, shook her head.

From where they stood, they heard Edwin say brightly, 'I'll look after that money, if you like. I can share it with Etta later,' but Philip Ottram's generosity didn't extend that far. He made one attempt to pat the flaxen head but Henrietta jerked away and this time Edwin said sturdily, 'Leave her alone! She doesn't like you!'

'That's it, son, you tell him!' Albert whispered. He felt Esther slide her arms round him.

'I'm so terribly sorry . . . it's my fault, asking you to write to him.'

'He would have found her, eventually. As he said, his sort don't give up. We couldn't prevent him coming here.'

'He can't take her away, can he?'

'I don't know, old girl.' Albert squeezed her hand tightly. 'My God, I hope not! I couldn't bear to lose Etta!'

'It wasn't just our letter that brought Mr Ottram today. Sybilla went to see him this morning.'

'One of these days I'll do for that old varmint,' Albert began but Esther was kissing his ear and whispered to distract him.

'I want you to write to Henry, tell him what's happened and invite him to stay. You and he can put your heads together – you're bound to come up with something. Oh, Albert, I was so proud of the way you spoke to Mr Ottram.' Her eyes were shining as she kissed him again and again. 'It really is paradise here, with you and the children.'

Chas had decided not to rush. He didn't want to be taken by surprise. Whatever was wrong with Albert, he intended to discover for himself first. How, was a problem.

Think matters out, Bella had taught him. Discover the facts then make some kind of plan. He'd have a good dinner, a decent cigar and a stroll in one of the parks while he thought about it. He missed the excitement of New York; the pace was slower but in a sense it suited him better. He felt more in tune with the tempo of London. Everywhere was so much greener, he'd forgotten the intensity of it, and the many song birds. It revived his homesickness for Suffolk.

In the end he decided to travel to Thetford and walk. There was a station at Brandon, his luggage could go direct, but the weather was fine, there might be some former acquaintance or a passerby glad of a gossip. He could glean more that way and adjust to all the changes gradually.

Bella always went first-class but Chas preferred to

441

arrive without fuss. Besides, Bella had gone from his life
for ever. The ache had been sore at first but was growing
easier with every day that passed.

The long straight road built, some said, by the Romans,
stretched ahead. Where once there had only been ancient
forest now all the empty spaces of the Breckland were
being filled with pine. Chas came across men planting
saplings in regimental lines and listened for a moment to
the soft Suffolk voices.

'Hey, Laxsey, careful with tha'. Man could damage
hisself usin' tha'.'

'I'm mindin'. Where's Nocky?'

'Gone back for another load along o' Biker.'

Chas was invited to join them at their midday bread
and cheese. He learned much without revealing who he
was. When one woodman summoned up the courage to
ask the smart stranger's credentials, Chas told them he
was returning home but left them to ponder which that
home might be.

Arriving in Brandon, he enquired Albert's whereabouts at the Post Office and set off on the final stretch,
picking his way through half-remembered streets.

Pausing outside the rickety gate at Willow End, he
watched a black kitten chase a butterfly. The two
gardens had been made one and a brick path led up to a
porch which framed the remaining front door. On either
side, cottage garden flowers crowded in on one another,
spilling their colour and fragrance, competing with a
pungent clump of lavender.

A fork stood upright at the end of a row of half-dug
cabbages. Albert obviously managed to cultivate his
garden. Chas breathed deeply. His heart was thudding
despite his sophistication. He hadn't managed to discover
anything from the workmen on the Thetford road. Now,
he would have to cope with the situation as he found it.

He'd rehearsed this encounter all the way across the
Atlantic, throughout his stay in London and today on the
train. He'd tried hundreds of ways to find the words
which would bridge the gap of so many neglected years.

442

'Yes?' She'd appeared in the doorway, a comely young woman with dark curls and a lively face with dark blue eyes. At first her glance was polite but now she stared openly. 'You're ... Aren't you ...?'

It was the way she tilted her head which brought memory alive and transformed him back into a gawky youth. The words tumbled out.

'I remember you – you're the girl from The Coachman's!'

'I'm Albert's wife,' Esther said, a trifle indignantly. Then, 'You're Chas.' He was so much broader, distinguished even – and whatever had happened to those flamboyant moustachios!

'Where's Albert?' Remembering his manners, Chas apologized in confusion, 'I'm sorry, it's been so long. How d'you do, ma'am. I'm very pleased to meet you again.' He held her hand in a firm grasp as he raised the broad-brimmed hat. 'Albert's wife, is it? He couldn't have chosen better if you'll permit me to say so.' Esther overcame her awe at the smart appearance and relaxed.

'You have changed, Mr Unwin.'

'Chas, please!'

'Chas, then.' Her wonderful eyes sparkled in a way he remembered. 'I don't think you'd have risked a compliment in the old days.'

Oh, but I've risked far more since, Chas thought a little ruefully. He smiled at the bright, warm face. It hadn't been flattery; Albert had chosen very well indeed. She'd filled out but still had her bobbishness that he remembered.

'Where is he?' he asked again. 'I've been the most rotten brother a chap could have but I hope Albert won't hold it against me.'

'I doubt it,' Esther chuckled. Albert would be bowled over by this wonderful vision of success. 'You'd better go and ask him. He's down at the staunch. He's taken Edwin and Henrietta for a swim.'

Here the river bank was flat without a single tree. Chas walked across the meadow to where the huge wheel operated the wooden sluice, trying all the while not to

hurry. It was a popular spot, he noticed, with plenty of
children perched on the frame ready to dive, watched over
by indulgent parents. He strove to make out one particular face among the squealing, wriggling bodies.

'Look, daddy, look!' A boy was on the top bar, hopping
from foot to foot, wet hair plastered in his eyes. The voice
was so familiar, it tugged at the heart. The boy wasn't
skinny or shivery – he had on proper bathing drawers
these days, not old threadbare shorts.

'I can do that, I can dive!' The girl was hoisting herself
up beside him. She was taller than Chas remembered, her
hair in a thick wet pig-tail but her eyes were the same,
huge and shadowy.

He forgot the passage of time, commonsense disappeared as he ran towards them, desperate to belong
once more.

'Polly!' Chas cried, 'Albert – it's me! I've come home.'

On the bank a man paused in towelling himself dry.
Thick grey hair framed a lined face with surprisingly
youthful eyes. The man frowned because the voice he'd
just heard couldn't possibly belong . . . not to that broad-
shouldered stranger?

'Chas?'

Chas halted. That couldn't be . . .? He was skinny
enough. The face was so much older! But it contained the
same honest blue gaze he'd always remembered.

'Hello, Albert. Yes, it's me. I've come back.'

Esther was ready when the procession finally appeared at
the top of the lane. She'd been preparing the best feast in
her power. Their approach was the triumphal return of a
hero: Albert, bursting with pride on one side of Chas,
Edwin on the other. The likeness was far more apparent
now the brothers were side by side. Albert was shedding
care and age by the minute, shouting the wonderful news
to every neighbour and friend, exhibiting Chas proudly.
Henrietta was dancing round this handsome new-found
uncle full of excitement. It sickened Esther that all this
happiness, anticipated for so long, was now under threat.

'Uncle Chas has come all the way from America!'

444

'Yes, dear, I know.'

'He's driven a mule train through Death Valley – he's been down a silver mine!'

'Has he, Edwin?'

Close to, Esther could see Chas was subdued although concealing it from the children; Albert has told him about Polly, she thought, but he's not letting it spoil their excitement. She would do the same. She would wait until the children were in bed before telling Albert the bad news. Let him enjoy what he'd been waiting for so long. 'Welcome home, Chas,' she said shyly.

The children poured past her into the cottage, bubbling with wonder, making Chas repeat what he'd done, over and over again. As for Albert, he alternated between exhuberant whoops: 'There, didn't I tell you he'd come back one day!' and melancholy: 'Just think, love, Chas never knew Pol was dead.'

It was when the special supper was over and the children on their way upstairs, that she murmured, 'A letter came in the afternoon post, Albert. From Mr Ottram. He says you and I are to go and sign some papers and he wants us to take Henrietta.'

There was much marvelling to be done upstairs before Chas was permitted to go back down. He had to admire every detail of Albert's handiwork. How one bedroom had been divided and cupboards fitted as well as shelves for books. In a corner of the smaller room was a pram with the most heavily welded chassis he'd ever seen – Albert had modelled it on the phaeton – for Henrietta's dolls.

Edwin demonstrated the desk which could be slotted between the sloping eves – even the brass nails trimming his boots.

'Your father learned to do that in the army. He used to repair boots for anyone who asked. Has he still got his tools?'

'Yes. Was he really in India, Uncle Chas?'

'Really in – ? Good heavens, young 'un, your father held the British Empire together, didn't he ever tell you?'

'No . . .'

445

'He stopped the fuzzies storming the pass. Blew 'em to smithereens, Albert did.'

'Tell us, tell us!'

'Tomorrow.' He was hoarse. 'We've got to leave something to tell. Can't hear everything tonight.'

As he descended the awkward stair Chas marvelled at their disparate lives. Any account of his own would have to be carefully tailored if he weren't to offend Esther. Which meant Bella Miller would have to remain a secret.

Bella had once complained that the army had sapped him of ambition. Maybe it had done the same for Albert; neither of them had ended up rich, not by American standards. Chas thought of the expensive furnishings in the house in New York. There was nothing here that could compare. At supper tonight, the cutlery was battered, even the tablecloth was darned.

He stopped in his tracks. He'd been blind! Albert was wealthy in the only way that really mattered. While he, Chas, had been chasing rainbows, trying to see beyond the next horizon, Albert had been laying up for himself real treasure upon earth.

Back in the shabby living room Chas suddenly caught sight of their two sad faces.

'What on earth's wrong?' Esther was near to tears. She turned to Albert who handed him a pile of paper bound with string.

'First things first. This is the letter I told you about. Esther suggested I begin it years ago when we didn't know where you lived. You can read it later . . . it'll fill in the bits I forgot. Things that happened when we used to live in London . . . usually me losing my situation.' Albert tried to summon a smile from Esther but couldn't.

'But we've had another letter today, concerning Henrietta.' He sighed. 'I'll have to explain what's behind it . . . I hope it doesn't make you think too badly of Polly, for she always was the dearest girl.'

Chas settled on the wornout sofa and took out his pipe. The kitten snuggled into his lap and as he tickled her ears absent-mindedly Albert began his tale.

When he'd finished he said sadly, 'So that's the top and

446

bottom of it. And when Ottram came here, he spotted the likeness straight away. Claimed Etta looked the image of her father.'

'He was bound to say so, Albert,' Esther pointed out.

'Maybe, but she certainly don't look a bit like old Henry.'

'She takes after Polly. As soon as I saw her, I remembered that day when you nearly drowned.'

'I was remembering it, too! And she does look like Pol, you're right. Sounds like her too when she's bossing Edwin about.'

'You must fight,' Chas urged. 'You can't give her up.' He couldn't bear to think this precious new-found family might disintegrate. 'I'll help you all I can.'

'That's it!' Albert promptly seized this new lifeline. 'Come with us on Monday, Chas. When Mr Ottram finds out Etta has a new uncle who's rich – '

'Not that rich!'

'But you can give her all the bits and pieces he said she needs.' Albert saw life in simple terms. 'He might not be so set on taking her away once he discovers that. Why, Etta might even have piano lessons now you're here!'

Esther believed Mr Ottram much more ruthless but didn't want to hurt Albert's feelings. 'You will let Henry know,' she reminded him. 'He particularly wanted to be there when we go to Norwich.'

Chapter Twenty-Five

Called to Account

The appointment was for Monday. Before that there were two whole days for Albert and Chas to savour things past and talk in cautious terms of the future. Two uninterrupted days, Albert had anticipated, but he hadn't allowed for general curiosity.

Word spread concerning the returned hero, especially when Albert began to parade Chas round the town. And after so many years, there were changes which had to be seen.

'Imagine, Esther, Chas never knew Victoria Avenue had been planted for the old queen's Jubilee. Come on, old chap. We can go past the new cinema on our way. Don't suppose you'll recognize anything in that part of the town.'

Their progress was slow and, once back home, old acquaintances came to call. The trickle became a stream and by Saturday evening Esther declared she wasn't making another cup of tea, no matter if King George himself turned up to shake Chas by the hand.

'Some of them today said they were at school with us. I can't hardly remember.' Chas eased his buttocks on the hard garden bench.

'They haven't changed. You have,' Albert said sagely. 'When you left that night for Liverpool, you was skinny as a rake. D'you remember, Esther?'

'Those moustaches were weighing him down,' she giggled. 'I've been dying to ask – when did they disappear?'

'Oh, during my time in New York, I guess,' Chas

drawled. 'Gel I knew told me I'd be better off without 'em.'
Funny how he'd scarcely thought of Bella since he'd
arrived.

'Plenty of gels, were there, old chap?' Albert gave a
knowing wink. 'Fillies with neat pairs of calves, eh?'

'One or two.'

'Now then,' Esther warned, 'little pitchers . . .'

They were in the garden enjoying the last of the sun
while the children teased the kitten.

'Tell you someone I haven't yet seen: old Syb. She's not
upped sticks and gone to London by any chance?'

'Wish she would!' groaned Albert. 'If I had a hundred
pounds it would be worth giving fifty to Syb, to send her
packing.'

'If she knew you had a hundred, she wouldn't budge till
she'd got her hands on the rest of it,' Esther retorted.

'What about Enoch Porrit, is he still around?'

'Oh, yes. That's why she daren't budge. She's too scared
of what he might do.'

'Make off with her property, you mean?'

'Something like that,' Albert agreed.

'Did you know your aunt once had her eye on Henry
Durrant,' Esther asked.

'Did she really?' Chas was amazed. 'I thought you said
Syb had gone religious? How did she reconcile lust with
church-going?'

'Henry inherited a tidy sum,' Albert explained, 'that
must've been the temptation.' Chas eased his posterior
again; Albert really had managed to fashion a most
uncomfortable garden seat.

'I reckon of all the people I've ever met, Aunt Syb was
the worst,' he grumbled. 'I'll never forgive her for being so
cruel when we were children. The only time she redeemed
herself was when she gave me that fifteen pounds.' There
was a tiny pause.

'Enoch Porrit was worse,' Albert said hurriedly.

'They were both as bad,' Chas announced decisively, 'I
hope I never meet either of them again.'

'You can't miss 'em if you intend staying on here,' Albert
protested. 'You made any decision yet?' Chas tamped

down the tobacco in his pipe.

'I'm still considering the possibilities,' he replied, non-committally. 'Let's get Monday over first, eh?'

'Yes . . . ' Esther gazed at Henrietta with troubled eyes. There was no escaping the fact; the impending visit to Norwich hung over them like a cloud.

When Sybilla returned home that evening the house was empty. This wasn't unusual but she wanted to vent her anger on someone and Enoch was as good as any. She'd heard the gossip that Chas was back – looking every inch the wealthy gentleman according to her neighbours – and that was enough to infuriate Sybilla. Why hadn't he had the decency to come and visit his aunt? They could have discussed that ever-important topic, the outstanding interest.

'Evening, missus.' She looked up from stirring a pan.

'Yes?' A policeman stood outside the back door, leaning on his bicycle.

'I've come about Porrit.' Sybilla stared.

'Is he dead?' Had a merciful God finally answered her prayers? The constable's mouth twitched.

'No such luck, missus. He's been caught poaching, that's what. Down Santon Downham way. He ain't as fast as he once was.'

'Stupid beggar,' said his wife, mechanically.

'He's up afore Thetford magistrates, Monday morning. Eleven o'clock sharp.'

'What you telling me for? It's nothing to do with me.' She'd offended his sense of propriety.

'Jus' keeping you informed, Mrs Porrit. You might want to be there, to give your man your support.' By way of answer, Sybilla snorted and turned her back.

As the constable told his desk sergeant, 'I reckon Porrit might ask to go inside when you think of what's waiting for him back home.' Later that evening, off-duty and in the privacy of The Ram, the same constable confided what had happened to one or two friends. By Sunday morning the whole of Brandon knew.

On her way to the Salvation Army Citadel, Sybilla was

450

waylaid by Mrs Heyhoe.

'I hear Porrit got catched. He's had it coming to him and no mistake.'

'What off it?' demanded Sybilla, ' 'taint my affair.' Her temper increased; if the news had reached the vicarage, it wasn't a secret any longer.

Mrs Heyhoe said speculatively, 'You're going to court, I hope?'

'Why should I?' Cook drew herself up.

'Because it's your duty, Mrs Porrit, that's why.'

Furious, Sybilla swallowed her reply and hurried off. But once installed in her pew she wasn't allowed to forget the subject. The sermon that morning extolled the virtues of repentence, with particular emphasis on the responsibility of those present to lead any erring sheep back to the fold. The entire congregation turned to stare at Sybilla. She knew what was expected, she daren't offend so many people. Affecting humility, she inclined her head towards the preacher. There were rustles of satisfaction. Mrs Porrit had tacitly agreed to behave like a Christian.

On Monday morning, Esther declared she would stay at home with the children. She was on tenterhooks as to what might happen but attempted to sound calm.

'You won't let Chas do anything rash? I mean, him being in America so long, he might not understand.'

'No, love.'

'Listen to what Henry has to say first.'

'Of course. You're sure we needn't take Etta? It's what Mr Ottram says we should do in his letter.'

'No.' Esther didn't trust the man an inch. It was safer if Henrietta remained at home.

The small courtroom was packed. If Sybilla imagined that by slipping in discreetly dressed in her oldest, most unbecoming clothes, she could attend without anyone noticing, she hadn't allowed for human nature. Everyone who could get to Thetford that morning was there. All those who'd suffered in the past from her vituperative tongue were out to enjoy the fun.

An expectant murmur rose as she entered. She found herself being pushed unwillingly to the front, past a crowd who sniggered just as they had on the day of her marriage. She was shown to a seat far too close to the dock. Enoch grinned when he caught sight of her. Sybilla wanted to scream that the affair was none of her doing! Her humiliation had already begun; merely the sight of him – unkempt, unshaven, his belly hanging over his belt and clothes torn and dirty from the scuffle – was enough to make her eyes smart.

Sensing her rage, her husband jeered loud enough for everyone to hear: 'You're in for a disappointment, Syb. Poaching ain't a hanging offence no more,' and from the body of the court, his cronies raised a derisive cheer.

'Silence!'

Anger sent blood pounding in her temples. Sybilla scarcely heard the preliminaries, nor the police evidence. Words broke through, descriptions of traps and of that most heinous of British crimes – damage to a gentleman's property.

The magistrates retired for an extremely brief period before pronouncing their verdict: 'Guilty. Fined five pounds. Alternatively, seven days confined to prison.'

'Permission to speak, Your Honour.'

'Well, what is it?'

'I don't have a penny, sir, but my wife here will be glad to pay –'

He was interrupted by a shriek which had the magistrate nearly falling from his chair.

'What the devil . . .?'

'That was my wife, Your Honour. It's her way of letting you know she couldn't bear for me to go to prison. She's got plenty of money. Five pound don't mean nothin' – Aah!' Enoch Porrit put up a hand to save his eyes while startled court officials attempted to restrain his wife.

Chas realized the diffident figure waiting on the pavement outside the office must be Henry Durrant. Albert was already wringing him by the hand. 'It's good to see you, old chap. We've had a marvellous bit of luck.

452

Here's my brother Chas, come home from America. He'll convince Ottram if anyone can.'

Introductions over, the three of them mounted the stairs. Chas in his light American suit and hat, Albert in an old-fashioned curly brimmed bowler and Henry in inconspicuous subfusc.

They were shown inside and Philip Ottram demanded impatiently, 'Where's the child?' He refused to use her given name.

'Etta's at home with my wife,' Albert replied.

'No matter. Simmons can take the maid to fetch her. We are having a small dinner-party this evening, to introduce Philippa to our friends.'

'Philippa?'

'A – slip of the tongue. Now, these are the forms I've prepared for you to sign, Unwin.'

'This is my brother Chas, Mr Ottram. He's back from America and can provide those extras you thought Etta should have.' Albert looked expectantly at Chas. 'He'll tell you that himself.'

Chas was uneasy. He didn't like what he saw: a smart office, a tall man with a determined expression – he was uncertain how they stood. In America they would have had their own solicitor to protect their rights. He suddenly realized how naive Albert and he had been; they'd come here totally unprepared. Chas had no idea whether Albert was entitled to keep the girl. Was a grandfather closer in law than two uncles, however loving? But even as he hesitated, Henry Durrant gave a quiet cough.

'May I see the form you wish Albert to sign?'

'Mr . . .?'

'Henry Durrant. Husband to Mrs Polly Durrant, father of Henrietta.'

The cuckold. Philip Ottram smiled, a little contemptuously.

'Of course, Mr Durrant.' He concentrated on Chas, who looked more businesslike. 'I have decided to make a reasonable offer, one that I'm sure all parties will consider fair. Fifty guineas. In return, my son's natural daughter will become the ward of my wife and myself.'

Albert went white. Chas felt helpless. This man was so confident. What could they do to prevent it?

'I don't know as how we could agree to that, Mr Ottram . . .' he began, anxious to gain a little time. He looked at Albert, uncertain what to suggest next.

'Excuse me. There is something here I do not understand?' Henry had removed his spectacles and was quietly pedantic. 'These two sheets of paper refer to the sale of my daughter Henrietta Durrant – '

'Not a sale, Mr Durrant. A – consideration – of fifty guineas, to Mr Albert Unwin here – '

'In exchange for a female child, namely my daughter,' finished Henry. 'Yes, I can read, thank you Mr Ottram. The suggestion is completely unacceptable. I bid you good day, sir. Come Albert, Chas.'

'Now, look here – '

'You bade us attend these premises in order to propose an illegal transaction. I advise you to be silent, sir. We will take our leave and say nothing more on the subject.' Philip Ottram was choleric.

'That child is not your daughter! She is the result of a liaison between my son and your wife – I am her grandfather!'

'No,' Henry strove to overcome natural diffidence and sound authoritative, fully aware everything depended on it. 'She is the child of my late dear wife and myself and you will never prove otherwise. I have, of course, heard scurrilous rumours in the past. In a small town such unkind gossip occurs from time to time. But I will explain to you once and for all Mr Ottram, why you have no claim whatsoever to my child.

'The third night following her birth, the doctor informed me Polly was in danger. On her deathbed, surrounded by medical staff, I asked if the child were mine and with her last breath, my dear wife gave her answer plainly: the child was to be called Henrietta. In other words, to be named after her father.'

In the silence Albert stared at his boots, unable to look Henry in the face. Polly had told such a whopper, bless her!

Philip Ottram leaned across the desk, both fists clenched as though he would smash the insignificant figure to pulp.

'She doesn't resemble you in the slightest!'

'No,' Henry replied steadily, 'she resembles her dear mother. For that, we are truly thankful. Never can any of us forget Polly while we have Henrietta.'

They watched, mesmerized, as he took out two photographs. One was his wedding picture, the other a formal solemn portrait of Henrietta. In sepia, without the flaxen coloured hair, she was indeed the image of Polly.

They could hear the traffic outside. In the office no one spoke. A fly began the long crawl up the window pane. Henry slipped the photographs back into his pocket. His quiet voice continued as evenly as before.

'My dying wife made one further request. Knowing I would be an elderly widower, she bequeathed her most precious possession into her married brother's care. I have carried out her wish. As Henrietta's father . . . ' he let the word linger a moment, 'I am completely satisfied that Mr and Mrs Unwiin, who are so devoted to her, should continue to care for her.'

He pushed the foolscap sheets back across the desk.

'Rumour carries no weight compared to the words of a dying woman, Mr Ottram. You have lost a son, I a wife; we must learn to bear those losses with fortitude, not seek replacements. Henrietta is better off with those who love her – for her own sake.'

In the silence, Henry walked to the door, opened it and went outside leaving it ajar. After a moment or two, Chas and Albert stumbled to their feet and followed.

Albert's trembling fingers gripped Chas's arm as the two of them descended the staircase. 'It's a bloomin' marvel,' he whispered over and over, 'that's what it is . . . a marvel.'

Outside, standing on the same piece of pavement, it felt as if an eternity had passed. Strangers ignored them, hurrying by on either side. Chas's mouth was dry; it was exceedingly difficult to find the right words but he was less involved emotionally. Breaking the silence, he clasped Henry.

455

'Well done. Very well done indeed. We were proud of you in there.' Lavish gestures served only to confuse and embarrass Henry. He retreated into stiff formality.

'Kind of you, I'm sure.'

For once, Albert wanted to tell his beloved brother to be silent. He understood the sensitive nature of this man. What an effort it must have taken – Polly owed him so much. Albert dearly wanted to tell him so. In the end all he could manage was a heartfelt, 'Esther and me, we shan't let you down, old chap.' Henry, devoid of expression, nodded briefly and walked away.

'Here . . .' Chas was astonished, 'aren't we going to celebrate?' Albert shook his head.

'Leave him be. When you think about it, there's nothing for Henry to celebrate, is there?'

On the train, they were deep in thought but then Albert began to recover.

'Thanks be, dear old Pol did tell that fib, though,' he said finally. 'I 'ope she hasn't got into trouble in the hereafter.'

'I don't suppose St Peter would be that mean,' Chas replied easily, remembering the many other sinners he had known. 'She wasn't really wicked.'

'No,' said Albert, adding carefully, ' 'sfar as I know.'

'Well, then.' Chas's own record was infinitely worse; he preferred not to dwell on it.

'Henry worked out how to tackle Ottram all right.' Albert marvelled again. 'He really is a clever old stick.'

'He took my breath away. You reckon he always knew?'

'We decided he must've done. But if Polly could perjure herself in a good cause, so could Henry, bless him. We ain't complaining. D'you know what I was remembering on the way here this morning? The night you, me and Pomf went after those fuzzy-wuzzies. That was another tight spot only we managed, thanks to Pomf.' Fond tales of past times blotted out the present.

As for Henry Durrant, travelling in a different direction, he felt a quiet satisfaction at discharging his debts. From now on the ghosts would let him enjoy his garden in peace.

The two brothers stood beside a pile of flints that marked the spot where their home had once been.

'Did anyone ever come and live here afterwards?'

'Not as far as I know.' Albert kicked at a stone. 'The doctor got his wish. He said it should be razed to the ground. The weather did that eventually.' He sighed. 'I wish it hadn't been necessary to burn those books though.'

'When you think about it, we were lucky to have such fine parents.'

'Wish I'd had an inheritance like father, to buy Edwin and Henrietta things,' Albert said wistfully. 'Etta should have pretty frocks and a governess. Gone to finishing school like Ottram said. She'd be a little princess.'

'She'd be a spoilt little madam,' Chas said with feeling. 'I've met enough of those in New York. You leave her be. She can have her piano lessons and as many books as she likes, but I'm not paying for no finishing school.'

'What about you, Chas? You decided yet what you want to do?' Chas gazed at the bleak fenland and the new plantations of saplings beyond.

'It come to me when I was in the hottest place on earth – Death Valley, that was – I might one day buy me a piece of land. Seems like no one else wants this place. So . . . I shall make an offer. I might build a little property.'

'You mean, live here – and farm? But that was why you ran away in the first place!'

'Not from here, Albert. This place was always home. It was misery and poverty I was escaping from. All that's changed for me. This time I shall *own* the land. I've learned a lot in America . . . how to farm and make land pay. I shall use machinery, not half-starved boys. And I shall need a helping hand – yours, bor.' He laughed self-deprecatingly. 'I haven't a notion what to do when those damn machines break down. It's not much of a job, I'm offering.' He pushed at the peaty soil with his foot. 'Would you feel like joining me?' Albert was overwhelmed and downcast, all in the same moment.

'I couldn't travel this far on my bike.'

'What's wrong with a motor car?'

'A motor . . . !'

'And a tractor. And a combine. We've got to move with the times, bor.'

'Well!' Albert was temporarily bereft of words. 'A combine – my, oh my!'

Chas surveyed the land from horizon to horizon. 'That's what it's about. Handing on to those who come after. It's taken a few years before I finally understood – that's why I came back. I didn't know Edwin and Henrietta existed but it's for them and those who come after. That's if you and I can make a go of it.'

Overcome at the thought Edwin's future was secure, Albert insisted on shaking him by the hand.

They were in a euphoric, sentimental state as they approached Willow End, unaware of events in Thetford. Sybilla had been forced to pay the fine because of the collective indignation of those in court. She had never in her wildest imaginings dreamed she'd *hand over* money on Enoch's account. In vain did she protest that he'd robbed her for years. No one wanted to hear; hadn't she also robbed them?

She was reminded how she'd made some of her money – 'You was there afore the corpus was cold, persuading that widder to hand over her home!' And when she began to protest she hadn't five pounds on her person, Enoch jeered that his wife was known to keep a five pound note in her secret petticoat pocket.

Finally, when justice was satisfied, the crowd followed her outside, intrigued to know what Mrs Porrit would do next.

Sybilla was white-hot with anger. There was no question in her mind: she must make good her loss immediately and the way to do so was plain. She returned to Brandon as fast as she was able and went directly to Willow End. A short distance behind came a few who'd been in court.

They watched as Esther refused to admit her. The children were shooed inside and they found an observation post at an upstairs window. Sybilla stood, fuming, beside the gate as Chas and Albert rounded the corner. Edwin spotted him.

'There's daddy now.' He saw his father groan at the sight of her. She waited, arms akimbo.

'So you finally came back from 'merica, Chas . . . like a bad penny.'

'Hello there, Aunt Syb. Yes, I'm back for good. I see you haven't changed, 'cept for looking older, of course.'

'I ain't wasting my time on compliments neither. I've been waiting for you to call and repay your debts. Seems you don't believe in being honest. Well, I can't wait no longer. I've had unexpected expenses today due to Porrit, now I wants the rest of my money. Seven per cent. You can hand it over afore you steps through this gate, d'you hear.' Albert gave a sharp hiss.

'Go away!'

'Your – what?' Chas stared.

'You know what I'm talking about. Interest on that money you borrowed.' Sybilla jerked a thumb at Albert. 'He paid the capital, now I wants the rest. Compound. I've worked it out and wrote down, businesslike.'

'Chas asked slowly, 'What the hell is she talking about?'

'I didn't like to worry you,' Albert muttered, and to Sybilla, 'Get on home, will you!' but Chas spoke, and his voice was hard.

'The only money I ever had from you was that fifteen pounds, which I thought was a gift . . . to make up for the way you treated us when we were children.'

'Gift!' she shouted, 'I never give gifts. He signed the paper.'

'I've paid enough. It never was compound interest anyway.'

'Just a minute,' Chas was staring at each in turn.

Albert said through clenched teeth, 'I had to sign, otherwise she wouldn't let me have it.'

'My stars!' Chas stared back at Sybilla. 'Albert was penniless. You knew that.'

'So? 'Twas his business. I'm a poor working woman, not a charity –'

'You're a witch! You're worse, you're a leech, sucking blood from everyone you meet!' The absolute cruelty of what she'd done unleashed a murderous rage. Chas advanced.

459

At the sight of his face, Albert cried in alarm, 'Careful, bor!'

'I am going to kill her!' Sybilla began to shriek. At their upstairs window, Edwin and Henrietta were fascinated.

'She's gone a funny colour,' said Henrietta, 'sort of pinky-purple.'

'Will he scalp her the way he did those Indians?'

She pursed her lips and considered. 'He hasn't got his hunting knife.'

'I can fetch it,' Edwin was eager, 'I know where he keeps it, beside the bed.'

'Better not. There'd be a bit of a mess. Aunt Esther might be upset. Shall we tell her?'

'Come and see, mummy,' Edwin called, 'Uncle Chas is going to kill Great-Aunt Syb.'

'What!' Esther came flying out of the kitchen. 'Where?'

'By the gate.' She was already halfway down the path.

'Albert, Chas – what's going on?' Albert had his arms round the kicking, squealing Sybilla as Chas attempted to heave her onto his shoulder. There were shouts of encouragement from the ever-increasing crowd. 'What are you doing!' Esther cried, for Sybilla now dangled down his back.

'Go on, lad, kill 'er,' shouted an elderly champion of justice, 'she deserves it!' On every side, others yelled excitedly as Mrs Heyhoe finally arrived on the scene. She stopped in amazement.

'Well, I never! Is that Mrs Porrit?'

'Of course it is – Help! Murder!' screeched the upsidedown Sybilla, 'POLICE!'

Across her wriggling body, Chas said, 'Albert, let's see if she floats.' Sybilla tried to break free, he slapped her rump hard. 'Oh no you don't!' In the old days, they tied witches to a stool . . . I shall manage without.'

Past the willows he tramped, Albert beside him, the crowd in wild pursuit with Edwin and Henrietta rushing to catch up. At a point where the river bank jutted out above the main stream, everyone halted. Chas teetered to the very edge with his burden.

'This is for all the misery, to Polly, Albert and me, and

everyone who's ever had the misfortune to meet you Sybilla Porrit – I hope you bloody well drown!'

'Aah!' The splash followed by her hysterical scream made roosting birds rise in a cloud, their squawks adding to the confusion as Sybilla sank, only to rise again, crying out in genuine terror as the sluggish current began to drag her downstream. 'I shall have the law on you . . . you murderer!'

'I don't know if she can swim, old chap.' Chas surveyed the pattern of the water with an experienced eye.

'She should drift as far as that overhanging branch. She's strong enough to catch hold, I reckon.' Nevertheless they waited until the flailing arms grabbed the willow. 'Right, that's it.' Chas promptly turned his back.

'Maybe we should go and help?' Albert suggested.

'No,' he was firm. 'Let her friends do that, if she's got any left. I'm hungry. Come along, Edwin, Henrietta, it must be nearly time for supper.'

'Is Great Aunt Syb *really* a witch, Uncle Chas?' He looked down in mock surprise.

'Why bless my soul, Edwin, of course she is. You saw for yourself, didn't you? She didn't drown, she floated.' And winking at Esther, Chas led the way back to the cottage.

Later, when the children had gone to bed, he growled, 'Why did you never tell me the truth about that money?'

Albert said simply, 'You might not have gone.'

'How long did it take?' Albert attempted nonchalence. 'To pay it back? Oh, a while.'

Esther murmured, 'Quite a long while, actually.'

'Oh, Albert!' Chas grabbed him in a fierce hug. 'What I owe you, bor!'

Much affected, Albert blew his nose. 'You've come home safe and sound, Chas. That's all the repayment I've ever wanted.'

Epilogue

Soldiering On, Summer, 1940

Under a dark sky on the lip of one of the ancient flint workings, an old bald-headed man sat watching the aircraft heading east. Leaning heavily on his stick, his brother approached and sank down awkwardly beside him, his lame leg obviously giving him pain. For a while, neither spoke.

'I guessed you might come up here.'

'I couldn't sleep, not after hearing the news.'

'Don't suppose anyone can tonight,' Albert sighed. 'We're on our own now seemingly. Nothing but us against the mighty forces of evil, according to Mr Churchill.' He gazed up as more aircraft thundered overhead. 'Edwin's lot have gone tonight.'

'I'm sorry to hear it, bor.'

'Thank God there's no moon.' Albert's mottled hand trembled as he attempted to light his pipe. 'Bloomin' matches. Must be the damp.'

'Here.'

'Ta.'

'Nothing changes, does it?' Chas burst out angrily, 'Remember father telling us about invaders with their swords of iron?'

'Mmm.' Albert's thoughts were still with the aircraft.

'Any word from Etta?'

'She's decided to come home. Safer than staying in London. Stops her brooding about her chap.'

'Reckon he's been captured?'

'Esther prays every night that he has . . . she's nearly as fond of him as Etta is.'

Chas stared at the mysterious shapes and hollows surrounding them.

'I wonder if the Old Uns ever sat here like us, waiting for the enemy to arrive?'

"course they did.' Albert was surprised. 'You remember Queen Boudicca – "the land red with Roman blood"?'

'Trust you to think of a few comforting words!'

'If Jerry does come at least we've got a secret weapon: Syb.' Albert went into a wobbly imitation of Hitler. 'Zis is an Englishwoman? *Mein Gott* – halt the invasion immediately!'

'Syb ain't got no chariot.'

Albert was more cheerful. 'We could weld knives onto your old tractor – not that we'd qualify for petrol coupons.'

'She's let her two rooms again.'

'Never!'

'She told the RAF she wanted coloured blokes because they're willing to pay double the rent.'

'The old varmint!'

'Only she forgot to tell Enoch what she'd done and he met one of 'em coming out the lavvy. Never stopped running till he reached the Five Bells.'

'At least she ain't fretting. Bet she sleeps at night, with her bank book under her pillow. All she cares about is Porrit getting a-hold of her money.'

'And he's not giving up 'till he does.'

'With people like Syb, we ain't going under.'

'I think we are,' Chas was suddenly bleak, 'this time. What a waste. Men like Edwin – the farm made into an airfield – '

'Now, then.' Albert eased his stiff leg. 'Remember what Pomf used to say?'

'Pomf . . .?'

'In India.'

'Ah, yes . . . Pomf.'

'All part of the great game.'

'Well I don't want to take part no more.'

'That's bloomin' daft . . . ' Albert looked at him steadily. 'It makes a nonsense of what we're trying to do . . . I got to believe in it for Edwin an' Henrietta's sake.'

'You going back?'

'No point in listening if you've got the collywobbles,' Albert winced. 'My arthritis is bad tonight. An' I don't like leaving my dear old gel too long. She'll be sitting there, waiting, till Edwin phones.'

'I don't lie awake 'cause I'm frightened,' Chas lied, 'I just don't fancy getting caught in bed if Jerry comes.'

'First German I see, I'll blow me ARP whistle extra loud. Give you time to get your trousers on. Then I'll bash 'im on the head with me stick. Come on.'

Side by side, the two old men stumbled across the ancient landscape. Behind them, the Old Uns paused in digging for flints to see them go.